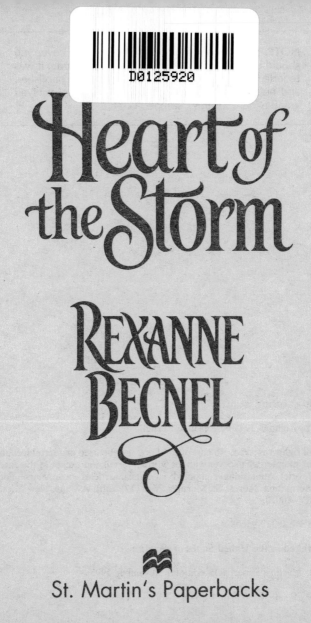

Heart of the Storm

REXANNE BECNEL

St. Martin's Paperbacks

HEART OF THE STORM

Copyright © 1995 by Rexanne Becnel.

ISBN: 0-312-95608-8

Printed in the United States of America

St. Martin's Paperbacks edition / November 1995

10 9 8 7 6 5 4 3 2 1

For David,
the real romantic in the family.

Special thanks to Kent Treadway, M.D. for sharing
both his knowledge and his enthusiasm with me.

Chapter One

London, England, 1844

The formal dining room at Diamond Hall was Eliza's least favorite room in her parents' London residence. It was too cavernous. Too ornate. And on this particular evening, despite the many good wishes directed her way, far too crowded with people.

Across the polished mahogany table and its gleaming array of Emes silver, Waterford glass, and Chinese Trade porcelain, she saw her father surreptitiously nudge Michael, and after a moment the younger man rose dutifully to his feet. All eyes turned expectantly toward him. And why not? Michael Geoffrey Johnstone, sole heir to the Earl of Marley, and Viscount Cregmore in his own right, had a natural charisma that commanded attention wherever he went. It was aided, of course, by his broad shoulders, his golden hair, and a profile reminiscent of numerous Greek statues Eliza had studied.

Everyone listened when he spoke. Her father was forever quoting some opinion of Michael's to her; her youngest brother Perry emulated the way he wore his hair and tied his cravat; while LeClere, her oldest brother, did a faithful imitation of both his walk and his talk. It was enough to make a girl plead a headache and retire to her room. Only she couldn't do that tonight. It was her birthday. Everyone had gathered here to celebrate and she must appear pleased.

"To Miss Eliza Victorine Thoroughgood—"

"Soon to be Lady Cregmore," LeClere threw in from his place halfway down the table.

"Here, here," Perry added. "My big sister shall no longer be here to order me about. She shall order you about instead," he finished, laughing at Michael.

Michael winked at Perry, and a smile curved his well-formed lips. Socially adept as he was, he waited for the wave of chuckles from the other guests to subside before continuing. "To my dearest Eliza on the occasion of her nineteenth birthday. Many happy returns of the day."

He lifted his gold-rimmed crystal wine glass and polished off the contents, then smiled directly at her. "Next year I shall attempt to host a party just as jolly as this one for your twentieth birthday, only it shall be at our home." He swept the attentive group with his clear gaze. "You are all invited to join us there."

Eliza's headache had been real enough before. Mentioning her forthcoming marriage to one of the most eligible and handsome bachelors in the entire British Kingdom set her head to pounding in earnest. In the hubbub that followed—more toasts, the bevy of servants refilling glasses with Veuve Clicquot champagne, and the numerous voices growing ever more boisterous with the free-flowing spirits—Eliza came near to panicking. Her head throbbed and her breath seemed to catch in her chest. Notwithstanding her recent good health, she feared she might have one of her attacks at any moment. She cast a desperate look toward her mother.

Despite her distance down the absurdly long table, Constance Thoroughgood recognized the look on her daughter's face. With her gracious smile kept serenely in place, she signaled the majordomo, and when he rang his bell, she stood up. "I believe the ladies will retire for a few minutes. Mr. Thoroughgood?"

Gerald Thoroughgood gulped down the rest of his champagne, then also rose, dabbing at his mouth with his embroidered linen napkin. "Very good, my dear. Gentlemen, let us adjourn to have a smoke. I have some very good cigars from the West Indies."

In spite of Eliza's earlier irritation with Perry, she was inordinately grateful when it was he who helped her from her chair and not Michael. If the perfect Michael Johnstone had taken her arm, she feared her lungs would have exceeded their meager abilities and she would have suffocated on the spot.

Why had her parents ever insisted on pairing her with such a paragon? Yes, the two of them were well suited on the surface, equals in both social standing and wealth. But he was incredibly handsome, excessively so. And while she was attractive enough—or so her several other suitors had vowed—she was hardly up to Michael's standard. Added to that, he was smart, quick-witted, and comfortable in any social situation. Whatever the circumstances—at a hunt, in the game room, handling his family's properties, or expounding in the House of Lords—Michael was the master of every domain. She knew because her parents and brothers—and every other relative she had—constantly pointed it out to her.

By contrast she was a shy and retiring little mouse, content to sit and read or do decorative needlework. She was neither flashy, nor even very amusing. Her cousin Jessica Haberton fit that description far better than she. Why Michael had pursued her instead of Jessica was quite beyond her understanding.

At first, of course, she'd been flattered when he'd singled her out for attention. During her season he'd attended every party she did, dancing with her as often as was deemed socially acceptable. He'd called on her at least once a week and brought her several thoughtful gifts, including an enameled thimble, an inscribed needlecase book, and a pincushion decorated with tiny shells. It was at that point, when his intentions became clear, that she had begun to panic. If she married Michael she would have to run his several households, entertain his vast array of friends and associates, and generally perform the same sort of role in his life that her mother did for her father. Only on a larger scale.

While Eliza took pride in her home and loved making it beautiful, she was not good at the entertaining end of it. Her mother was; she drew people in effortlessly and had the knack of putting everyone at ease. But Eliza knew she could never do that. She didn't begin to know how.

And besides, she was ill. She'd been sickly all her life.

Oh, why must she marry Michael? Why must she marry anyone at all? She'd much rather remain at home, at least for a few more years.

"Are you all right, my dear?" her mother asked as she supported Eliza's arm and directed her toward the drawing room. "Can you breathe all right?"

"If I could just have a minute's privacy," Eliza murmured, her voice shaky and thin.

Her mother steered her without further comment toward the special bedroom they kept for Eliza on the main floor of the enormous residence. They still felt she was not strong enough to use the stairs on a regular basis. Too hard on her weak lungs, they said. It might bring on one of her attacks of short breath, they warned her. But Eliza would far rather endure the rigors of stair climbing than the rigors of marriage to Michael.

"Clothilde, do you think we should prepare a steam tent?" Constance asked once the doors were closed behind them. "Maybe if I just loosen her gown and bathe her wrists and neck. Quick, now. We have only a few minutes."

Constance Thoroughgood turned her gentle brown eyes on her daughter. "Now Eliza, you must not let yourself become overly excited. It's only a birthday party."

"Yes, Mama," Eliza dutifully replied. But she leaned her head back against the gilt-stenciled Grecian couch and let her eyes fall closed. "I'll try," she added, her voice even more faint.

It had the desired effect. Her mother pressed her fingers against Eliza's wrist and silently counted her daughter's heartbeat. "Can you breathe better now? Slowly. And count your breaths as Dr. Smalley always advises. Just calm yourself. It's only a birthday party," she repeated, though she didn't sound nearly so certain this time.

Eliza seized upon the moment. "I know it's just a party. But Michael . . . the wedding . . . oh, Mama, please speak to Papa again." Eliza opened her eyes and stared beseechingly up at her mother. "Please say you'll try to make him reconsider."

After a moment's pause Constance frowned. "Leave us, Clothilde." Once the maid was gone, Constance took Eliza's two hands in hers. "It is your duty to marry. You know that. Your father has gone to great pains to find someone as fine as Michael. Someone gentle and well-read. Someone whose bloodlines are complemented by our financial resources."

"Yes, Michael is certainly perfect in every way," Eliza conceded bitterly.

"I don't understand you, daughter. You act as if that is a flaw."

Eliza pushed herself upright on the cream and gold cushions of the reclining couch and swung her legs around so that her feet rested on the antique Aubusson carpet. "He is perfect and I . . . I am pitiful by comparison."

"Eliza! That simply is not true. You are lovely. Any man would be happy to marry you."

She gave her mother a pained smile. "I admit that we make a 'lovely couple.' I've heard it said constantly by everyone I know—and from an endless number of people I don't know—ever since you and Papa announced our engagement. But it's not that, Mama. It goes deeper. He is—" She broke off, unable to find just the right way to explain it. "Michael is just . . . just too grand for me."

"That's simply not true," her mother repeated.

But they both knew it was. Eliza Victorine Thoroughgood was unarguably one of the wealthiest heiresses of marriageable age in England. But she'd been a sickly child and had grown up to be reserved, rather bookish, and when compared to the popular and outgoing Michael Johnstone, very nearly a recluse. He shone as brilliantly as the beacon light at home on Lantern Rock, while she sputtered like a yellow tallow candle.

"Michael does not evidence any hesitation whatsoever," her mother admonished. "Nor should you."

"That's because he shall outlive me," Eliza stated. She was grasping at straws now, shamelessly trying to sway her mother by frightening her. But what other choice did she have? And given her medical history, it might very well be true.

"That's a dreadful thing to say!"

"But probably true! I shall never survive the rigors of childbirth—assuming I even survive the rigors of his husbandly attentions." *Assuming he was even remotely so inclined toward her,* a miserable voice in her head added. After all, he'd not so much as begged one single kiss from her. Only at their engagement party had he kissed her, and that had been a chaste and perfunctory peck, as had been expected by their audience of well-wishers. It had certainly not been anything like the passionate kisses she'd read about in Lady Morgan's book or in her brief glimpse of LeClere's tattered copy of *Aristotle's Masterpiece*.

"Eliza Victorine. I will not hear of such talk. Marriage will be good for you. A change of scenery. A tour of the continent. Why, we shall hardly recognize you when you return, for you shall be much stronger by then. I'm certain of it."

But Constance Thoroughgood was not nearly so certain as she feigned. Eliza had never been strong. Though she hadn't suffered one of her horrible attacks of asthma in a good while, it was only because they were so careful of her. Dr. Smalley attended to her condition and they followed his instructions strictly. No riding. No walking outside on any but the warmest and calmest of days. Keep her warm and keep her quiet, so that her lungs were not overtaxed. Constance had only to recall her daughter's face turning blue from lack of oxygen and to remember that dreadful gasping sound as she fought for breath to grow afraid for her all over again.

LeClere and Perry had been blessed with robust good health. Only her darling Eliza suffered ill health. The entire family took great pains to protect her. She had but to ring her special bell and someone was at her side. Confined as she was, however, she had turned at an early age to books for company. Now she drew, painted, and read, and except for a brief morning sojourn on the terrace when the weather permitted, she spent all her time indoors.

She was beautiful in a delicate way with her fair complexion, expressive gray eyes, and gleaming dark hair. Though she was petite in stature, she'd nonetheless filled out most becomingly. Yet in spite of her feminine beauty, there was a fragility about her, as if she were a lovely doll which, if handled too roughly, might break.

Most of the time her family simply took her delicate constitution in stride. They included her in what activities they could, and did not worry when she escaped to the quiet of the library. This business of her betrothal, however, had sent Eliza into a new sort of decline.

As Constance helped her reluctant daughter to her feet and guided her back to their guests, she couldn't help but wonder whether she *should* speak to her husband one more time.

In the dining room Eliza chose one of the Chinese Chippendale armchairs near the immense hearth, for she was always a little cold in this house. She bade her mother's sister Judith to sit beside her—anything to make sure Michael did not. Perry wheeled young Aubrey, Judith's son, over to them when the men rejoined the women, and for a few moments Eliza forgot all about Michael. Her ten-year-old cousin Aubrey had become confined to a rolling chair ever since he'd broken his foot in a riding accident during the summer. It had not healed well and he still could not walk. His father, Sir Lloyd Haberton, had had the contraption specially designed, but the boy clearly resented being seen in it.

"Hello, Aubrey. I don't believe I thanked you yet for coming to my birthday dinner. And also for the—"

"When can we go home?" Aubrey cut her off, addressing his mother instead. "Everybody's staring at me. I want to go home."

"Shh," Judith admonished, glancing furtively about. "You mustn't behave so, dear."

"But my foot hurts," the child insisted, his wan face drooping in a frown. "You know it hurts more when I'm cold."

"Let me push you nearer the hearth," Eliza said, rising to help him.

"Now, Eliza. You know you're not strong enough." Judith signaled a manservant to assist her. At precisely that moment Eliza's father strolled up with Michael in tow.

"There you are, daughter. Michael and I were just—"

"Oh, Michael. Just the person I was looking for," Eliza fibbed as an idea occurred to her, inspired by her desperation. He was always so infernally kind to her, he'd be completely unable to turn down her request. "Aubrey is rather uncomfortable. I thought he might enjoy playing with Tattie. Would you see if you could find her?"

"But Eliza," her father began.

"No, no. I'd be happy to find Tattie for Eliza. And for Aubrey." Michael gave an abbreviated but gallant bow, sending her a truly devastating smile at the same time. "Any suggestions as to where she might be hiding?"

Eliza frowned as if thinking, though it was actually to cover the panic that always set in when he turned his easy charm upon her. "Very likely in the morning room," she lied again. But it was a matter of self-preservation, she told herself when Michael moved away to do her bidding. Eliza's old cat was more probably in the kitchen, nestled in the small space between the coal box and the stove's water tank, warm and snug and hidden to anyone who did not know precisely where to look. Michael would never find her and perhaps she'd be spared having to spend any further time with him tonight.

But that did nothing to address Aubrey's peevishness.

"You will like my cat," she ventured, though the boy's face was closed in a pout.

"I hate cats," he replied.

"So do I. So do I," Gerald Thoroughgood muttered, glaring at Eliza. "Especially when they're used on such a petty pretext—"

"What animals do you like?" Eliza asked the child, determined to ignore her father completely.

"He used to like dogs. And horses," Aunt Judith answered for her son.

"Cats can be fun," Eliza persisted, trying to get the boy to speak for himself. "Kittens especially are so comical. Like little monkeys twisting and wrestling all the time."

"We offered him a small lap dog." Judith reached out to push a black curl back from Aubrey's brow, but he turned his head sharply away, and Judith reluctantly withdrew her hand.

Eliza hadn't seen her young cousin much in the four months since his fall, though her mother had kept her apprised of his progress—or lack thereof. As Eliza stared at the sullen child now, confined to the bulky rolling chair, forced to participate in a society he no longer felt included him, she knew exactly how he felt. Though her physical limitations were not so immediately visible as Aubrey's—she at least could get up and walk—she felt no less cut off from the main stream of daily life as he did. Too bad there wasn't a place for pitiful creatures like them to congregate, where being sickly or maimed or just different was the norm and not considered odd at all.

All at once a preposterous idea popped into her head. What its source was, she could not say. Perhaps from something she'd read. It might have come from the *Times* which her father brought home to her every evening. It could have appeared in the travelogue she'd read last spring, the one written by that eccentric duchess who lived down in Cornwall. Or perhaps when she'd studied that book on migratory birds of the Atlantic coastline.

Whatever the source of her inspiration, Eliza suddenly knew the answer to her dilemma. Madeira. The island of Madeira, haven to myriad migratory birds, and haven as well for numerous travelers searching for escape from England's cold damp winters. The island's balmy southern shore had made of it a winter colony for ailing British citizens. If she and Aubrey could go there, they'd be with others like themselves—and she'd be away from Michael and her father's determined matchmaking, at least for a while.

She leaned forward, her gray eyes alight with hopefulness. "I have the most wonderful idea," she began.

Long after most of their guests had departed, Aubrey, his parents, and Michael lingered. Aunt Judith had very early on retired from the debate. She sat on the hearth bench, just listening. But Eliza felt sure she was on her side. Michael lounged near the mantle, one elbow propped on it, a drink forgotten in his other hand as he stared at her. Eliza's mother, too, was quiet. Only Uncle Lloyd and Eliza's father voiced their opinions, and they were both opposed.

"If it's the cold, we can send him to St. Mary's, down in the Isles of Scilly," Sir Lloyd said. His thick mutton chops seemed almost to flap independently of the movement of his jaw.

"Madeira is far too . . . too far," Eliza's father added.

Not far enough, Eliza wanted to retort, but she wisely held her tongue. "You and LeClere have sailed to Portugal. Several times," she argued instead.

"Yes, but though Madeira is Portugese, it's several hundred miles farther out. And besides, that was business."

"And business is more important than Aubrey's health? And mine?" Eliza demanded an answer, her cheeks flush with emotion. She did not even try to hide her frustration with them.

"She has a point, Gerald." All eyes turned toward Constance. "Though I cannot help but dread the thought of them undertaking such an arduous journey, I think both Eliza and Aubrey might benefit from a winter in Madeira. Dame Franklin sent her son-in-law there—the one who suffered from the foxhunting accident. She told me once that it worked miracles for him."

Gerald Thoroughgood frowned. "But what of her wedding?" He gestured toward Michael. "It would hardly be fair to the groom."

"I think she should go."

Michael's surprising comment drew every eye in the room to him. His posture straightened and he set his glass down on the marble mantle. But although he addressed her father, he kept his clear gaze directly upon Eliza. "I think her idea is a sound one. What nobler endeavor could there be than to improve a child's life? I understand that Eliza has known illness in her own life. Who better to accompany Aubrey? Who better to understand and help him regain the use of his injured foot?"

Even Sir Lloyd could not hold firm when society's shining star turned the full force of his persuasive personality on him. Michael's smile was disarming, but it was his words which ultimately carried the day. Who could deny a suffering child perhaps his last chance to heal?

When the two fathers finally agreed, Eliza could only gape at Michael, quite dumbfounded. Was it because he wished to be rid of her for the several months the journey would take? Or was he hoping for a way for him to cry off that would be less humiliating for her? Or allow *her* to cry off? It would be quite like him to do such a gentlemanly deed.

But the intent expression on his face as he stared at her put the lie to those possibilities. He studied her so oddly, as if he'd never really looked at her before now. Nor was she nearly so disconcerted by his attention as she usually was.

But then, she'd been caught up in her passionate argument with her father and Sir Lloyd.

"I'll check the ship logs in the morning," Sir Lloyd stated as one of the servants helped him into his heavy overcoat. "I believe one of my vessels can carry them there without much trouble."

"And we must see to a chaperone," Eliza's father added.

Eliza stood and crossed slowly to Aubrey who'd been silent through the entire discussion. "We shall have ourselves quite an adventure, you and I." She covered his thin hand with one of hers. "Sailing to an exotic island. Enjoying a warm, sunny winter instead of a cold, dreary one."

"I'm not going if I have to take this bloody chair," the boy snapped.

"Now Aubrey," Sir Lloyd began. "You shall do as we deem best, and I—"

"Before long Aubrey may not need that chair at all." Once again it was Michael who came to the rescue, ending the debate before it could properly begin. Then with that smooth manner that had disarmed Sir Lloyd, he drew Eliza a little aside from the others. To her utter shock, he placed a hand on each of her shoulders then bent his head nearer hers and addressed her in a tone reserved for her ears only.

"And perhaps by the time she returns to us, my bride-to-be will be more eager for our marriage."

"I . . . it's not . . . that is—"

He cut her stuttering off with a light, pleasant brush of his mouth against hers that threw all her senses off-kilter. But she could feel the smile on his well-formed lips, and when he straightened up again, she wondered disjointedly whether he could feel the round O of astonishment on hers.

"I'll be there to see you off, Eliza. But I will also be there to greet you when you return," he said, his handsome face hovering above hers. "I am hoping, dear girl, that your doubts about our coming marriage will ease during your sojourn, and that by the time you return, you will anticipate our union just as eagerly as do I."

Chapter Two

"*H*e has three daughters and one son."

"How old? The son, not the daughters."

The skinny solicitor had to force down the gleam of unholy interest that lit his eyes. Why would this man want to know how old Sir Lloyd Haberton's one male heir was? But he was not about to ask the question out loud. He had a nose for trouble, he did. And it was clear this particular chap was nothing but trouble. Not loud rowdy trouble, but the deep, silent kind. The very worst sort. Pity this poor Sir Lloyd Haberton.

"Nine. Ten. Does it matter how old he is?"

Stupid question, he quickly realized. For the man raised his head from the single sheet of paper he'd been studying, the one listing Haberton's several business and residential addresses, and fixed his cold eyes on him. Deadly, those eyes were. Cold and deadly as death itself. The solicitor swallowed and shifted on the hard wooden bench. "He's ten. Yes, ten. That's what the scullery maid told me. Oh, and he's being sent away for the winter."

One dark brow arched but the man's eyes reflected no discernible emotion.

"He's had a fall and he's being sent to some island to heal," the solicitor continued.

"How fortuitous."

Cyprian Dare did not believe in fate or in luck. He neither wished for things nor prayed to anyone or anything. A man made his own fortune, good or bad. He took advantage of what was happening around him and he shaped his own fate. Cyprian had waited all his life for the chance to even the score with Haberton. Now his persistence would pay off. The time had come.

He pulled out an envelope and slid it to the center of the scarred tavern table. "Your payment. Speak a word of this to anyone, however . . . "

He didn't need to elaborate. Behind him Xavier shifted his considerable weight from one leg to the other, and Cyprian watched the sallow-faced solicitor go two shades paler. Xavier had that effect on people.

Once the solicitor scurried out of the room, Cyprian signaled his two men to join him at the table. At the same time, the serving wench stuck her head in the door.

"Can I fill you up again?"

The younger of Cyprian's two men, Oliver, waggled his brows at her. "What a jolly idea. You can fill me up. I can fill you up." The boy grinned. "I'm certain we can work a trade of some sort or another."

She giggled and sidled into the room. She was a short brunette with huge breasts threatening to burst the seams of her tightly laced bodice at any moment. Completely unlike the slender blonde dairy maid Cyprian had dragged Oliver away from not an hour past, and that after the rapscallion had spent the night in the company of a rather refined widow nearly twice his age.

"Fill up our cups and leave," Cyprian growled impatiently. Now that his revenge was so close at hand, Oliver's renowned appetite for the ladies would have to wait.

The maid was quick to do as Cyprian ordered, but she leaned low over the table as she poured, offering Oliver and the others as well an ample view of just what she had to offer a man. When Oliver slid one hand up her skirt, she let out a pretty little shriek, and then a softer gasp. But she was careful not to slosh the wine. As she flounced away, casting a long meaningful look back at Oliver before closing the door, Oliver held up his center finger and grinned.

"Caught a dip, I did. And she's wet and ready for me, just that fast." He sniffed his finger and let out a heartfelt sigh.

Xavier shook his head at the younger man. "She's probably still nasty from the leavings of some bloke who had her under the stairs. Or in the barn. Or out in the meadow."

"Screw you," Oliver retorted flippantly. He stuck his finger in the other man's mug and stirred it around. "You're just jealous because that's the closest you'll get to any quim this trip out."

"My Ana's worth a hundred of your doxies. A thousand. It's no hardship a'tall to be waiting for her. You're young yet—only a lad," he added, clearly to irritate Oliver. "You'll learn that there's more to a woman than the place between her legs." Then Xavier turned from the boy to face Cyprian. "Will we be turning for home now?"

Cyprian drummed his fingers idly on the table. "Soon," he mused out loud to his first mate and oldest friend. "Very soon."

Then he straightened up and smiled, a cold, calculating smile that drove any thought of women from the minds of his two men. When Cyprian Dare wore that expression, best for the whole world to beware.

Xavier and Oliver shared a look. They knew little of this Sir Lloyd Haberton whom Cyprian hunted so fiercely. But they knew the man must have done something extremely foolish to have stirred such intense emotion in their captain. Whoever he was, however, he'd soon know why no one ever trifled twice with Cyprian Dare.

The sky hung ugly and low, and mist coated everyone in the Haberton and Thoroughgood party with beads of moisture as fine as diamond dust. They'd smelled of damp wool on the crowded coach ride to St. Catherine's Dock. Now, however, a rank fishy smell dominated. Eliza heartily hoped they'd not be forced to endure that smell the entire journey.

She'd never been to sea. Never stepped foot on a boat, let alone a sea-going ship. But she'd imagined it. She'd read once that the sea smelled of salt and other strange things, altogether different from the land. Despite her recent doubts about this harebrained scheme of hers, she couldn't deny the budding curiosity growing in her. She wanted to smell the sea, and stare across the living, writhing swells of it. She wanted to see where and when the moon rose, and figure out how the tides were affected by that distant orb.

She just hoped it wasn't always as cold as it was today. She felt that her skin surely must be turning blue.

"You know, it's not too late to change your mind," Eliza's mother murmured for her daughter's ears only. "Your cousin Agnes could manage—"

"No, she couldn't. Besides, I *want* to go."

Perry jostled his way between them and threw one arm around each of their shoulders. "Here now, Mum. She wants to go. *I* want to go."

"You have school, little brother," Eliza taunted, but gently. Younger brothers were almost as much trouble as older ones, but she knew she would miss both of them enormously.

"I'm hardly little," he said, staring down at her from his lofty height. "Besides," he added, "I'd learn ever so much more if I went—geography, history." He sent his mother a pleading look but his argument fell on deaf ears, as it had often in the previous two weeks. With a grimace of resignation he gave Eliza a kiss on the cheek. "Take care of yourself, paleface," he ordered sternly, using the name he'd given her after reading stories of America.

Eliza gave him a wan smile. This was turning out to be even harder than she'd guessed. "Don't grow too much while I'm gone."

LeClere was next, giving her a fierce hug. He was the one who always looked out for her, and she realized only now how much she had always relied on him. Could she truly manage this?

Then Michael came up and a new wave of doubt assailed her. Why was she running away from him? He was such an utterly perfect human being. Her brain must be even weaker than her lungs to think of turning down such a paragon among men.

When he smiled that paragon smile, and kissed her brow with his paragon lips, she wondered if perhaps she should reconsider this trip to Madeira after all. Then her father cleared his throat and Michael stepped back. "Have a safe trip, Eliza. I'll eagerly count the days until you return to me."

Until you return to me. His words lingered in her head through the rest of their goodbyes. Her father hugged her, so hard and long that she thought she'd never catch her breath again. Her mother held Eliza's face in her hands while tears sparkled in her eyes. "When you return it will be time to get on with the wedding. You understand?"

"Yes, Mama. I understand. And I'll be ready." And she would, she told herself.

In the past two weeks Michael had been even more attentive than he had before, coming to dine with the family, escorting them to the theater. She'd been disconcerted by his presence, as always. But now it was somehow different. Before he'd behaved as if he were fond of her, but not particularly drawn to her—as if their marriage were a business arrangement, which it was. Now, though, his interest in her seemed more personal. More physical, too.

Once, when he'd helped her down from his carriage, she'd known by the look in his eyes that he'd wanted to kiss her. And if she'd paused just a moment, he would have taken that kiss. But she'd turned away, flustered, and the moment had been lost. Afterwards she'd recalled the one time he had kissed her and berated herself for missing the chance to satisfy her curiosity with a second kiss. Today, of course, with her family here, he'd had to confine himself to kissing her brow. But that only increased her curiosity.

She stared past her mother to where Michael stood watching her with a half-smile on his face. Despite the cold, hot color flooded her cheeks. Soon enough they would be married and then her curiosity about kissing— and other things—would be answered. Perhaps this trip would be good for them both, whetting their appetites for the coming ceremony.

The goodbyes might have gone on endlessly had the captain of their vessel not implored his employer, her Uncle Lloyd, to intercede. "The tides do not wait for the *Lady Haberton*."

"Yes, yes," Sir Lloyd conceded. He'd arranged for one of his regular vessels to stop over in Madeira. Now he looked none too pleased with the entire venture. "Come on," he muttered. "Let's be done with it."

A scared-looking Aubrey was carried up the gangplank by his servant Robert. Eliza's maid Clothilde followed them, as did an army of baggage carriers and a perplexed sailor pushing Aubrey's chair. Cousin Agnes was assisted aboard, grumbling about the rain, the stink, and the paltry size of the ship.

When it was Eliza's turn to mount the ridged gangplank, she steeled herself not to stumble or hesitate or look in the least overwhelmed. Madeira would be good for Aubrey's condition and very likely hers too. She must approach everything about their journey with a positive outlook. But once LeClere released her arm and returned to the dock, she was not quite certain she could succeed. Waving madly with her damp hankerchief, she stood at the rail as the gangplank was pulled up.

But Agnes herded her away from the deck. "You'll catch your death, child. Your lungs are weak enough as it is. Come along, come along."

The last view of her family that Eliza had was of her parents standing arm in arm, her mother dabbing at her eyes. LeClere and Perry and Michael had their collars turned up and their hats pulled down against the cold and the rain. But they were smiling and she gulped down a hard knot of emotions. Six months until she saw them all again. Six long months. Who knew how things might change by then?

The *Lady Haberton* slid out of St. Catherine's Dock and into the Thames at nine o'clock. A bare half hour later the *Chameleon* followed. Cyprian Dare stood at the forward bow, leaning out over the bow sprit, just above the weathered carving of a woman with a thick serpent twined about her.

Not much longer. Not much longer at all. He would let them get well out to sea. Perhaps as far as the Channel Isles. Then he would pounce and Sir Lloyd Haberton's child would be his.

A sheet of rain gusted over him, stinging his face, then rippling across the deck. Another came, and then another, until the entire world was a cold wet blur of rain and deck and murky river. But the wind blew strong from the north and they made good progress. He shrugged off the hood of his rain slicker and turned his face up to the sky. The violent rain plastered his close-cropped hair to his skull and icy fingers of water worked under the collar of his coat and shirt.

But Cyprian didn't care. If anything, the freezing rain helped cool the terrible fire that raged in him still. Finally, twenty-eight years would be avenged. He'd begun his search the day his mother had died—fifteen years it was now. But the memory of it was as fresh in Cyprian's mind as ever. Up till then she'd never spoken of his father, not even when he'd asked. Only as she lay dying had she finally revealed his name—Sir Lloyd Haberton —and cursed him for abandoning both her and their child. Then she'd abandoned Cyprian as well. He knew now, of course, that she'd wanted to stay. But back then he'd felt abandoned.

Cybil Burns probably had been a handsome woman once upon a time. But a youthful indiscretion and the resultant pregnancy had turned her family from her in shame. Alone, abandoned by everyone, she'd had her child and made her way as best she could. But the music lessons, private tutors, and polite manners she'd been taught were no help when it came to keeping a child fed. Though raised a well-to-do vicar's daughter in Newport, she'd been reduced to working as a maid in dockfront taverns. She'd whored too, Cyprian had realized years later. She'd slept with anyone who'd promise a better opportunity for her child. He'd gotten his first position as a cabin boy that way, and God only knew what else. Because his father hadn't cared at all that she'd borne him a child, she'd been forced to sell her body so that she could make a life for herself and her son.

He'd never been able to use a whore with complete satisfaction as a result.

Thank God there were enough other women who were willing to lay with him without benefit of money, else he'd be as celibate as a monk.

If monks were truly celibate.

A shiver wracked him but he ignored it. Somewhere ahead of him was the means to his revenge. Once he had Haberton's son in his possession, Cyprian could finally begin to purge himself of the hatred that sometimes threatened to consume him. The boy would suffer as Cyprian had suffered: the pain of abandonment; the frustration and the helplessness; the humiliation of making his way as a child in a cruel world that made no allowances for childishness or weakness. And Cyprian would see to it that Sir Lloyd Haberton was kept informed of every sordid detail. From port to port they would move, and from each new place Cyprian would write Haberton.

The man would know how his beloved child shivered under a thin blanket, sleeping in the shed behind the home of his latest employer. He would be kept informed about how his son was reduced to fighting dogs for their food in order to fill his stomach adequately. Wearing rags on his feet when his one pair of shoes grew too small.

Cyprian gritted his teeth and his fingers tightened on the wet rail as he remembered his wretched childhood. But he had learned to fight. He'd learned how to stay alive, and he'd grown stronger for it. So would this boy, cripple or no. It was Haberton who would suffer more. With every letter Haberton would die a little more, just as Cyprian's mother had. The man would still be wealthy, well fed, and well respected in his own circles. But Cyprian knew he would be dying inside. Not knowing where his son was would destroy him.

It was a revenge Cyprian had relished all the years he'd searched for his bastard father—for that's how he termed the man. Cyprian may have been born the bastard, but it had been his father's choice, not his own. Nor even his mother's. His mother had told him he had no surname. She'd lost hers, when her family disowned her, and his father had not given him one. So Cyprian

had named himself Dare. Even when she'd told him his
father's full name, he'd refused to take it as his own.
Nor would he ever. He didn't want the man's name nor
his wealth. Not a farthing of it. But his only half
brother . . .

   Yes, to control the destiny of Haberton's one true
heir—to steal Haberton's pride and joy away from him
—that didn't seem an unreasonable payment for twenty-
eight years of abandonment.

Chapter Three

The river Thames and the long day they spent traversing its length to the sea made for as awful an experience as Eliza could remember. The rain came down intermittently so that they were confined to their chilly cabins. The view outside was of a dirty trash-filled waterway that looked more like a sewer than the greatest river in the land. And it stank.

"God in heaven, please save us from anymore of this . . . this odor," Agnes intoned, clutching her prayer book to her ample bosom. First cousin to Sir Lloyd, Agnes lived on the meager allowance left to her by her own wastrel father. Sir Lloyd's generosity to her these last eight years had been a blessing to her, and in her eyes at least, the man could do no wrong. Though she'd been terrified crossing the gangplank and now pressed a lilac-scented handkerchief to her nose, Eliza knew the woman would voice no harsher complaint than that murmured prayer.

Eliza, Agnes, and Clothilde shared a cabin that was not even a quarter the size of Eliza's opulent bedchamber at home. The beds, though generously provided with plump pillows and thick coverlets, were nevertheless rather narrow. They were built into the walls with storage underneath and railings made to hold a sleeping body in place no matter the pitching of the vessel. Their trunks were lashed to the outside wall and everything else—pitcher, bowl, chamber pot—was stowed in small teakwood compartments that had been specially sized with locking latches. A brass lantern hung from a hook in the middle of the coffered ceiling, and two glass prisms flanked it, bringing light down through the deck, though with this rain there was little enough light.

"Shall I unpack, Miss Eliza?" Clothilde asked.

Thank heaven for Clothilde, Eliza thought, sending her sturdy maid a smile. With her good sense and ebullient spirits to buoy them up they'd all do fine. "If you'd like. But not everything. Bed clothes. A few day dresses. Oh, and my tablet and pencils. I'd like to do some sketching when the weather improves."

But the weather stayed grim and cold. They ate a light lunch in their room and then dinner in the captain's cramped dining room. Aubrey sulked and Robert appeared put out with the boy. In the name of peace Eliza paired Robert with Clothilde and then put Agnes next to the captain so that he could entertain her. She sat next to Aubrey.

"How is your cabin?" she asked the child. "Ours is small but charming, and most cunningly designed."

"Too small," he muttered, sticking his lower lip out. "And it stinks."

"By tomorrow we should be out to sea. The air will be clean and bracing there."

Aubrey didn't look up. He just pushed his leeks around the plate with his fork.

"I plan to sketch tomorrow. Will we pass Dover during the day?" she asked the captain.

"Aye, miss. The white cliffs will be just off starboard. And a magnificent sight they are."

Aubrey looked at the captain too, though his expression didn't improve in the least. "Are they truly white, then?"

"White as chalk, for that's what they are," Eliza replied. "I read that," she added, glancing shyly at the Captain.

"Well, you read correctly, for they're so white you can scarcely believe your eyes."

"Perhaps you'd like to try some sketching also." Eliza turned back to Aubrey. "I've scads of paper and pencils with me. You're free to use as much as you like."

"Not in that chair." He poked at the leeks again.

"Now, Aubrey." Cousin Agnes leaned forward and gave him an earnest look. "You know what your father said. A good bracing turn about the deck each day. Robert will push you—"

"No!" The fork hit the plate, and leeks and carrots flew across the table. "No rolling chair!" the boy shouted, his face going red and his eyes glinting suspiciously with tears.

Eliza hated emotional scenes like this. They always made her heart pound and her breathing come too fast. Yet she could see that someone would have to intercede. Cousin Agnes meant to carry out Sir Lloyd's precise instructions as if they'd been sent down with Moses along with the commandments. And Aubrey would fight her just as fiercely as he'd been fighting his father at home. It was, unfortunately, up to her to keep some sort of peace between them.

"Once at sea, the pitching of the ship may make the rolling chair a trifle unsafe. Isn't that right, Captain?"

He had leaned back in his chair at Aubrey's outburst. Now he faced her. "Depending upon the swells, of course, it could certainly be a bit of a problem."

"You see?" Eliza switched her gaze back and forth between the scowling child and the self-righteous Agnes. "To be safe we'll have Robert carry—I mean help Aubrey above decks and settle him in a nice secure chair. That way Uncle Lloyd's wishes shall have been carried out and Aubrey will also be content. That is all right with you, isn't it, Aubrey?"

"I want to go to my room," he responded, refusing to answer her question. "Now," he added, glaring at Robert.

So the day ended, with everyone grumpy and uncomfortable. But as Eliza lay in her unfamiliar bed a short while later she vowed that tomorrow would be better. She'd have to keep Agnes away from Aubrey and have the rolling chair he so despised stored out of sight. Whyever had Uncle Lloyd thought his fussy spinster cousin the right chaperone for a ten-year-old boy?

Yet as her mind drifted toward sleep, it was not her young cousin or anyone else on the ship she dreamed of, but rather a tall, strong man holding her by the shoulders and bending down to kiss her. And in her dreams she smiled and stretched up on tiptoe to kiss him back.

"Your sketch *is* every bit as good as mine," Eliza assured Aubrey.

" 'Tis not. I can't draw worth a fig." With a frustrated cry he crumpled the paper and flung it away. It caught in the crisp sea breeze and flew out over the rail and into the choppy waters of the Channel. Fading off to their right were the cliffs. By tomorrow they'd reach the Channel Islands where they'd dock for just one night at St. Peter Port in Guernsey. But although their trip had just begun, Eliza was not sure she could endure even another day with Aubrey. He was extremely sensitive and angry at the world. It took only the slightest provocation to spark his volatile temper and then they all must suffer it.

"No one draws a masterpiece on their very first effort," Eliza gritted out, trying to sound pleasant, though she felt anything but. "It requires a considerable amount of practice."

"Well, I don't want to practice!" He swung about on

the lounge chair Robert had settled him in and placed both feet on the ground. Before Eliza could stop him he lunged upright, then with a cry of pain, collapsed in a heap on the deck.

"Aubrey! Aubrey!" In an instant she was kneeling beside him. "Are you all right? Tell me you are. Oh, please."

To her utter surprise, he burrowed into her arms and burst into tears. Gone was the dreadful little tyrant of only minutes before. Instead he was a frightened child, hurt and confused, sobbing in her arms. She gathered him up and pressed a kiss upon his dark curls.

"Hush, sweetheart. It will be all right. You'll see."

"No." He shook his head. "It will never be all right again. I'm always going to be a cripple. A cripple! I'll never be able to walk or ride or do anything at all!"

"That's simply not true, Aubrey. There are lots of things you'll be able to do. You just have to give yourself more time and try harder."

"But I can't. I can't," he sobbed.

"Yes, you can," she vowed, waving a concerned Robert away. "Everything will require practice, however. Many hours of practice."

"I don't mean drawing," he complained, pulling back from her and wiping his face with his sleeve. "Drawing is for girls—and sissies. I want to be like before. I want to walk and run—" He again burst into heartwrenching sobs but this time Eliza simply held him as he wept. What could she possibly say to console him? Any promises she made would be no more than empty conjecture. Hopeful thinking. For she did not know whether he would ever be able to do those things again.

She'd struck upon this journey with Aubrey as a way for her to escape Michael. Aubrey was merely the excuse she'd used. But everything had turned upside down since then. Aubrey's plight was ever so much worse than hers. And as for Michael . . . she was as awed by him as ever, but she actually was beginning to believe he cared for her. At least a little. Marriage to him might not be so terrifying as she'd previously feared. But there was still Aubrey and the next six months to muddle through.

"Now you just listen to me, Aubrey Haberton. I think we should make a pact, you and I. You shall act as my nurse, and I as yours." She patted at his damp cheeks with her lace handkerchief. "For part of each day—say an hour—I shall be completely in charge of your activities, and for another hour, you shall be completely in charge of mine."

"Wh . . . what do you mean?" he asked, hiccuping.

"I mean that we each have an hour a day to make the other do whatever we think is best for the improvement of their health."

He thought a moment. "What's wrong with you? You don't look sick."

What indeed? It was such a part of her existence that she often forgot. "I have an illness called asthma. It was much worse when I was your age. But my doctor advises me that I must always be very careful not to overexert myself. Breathing too deeply is not good for me at all."

"Why?"

Eliza shrugged. "My lungs are weak. I was born that way. Sometimes when I was younger they would stop working altogether, and I would faint and then turn blue."

"Blue?" He looked at her doubtfully.

"Well, that's what LeClere and Perry have told me."

"Is that going to happen to you while we're on this trip?"

She smiled at his curious, almost hopeful tone. "I don't think so. In fact, I haven't had a full-fledged attack of that sort in, let's see . . . four years or so. Now, do we have an agreement?" she asked, returning to her original idea.

He let out a great gust of a sigh, but he looked far cheerier than before. "Oh, I suppose. It's only an hour. Besides, there's nothing else to do."

Together they managed to get him back up onto his chair, and just in time for Agnes came up from below decks, huffing from the short, steep climb. "Aubrey needs his medicine," she announced, fishing a brown bottle from her pocket. "And it's time for him to rest."

Eliza stopped Aubrey from snapping at the older woman with a warning hand to his arm. "Give it to me, Agnes. I'll see he gets it in a moment. We were just in the middle of a . . . of a geography lesson," she fibbed. Anything to prevent another row between them.

To her relief, Agnes handed over the bottle without argument. Then the woman grabbed for the nearest railing when the ship slid down a steeper than normal trough. "Oh, dear. Oh, dear," she murmured. "I don't feel well. No, truly I don't."

Her face did look a trifle pale. Green even. Eliza signaled for Robert, and in a moment he guided the woman back toward her cabin. Poor Agnes, it must be *mal de mer*. But Eliza's sympathies were cut short by a hoot of boyish laughter.

"She's seasick," Aubrey crowed. "What luck! She shan't be ordering me about at all!"

Eliza had to force down her own giggle. It wasn't really funny, but then, Agnes was rather stuffy. Aubrey was right. They *were* in luck.

She cleared her throat. "She may not be here to order you about. But I plan to do so for the next hour."

The western sun was just dipping toward the sea the next day when they tied up at St. Peter Port in Guernsey. Though it was one of the Channel Islands and still good English soil, England was quite beyond their view. Instead it was the French coastline they'd seen off the port side of the ship earlier in the afternoon, and now as

Eliza peered out at the village that crowded the island's shore, it all appeared quite foreign. More French than English, she decided.

"You're not holding your breath," Aubrey accused, drawing her attention away from the fascinating view of white-washed cottages, tiled roofs, and stone-paved streets. "I'm in charge. Remember?"

"Isn't your hour almost over?" she asked hopefully. Aubrey had taken her proposal more seriously than she'd expected. He'd worked hard the past two days at every task she'd given him: counting the balusters of the side rail by pointing his toes at them; singing a song and conducting imaginary musicians with his injured foot. He'd let her look at his poorly healed ankle after only a brief objection, and he'd answered all his questions about what parts hurt most, what he could feel and what he couldn't.

But eventually her hour had ended for today, and his had begun. It seemed he'd had her singing and blowing, and holding her breath off and on for much longer than sixty minutes. She'd even become dizzy once or twice.

"Just one more time," Aubrey demanded. "Let me time how long you can hold your breath, and then we'll stop."

She dutifully took a deep breath then held it while he counted at a slow steady pace. At thirty she wanted to stop. At forty she crossed her eyes and he began to laugh. But he kept on counting through his giggles. At fifty, however, she released a huge gasp.

"Enough! Enough. I can't do any better than fifty, I'm certain."

Aubrey grinned. "You did very well today, Eliza. If you keep up the good work and practice everyday," he said, imitating the exact words she'd used with him just an hour earlier, "you're bound to get better. I bet your lungs will stretch bigger and bigger and get stronger and stronger."

It sounded so logical Eliza could almost believe it. And perhaps if Aubrey worked hard and practiced enough, he could be the ring bearer at her wedding, she fervently hoped. But it was far too soon to mention that possibility. Still . . .

Robert took Aubrey to his cabin to prepare for dinner. They would be dining off the ship tonight, the last time for quite a while. But Eliza waved Clothilde off when she came for her, bidding her to help Robert, saying she wished to sit quietly for a short time. The fact was, Eliza had noticed Clothilde's interest in Robert, and she thought it quite sweet. Besides, the air was so clear and the evening sky so spectacular in hues of violet and salmon, like streaks of color painted by a bold, heavenly hand. Was Michael viewing this same vivid sunset? she wondered.

Then a ship moved into her line of sight, cutting off her view of the sky and her thoughts of Michael. The vessel eased right up beside theirs, bumping up against the timber dock and swinging around slowly so that she thought they might even collide. But it righted itself—or rather, the burly navigator she could see at the helm righted it. Eliza stared in awe at both ship and navigator, for never had she seen such a unique pairing. The ship was a very dark wood, with round gun portals painted red running in a row down the side. At the front of the ship—fore, it was called—was a most revealing carving of a woman. A naked woman. The most private portions of her anatomy were concealed by a thick snake which coiled itself about her. But Eliza couldn't help thinking that the snake made the sculpture far more lewd than if it had been just the naked woman alone.

Then there was the huge man handling the ship's wheel. Eliza could not stop herself from gaping, though she knew it was horribly rude. It was just that she'd never seen a Negro before, for that's what she thought he must be. A Negro from the African continent. And what a magnificent sight he was. Tall, with arms as thick as tree branches, and short hair curling tightly around his dark face. Other sailors clambered up in the riggings as they did on the *Lady Haberton,* but the man at the wheel had captured her attention completely.

"Miss Eliza. Come along, miss. Please." Clothilde had to give Eliza a sharp pinch on the arm to break her spellbound fascination with the man. "Captain says you shouldn't be up here alone. Not while we're in port anyways. St. Peter Port is a rather rough town, what with all these ships comin' in and out—oh, my sweet Lord! Would you look at him!"

The dark-skinned man turned at that precise moment to stare at them across the short space between the ships, and both Clothilde and Eliza stepped back. He was no threat to them, so it was all quite illogical. But Eliza did not protest when Clothilde hurried her through the low hatchway and down the stairs to their cabin.

On the neighboring ship Cyprian was acutely aware of the *Lady Haberton's* proximity. He looked up at Xavier's approach after the first mate had tied the wheel in place.

"I don't like it," Xavier muttered to him. "We should not take the boy here. We are too well known in this place."

"What difference does it make?" Cyprian replied, unperturbed by Xavier's concern. "Once Haberton receives my letter, he'll know who has his son."

But that did not appease Xavier, judging by the man's downturned mouth. "I cannot like this plan of yours, Cyprian. To harm a child is not your way—"

"He won't be harmed."

"No?" The big man's jet black brows raised in skepticism. "There is no way the child cannot be hurt. You are tearing him from his family, and that after he has already suffered some misfortune with his legs."

"You worry without reason. I plan to take very good care of my brother," Cyprian assured him. He took a grim pleasure in the surprised look that came over Xavier's face.

"Your brother? But you've never spoken before of a brother."

"My half brother, sired by the same man. So you see, Xavier, you need not worry about him. I personally shall see to his education and upbringing. He shall learn, as you and I did, how to survive in this world. And how to succeed."

The first mate rubbed his jaw thoughtfully. "So. This Haberton is your father. Does he know?"

"He does not. Nor does anyone else but you, and I would keep it that way." He eyed his good friend assessingly. "Are you with me, Xavier?"

There was a long pause before Xavier answered, but Cyprian never doubted his friend's response. "Aye, you can count on me. It will be good for you to have family again. It has been—"

"He's not my family!"

This time Xavier shook his head and sighed. "Do you plan to ask for a ransom?"

Cyprian shrugged. "Perhaps, just for the frustration it will give Haberton to fail in his efforts to reclaim his son."

"And will you explain all this to the boy so that he will understand and not be afraid—and not hate his brother?"

Cyprian laughed, though he felt no humor at all. "He can hate me for all I care, and he probably will. I'll leave it to you to play mother to him. Just as you did for Oliver."

Xavier snorted but he was not distracted. "You would have this titled young man become a rowdy sailor like

Oliver—like you and me—when he could be anything else?"

"What I want is for Haberton to exhaust himself searching for his son. His *sons*," Cyprian amended bitterly. "The one son who he'll want back at any cost, as well as the other son he'll never be able to ignore again."

Chapter Four

*T*he boy was surrounded by people. But the aging captain, the single manservant, plus the maid, the older woman, and the petite young woman accompanying him would prove no impediment at all to Cyprian's plan. Oliver had easily befriended a few of the *Lady Haberton*'s crew at a nearby tavern. He had come back with the news that the captain meant to take them to dine at Duffy's Lodgings in a private room, then return to their ship.

But when they set sail at the turn of the tide, just before dawn while the passengers yet slept, they would be missing one of their number. Young Master Haberton would be safely ensconced in the *Chameleon*'s hold. Let them think the boy had drowned for now. It would only increase Haberton's suffering.

Cyprian took a long pull on the cheroot he held. All was quiet. The sun had set and most of his men had been granted shore leave, though they had strict orders to be back before the changing of the tide. Should they need to cast off early, he wanted the entire crew already aboard.

He watched the small party depart the ship and saw Oliver stroll along after them. Oliver was to keep a watchful eye on them. Later he and Ollie would board the ship and snatch the boy.

Cyprian finished his smoke and promptly lit another. He coughed once, but the burning smoke filled his lungs and soothed his raw throat. He thought of the small chest of opium in his quarters and for a moment he almost succumbed to the temptation. But experience had taught him—the hard way—that deadening his senses with that seductive drug always came with a cost. He needed to be alert tonight. If, as it happened, he were primed more tautly than the most hair-triggered of his ship's several guns, that was to the good. Time enough later to numb himself. He would save that for three days from now, the anniversary of his birth. The official anniversary of his abandonment by the man who'd sired him.

The night grew black. Clouds scudded in from the west. Yet still he sat alone on the deck. Two lanterns bobbing along the sloping street that led down to the docks marked the early return of the diners, and Cyprian shifted his position to the fo'c'sle head to better view their progress.

The boy was easy to see, for he was carried in the servant's arms. What was wrong with him, anyway?

Cyprian flung his cheroot in the water and squinted at them. If the boy didn't recover from whatever ailed him and never relearned to walk it would complicate things. But then, he could always become a street beggar. Wouldn't *that* destroy Haberton.

Cyprian clenched his teeth in rhythmic spasms and for a moment he paused. He'd seen beggars in ports all over the world. The pitiful dregs of society, missing eyes or limbs and inevitably covered with sores. Like street rats they were, scurrying in the shadows, eking out whatever miserable life they could. Surviving on what others threw away.

He'd begged for awhile—until he'd learned that

thieves ate much better than beggars. He'd survived, he reminded himself, doing whatever he must to stay alive. Haberton's son deserved no better opportunity than he'd had. He suppressed any sympathies he might have for the ailing boy beneath that one overriding conviction.

Aboard the *Lady Haberton*, Eliza held the hatchway door wide for Robert's descent. In his arms Aubrey lay, rigid as stone. Gone was the laughing child of the past two days. Agnes had but to complain that the rolling chair would have been easier on Robert, and the boy had thrown a tantrum. The entire meal had been ruined and by unspoken consent they'd decided to leave the lodging house early. Now, however, though she was relieved to be rid of Aubrey's unhappy presence, Eliza was no less eager to be confined with Agnes in the close quarters of their cabin. The woman was certain to expound relentlessly on how Aubrey should mind his father's instructions. It would take all of Eliza's effort not to snap at her, and at the moment she wasn't sure all her effort would be enough.

"I think I shall linger a short while on deck," she told Clothilde. "You go on down and tend to Agnes. I'll join you both soon."

"But miss, you shouldn't be alone."

"I'm sure it's perfectly safe. Isn't it, Captain?"

"We've the watch posted. And I'll have the gangplank pulled up."

"There, you see?" Eliza patted Clothilde's arm. "Don't worry. I just need a few minutes to myself."

The maid gave her an astute look. "Away from her, you mean," she whispered wryly.

Once everyone had descended and the hatch door was closed, Eliza sank down upon the steps that led up to the quarterdeck. Nothing was going quite as she'd expected. Aubrey was impossible, though he was perfectly capable of being charming when he so desired.

Cousin Agnes, however, was surely the most insensitive of women. Why must she constantly bring up the one subject certain to set off Aubrey's temper? How Eliza wished she could simply push that confounded rolling chair into the sea!

At the edges of her vision, a small light suddenly flared, then just as swiftly faded. It was on the ship nearest theirs and Eliza squinted toward the hulking shadow of it. The *Chameleon.* A lantern hung aft, and a light gleamed from one of the intimidating vessel's lower decks. But like the *Lady Haberton,* it lay mostly in darkness, save for the tiny glow from the deck that she supposed was someone smoking. Was that their watchman? And could he be watching her?

Eliza drew her boxcloth mantle closer around her neck. The sea air was cold at night, even this far south. But it wasn't the cold that made her shiver. There was something about that ship and its invisible watcher that struck a disturbing chord in her. It was so dark and bristled with so many guns. And then that vulgar figurehead. The ship and its crew seemed deliberately to flaunt the rules of good society. Why, they might even be pirates, for all she knew.

At that daunting thought Eliza rose to her feet and backed uneasily toward the hatchway. But she kept her eyes fastened upon the flickering glow from the other ship, and when it too started to move parallel to her, her heart began a fearful thudding. He *was* watching her! Could it be the fierce-looking African she'd seen earlier?

Then the tiny spark arced out toward her and she stumbled backward in fear. It fizzled out, of course. It was, after all, just the man tossing away the remains of his cheroot. But the darkness that remained afterwards spooked her even more. With a muttered imprecation— words she'd heard her brothers use but had never uttered herself—Eliza turned and fled.

* * *

Cyprian stripped down to swanskin breeches as he gave Xavier his last minute instructions. "Bring the dinghy aft, beneath his cabin. We'll drug him to keep him silent and lower him to you. If anyone raises an alarm and you're spotted, abandon the boat and swim to shore. It's dark enough that no one should see you."

"Am I to allow the poor tyke to drown, then?"

Cyprian slanted his first mate an aggravated stare. "Let him drown and I'll drown you," he muttered. And at that moment he meant it. He should never have revealed his reasons for this kidnapping to Xavier, but he'd needed to talk to someone. It had not changed Xavier's opposition at all, however. That's why Cyprian had decided to take Oliver on board the *Lady Haberton* with him and leave Xavier to man the boat.

"Try not to kill anyone," he told Oliver, even as he strapped a sheathed knife onto his calf. "But if that's what it takes to get the boy . . . " He trailed off, meeting Xavier's frown with a mocking stare. Then he picked up a jug of Madeira wine and took a deep pull. "To success," he said, passing the jug to Oliver.

"To the hunt," Oliver added, an eager grin on his young face. He drank and handed the wine jug to Xavier.

The African held the jug in his wide hands for a long moment. Then he gestured toward Cyprian with it. "To our captain and to peace. May you find it someday."

When Cyprian slipped from the dinghy into the icy waters of St. Peter Port Bay, Xavier's words rang still in his ears. The man was clearly turning pious on him. Ever since he'd married that waif he'd rescued, Ana, the soft spot in Xavier's heart had grown bigger and softer. But Xavier's overdeveloped conscience was *his* problem, not Cyprian's. As he and Oliver swam silently toward the sleeping ship that held his quarry, Cyprian buried all thought of Xavier and his disapproval. No matter what his first mate thought, he could always be trusted none-theless to follow Cyprian's orders. Cyprian would stake his life on that fact. After all, they'd both staked their lives on each other too many times to count already. Xavier's disapproval of this particular scheme would fade in time.

At the corner of the *Lady Haberton,* starboard side, Cyprian and Oliver tread water. "There are two cabins aft. He's on the starboard side. But we'll have to shimmy up the tie out for that rowboat."

It was no task at all for them each to pull themselves up the coarse rope that kept the small boat alongside the taller ship. Oliver scaled it like a monkey, using all fours, while Cyprian just hauled himself up hand over hand. Years manning the riggings had developed his up-per body so that such a climb took no real effort.

They hoisted themselves over the rail and crouched in the shadow of the poop deck, getting their bearings. Cyprian had spied someone in the shadows earlier, a woman, judging by her silhouette. But she'd not lingered long. Now there was only the solitary watch-man, and he kept watch for a shore approach. If all went as planned, they would have the boy locked aboard the *Chameleon* before anyone raised the slightest alarm.

Across the sky a dull light flickered, followed a few seconds later by an unfocused rumble from the heavens. Good. A storm would cover any sounds of struggle with the boy's servant. The wind blew, raising goose bumps on Cyprian's wet skin, but he didn't notice. The time for his revenge was at hand.

In her cabin Eliza heard the same roll of thunder. Another flash of light soon followed, and this time the thunder crackled its threat. A muffled cry sounded. Au-brey, she realized. She sat up, hoping Robert would be able to appease the child. But Aubrey's cry came again. Should she see to him?

When lightning flashed another time, however, illuminating their narrow cabin with its unearthly light, she knew she'd have to go. For although Cousin Agnes slept blissfully in her bed, Clothilde's narrow bunk was vacant. If she were out, it could only be with Robert. And that, Eliza realized with a sinking heart, meant that Aubrey was alone.

A panic-stricken cry prodded her, despite her reluctance, to crawl from her bed. She donned her soft kid slippers and her pink quilted wrapper, and with a muttered oath about derelict servants, let herself out of the room.

Sure enough, Aubrey was alone. Both Robert and Clothilde would catch the rough side of her temper tomorrow, that was for certain, she decided as she hurried to his side.

"It's just a storm, Aubrey. That's all. There's no need to be frightened," she reassured him once she located him in the darkened cabin.

He was sitting up in the bed and at her touch, he grasped her around the waist. "I hate storms. I hate lightning. I hate thunder—"

He broke off at another ear-splitting crack and buried his face in her arms, and it was then Eliza recalled why he feared storms so. His horse had panicked and thrown him during a sudden summer storm. It had been brief but quite violent. A number of trees on their properties had been torn right out of the earth, she remembered. But the aftermath for Aubrey had been ever so much worse.

"Shh, shh," she soothed, holding him close. "It will soon pass us by. You'll see." As she said the words, a quick patter of raindrops on the thick-paned rear-facing windows signaled an advancing wave of rain, and in a moment they were cocooned in the rush of sound. Aubrey's thin shoulders heaved with his sobs and his tears soon turned her wrapper and gown quite damp. But Eliza could sense his emotional storm changing, just as

the storm outside shifted. Less furious sound and outrage; more muffled weeping and sorrow.

But it was awkward for Eliza to bend down to the
level of his bed, and after a few minutes she sat down
beside him. At once Aubrey curled up beside her, his
sobs easing to occasional shudders and unpredictable
hiccups.

"There. Better now?"

He shook his head. "It might come back."

"Oh, I don't think so," Eliza countered. "The lightning is just at the beginning of the storm. Once the rains
come the lightning and thunder always stop—"

A flash of brilliant light, followed immediately by a
deafening crash made a liar of her. They both jumped
and Eliza was certain her heart stopped.

"You see!" he cried, clinging to her in terror.

Eliza was not about to argue. Without thinking she
huddled down beside him and drew the covers over
their heads. Though she was not much taller than him,
he curled into her arms like a petrified kitten. But he
seemed marginally reassured by her nearness, and as
the storm raged outside, rocking the ship at its moor-
ings, they lay side by side in the warm nest of the boy's
bed.

"Tell me a story," he whispered after a while of hearing only the rain and wind pounding against the windows.

"A story? I don't know any stories."

"Everybody knows stories."

Eliza sighed. "Oh, all right. Let's see . . . once upon
a time there was a little boy who refused to grow up."

It was her own disjointed retelling of an old story one
of her nurses used to tell her. An island where boys
never had to grow up, where magic was not unheard of,
but where boys still must eventually face the conse-
quences of their actions. She told the story slowly, whis-

pering and pausing to remember or to make up some new twist to her nurse's tale.

It wasn't long, however, before she realized that Aubrey was asleep. His breath came faint and even against her neck. His tousled head rested heavily on her shoulder. And as she let her story trail away, she couldn't help smiling. He really was a sweet child. Before his accident she'd not known him very well, for he'd always escaped outdoors whenever his family came to visit, to the stables or the fields. But he'd seemed a nice enough boy. It was only his unhappiness with his recent injury that brought on his bouts of ill temper.

She pressed a kiss to his warm brow and said a prayer on his behalf. Let the warmth of Madeira mend his foot. Let the winter sunshine heal him, both inside and out.

And let her someday have sweet children of her own.

She yawned and smiled to herself. Just look at her. Three days gone, fleeing her bridegroom, and now dreaming of the children they might have together.

She shifted, sliding Aubrey off her shoulder. He murmured something unintelligible and rolled over onto his side, but still she didn't leave his bed. Outside, the rain beat fitfully at the window. She should return to her own cabin, she knew. But she was warm and comfortable, and oh, so sleepy. . . .

Eliza dreamt of children running across a flower-strewn meadow as she laughed and chased them. But the dream shattered when the covers were ripped back and a pair of powerful hands tore her from the bed.

She screamed. But nothing came out. One hand clamped around her mouth. Another clutched her waist, holding her off the floor as easily as if she were a slight child.

She screamed again, choking on the terrified effort, then bared her teeth and bit down. She tasted blood. The one rational remnant of her mind recognized the strange taste of salt water mingled with blood. But if she

hurt the unholy wretch, he ignored the pain. He only
yanked her more cruelly to his hard, unyielding chest.

Then something cold and round was pressed to her
mouth. "Hold still," he muttered in her ear. "Just drink
this."

She fought with all her might, kicking, flailing about
within his murderous embrace. He meant to drug her!
To kill her! But why?

"Hold still, boy," he hissed near her ear. Then he
abruptly let out the vilest string of oaths she'd ever
heard. Still, the shock of hearing that was nothing compared to the appalling feeling of his hand sliding up to
her breast and then sliding over to the other. As if to
make sure she had the two of them!

"May I be Jonas-fucked!" Cyprian spat as he recognized just what lay beneath his right hand. One soft and
decidedly feminine breast. And a matching one beside
it. They'd been told the wrong cabin! "Son-of-a-fucking-
bitch!"

The woman in his arms bit down again and with another curse he yanked his hand away from her lethal
mouth. Disaster. Yet in a flash of insight he realized that
if no one guessed his true motive for being here, perhaps all would not be lost.

Without further pause he jerked her around, and
catching her long solitary plait in one hand to tilt her
head back, he kissed her.

She'd foiled his plans. No, he'd done that himself.
Nevertheless, she received the brunt of his frustration.
He wanted her to believe him to be just some drunken
sailor bent on ravishing her, and so he played the role to
the hilt. He captured her mouth with his, parting her
lips and thrusting his tongue deep. He roamed her body
with his free hand, cupping an unexpectedly well-shaped
bottom.

Only when his own body reacted physically to hers
and he thrust instinctively against the softness of her

belly did he snap out of it. Christ, was he out of his mind?

He shoved her rudely away, willing his body to concentrate on what was important: escape, not how good she felt in his arms. Then he spun around, and no longer caring about silence, tore from the darkened cabin.

Oliver had his dagger drawn and nearly struck at Cyprian when he burst from the cabin. But the young sailor had no need of words to know the plot was foiled. As one the two flew up the short steps to the deck, then launched themselves into the stormy waters of St. Peter Port Bay.

The last thing Cyprian heard before his tense body cut into the surging waves was a woman's scream: high-pitched, terrified, and outraged.

Chapter Five

The island of Madeira rose like a jagged jewel breaking the vast reaches of the endless sea. Green and misty, with clouds shrouding its soaring peaks, it commanded the attention of every eye on the *Lady Haberton*.

Eliza had stood upon the forward deck ever since the first cry, "Land ho." Ten days they'd been without any sight of land; ten days that she'd spent reliving that terrifying night in excruciating detail.

Clothilde had fussed at her to put it out of her mind and to eat better. Cousin Agnes had decried the state of the world and admonished Eliza to find comfort in prayer. The captain, of course, had ordered a thorough investigation. But the results had been inconclusive. The watch had seen no one. And yet none of the *Lady Haberton*'s crew had been wet, as she'd recalled the man being. Salty, she'd remembered, though she'd not confessed that to anyone. Bad enough for the entire world to know she'd come that close to being forever ruined. Heaven forbid that they know he'd gone so far as to kiss and fondle her. And that she remembered how he'd tasted.

And that a tiny, wicked part of her had been tantalized by the entire experience.

Eliza let out a groan of denial. She hadn't been tantalized. No, not at all. She'd been paralyzed with fear at the time. But later . . . later in the privacy of her thoughts and even her dreams, she'd recalled the most disturbing details of those few moments. Details she'd kept strictly to herself.

He'd touched both her breasts, first one and then the other. Almost as if they'd come as a surprise to him. No one had ever touched her there before and it had been altogether shocking to her. But that had not begun to compare with the feel of his tongue invading her mouth. She hadn't liked it at all. How could she? Yet ever since then she'd done nothing but think of . . . of sex. Of what went on between men and women in the privacy of their marriage bed. Of what she and Michael would eventually do together.

When she thought of the very proper Michael Johnstone pushing his tongue inside her mouth, it didn't seem quite so frightening. In the past few days, in fact, she'd spent more and more time thinking about him doing that very thing. Kissing her with an almost violent fervor. Pressing up against her belly until she could feel the bulge of his . . . his thing.

She shook her head, wanting to deny such perverse thoughts. But she couldn't. She kept imagining Michael kissing and touching her with that explosive passion. Except that he invariably tasted of salt, and that always destroyed her fantasy. He always turned into her midnight attacker. Wet and salty. Powerful and unrelenting.

But he *had* relented, and every time she tried to figure out why she ended up going in the same circles. He'd spoken of a drug. He'd begun to ravish her. Then he'd fled. Had he said anything that might reveal who he was, or why he'd done it? Anything at all?

"Put me beside Eliza."

She turned at the sound of Aubrey's voice to see Robert carrying him toward her. The little boy had probably

been of more comfort to her than anyone else during
these past days. He'd awakened to her screams that
night, and despite his own fear, he'd comforted her in
those first few moments until help came. Since then
he'd been most solicitous of her. But unlike the others,
he'd encouraged her to get up and walk about and participate in what limited activities there were on board.
When Agnes would bid her rest and Clothilde would
offer the calming influence of her medicine, Aubrey insisted that she hold fast to their agreement. An hour a
day each.

She smiled fondly at him. He'd latched on to her off-
hand idea with a doggedness that mirrored his father's
bullheadedness. Despite her initial reluctance, she went
along with his demands and now she actually thought it
might be working. Even considering her dull spirits of
late, she felt physically stronger than she had in years.

Robert lowered Aubrey to a chair beside her, then
fussed when the boy nearly tumbled over. "Be still, boy.
Let me get you situated."

Be still, boy.

Eliza tensed. Someone else had said that, but in a
harsher, rumbling tone. The night of the attack! That
man had ordered her to be still. Be still, *boy*.

Had he expected her to be a boy? Was that why he'd
seemed surprised to discover she had breasts?

She bit her lip in concentration. None of this made
any sense. Why would he break into the cabin of a boy?
She stared at Aubrey, her brow creased in thought.
Could he have been searching for Aubrey? Perhaps to
steal him away? But where was the logic in that?

"You can just stop frowning at me, Eliza, for you
shan't frighten me away. You still owe me an hour. So
why don't we start with a song? As loud as you can
manage."

He led her in a French children's song about a little
frog who lost his tail, and after the first verse she was

able to suppress the disturbing thoughts that had been troubling her. But she didn't forget them. And as they drew nearer and nearer to their winter quarters, she resolved to speak to Robert and perhaps hire another man to ensure their security during their extended stay in Madeira.

"Shall I lift a few things, then? A coin here or there. A pretty bauble. They're not likely to miss them," Oliver finished, a hopeful look on his boyish face.

"And give them reason to suspect you?" Cyprian fixed Oliver with a warning stare. "Just ingratiate yourself with them, Ollie. Once I have the boy, you can fleece them of their every earthly possession. But until then, keep your light fingers to yourself."

"Ingratiate myself, eh?" Oliver's eyebrows waggled suggestively, eliciting a groan of dismay from Xavier, who sprawled in a wide sturdy chair in the corner of Cyprian's spacious cabin. Oliver's grin only widened at the older man's expression of disapproval. "It shall be my pleasure to ingratiate myself, especially with the lad's rather comely cousin."

"Comely cousin?" Once more Xavier groaned. He knew just as well as Cyprian what that meant. But instead of thinking Oliver's lusty intentions humorous, as he usually did, Cyprian found them irritating.

"Stay out from under her skirts," he snapped, more anger in his tone than he'd intended. Then before either of his surprised crewmen could question him, he pushed out of his chair and escaped to the deck.

What the hell was wrong with him?

Ten days they'd been dawdling behind the slower *Lady Haberton*. Oliver had pushed him to simply overtake the vessel and seize the boy in a show of force. He, like the rest of the crew, was eager to add a little open sea piracy to their more sedate role of smuggling. They'd spent the past eighteen months shuttling black market goods into both England and France, and in all that time they'd not had even one close call. The entire crew was spoiling for a fight, and in his own way, so was Cyprian. Such an open act of hostility would be the ultimate slap in the face to Haberton.

Yet something in him balked, and Oliver's vulgar comment made it clear what. That comely cousin of the boy's—the one whose face he'd yet to see, but who possessed a petite and slender body, firm young breasts, and the most exquisitely shaped bottom—had roused an unexpected fire in his gut. And it had yet to burn out.

It was all due to the circumstances, he told himself. The pent up energy, the repressed emotion he'd focused on capturing Haberton's son that night, had been diverted in that one moment when he'd realized he had the wrong person in his grasp. The charade he'd played in kissing her to mislead her about his motives had been conceived in a split second, and even now he considered it rather inspired thinking. Only it had come with unexpected repercussions.

He'd been aroused by the woman in his arms. Painfully so. She'd been small and sweet, and had smelled of lemons. Lemons.

He stalked the length of the quarterdeck, his hands knotted together behind his back, his face darkened in a scowl. He should have stayed in St. Peter Port long enough to relieve the frustration he'd felt ever since the wench had foiled his plans. He should have ignored his scruples and simply hired the finest whore the island had to offer. Or the raunchiest. Raw, unbridled sex with a woman who knew every dirty secret there was. That's what he needed to make him forget the faceless woman he'd kissed so hungrily in that dark cabin. Tonight, once he knew Oliver had gotten the job as bodyguard to the boy and his cousin, maybe he would ignore his usual compunctions and find out if Funchal's Portugese whores were as good as rumored.

* * *

"I don't know why anyone would want to hurt him," Eliza said to Aubrey's new bodyguard. New servant, she amended. There was no need to frighten the boy by terming this Oliver Spencer anything other than another manservant hired for the duration of their stay. But she wanted to be sure the new man knew precisely what his duties were.

"Aubrey has come here to heal, we hope. We shall keep to ourselves in the villa most of the time." She indicated the rambling hillside house they'd taken above Madeira's capital city of Funchal. "Only occasionally will we venture into town. For church, of course, and perhaps to shop now and again. Mostly, however, we will stay on our own grounds."

"Yes, ma'am," the polite young man answered. He was tall and lean, with a build that reminded her of Michael. He was almost as handsome as Michael too, she noticed, though she knew she should not. They were different in coloring, however, and Oliver Spencer appeared somehow more dangerous. She didn't know quite why she felt that way, for he was neatly dressed and groomed, and hardly appeared the ruffian. Yet there was something in his eyes, something a little wild and reckless. Still, it was those qualities which would probably make him a very good bodyguard.

"Where am I to sleep?" he asked.

Was it only her imagination, or did the faintest smirk curl his lips? Eliza blinked and stared, but saw nothing but a serious look in his eyes. Lately it seemed she read something lurid into every look and comment.

She cleared her throat. "Aubrey's suite includes an antechamber for you and Robert." His gaze flickered momentarily over her and she had to fight down a sudden blush as she imagined him staring quite past all her clothing right down to her skin. What on earth was the matter with her these days? But ever since that man had kissed her so forcefully—no, ever since *Michael* had kissed her so sweetly, she amended—her thoughts were always turning toward the most improper subjects. Once more she cleared her throat. "Can you start right away?"

"Yes, ma'am. Right away."

Had there been another choice, Eliza would have reconsidered her decision to hire this particular young man. Somehow she suspected that Oliver would prove a handful. But Robert had approved him as a bodyguard, while Cousin Agnes had approved him as the servant they'd told her he was. Eliza shook off her doubts as she led him to meet Aubrey. He was strong, he was presentable, and he was available. Those were all the qualifications he really needed.

By the next evening Eliza's nagging doubts about the new man seemed so much foolishness. Oliver had proven already to be just the breath of fresh air that Aubrey needed. After watching her work with Aubrey just once, the man had quickly taken up her approach, making the boy use his weak foot in all sorts of creative ways. Unlike her, however, he did not respond to Aubrey's complaints that it hurt. Perhaps it was that he was little more than an overgrown boy himself. But for whatever reason, Aubrey responded to Oliver's demands as if they were each a personal challenge he must meet and exceed.

"Kick it, laddie. C'mon, mate." Oliver positioned a rounded stone near Aubrey's leg. "Pull your foot back and shove the thing right off. Make it walk the plank. Pretend it's your old biddy cousin," he added in a stage whisper.

Eliza looked up from her sketch, grinning at Oliver's cheeky comment about Agnes. It also worked with Aubrey, for he laughed and tried even harder. A warm gust of air lifted a strand of her hair from its loosened bindings and she absentmindedly thrust it behind her ear.

She focused back on her drawing. She was trying to capture the spectacular spatial disparities of their surroundings. The stone terrace of their villa jutted right out to the edge of a steep rocky hill. Below them the land spilled down, a blend of rock outcroppings and luxuriant tropical growth, to a ribbon of beach and then the brilliant surging sea. A person could see forever from this spot. Just stare off to the southwest, past the edges of the island and all the way to the ends of the earth, she fancied. But her drawing didn't quite capture it.

Perhaps the line quality in the foreground of her sketch needed to be bolder. And sharper, she decided. Then the distant scenery could fade a bit. Perhaps a ship on the horizon would help convey the sense of space which somehow seemed lacking in her sketch.

"Avast, me hearties," Aubrey cried. Eliza looked up just as the stone tumbled from the end of his chaise lounge.

"I'll make a first class sailor of you yet," Oliver bragged. Then, as if aware of Eliza's attention, he turned and sent her a lopsided grin. "Beg pardon, miss."

"Oh, that's quite all right," she replied. But she felt a sudden unease. He stared at her so oddly sometimes. Did he look at every woman that way? But it wasn't just that, she realized. "Have you spent much time at sea? You use quite a lot of nautical terms."

"Do I?" For a moment he looked nonplussed. "Well, I didn't swim here, as you can guess. 'Course I came on a ship."

Eliza didn't press the issue. But she was certain he was being evasive, and her sense of unease about him returned. Something was not quite right, but for the life of her she didn't know what.

They ate their evening meal in the baronial-sized dining room. Eliza had wished to eat on the terrace, but Cousin Agnes had already made her feelings quite clear

on that point. Tea might be had on the terrace, and
luncheon. But not dinner. So she, Aubrey, and Eliza sat
in the room, waited upon by the three servants in can-
dlelit splendor.

"Now, isn't this nice?" Agnes pronounced, beaming
at her reluctant companions. "Just because we are not
currently resting upon good British soil does not mean
we should abandon our good British manners. Don't
you agree, Eliza?"

"Yes, ma'am," she murmured. Clothilde poured wine
for her as across the way Robert poured cider for Aubrey. The new man Oliver stood in the corner, observing
the more experienced servants so that he might better
learn his duties, as Agnes had instructed him.

When Eliza glanced at him, however, she could have
sworn he winked at her. She stiffened and stared at him
all the harder, but in the flickering candlelight it was
hard to be sure. Still, there was something mightily suspicious about his behavior. Good thing he was not truly
hired as a servant but rather as a bodyguard, for she
would be hard-pressed to offer him a good reference.

"Let's have a bout of chess," Aubrey suggested when
the meal was done. "Do you play, Oliver?"

"My game is backgammon," he answered, lifting the
boy to carry him into the parlor.

"*I'll* play chess with you, Master Aubrey," Robert interjected.

To Oliver's credit, he accepted the older servant's
subtle rebuke without comment. Eliza kept silent as
well, but she dearly hoped Robert was not becoming
jealous of Aubrey's quick affection for the new servant.
The last thing Eliza needed was to referee a tug of war
between those two.

Once he had settled Aubrey on a chair at the game
table, Oliver approached Eliza. "Would you like to play
at backgammon, miss?"

Eliza glanced up at him from the wide Mediterranean

chair she'd chosen and nervously cleared her throat. "I . . . um . . . I don't believe I know that game."

"I'd be pleased to teach it to you."

Eliza frowned. "Shouldn't you be checking around outside instead of playing games in here?" she whispered, so that Aubrey would not hear. "Making sure we're safe?"

"I have things well in hand, Miss Eliza. Don't you worry about that at all. I have things very well in hand."

Aubrey and Robert settled into their game of chess. Clothilde attended Cousin Agnes in her evening ritual of creams and arthritic potions, all in the privacy of her bedroom suite. The Portugese cook and her staff finished their work in the expansive kitchens. Everyone was occupied in some way, and it pointed out all the more awkwardly that only Eliza and Oliver were without any occupation or entertainment. It made her look foolish to have turned him down, and rude as well.

Annoyed with herself, she rose to her feet. "I think I shall retire," she announced. "You'll see to Aubrey?" she added, though unnecessarily, to Robert.

"Yes, miss. Aha! Knight captures Queen's rook!"

Eliza flipped a heavy lock of her hair back over her shoulder and let out an exasperated sigh. She would obviously not be missed. What a long and boring winter this was going to be. "You are dismissed for the evening, Mr. Spencer," she said in a conciliatory tone. Then, feeling unaccountably sorry for herself, Eliza escaped to her spacious, solitary bedchamber.

Unfortunately she was not in the least bit sleepy. Even after lingering at her ablutions, brushing her hair twice with lemon water, then sprinkling her sheets with more of her favorite fragrance as well, she was still quite wide-eyed. She paced barefoot across the huge Turkish carpet and then across the smooth stone floor to the bank of east-facing windows. After opening one pair of

the casement windows she leaned out, breathing in the
cool night air.

Beyond, all lay in darkness. A light glimmered somewhere in the hills above the house and the stars offered
their cool silver light. But she could see very little.

What was Michael doing right now?

Dancing at a ball, very likely. Besieged by a bevy of
young women and their predatory mothers, all of whom
no doubt wondered why such a handsome man had
been abandoned for so long by his fiancée.

What had she been thinking, to leave him these long,
long months? Though she'd hoped he might cry off at
the time, now . . . well, now she wasn't so sure about
anything.

Oh, but it didn't bear thinking about.

Eliza turned away from the window and resumed her
pacing. She was an idiot ever to have suggested this trip.
Yet even as she rebuked herself, she had to admit that
already she saw its benefits. She was stronger, and so
was Aubrey. And that due solely to the two weeks they'd
spent on the ship. Rather than succumbing to self-pity-
ing thoughts, she should resolve to become completely
well—and make sure Aubrey did too.

With that thought firmly in place, she pulled the tall
windows closed and turned toward the bed. But the
massive sleigh bed, piled though it was with feather mat-
tresses, a wealth of pillows, and a luxurious down-filled
coverlet, held no appeal. What she needed was a book.
She could fall asleep if she had a book to read.

The house was quiet. And dark. One brace of candles
flickered at the top of the stairs, but Cousin Agnes's
room was dark and so was Aubrey's. She hoped he did
not yet linger at chess with Robert, though she knew it
unlikely. Once Clothilde was free of Agnes's demands,
Robert would have ended the game. Eliza wasn't sure
whether she should discourage the blossoming romance
between the two servants or not. But she would worry

over that problem tomorrow. For now she meant to find some interesting volume to read. Hopefully the library was not restricted to purely Portugese tomes.

As she made her way down the stairs, however, she spied the four sets of glass doors that led to the terrace. One pair yet stood ajar.

Unlike her bedroom, the view beyond the doors and the terrace wall was well lit. The town lay off to the left, its streets still discernible by the lights that burned here and there. In the harbor, too, lights marked the many ships and boats at rest.

Had the *Lady Haberton* departed yet? Eliza leaned her elbows on the carved stone railing and stared out toward the harbor. Some sweet scent drifted on the breeze. Gardenias perhaps? Or roses? She wiggled her bare toes against the grainy stone terrace. Tomorrow she would propose an adventure into the hills. Perhaps she'd discover the source of that beguiling fragrance. Between Robert and Oliver they could easily carry Aubrey.

Oliver. As if beckoned by her very thoughts, Oliver's voice came out of the darkness. "Be careful of him, you oaf. Here. Give him to me."

Was that Robert he was calling an oaf, she wondered indignantly. Really but that young man had a lot to learn about dealing with his betters. Vowing to give him a firm talking to, she straightened and turned.

But the sight that met Eliza's eyes drove every thought of reprimand quite out of her head. For there, filling the doorway and blocking any hope of her escaping unseen was a huge black man. The African. The one from the other ship. And he was handing what could only be the inert form of Aubrey to Oliver.

She must have gasped. She knew she nearly fainted, for she fell hard against the rail in absolute terror. For whatever reason, both men looked up at her in the same moment.

"Bloody hell," Oliver muttered.

"What have we here?" the other one said.

Before the first logical thought could form in her head—before she could scream or run or do anything at all—the immense dark-skinned wretch had her fast in his grasp. As if she were no more than a frightened kitten, he held her off the ground with one arm while his other hand prevented her from making a sound. Oh no, not again, the frozen thought came.

"I thought you said everyone was asleep," the man muttered.

"She was," Oliver swore. "Bloody hell. Now what are we to do?"

"I could toss her over this wall and down the hill."

Eliza's heart stopped. It had been thundering until he said that. Now it stopped. He hefted her higher in his arm, and despite her struggles, held her just above the rail.

"Stop fooling around," Oliver ordered. "We've got a real problem here."

She felt her captor shrug. "Give her the same drug we gave the boy. Put her to sleep."

At once it made sense. They'd drugged Aubrey and meant to kidnap him, just as the same pair must have tried to do back at Guernsey. No wonder she'd felt so uneasy about Oliver. And now, just like before, she'd managed to stumble into the middle of it.

She began to struggle in earnest now, kicking and clawing at the man who so easily held her. But with only a quick flexing of his thick arm he squeezed her tighter until she feared she would faint from lack of air.

"We used all the stuff on Aubrey," Oliver answered.

"Well, we can't leave her here to rouse everyone."

"Then we'll just have to bring her with us."

Eliza felt the silent shaking of the man's laughter before it came out. "The captain shall have our hides for bungling this."

"Well, *he* was the one who bungled it the first time," Oliver retorted. "He can hardly blame us if she interfered with us."

The two men moved swiftly after that. Over the rail and into the lush landscape of the hillside, Eliza bumped along in her captor's unyielding grasp, terrified. Furious. Oliver Spencer was a ruffian of the worst sort and she should have known better than ever to have hired him. Yet it was clear they'd plotted this a long time. And now she and Aubrey were being dragged to meet this . . . this captain of theirs. This captain who'd bungled it once before.

As if her fear were not profound already, a new layer of panic overwhelmed Eliza. This captain must be the one who'd crept into Aubrey's cabin that night. The one who'd hauled her so rudely from the bed. The one who'd touched her body and kissed her—

Eliza squeezed her eyes tight, though the black night already hid as much as her eyelids did. But nothing could blot out the terror that had her in its foul grip. She was being dragged off by two of the vilest cads in the entire world to be given over to the clutches of their even viler captain.

Eventually her hands were tied before her and both her eyes and her mouth were bound with rather smelly handkerchiefs. She was lifted and placed on a bench—in a boat, she realized from the sound of waves slapping against the shore. Aubrey was stowed in the boat as well and the men pushed off. They rowed in silence, but though she could hear little and see nothing, she knew where they were headed. To that ship with the naked woman on the front. To the wicked ship *Chameleon*. To its unholy captain with his bold hands and even bolder mouth.

He would finish what he'd begun that night, of course. He would ravish her and she would be ruined for marriage. Michael could not be expected to wed a ruined woman.

Then the small boat bumped up against a larger object and her fears doubled. Ravishment could very well be the least of her troubles. And Aubrey's.

Chapter Six

"**W**hat do you mean, you brought his cousin too!"
Eliza could hear the shouting even from the
small cell they'd confined her to, deep within the bowels
of the ship. She and Aubrey were locked in a dark,
damp chamber and she sat now with her back against a
chilly wall and Aubrey in her arms. Despite all his handling, the boy still slept, breathing even and slow. She
smelled an odd flavor upon his breath, something sweet
and medicinal. But at least they'd not hurt him, she consoled herself as she hugged him close. No telling why
they'd stolen him, but at least that pair of thugs had
seemed intent on keeping him safe. Until their captain
ordered otherwise, she worried. Judging from his bellowing anger, she expected only the worst from that
quarter.

"You could have tied her up and left her there—"
Eliza strained to hear the reply to that, but without
success. Clearly this captain cowed his two men with his
fury. She shivered and hugged Aubrey even closer to
her. What sort of man could intimidate the flippant Oliver and that hulking African?

She was soon to find out. Every muscle in her exhausted body tensed at the sound of approaching foot-

steps. A key rattled in the lock, followed by the blinding light of a lantern held high.

"Come along, Miss Eliza," Oliver ordered, though in a rather subdued tone.

She blinked against the strong light but sank back all the harder against the wooden wall. "Come along where? To face that monstrous captain of yours?" Her voice shook with both fear and fury. "How could you do this to us, Oliver? How? And why?"

He hunched his shoulders and glanced sheepishly at his silent companion.

It was the African who finally answered. "You've nothing to fear, miss. He doesn't mean to harm you."

She peered up at the huge fellow. For such a frighteningly large man his voice was surprisingly gentle.

"He doesn't mean to harm me? Then why did he treat me so . . . so abominably when he broke into Aubrey's cabin back in St. Peter Port?"

The two men exchanged puzzled glances. "That was you who foiled the captain in Aubrey's cabin?" Oliver asked.

But the other man cut him off. "What do you mean, abominably?"

Encouraged by their curiosity and nonthreatening attitudes, Eliza gave vent to all the frustrations that had been building in her. "He mauled me! He treated me as I were some . . . some tavern girl. A woman of loose morals!"

Once more the pair exchanged glances. Then the African drew nearer and squatted down before her. "Could you please be a little more specific?"

Eliza frowned in confusion. Could she *please* be a little more specific? Maybe this was just a bizarre dream about polite kidnappers or something. But when he just gave her an encouraging smile, she knew it was no dream. She'd been stolen from her home by a pair of ruffians; it just so happened that one was a charming flirt, and the other was a polite black giant. Truly the world beyond Britain was filled with the oddest people.

She ducked her head and pressed her cheek against Aubrey's dark curls. "He grabbed me. And . . . and touched me. Places he had no business touching me," she added belligerently. "Then, well . . . then he kissed me."

"He kissed you?" the pair chorused.

"Could you please be more specific," Oliver echoed Xavier's words.

It was the last straw. "He stuck his tongue in my mouth," she snapped. "Is that specific enough for you, Mr. Spencer?"

Oliver backed away, but the African only grinned. "That explains his bad temper," he said over his shoulder to Oliver. His grin turned to a friendly smile when he returned his gaze to her. "I know you're frightened, Miss Eliza. But I assure you, you shall come to no harm at the captain's hands. Xavier will see to that," he vowed, tapping his broad chest. "Xavier *and* Oliver."

Eliza had no reason whatsoever to believe him. Hadn't he threatened to toss her over the terrace railing earlier? But there was something in his dark face, something in his jet black eyes that reassured her. Though he looked easily able to crush her with only one hand, his voice was as gentle and clear as an angel's might be. It made no sense at all, but despite his role in kidnapping her and Aubrey, she *did* believe him.

Still, there was Aubrey to consider and he apparently was at the heart of this scheme.

"Will you protect Aubrey from him as well?"

The glances the two men shared this time answered Eliza better than words could, and her fear returned tenfold. "Why should he want to harm such a little boy?" she cried, clutching the sleeping child to her. "He's only ten years old, and he's crippled. You know that, Oliver. He can't even walk on his own!"

But the glib Oliver had no reply this time. Xavier stood up and extended a hand to her. His face was creased as if in thought—or worry, she feared.

"Come along, miss. You cannot put off this meeting with the captain. Keep this in mind, however. He carries much anger in his heart, much anger and much pain. Heal that pain, however, and the anger will disappear."

Heal *his* pain? Had she not been so terrified, Eliza would have scoffed at Xavier's words. What about Aubrey's pain? And hers? But as Oliver took Aubrey in his arms and Xavier pulled Eliza to her feet, she was unable to verbalize her fears. They led the way down a low-ceilinged companionway toward their ominous captain, and Eliza felt for all the world like one of the early Christians being led into the lions' presence. Even the promise of a heavenly reward could not still her fear of the coming confrontation.

The chamber she was ushered into was much larger than she expected, and much better furnished. It wasn't lavish. Hardly. Rather it bore the look of a well-used office, complete with a polished mahogany desk and a pair of leather chairs. But under the rear-facing diamond-paned windows was a huge bed, furnished with silk bed hangings, fringed pillows, and an immense, pure white fur throw. It was like a decadent slap in the face to an otherwise purely utilitarian space, and it sent an icy frisson of fear up her spine.

"Let me see the boy."

Eliza gasped and spun around. Xavier had blocked her view, but now he stepped back and she had her first glimpse of the man who was the source of her present predicament.

The captain of the *Chameleon* was a tall man, nearly as tall as Xavier. But he was lean and much harder looking than Xavier. Nor did he have any of Oliver's carefree manner. From his black close-cropped hair, to the rigid set of his square jaw, to the burning intensity of his dark eyes, he looked ruthless and unyielding, and her heart sank.

He glanced at Aubrey, as if to assure himself that the child was indeed there. But then he turned his gaze upon her and she felt the full force of his animosity.

He carries much anger in his heart. Xavier's words echoed in her head. Yes, very much anger, she realized. The fact that it might be caused by much pain was no reassurance at all, however. It was the pain he meant to inflict upon her and her defenseless cousin that worried her far more.

"I demand that you return us to our home."

Was that her voice so high and shaky? Eliza tried to swallow the lump of fear that lodged in her throat, but to no avail. If the captain heard her words he gave no indication. He just stood there, leaning back against an intricately tooled leather trunk, his legs crossed at the ankles and his arms crossed over his chest. It was a pose that would have been considered attractively nonchalant had he been a proper gentleman. Like Michael, she thought in vain hope. But this man was like a coiled spring, waiting to explode, she feared. On him that casual pose was nothing but threatening. He radiated pure menace; there was no other way to describe it.

And she'd just *demanded* that he set her free.

When he straightened up suddenly, she gave an involuntary jerk.

"Which home is it you wish to be returned to, Miss Thoroughgood? Your villa in Funchal? The *Lady Haberton?* Perhaps your family's home in London? Or, no, you look the rustic sort. Perhaps your country place?"

Eliza's gray eyes grew round as saucers. How did he know so much about her? Her name was one thing. But where she lived? Without thinking she turned a panic-stricken face to Xavier. But the captain cut off that avenue of support with a sharp order.

"Leave us."

"But Cyprian—" Xavier began.

"I said leave us." He bit out the words slowly. "Put the boy in the cabin prepared for him. Miss Thoroughgood and I will have a brief chat. Then she shall have her wish and be put ashore. Not too far from her home," he added, giving her a chilling smile.

Xavier disentangled Eliza's frozen fingers from his sleeve. When had she knotted her fist around it? "It will be all right, little one. Just be brave," he murmured to her.

Be brave? When she was certain the man meant to finish what he'd begun before?

Before Oliver could follow through with his captain's orders Eliza tried to snatch Aubrey from him. "Don't take him from me. Don't you dare!"

But he had no more choice than did she, for with one unyielding hand around her upper arm, the wretched captain yanked her away from Oliver. The younger man gazed at her regretfully. He glanced from her to his captain and then to Xavier. But Xavier shook his head. So much for the man's vow to protect her, Eliza thought as she fought down hysteria. Then the two men backed from the room, taking the still sleeping Aubrey with them and leaving her alone in the lion's den.

When the door closed, the click of the latch was as ominous a sound as she'd ever heard.

"Now, Miss Thoroughgood." He released her and Eliza stumbled back. There was no way out, though. He stood between her and the only door, and the enormous bed lay between her and the windows. Trapped like a feral kitten she'd once seen her brothers corner in the walled garden at home, Eliza stared about wildly, all the time shaking like a leaf.

"Rest assured, Miss Thoroughgood," he said in a cool mocking tone. "Your reputation is perfectly safe with me."

That statement was so ludicrous that Eliza came perilously close to laughing. But she was afraid it would turn to embarrassing tears. She drew herself up as best she could, straightening her posture and wrapping her arms protectively around herself.

"I have no reason whatsoever to believe you," she managed, though in a rather strangled tone.

He smiled ever so faintly, then pulled one of the leather chairs in front of the door and sat in it. He gestured to the other chair. But instead of sitting in it, Eliza backed around it.

As if it would keep her safe from the likes of him!

"As you wish. Now, I have a message for you to deliver."

Eliza stared at him suspiciously, but his expression gave nothing away. "A message," she repeated.

He steepled his fingers together, watching her all the while with eyes that seemed far too observant. Eliza was suddenly cognizant of the fact that she wore nothing but an embroidered flannel gown. She was covered from chin to wrists to ankles, of course. Nonetheless it was night apparel, not her proper day clothes. And her hair was unbound, fallen during her ordeal into a tangled mess around her face and shoulders. Alone with a man in his bedchamber, and dressed this way. Her reputation was already irrevocably destroyed.

But her reputation was of less moment than the danger that dear Aubrey might be in. "A message to whom?" she repeated in what she meant to be a scathing tone of voice.

His black eyebrows raised, mocking her again. Somehow that roused her ire as nothing else could. He thought her amusing. She'd been threatened, manhandled, and kidnapped, and now he found her amusing! The utter conceit of the man!

"To Aubrey's father, of course."

As quickly as that, her outrage changed to dread. "Uncle Lloyd?"

"So he *is* your uncle."

"He's married to my mother's sister. But what has that to do with you? Why should you want to harm an innocent child like Aubrey?"

"My reasons have nothing to do with you. It is enough that you tell the man that I have his son."

Eliza gripped the back of the chair. "But why? Why would you do such a horrible thing? What has Aubrey done to deserve such cruel treatment at your hands?"

A muscle flexed in his jaw. Once, then again. But he gave no other sign of his feelings. His voice remained low and even. Still, Eliza knew some violent emotion seethed inside him. A deep, poisonous fury.

"The child means nothing to me," he vowed. " 'Tis the father. The father."

Eliza swallowed hard. "You would hurt the boy to get back at the father? Oh, what kind of monster are you?"

He leaped from his chair with an abruptness that sent her backing away in terror. Like an overflowing cauldron, his emotions erupted, threatening to scald anyone in their path.

"I am the monster Haberton made of me! The same sort of monster I shall make of his one male heir. Tell him that. And tell him also that it will be a very long time before he sees his precious son again!"

He stood tall and utterly forbidding, his fists knotted at his side, and every muscle in his lean frame tensed and angry. "Now go, Eliza Thoroughgood. Run back to your mother and father and the safety of your little family. But don't forget to give Haberton my message."

He stepped away from the door and with a sharp gesture dismissed her. But Eliza could not move. Nothing about this made any sense. "You can't send me back to him with no more message than that. What could he possibly have done to provoke such . . . such *evil* from you? I don't even know who you are."

She caught a glimpse of stark pain in his eyes. Or she thought she did. But before she could be certain, he bent low and gave her a sweeping bow that would have done any nobleman proud, had it but been sincere.

"My, but I do forget the manners my mother drilled into me. Cyprian Dare at your service, madmoiselle." He straightened and stared boldly at her. "Now, if you would please get the hell off my ship."

It was positively the last straw. With a cry of pure outrage Eliza snatched up the nearest object she could find—a heavy navigational tool of some sort—and threw it straight at his head. How dare he order her off his ship so vulgarly when it was he who'd had her dragged here in the first place! She grabbed a book from the desk and threw it at him as well.

Cyprian avoided the bit of brass by ducking, and deflected the book with one arm. Then before the chit could send a heavy glass tumbler sailing at him, he launched himself at her.

All things considered, he thought he'd handled things in a fairly civilized fashion. Any other man, knowing what lay beneath that frumpy gown, would have tossed the cheeky wench on her back straightaway and taught her just who was in charge. Any other man who'd spent the last ten days frustrated just because he'd kissed some faceless woman who'd possessed a rather luscious body, would have made quick and satisfying use of that body. But rape was not his way. He'd only wanted to see her, to see if her appearance was as stimulating to his senses as the feel of her had been.

When she'd sidled into his cabin alongside Xavier and Oliver, he'd been disappointed. At least at first. But as he'd threatened her, her trembling fear had squeezed a reckless sort of bravery out of her. The prudish gown had begun to whet his appetite for the delights that lay beneath it. Her wealth of dark brown hair had begun to beckon him to reach out and touch it. Then she'd thrown the sextant at him and his initial opinion of her had given way entirely. Eliza Thoroughgood was quite a piece of work with her huge eyes glittering in fury and her pale complexion flush with emotion.

Now, as he caught her around the waist and fell onto the chair with her on his lap, he hoped the sextant hadn't broken. But it was not to prevent any further carnage that he'd trapped her in his arms. No, it was to have his hands on her once more. She was smaller, weaker, and scared to death of him. Yet he felt as if in her he'd met an adversary unlike any he'd ever faced before, and he felt the urge to take their battle to a new and more stimulating level.

Not to hurt her, though. Hardly. What he'd discovered, to his dismay, was that he wanted to seduce the very proper Miss Eliza Thoroughgood. To enjoy her sweet young body. And in the process she would learn a few things as well. First, the pleasures to be had between a man and woman, something a sheltered young woman such as she had undoubtedly been well-protected from. Second—and more important, he told himself—was how it felt to be at someone else's mercy, to survive purely on the whim of someone more powerful than yourself. She was used to being part of the ruling class. Now she would have a taste of life as it was for the poor, the weak, and the helpless.

"Be still. Be still, by damn, and I won't hurt you," he growled as he forced her hands to her sides and held her on his lap. "I said be still."

He couldn't see her face beneath her tangled hair, but even so he could feel her panic. She struggled against him, kicking fruitlessly with her heels against his booted shins, and her heart beat a thunderous pace beneath his tight embrace. "You're only hurting yourself," he taunted, murmuring the words somewhere in the vicinity of her right ear. "Just calm down."

"Go to bloody hell," she muttered back, kicking once more.

"I bloody well intend to," he replied, smiling as her delectable bottom shifted across his lap. What would it take, he wondered, to make her more amenable to his overtures?

Only when she had exhausted herself did her struggles against him finally subside. For a moment Cyprian simply enjoyed the feel of her in his arms. Her breath came in quick, deep gasps. Her exertion had released that same lemony scent he remembered. It was in her hair, he realized, nuzzling his nose into the silky thickness of it.

She reacted as if stung, starting to struggle once again. "Let me go you . . . you bloody monster! You horrid child stealer! You . . . you—"

"You smell of lemons," he said, paying no mind to her anger. "How do you manage that?"

She strained away from him, but it was a futile effort, for he had no intention of releasing her until he was good and ready. Yet how was he to get her to relax her guard long enough to make her willing?

"Listen to me, Eliza. You don't mind if I call you Eliza, do you? Considering how well acquainted we became at our last meeting."

"I hate you," she swore.

"No doubt you do," he mocked. "Especially since I intend to take your cousin away from you. I suppose your uncle asked you to watch over him, didn't he? To chaperone and protect him. I'm sorry, but it will now be impossible for you to carry out those instructions."

"If you were truly sorry you wouldn't be stealing him this way. No, nor treating me so cruelly. Let me go!"

But he ignored her last remark. "I'm not trying to be cruel. But I can't have you throwing my belongings about, can I? If you'll promise to behave I'll release you." He paused, waiting for her answer. "Well, will you behave?"

He could feel her heaving breaths against his arm. "What are you going to do with Aubrey?"

Aha. So the chink in her armor was her responsibility for the boy. Just as he'd suspected. Loyalty was a good quality in a person, something he highly valued. In this case, however, it was a virtue he could use against her.

"I haven't decided what I shall do with him. Yet."

She was still a long moment and he guessed what she would say before she phrased the first word. "If you would just return him unharmed, I . . . I would make a bargain with you."

"A bargain?" Again he smiled. Yes, she was nothing if not the loyal guardian.

"I will . . . I will—you know—do whatever it is you wish to do."

He nuzzled his face against her hair again, searching out the rim of her ear with his lips. When she jerked her head away he laughed. "But would you do it willingly? Somehow I don't think so. Besides, I'm not in the mood to bargain. I have the boy and I also have you, if I want to keep you. I can do whatever I wish with either of you and there's no one to say me nay."

She shuddered and Cyprian felt a vague and unfamiliar regret for his words. If he was going to seduce her, scaring her was probably not the right approach.

"Then get it over with," she muttered. "Just do it and get it over with."

"Do it?" He laughed, but ruefully. Seducing her obviously would take more time than he had to give and raping her held no appeal at all. These ten days of frustration had all been for naught, he realized. Suppressing a frustrated oath he continued. "I'm a discriminating man, Eliza. I like my women willing. And you, it appears, are not entirely willing."

She snorted in derision, but he also detected a slight easing of the tension in her back.

"So," he went on. "Best to put you ashore now and get on with my plans for the boy." He let loose her arms and gave her a little shove.

She leaped away from him as if burned and backed into a corner. But her face reflected her confusion. "Just . . . just what *are* your plans for Aubrey?"

He shrugged and sprawled back in the chair. But though he affected a casual air, he studied her closely, watching every flicker of emotion on her lovely face. Though she was still terrified, she was not about to back down from him. She appealed to his tastes more and more. How unfortunate for him. "I haven't yet decided what my plans are for your young charge."

She swallowed and he waited for the plea he was sure would come next.

"Oh, please," she begged, wringing her hands together. "Can't you see that Aubrey is the wrong person to wreak your revenge upon? He's just an innocent child."

"He gives me access to his father."

"But what could Uncle Lloyd possibly have done to you that you would react in so heartless a fashion as this?"

Cyprian stiffened, but he bit back the angry retort that rose to his lips. That was not what this little exchange was about. He had the boy in his possession, so his revenge on Sir Lloyd Haberton was well underway. Now he could relax and concentrate on this new diversion, in the form of Haberton's niece. Maybe he still could seduce her, if he put his mind to it. But no matter what might eventually pass between them, he had no intention of defending his plan for revenge to her.

"I'm sure you cannot imagine the man being less than the perfect uncle, Eliza. The perfect father," he added, a trace of sarcasm creeping into his voice. "But if you knew him as he truly is, as I know him . . . " He trailed off, unable to control his seething anger whenever he spoke of Haberton.

He saw her compress her lips tightly and nervously weave her fingers together. She should wear red, the unwonted thought came to him. Not a hot Chinese red, but a deep, shadowed scarlet, verging on purple. Her hair would gleam like dark, lush velvet against it; her gray eyes would glitter like diamonds.

She averted those eyes, breaking away from his avid stare. "I . . . I admit that he can be distant. Remote. He is a stern taskmaster to his children, and . . . and ever since Aubrey's accident, well, it sometimes seems that he is angry with the child. But it's only that Aubrey had been warned time and time again not to go riding alone. When he disobeyed and then was thrown and dragged—" She broke off, but the appeal in her huge eyes was almost enough to make Cyprian reconsider his plans. Almost.

"So, he has no pity for his crippled child."

"No, that's not it at all!" she cried. "And anyway, who are you to criticize him, when you are so much worse? You're the one who has torn the boy away from his home and family. You're the one with no conscience whatsoever. Don't you see how wrong this is? How cruel? If it's the father you hate, then hurt the father. But not the son. Not Aubrey."

Cyprian stood up abruptly. In the face of her accusations he was unable to remain cool and aloof. How dare she defend Haberton to him! "It's time you were put ashore," he muttered in an icy tone. "You know what you're to do. Just tell Haberton that Cyprian Dare has his son."

He glared at her. If the wench said even one more word in defense of that bastard he'd have to shut her up. One way or another he'd have to shut her up.

But she glared right back at him, like a small wildcat

protecting her precious kit. Tears sparkled in her eyes, though they could not disguise her fury, and her petite form fairly bristled with animosity. "Send you vile communication through another messenger, Cyprian Dare, for I refuse to bear it. Uncle Lloyd asked me to watch over Aubrey, and so I shall. *I* will not leave this ship until he does too!"

The tears spilled past her lashes then, but she wiped them away with an impatient gesture. Then without waiting for a reply, she marched over to the heavy chair he'd abandoned, shoved it aside, and jerked the door open. It slammed as she stamped out into the passageway, a sharp exclamation point to her angry vow. "Xavier!" she cried in a furious tone as she hurried away from him. "Oliver!"

Cyprian's first inclination was to charge after her and throw her off his ship himself. Who in the hell did she think she was, making such farfetched pronouncements? He was captain here and she was worse than a fool to demand to stay on a ship full of men who'd as soon tumble her as look at her.

But instead of storming after her, he just sat down, a little stunned, a little amused—more than a little aroused—and enormously pleased, if the truth be told. Brave little fool that she was, she demanded to stay, and whether it was foolish of him or not, he was going to let her. She was a strange combination of fear and fearlessness, of proper behavior and hidden lushness. Of fury and tears.

Of all those qualities, however, it was the tears that ultimately swayed him, he realized. Most women cried at the drop of a hat. It was a weapon they used to get their way. But when overused, that particular weapon lost its effectiveness. He'd seen his mother cry less than a handful of times, though she'd had reason enough to spend half her life in tears.

This Eliza Thoroughgood had impressed him, despite

all the reasons he instinctively disliked her. She was a highborn woman used to everything going her way. But she was also a brave little hellcat. Though her claws could do little enough damage—she would never win against him—she nonetheless would not give in. Despite the fact that he'd manhandled her, threatened her, and then ordered her off his ship, she'd stood up to him and demanded to stay with her cousin. You'd think the boy was her own child, so fierce was her need to protect him. Yet he was only her cousin.

But then, what did he know of the bond that existed between cousins, Cyprian thought. If he had any he didn't know about them. But that was neither here nor there, and as quickly as his anger had risen then fled, so now did a new buoyancy lift his spirits. Everything was going as planned—better than planned. He hadn't felt this invigorated in a long time.

Cyprian pushed himself up off the desk and began to pace. Yes, he would let her stay after all. They would be at least a week sailing to Alderney, and that should give him plenty of time to seduce her. Then he grinned. Miss Eliza Thoroughgood was going to be just the diversion he needed while he waited for Haberton to make the next move.

Chapter Seven

*A*ubrey didn't awaken until midmorning. By then the *Chameleon* had been under sail for at least four hours. Eliza had lain awake the entire time, relieved that the captain had not put her ashore as he'd threatened, yet nonetheless alternating between fury and hopelessness. That man. That awful, wicked . . . pirate, she decided he was. She'd read all about pirates, both real ones and fictional ones, and she fancied he must be the epitome of them all. Completely immoral and without a shred of compassion in his heart.

Oh, yes, his heart which Xavier insisted was filled with pain. Ha! In her opinion, he probably had no heart.

"Mother?" Aubrey murmured, trying to roll over in the hammock he'd been placed in. "Mother?" Before Eliza could reach him, the hammock flipped over and with a thud, poor Aubrey landed on the bare floor—a thud followed by a howl of pain.

Eliza gathered the sobbing boy to her, and once she ascertained that he was not actually injured, she tried to comfort him. But it seemed an impossible task, and equally impossible for her not to be affected by his tears of fright once she explained their abrupt change of circumstances.

"I want my mother."

I want my mother, Eliza echoed, sniffing back the threat of her own tears. "We'll get home eventually, Aubrey. Just see if we don't. These awful men are just trying to scare your father. That's all. But Uncle Lloyd will come to our rescue. I *know* he will."

They were a rather pitiful sight when a key turned in the lock and Oliver poked his face into the cabin. "Are you decent?" he asked, sweeping Eliza with a gaze that would have called for a sound slap had they been in London. But they weren't in London, nor in any civilized society whatsoever. They were at the mercy of a rogue captain and his rogue crew. And Oliver needed a proper set down by someone who knew how to do it.

"What do you want?" Eliza snapped, scooting between Aubrey and the young sailor.

"D'you want the whole truth?" he answered, grinning and waggling his thick brown eyebrows at her.

"Oh, do be quiet, Oliver. This is all your fault."

"Are you a pirate, then?" Aubrey asked, peering around Eliza's back at the man whom he'd simply thought a particularly entertaining manservant.

"A pirate? Why, never think it, mate. I'm just a happy sailor who delivers goods to people, goods that make them happy too."

"Well, why'd you steal me out of my very own bed if you're not a pirate?"

For a moment Oliver's ebullient spirits faltered and he looked more like he had last night when he and Xavier had responded to her furious call once she'd stormed from their captain's cabin: ashamed of himself. It hadn't stopped him from locking her in with Aubrey, of course. But at least she knew he still retained the smallest bit of conscience—unlike his vile captain. Eliza meant to use that bit of conscience to torture the young sailor as much as possible.

"Yes, Oliver. Explain to poor Aubrey why you stole

him from his bed. Explain why you lied to him. Why you drugged him and brought him here."

Oliver bit the side of his lower lip and his no longer merry gaze flitted back and forth between the two of them. "It's like this, my boy . . . that is . . . " He trailed off, then turned back to the door. "Xavier! Where in the blazes are you?"

Aubrey stiffened when the tall African stooped to enter past the low frame. But what Eliza felt was relief. She shouldn't, of course. Xavier was as much a party to this crime as any of them. But there was something in his bearing that reassured her nonetheless.

"Good morning, miss. Ah, so this is young Master Aubrey." He gave the boy a gleamingly white smile and extended his hand in greeting. "I'm Xavier, first mate of the *Chameleon*. Ever slept in a hammock before?"

Aubrey glanced at Eliza, but at her nod of approval, hesitantly took the man's hand. "No, I never did. If I had known it was a hammock I was in, however, I wouldn't have fallen out."

The sight of his pale childish hand resting in that giant black grip gave Eliza even more confidence that Xavier was an ally, not an enemy. Not like Oliver, she thought, sending that traitor a scathing look.

Oliver had been staring at her—at her rumpled dishabille, no doubt. But he averted his eyes at her contemptuous glare. "I thought you might like something to eat," he murmured sheepishly.

Eliza tilted her chin at a pugnacious angle and tried to remember how their housekeeper at home dealt with recalcitrant servants. "First bring us water to clean ourselves with. And I'll need a brush and comb as well. This chamber," she added, really warming to her role, "will never do. We'll need an adjoining suite with separate rooms for each of us. We'll have our breakfast there, though you can bring the water here," she finished.

"Well?" She gave him an arch look, quite satisfied with his suitably cowed expression. "Get on with it."

Oliver backed from the room, cracking his head against the top of the short door frame in the process. Once he was gone, Xavier began to laugh.

"Ah, Miss Eliza. I see you have determined how best to deal with our young Oliver."

She tossed a hopelessly tangled length of hair behind her shoulder. "You mean order him about like the lowly worm that he is?"

Again the man laughed, a deep rumbling chuckle that brought a reluctant half-smile to her lips too. "Oliver likes women," he explained. "Very much. And women like him too. They're always falling at the lad's feet and he prides himself on how well he pleases them—" Xavier broke off and cleared his throat. "If you know what I mean," he added a little awkwardly.

Eliza wrinkled her nose. She feared she knew exactly what he meant. But Oliver Spencer—if that was his real name—would never find *her* at his feet. "I can handle Oliver," she stated. "But . . . "

"But Cyprian?" he finished for her when she trailed off. He sighed. "Cyprian will be a little longer coming around. You'll need much patience."

"Who is Cyprian?" Aubrey asked.

A heartless wretch, Eliza wanted to say. But instead she forced a taut smile to her lips. "He's the captain of this ship. I imagine you'll be meeting him later today."

"Actually," Xavier said. "He wishes to speak to you now, miss."

A jolt of pure panic lifted the hairs on Eliza's nape and raised her pulse to a rapid tatoo. She'd been dreading their next confrontation since the moment she'd stormed out of his cabin last night. "Me? Now? But why?"

Xavier shrugged. "He didn't say. However, I think

you should view this as another opportunity to win him over."

"Win him over?" Eliza frowned and chewed on her lower lip. "I doubt I shall ever sway that man from his vile plan to use—"

She broke off before she could frighten Aubrey with the true facts of their abduction. But the boy obviously sensed her fears.

"Don't leave me, Eliza. Stay with me. Say you will," he pleaded.

"You mustn't worry, Aubrey, for I have no intention of leaving you. No, none at all." She sent Xavier a speaking look. "When our new quarters are ready and we've had our breakfast, I'll be happy to entertain your captain. You will make sure that Oliver attends to those matters, won't you?"

Xavier stared at her as if she were just a little bit mad. And indeed, she must be, she realized. That awful captain would not like her demands at all, or her refusal of his summons. But then, what precisely did she have to lose? His good will? Inwardly she scoffed. Hauteur had cowed Oliver. Maybe it would work on Cyprian Dare as well.

In less than an hour they had been transferred to a pair of outside cabins. The two chambers were connected by a skinny door, and neither of them was either spacious or particularly comfortable. But Xavier brought cushions while Oliver brought breakfast. By the time she and Aubrey were cleaned and fed, the rooms were nearly as pleasant as the ones on the *Lady Haberton* had been.

But there had been no grim shadow hovering over them on the *Lady Haberton.* No threat in the form of a vengeful sea captain. When he summoned her again it was via a sailor she did not know.

"I'm Mick," the man said in a broad Yorkshire accent. "The cap'n, he says yer to come wi' me now. If you please," he added, bobbing his slightly balding head.

"If I please," she muttered to herself. "If *he* pleases, you mean." But to the weathered-looking fellow she only said, "I refuse to leave Aubrey alone, so your captain will have to come—"

"Ollie!" the man cut her off with a bellowing cry. "Ollie, you gots to wait in here wi' the lad!"

"Kindly use a little restraint!" Eliza scolded, clapping her hands over her ears.

"Sorry, miss." He backed away a step, just as cowed as Oliver had been when she used her coolest, most well-bred tones. Could it be that these sailors—common men all—were intimidated by a titled noblewoman? It seemed more than ludicrous—but then, so did everything else associated with this misbegotten voyage.

"Well, just see that it doesn't happen again," she ordered, mollified by his behavior. If he'd known how to properly bow and scrape, she realized, he would have done so. Oliver, too, crept into the room like a dog fearing to be scolded. It boosted her confidence enormously.

"Stay with Aubrey while I'm gone," she instructed the younger sailor. "You already know how to exercise his foot, so do it. Once I'm finished with your captain we will wish to sit on deck for awhile." She glanced at the other man. "Be sure to have two comfortable chairs ready. And Mick," she added, enjoying the dismay on both their faces. "Don't forget blankets."

Then, not waiting for a reply, she gave Aubrey a reassuring smile and stalked majestically into the companionway.

Her triumph did not last long. She peered to the left and then to the right, only to be met by a deflating sight. Not twenty feet away, the door to the captain's chamber stood open. Just beyond the door, behind his handsome desk, sat Cyprian Dare, his feet crossed upon the edge of the desk as he stared straight at her. He gave her a faint smile, just the mocking curve of one side of his mouth. But it was enough to take all the wind out of her sails. The ship rocked smoothly along, creaking its unique rhythm as the muffled calls of the crew wafted down to them. But in the dark passageway, her world seemed to narrow down to that brief, smug smile.

She could order his crew around, but Cyprian Dare? Eliza feared she was no match for him at all. It occurred to her that she'd once felt the same way about Michael. Inadequate. Overwhelmed. But that seemed so inconsequential now. Only her self-esteem had been at stake then. Now her very existence hung in the balance. Hers *and* Aubrey's.

She steeled herself as best she could, and bracing herself on the rough plank wall, made her way toward him. Not once in those long seconds did he take his eyes from her, and that finished off completely what little there was left of her composure.

"Close the door."

Eliza stopped just inside the portal. "Why?" she managed, despite her fear.

One of his straight black brows raised in mild surprise. "Why? Because I told you to. I'm captain of this ship, Eliza. What I say goes, and no one questions me about why. We'll get along much better once you accept that." He paused. "Now, close the door. Please." He smiled again.

Despite her unreasoning terror, Eliza nonetheless deemed it wiser to comply. She swung the door closed with trembling hands, then stood before it, close enough to flee should that prove necessary.

But Cyprian Dare did not look inclined toward grabbing her as he had at their previous meeting—previous *two* meetings, she amended. He'd grabbed *and* touched *and* kissed her that very first time. Now as he studied

her with his dark enigmatic eyes, she feared he might be
remembering that same incident.

"Sit down." He gestured to one of the chairs, then
went back to studying her, one fingertip idly rubbing a
small scar on his chin.

Eliza sat down, but warily. He was dressed almost like
a gentleman today, with a crisp shirt of white lawn that
looked every bit as fine a garment as her brother
LeClere might choose. His boots too, were from the
finest London shoeworks, for she saw the distinctive
mark of Pickerings on the instep. Was he pirate or nobleman? she wondered. Could it be her Uncle Lloyd
had ruined him in some business venture and now he
sought to even the score?

She cleared her throat, growing more nervous by the
moment with his silence. If he meant to terrify her he
was succeeding awfully well.

"It's been so long since anyone has requested passage
on the *Chameleon* that I've almost forgotten my duties.
And you *did* request passage, as I recall." He stretched
back a little and rested his folded hands across his flat
stomach, all the while smiling at her. Once again she
was reminded of a coiled spring, a seething inferno, restrained—but barely—beneath a facade of deceptive
idleness and casual banter.

Eliza worried her lower lip with her teeth. She *had*
insisted that she be allowed to stay to protect her young
cousin from this vengeful man, and she would not
change her actions at this late date. Yet that was hardly
the same thing as requesting passage. Still, she had the
troubling feeling that he was well pleased that she had
elected to stay. What game did he mean to play with her
now?

"*I* may have chosen to stay on board your ship, but
Aubrey was given no such choice," she accused him, deciding to be blunt.

The spring uncoiled. With a jerk his feet came off the

desk and hit the floor so fast that her heart stopped. She feared that she would have one of her asthma attacks and expire right on the spot, as his searing gaze pinned her to her chair.

"I suggest you use a more pleasant tone when you speak to me," he bit out. "I suggest you display the good manners you were raised with, Miss Thoroughgood. Order my men about, if you like. Bully them with that hands-off tone you wield like a weapon. But don't ever think to use it on me."

His cold eyes bored into hers for one long uncomfortable moment, and more than anything Eliza wanted to flee. Had she been anywhere but on a ship somewhere in the middle of the Atlantic Ocean, she would have done just that. But there was nowhere to run. So she sat there petrified, gripping the carved wooden ends of the chair arms as if they could possibly lend her their support.

He gave her a cool smile. "That's better. I've decided to lay down a few rules for you. Xavier will see to most of your needs. But if you have any complaints, bring them to me, not him." Then his expression grew even cooler, if that were possible. "I suggest very strongly that you keep your distance from Oliver."

"But . . . but why?" she managed to get out in a shaking voice.

He pursed his lips and gave her an assessing look. "He can't be trusted around women. I wouldn't want him to do anything, shall we say, untoward."

No doubt you're saving that task for yourself, she thought. But she wisely did not say that out loud. Her tart remarks had always been forgiven at home. She was the pampered invalid. The only daughter. But here . . . She shivered to think how totally vulnerable she was here.

He seemed to be equally aware of that fact, if the sudden glitter in his vivid blue eyes was any indication.

"You needn't worry about me, Eliza. As I explained last night, I'm only interested in women who are willing. Or women I can make willing."

The challenge in his voice was unmistakable and it was made worse by the fact that he stared at her so boldly hot color burned her cheeks. Did he imply that *she* could be made willing?

She shook her head, denying to herself the curiosity his kiss had roused in her. "Then I . . . I suppose I have nothing to worry about, do I?"

His head dipped once as if in mocking acknowledgement of her feeble attempt at bravery. "We shall see, won't we? But I forget myself. Now that you are settled in your quarters, it remains for us to attend to other matters." His eyes slid over her, studying every aspect of her appearance until she squirmed in self-conscious dismay. Her face was clean, and her hands as well. But her hair, though combed, was styled only in one long, ragged plait down her back. As for what she was wearing . . .

If his goal was to keep her in a constant state of discomfort, he was certainly doing a very good job of it.

"Stand up," he ordered.

"Wh—what?"

"Stand up," he enunciated more clearly. "And turn around. Slowly."

"But . . . but why?" she asked, fighting back a wave of pure panic.

He sighed, as if she tried his patience to the absolute limit. *She* try *his* patience!

"Unless you wish to wear that hideous garment for the duration of your time aboard, you will stand up and turn around. Your nightgown, I believe?" He waited expectantly.

Was that all he had in mind, providing her with more suitable clothing? Despite Eliza's unwillingness to accept any kindness from him, an enormous wave of relief washed over her. She had been excruciatingly and constantly aware that she was dressed only in her nightgown. Desperate to be more properly clothed, she ventured, "Are you saying you have women's clothing on board your ship?"

"Actually, I was going to offer you one of my shirts and a pair of breeches."

At that she stiffened. She should have known he'd find some way to be insulting in the process of appearing to be kind. "Thank you, but no."

A mocking grin curved his lips. "I suppose I should have anticipated that sort of response from such a proper London miss as yourself. Would you like me to ask my crew if they have any women's garments?"

"Your crew? Why would any man carry women's clothing with him?" she asked suspiciously.

"They often purchase such things for their wives or other womenfolk when we're in foreign ports."

Eliza's heart leapt in hope. But she was wary, too. He seemed awfully accommodating this morning. Perhaps she should test the limits of his pleasant mood.

"I'd appreciate that very much."

His eyes, so dark and bold, held hers captive. "Good. So, stand up and turn around."

Once more a shiver of fear snaked down her spine. She was so completely at his mercy. Though he professed no interest in unwilling women, everything he did managed to be outrageously provoking and somehow filled with innuendo. She'd never been made so entirely aware of a man before. Not even Michael. Nor had she ever been so conscious of her own body. Worse, she feared that even a change of clothing would prove no barrier to that disturbing awareness. Appearing before him in her nightgown was not what was making her so nervous. It was him. Were she garbed in full winter regalia, she would still feel the impact of his eyes on her.

She cleared her throat, seeking a way to avoid al-

lowing him a full inspection of her person. "I . . . ah
. . . I'm sure I can alter any garments you may provide
so that they fit. What I'd rather discuss—"

"You can sew?" he interrupted her.

"Well . . . well, yes, of course I can sew."

"And here I'd thought you just a . . . how do I put
this? Just an ornamental sort of female. Unable to cook
or sew or do any of the ordinary domestic tasks. Has the
life of English nobility changed so much in recent years?
I would have thought you had servants to perform all
those little jobs for you."

Eliza didn't know whether to be angry or defensive at
his taunting appraisal of her and her sort. She sewed,
yes. But only embroidery. Ornamental detail. She'd
never once sewn a complete garment. Nor cooked a
complete meal, either. But that didn't mean she
couldn't if she tried.

"I'm quite able to alter any clothing," she stated, willing any tremble from her voice.

"Very well, then. I'll have Xavier see what he can find
for you."

"What about Aubrey?" she asked, for Aubrey was
what this was all about, not her. "Aubrey needs clothing
too."

She might as well have slapped him, she thought, in
the frigid moments that followed. His expression had
been relaxed, though still retaining that mocking edge.
Now, however, his brows pulled together and his jaw
hardened. "The boy has no need of additional clothing."

"But of course he does," Eliza insisted. Though she
was aware her words infuriated him, she was compelled
to continue. "He can't remain in his nightshirt."

"He *can* remain in his nightshirt. And he can bloody
well remain in his cabin, too!"

Despite the threat in his menacing tone, Eliza knew
this was one subject she must pursue, for his vengeful

treatment of Aubrey was at the heart of his vile scheme. "But he is only a child," she pleaded. "You cannot leave him locked up that way."

"I can do anything I bloody well please, Eliza. I suggest you not forget that. Anything," he repeated for effect.

It worked, for it struck fear in her very soul. She started to argue, but her mind seemed to freeze. When she finally found her tongue it was to stammer, "I wish you wouldn't curse."

To her shock, however, her foolish words turned his glower to amusement. "You wish I wouldn't curse?" He laughed out loud. "If you think to run me and my ship like you run your household, you shall be quite disappointed, my dear." He leaned forward, a wicked gleam in his eyes. "I say what I bloody well want and I do what I bloody well want. And nobody, not even a prissy little thing like you, tells me otherwise. So tell me, my delectable Eliza. Why aren't you married yet?"

His abrupt change of mood, followed at once by his equally abrupt change of subject, shredded the last of her composure.

"I . . . I'm engaged to be married. But . . . but that is neither here nor there. You cannot confine Aubrey to below decks. It is simply too cruel."

A muscle in his jaw flexed but this time his expression remained unchanged. "I'll make you a bargain, then. You dine with me this evening, wearing your new clothes, and I'll allow the boy on deck."

Eliza studied him warily. What was he up to? "You'll find him clothes and allow him on deck?"

He studied her right back and she saw a flicker of a smile in his eyes. Before when he'd smiled it had been overcast by a mocking sense of distance. He'd been observing her—baiting her—and amused by what he saw. This time, however, some stray bit of warmth showed in his vivid blue eyes. It lit them with just a hint of silvery color.

"Every day you share a meal with me, he shall be allowed on deck," he conceded, leaning back smugly in his chair.

Eliza swallowed the alarming shiver of anticipation that gave her. Did he think in this way he might "make her willing"? She wasn't sure she wanted to know. "What of his clothes?"

He nodded once. "He'll have clothes. Anything else?" he asked, raising one imperious slash of a brow.

Eliza deemed it best to stop while she was ahead. She still hoped to uncover his reason for kidnapping Aubrey, as well as his plans for the child. But that was a subject better left for another time. Perhaps tonight at dinner, she decided when she rose. His gaze slid over her once, very briefly. But it was enough to warn her to be on her guard. If he should behave in even the most mildly forward fashion, she would bring up her uncle's name. Hopefully his resulting anger would squelch any amorous intentions he might harbor. Better him furious with her than trying to seduce her.

With that one bit of security to sustain her, she moved nearer to the door. "If it's all right with you, Captain, I'll return to Aubrey now."

"As you wish. But Eliza," he added when she turned to leave, "I'd prefer you call me Cyprian."

Once again there was that flicker of heat in his eyes and it sent a disturbing quiver up her spine. Somehow it made him seem even more dangerous to her than before.

"And if I don't prefer it?" she whispered.

His smile did not change. "As I told you before, I never force a woman to do anything she doesn't want to do."

I just make her willing. The unsaid words rang as clearly as if he'd shouted them.

Eliza didn't reply. What would be the purpose? But as she pulled the door open, slipped out, and pulled it shut, the words echoed in her head. *I just make her willing. I just make her willing.*

Eliza squinted in the waning light. The skirt Xavier had brought fit well enough, though she'd had to pull the ties at the waist as snug as they would go. The chemise too was fine, though rather sheer for her tastes. But the blouse he'd given her was altogether something else. It was a fine quality cotton with a soft hand much to be admired. But it was cut wide and low at the neckline, with vivid colors in an unusual geometric pattern. Rather gypsyish. Xavier had said it came from Morocco and was of a style worn by many women there. But it was quite unlike anything Eliza had ever seen.

She was trying now to take it in at each shoulder so that it didn't gape so immodestly over her chest. Three more stitches and she'd be done.

"Ouch!" she yelped when the boat lurched and she jabbed her thumb. "Bloody hell," she added as she stared at the pinprick of blood that welled up from her offended digit. "Bloody, bloody hell."

Somehow it felt good to say such vulgarities out loud. If her current situation didn't warrant cursing, she wasn't sure what did. Still, she was glad no one was there to witness her profanity.

She finished the garment and donned it right away. Xavier had taken Aubrey above decks a short while before. The boy was clad in coarse wool breeches rolled up around the ankles. He wore his sleeping shirt over it and a loose knit cap covering his curly head. He'd wanted shoes—to cover his misshapen foot. But there were none in his size, so he was forced to remain barefoot. Still, his eagerness to leave the confining cabin, coupled with Xavier's reassuring encouragement, had eventually overcome his embarrassment.

How Eliza wished she could have the gentle giant Xavier with her when she joined the captain at dinner. The captain who preferred she call him by his given name. Cyprian Dare.

Eliza had thought about the enigmatic captain all afternoon. If she was forced to dine with him once a day in order for Aubrey to be free of his cabin, she must formulate a plan to gain whatever else she might from him. It was clear he expected to soften her opposition to him by their forced proximity, so that meant he would most likely be on his very best behavior. What she must do, she told herself as she tugged the neckline as high as she could get it, was beat him at his own game. He meant to bring her around, but she must bring him around instead. She must convince him not to use Aubrey as a weapon against her Uncle Lloyd.

Despite Eliza's firm convictions, however, it took only a sharp rap on the door to shatter her flimsy composure. She tugged at the offensive bodice again, then with a groan of dismay, pulled her unbound hair over her shoulders. Though it provided only a partial shield to her exposed collarbone and upper chest, it was better than nothing. The sharp rap came again and she pushed off the bed. Time to face her nemesis.

"I'm coming," she muttered, throwing back the door. To her relief, it was Oliver who stood there, not Cyprian. Oliver, whom Cyprian had ordered her to avoid.

"Holy mother," the young man murmured at the sight of her. His eyes raked her with a bold, appreciative stare. "Holy mother," he repeated as a grin lit his boyish features. "May I say, Miss Eliza, you are looking quite fetching tonight. Quite tasty, in fact."

She gave him a withering stare. "If your tastes run toward barefoot peasant girls, I suppose I am passable."

"Oh, more than passable. Besides, there's not a man aboard the *Chameleon* that wouldn't appreciate a comely peasant wench, barefoot or bare anything else," he added, a leering gleam in his brown eyes.

She let out a rude noise. "Your manners are worse than deplorable. Can I assume, however, that you are here for a reason?"

"A reason? Now that I see you, it's clear you're reason enough," he persisted, this time waggling his expressive eyebrows in so humorous a fashion she almost laughed. But that would only encourage him so she forced herself to be stern.

"The reason, Oliver. Why are you here?"

"Ah, yes. 'Tis Aubrey. He'd a splinter in his hand, though Cook has removed it. He's in the galley now, listening to one of the cook's farfetched tales. I just thought you'd want to know."

"Oh, dear. I'd better go to him," Eliza said. "Can you show me to the galley?"

"I can show you anything you want," he replied, his appreciative gaze sweeping over her again.

"I think I'm the one to do that."

They both jumped at that dark, imperious voice.

Oliver backed away, and Eliza would have also. But Cyprian stepped into the doorway and caught her by the hand. "See to your duties," he ordered Oliver without even glancing in the young man's direction.

Once the second mate left, however, Cyprian's keen observation of her turned positively unnerving. As Oliver had done, Cyprian's gaze swept over her, taking in every aspect of her gypsyish dress. But where Oliver's leering gaze only left her exasperated, Cyprian's started the most unseemly sort of clamoring inside her. Breasts, belly, thighs. Even her toes seemed to react to his brief but very thorough examination of her, for they curled against the smooth floorboards as if of their own volition.

Then he met her apprehensive eyes and gave her his most sincere smile yet. She felt his hand shift against hers—the hard, calloused palm slide upon her softer one, and his strong fingers flex around hers.

"Since it appears you are dressed and ready, why don't we adjourn to my quarters? Now."

Chapter Eight

"**B**ut I must see to Aubrey," Eliza protested as Cyprian drew her down the companionway toward his cabin. "Oliver said he—"

"Oliver said he was with Cook and in good hands."

"Yes, but—"

"And I told you to avoid Oliver."

Eliza tried to jerk her hand from his to no avail. Although his grip was not tight enough to hurt her, it was still too firm for her to evade. As he strode down the passageway, pulling her willy-nilly behind him, panic flooded through her. He wouldn't let her see Aubrey; he was dragging her into his private chamber; and his warm grip filled her with both dread and a perverse sort of fascination. It was how she'd felt about Michael, a vague part of her realized, only with Cyprian it was twenty times stronger.

"Wait!" she cried, grabbing the door frame with her free hand. "Wait!"

He stopped, but did not release her. "You agreed to dine with me," he reminded her, after turning to face her.

In the dim light of the low-ceilinged hall he appeared larger and more imposing than ever before. He was backlit by the lantern burning in his cabin, and his face lay in shadows. Despite that, she could feel the distinct touch of his eyes upon her.

She took a shaky breath. "If you're trying to be cruel, you are doing a very good job of it. But I don't understand *why* you're doing it."

There was a short charged silence. "Are you referring to my treatment of you—or of the boy?"

Eliza tried to calm her racing pulse. "Both," she answered, deciding there was no benefit in hiding the truth from him.

Again there was a pause. Then he lifted her hand and stared at it. To her utter surprise he shifted it to his other hand, gave her an abbreviated bow, and kissed her fingertips.

She jerked her hand away and for one panicked moment they stared at one another. She didn't understand him, the solitary thought repeated itself in her head. She didn't understand him at all. But she did know she was in a dangerous situation. This was the same brazen man who'd so boldly stolen into Aubrey's cabin aboard the *Lady Haberton* and then proceeded to kiss her and fondle her as if he had every right in the world to do so. If he were that daring on another vessel, what might he attempt here?

She drew herself up with an effort. Unfortunately, she had to break the hold of his compelling stare before she could speak, and she feared that weakened her show of bravado. "Are you going to explain yourself?" she asked, hitching the neckline of the blouse higher on one shoulder while she stared determinedly at the dangling ties of his collarless shirt.

But he would not allow her to evade him that easily, for with his thumb and forefinger he turned her face back up to his. Although his touch was light it managed nevertheless to command her attention, to focus all her senses upon him though it was merely that faint press of his skin to hers. For one insane moment she thought she actually might swoon.

"I had thought our dinner conversation could be more pleasant. But as it obviously means so much to you, I'll try to explain myself. But not here in the companionway. Come inside and I'll pour us each a glass of wine. Then we can sit down like civilized human beings and discuss it." His hand fell away from her chin and he gave her another mock bow. "Will you please join me, Miss Thoroughgood?"

It seemed pointless not to, Eliza rationalized past the thundering pulse in her ears. She stepped tentatively into the captain's quarters, fighting all the while to regain her composure. She heard him close the door behind her, but he did not lock it. Though she knew it was ludicrous to find any reassurance in that—it was not as if she could actually escape him for long on his own ship—it nonetheless helped her to take the seat he indicated. But she watched him closely just the same.

He took a bottle of wine from a cupboard and two heavy goblets. The bank of diamond-paned windows behind him framed a breathtaking sunset. They were headed northeast, she realized. Back to England? But Cyprian's excessively masculine form blotted out all thoughts of direction and sunsets. When he approached and offered the full goblet to her, she was conscious only of him. Golden sunlight glinted off his night-black hair. And golden lights seemed to glint as well in his dark eyes.

"To good seas and a fair wind," he murmured, lifting his pewter goblet half the way to hers.

Eliza gripped the spiral stem of her goblet tighter. "Yes." She cleared her throat. "I should not like for us to sink."

She touched her goblet to his, then following his lead, drank. But she watched him over the rim. When he too sat, she drank again in relief. He was so intimidating when he stood over her—not that he wasn't almost as intimidating sitting down. Cyprian Dare projected the most overwhelming aura of masculinity, whether sitting or standing, in darkness or in light, on his own turf or someone else's.

What a swath he would cut in society, she thought, beating down a giggle at the thought. Put those shoulders in an evening jacket, release him into a room full of women, and then just stand back and watch. It was a toss up who would salivate more—the mothers or the daughters.

"I assure you, Eliza, the *Chameleon* will not sink," he said, sending her a devastating smile that only reinforced her opinion. His teeth were white and straight in a face burned brown by both sun and wind, and when he smiled like that and stared directly at her, it was enough to convince a girl he'd never shared that smile with any woman but herself.

Get a hold of yourself, Eliza, a stern voice ordered. Blinking, she broke the hold of his eyes and drank deeply once more. The wine was cold and of good quality, she noticed. It went down smoothly—he probably hoped to get her tipsy, she realized. With a thunk she set the drinking vessel down on the table.

"You said you would explain yourself," she muttered, angry at herself for her meandering thoughts. He was trying to distract her and she was obliging him. But no more.

He stretched his legs out and crossed them. The wild beast relaxed in his own den, she imagined as they studied one another.

"Where shall I begin?"

Eliza had to give herself a mental shake. "You can begin by telling me what you intend to do."

"With you?" He grinned ever so slightly. A smirk, she termed it. Yet it served to remind her how he'd kissed her once before with those same curving lips.

"With Aubrey," she retorted in rising irritation. "I want to know what you intend to do with Aubrey. For I intend to stay with my cousin."

He took a slow considering sip of his wine. "I plan to reorder his future, that's all."

She let out a frustrated sigh. "What does *that* mean?"

He shrugged. "He shall earn his way in the world, not have it handed to him by his wealthy father."

Despite her frustration with his deliberate evasiveness, Eliza recognized the subtle emphasis when he said the word *father*. What was she to make of that?

"I take it you do not care for Aubrey's father."

The fact that he did not scoff at her carefully understated remark only served to emphasize to Eliza the depths of his hatred for her uncle.

"His father—" Again the same sarcasm, though less veiled than before. "His father can only raise the boy to become as vile and cruel as he is himself. The fact is, the boy will be better served in my care than in his father's."

"Oh, but how can you say such a thing? You cannot truly believe such a thing would be best for Aubrey."

She saw his jaw tense and his knuckles whiten around the stem of his goblet. But he kept his temper under control. Still, the fact that her defense of Sir Lloyd could so infuriate him fed her curiosity more than ever. "All right. All right," she conceded, unmindful that she took another sip of her wine. "It's clear you *do* believe it. But why? How do you even *know* Lloyd Haberton?"

"I've known him for many years."

Eliza bit her lip in thought. "For many years. But not in English society, for I would remember a family named Dare. So it must be through his business connections. Have you perhaps sailed upon his ships? Were you unfairly treated by one of his captains?"

He grinned, but it was the cold expression of a ruthless predator. "No, my lovely little meddler. Only by him. It's unlikely any of his ships are a worthy match for mine."

He thought her lovely? Eliza took a restoring swallow of wine and forced herself to ignore that completely unimportant remark. "What exactly has he done to you, then?" she asked, though her throat burned from her hasty gulping.

It was his turn to drink and as he drained the contents of his goblet, Eliza watched in fascination. His throat worked in smooth undulations. When he tipped his head back she could see the shadowed line where his facial hair ended and smoother skin began. When he met her gaze again, however, she saw the hard glint of hatred in his eyes. Not of her though, she realized, but of her uncle.

Anger caused of pain, she heard Xavier's words echo. Was the harsh face Cyprian showed to the world just a cover for a more hidden and vulnerable one? Like Aubrey at his most difficult, throwing a tantrum that overshadowed the simple fact that he was frustrated and afraid? Could it be that Cyprian was just like the smooth skin of his throat, well protected when his head was lowered, by the bristles of his beard stubble?

"What he has done is not pertinent to our conversation," he said in a tone so low and even—so menacing— that it lifted the hairs on the back of her neck. "He has wronged me grievously and now I shall return the favor."

Eliza averted her eyes from his penetrating stare. "But . . . but what precisely will you do to Aubrey?" she persisted. Though she feared his answer, she needed to know just how deeply his hatred for her uncle ran, and how much of it would transfer to his hapless child.

He reached for the wine bottle and refilled his goblet, then did the same for her. To cover her case of nerves, Eliza drank again. How was she to get through an entire meal in his presence when just sharing a glass of wine with him was so difficult?

"Drink up," he encouraged her in a more pleasant tone. When she glanced at him in surprise he lifted his glass and drank. She did as well, more by habit than anything else. Their eyes held throughout, however, and she rightly guessed that he intended to control his emotions better.

"Your cousin has a choice. He can become a cabin boy on one of my ships. He can work on land—perhaps in a stable or a tavern. I know any number of people who might hire him. Or he—"

"But he can't walk," she cried. "You've seen him. You know he can't do those things."

"If he will not work, then he can become a beggar."

"A beggar?" Eliza's anger rose too swiftly for her to control. The cruelty of the man! The arrogance! she leapt to her feet and in the process bumped the table and nearly toppled over her half-emptied goblet of wine. But she could not care about that, not when poor Aubrey's life was being ruined.

"You are the vilest, most horrible, monstrous man—" She broke off and turned, needing to be away from him —and close to Aubrey. But before Eliza even reached the door, he caught her by one arm and spun her around to face him.

"I did not give you permission to leave here." He thrust her roughly against the door. "Lest you forget, you are on *my* ship, in *my* cabin, and at *my* mercy. *I* am captain here, and I'm no fop or dandy whom you may control with only your smile."

Eliza glared up at him. She was terrified and yet fury governed her lips more than fear. "I will fight you," she vowed. "You may have us at your mercy now, but my father will come for me, as will my uncle and my brothers and . . . and my fiancé too. You'll never escape their wrath, Cyprian Dare. Never!"

His hands tightened so fiercely around her arms that she thought he might actually crush her bones. "If you want to fight me, fair Eliza, I suggest you choose your battles carefully. Forget your cousin. You can't win against me when it comes to him. But there are other battlefields between us where your chances are better."

He moved, just the slightest shifting of his weight. But it settled his hips against hers. Eliza's eyes widened in shock. His warm weight against her was a threat, pure and simple. He could do things to her and she couldn't stop him.

Then one of his knees pressed into the space between her thighs and she knew he meant to prove his mastery over her right now.

She shoved at him with a strength born of utter desperation. But it was like trying to move an oak tree. He did not budge.

"No," she gasped, staring at him in wide-eyed fear. "Don't do—"

But he cut her off. The firm press of his mouth against hers stifled all her protests.

Eliza tried to turn away, to avoid this beginning to the ravishment he planned. But he slid his long fingers into her unbound hair to keep her still.

She struck at him with her freed arm. Once, then again. But her blows were ineffectual, and anyway, his lips swiftly demanded her complete attention. For instead of forcing her mouth open and possessing it with his tongue as he'd done that other time, he was stroking and caressing her lips in a manner at once both relentless and tender. He wouldn't let her turn away, and yet he was not forceful. He kissed the corners of her mouth, sucked at her lower lip, and traced the seam of her tightly clamped lips with his tongue.

"Come on, Eliza," he coaxed, trailing kisses across her cheek, her jaw, and then up to her ear. "Come on," he breathed into her ear, causing her to squirm at the untoward feelings that roused in her belly. "Direct some of that fiery temper of yours at me now."

How dare he mock her! Yet Eliza could not deny that the fear she had of being raped eased enormously at his beguiling tone. It was almost as if he wooed her.

His tongue traced the patterns of her ear and she gasped at her inexplicable reaction to such a strange touch. "Stop. No—don't do that! Oh . . . "

His mouth returned to hers with the same devastating effect. But though he easily could have forced entrance between her parted lips now, he did not. One of his hands still tangled in her hair, and the other wound around her waist. Though her hands were free to oppose him, they didn't. One of her palms pressed against his solid chest. The other gripped his upper arm.

"So sweet," he murmured the words against her mouth. Then he licked her lips, wetting them before capturing them once more.

Eliza's lips were opened to him. There was no way she could pretend they were not. Her entire body had turned pliant at his touch, and . . . and willing.

The remnant part of her rational mind demanded that she break away. Yet another part of her marveled at the wondrous sensations building up inside her. And at his astounding restraint.

He was making her willing, the rational part realized. Just as he'd warned, he was making her willing.

But she shut out that irritating voice as she rose to answer his kiss. One of her arms wrapped about his neck, and as if that signaled her full acceptance, he finally deepened the kiss.

The feel of Cyprian's tongue filling her mouth, sliding along her incredibly sensitized lips, was unlike anything Eliza had ever known. The voluptuous quality of such unlikely behavior must surely be wicked, she vaguely determined. If it was all right to feel these astonishing sensations all over her body, someone would surely have spoken to her about it before now. But they hadn't and so she concluded it must be wrong.

Still, that line of reasoning did not prevent her from pressing up on tiptoe to have more of that feeling.

Cyprian obliged by slanting his lips, fitting the two of them even closer together. His tongue delved deep, sliding in and out in a rhythm that generated the most disquieting feelings inside her. There was an urgent rhythm to his kiss that managed to infect her until her entire being seemed to pulse with the same rhythm. Then his hand slid down from her waist and over her derriere, and deep inside her a veritable fire leapt to life.

He pulled away from their kiss but she pressed up to it. This time she stroked the seam of his lips with her tongue. He opened to her tentative foray and she grew bolder. He lured her tongue all the way into his mouth, teasing and taunting her, as if they were two combatants in a duel. She knew he was far beyond her in ability, but that didn't prevent her enthusiastic participation. When he pressed his knee higher between her thighs, however, until she practically straddled his upper leg, and his hand curved around her derriere from the back to meet his knee, she pulled her head back in shock.

"You must . . . you must stop," she murmured breathlessly.

"You first," he retorted, seeking her ear with his lips.

She shook her head, trying to avoid the undermining impact of his hot breath on her sensitive neck. But he found the tender skin there anyway, and in mindless reaction she moaned and arched nearer.

"God, woman." He bit the words along her neck and raised her higher on his knee until her feet left the floor and she was forced to cling to him as her only support in a world tilting right off its axis.

"Let me down," she protested, even as she pressed her belly against him.

"As you wish."

Before Eliza realized what he was about, she was flat on her back on his lavishly upholstered bed. And he lay above her!

"No! Let me up!" she protested, trying frantically to twist away. But she was caught between the deep feather bed and his solid weight, and tangled in her own skirts. She tossed her head wildly, seeking to avoid the kiss she was certain would follow. "Let me up," she cried, truly terrified now.

"Let you up. Let you down. Make up your mind, Eliza," he answered, a half-smile on his face.

From fear to fury that half-smile propelled her. How she wanted to claw it from his handsome face! But though he didn't let her up, neither did he try to kiss her again. He just held her down and studied her. Waiting for her to exhaust herself and give up, she suspected. Waiting until she no longer had the strength to fight him.

Her struggles subsided at once. She stared back at him, at his dark face just inches above her own, and she perversely thought of Michael. Michael was a gentleman. He would never behave this way toward her. Michael was more handsome as well, as if a golden aura surrounded him, while this man . . . if Michael was the sun, Cyprian Dare was the storm, violent and threatening.

Yet the look in his eyes right now was not threatening, but rather triumphant. Smug, and amused.

"I'm so gratified that you find this amusing," she snapped in the most scathing tone she could manage.

His grin came out full force. Was that a dimple in his left cheek?

"Any other maiden would be dissolving in tears by now. Why aren't you weeping—at least a little?"

Eliza swallowed hard. Why indeed? The truth was

that she hardly ever cried. She supposed she'd never had reason to in the past, and it hadn't occurred to her now. If it made her appear braver than she actually was, however, perhaps that was good.

"Is that your goal? To make me cry?"

He shook his head slightly and a sensual expression took over his face. "Actually, no. My goal is to . . . " He trailed off but the glint in his vivid blue eyes made his intentions clear.

"You cannot make me willing," she vowed, ignoring the fact that he'd already done so, and awfully fast. She felt his silent chuckle against her chest. "Get off me," she muttered, shoving at him.

To her utter shock—and immense relief—he complied. He rolled to the side, though he kept one arm across her waist to keep her still. Then he propped up one elbow and studied her. "Would it help if I plied you with pretty words?"

"Since plying me with wine didn't work as well as you thought it would?" She glared at him, conscious of the warm weight of his arm across her ribs. Just beneath her breasts.

"Oh, but it did work. I thought you kissed me with quite commendable enthusiasm."

"I did not!"

"You put your tongue in my mouth," he taunted, bringing his face closer to hers. "How sweetly and seductively you slid it in."

"I . . . I was thinking of Michael then. My fiancé," she added, relieved for such inspiration. When his features stiffened, she plunged on. "I only endured your unwelcome attentions by imagining you were Michael."

Her disparaging words had the desired effect—at least somewhat. For whatever his amorous intentions had been, they faded at her deliberate insult. Unfortunately his vengeful nature rose to fill the void. Though he stroked her cheek and pulled one tangled strand of her hair free and smoothed it upon the silken coverlet, his dangerous mood was apparent in the chilling silence that followed.

"For all your facade of good manners and polite conversation, you and your kind possess a cruelty not found among common people. Perhaps you need to be taught humility every bit as much as your uncle does."

He trailed one dispassionate finger along her neck, down to the low neckline of the blouse and beyond, all the way down, between her breasts to her stomach. Her breath caught when his hand splayed wide across her flat stomach and rested there, but her heart thundered as if it would explode. His amorous teasing was of less threat, she realized, than this terrifyingly calm anger.

"There are few options open to women. Ruined women," he added.

"So . . . so you intend to ruin me?" Her words were barely a whisper, so effectively had he managed to intimidate her.

He smiled, a cold grimace that made a mask of his harshly handsome face. "Could you survive it, I wonder? Would your family disown you? Would your upstanding Michael still want to marry you?"

Eliza did not know the answer to that, and her doubt must have shown in her expression. For Cyprian sat up then, a bitter smile of triumph twisting his lips.

"Enough of this." He stood and ran his fingers through his close-cropped hair. "I'm hungry." He extended a hand to her and then, when she flinched away, took her hand anyway. He drew her to her feet and with a slight shove pointed her toward the table. "Serve me my dinner. From now on that shall be a part of your duties. Keep my quarters neat. Tend to my clothes. All the domestic tasks you've had an army of servants to manage for you in the past."

When she would have protested he raised one black

brow in arrogant reminder. "Your good behavior as-
sures your cousin's good treatment, Eliza. In the coming
weeks we shall determine just how dedicated a guardian
you are, won't we?"

Chapter Nine

"You were gone so long," Aubrey complained when Eliza finally returned to her tiny cabin. The door stood open between their two rooms and he'd clearly been waiting for her, propped up in his narrow bed.

"Yes, well, I'm sorry. I would much rather have been here with you. But . . . but I couldn't," she finished as she sat down beside him. "Have you had your dinner?"

"Yes, but Cook said I had to earn my keep. He made me work in the galley—that's what a ship's kitchen is called, you know. I had to chop onions and potatoes. The onions made my eyes burn and I almost cried from it. But I didn't," he added boastfully.

"Are you all right?" she asked anxiously. She studied what she could see of him beneath the sheets, his dark uncombed curls, his dirty face, and his wrinkled night shirt. "I heard you had a splinter."

"Yes, but I got it out myself with Cook's little knife."

Eliza grimaced. "I bet it was filthy," she muttered.

"I wiped it on my sleeve first."

"Oh, that's just wonderful," she retorted.

Aubrey frowned. "What's the matter with you?"

"What's the matter with me! What's the matter with me?" She lurched to her feet and began to pace, gesturing furiously with her hands. "Oh, I've just been kidnapped, that's all. And by the way, in case you haven't noticed, so have you. We're stuck in the middle of the Atlantic Ocean on this stupid ship with a bunch of . . . of . . . of heartless pirates!"

Aubrey drew back and a frightened expression covered his face. At once Eliza regretted her outburst. She should not be ranting at him, for it was hardly his fault. No, it was Cyprian Dare's fault. Every single bit of it.

She crossed back to Aubrey, sat down, and drew him into her arms. "Don't be afraid, sweetheart. Everything will turn out all right in the end. You'll see."

The boy burrowed into her arms. "Do you think Father will rescue us?"

"Of course he will."

"But how will he ever find us?"

"I'm sure Cyprian—the captain," she amended, "will send word to him."

"But how long will it take?"

How long indeed? That was something Eliza was afraid to speculate about. But she could hardly tell a child that. It was her duty to protect him and to keep his spirits up. So she did the only thing she could. She lied. "Not long at all, dear. Not long at all."

He sighed, then disentangled himself from her arms. "The food here is not nearly so good as at home. Too salty."

"Is it? I hadn't noticed," Eliza replied. The dinner she had shared with the *Chameleon*'s difficult captain had been frustrating, infuriating, and frightening. But salty? She honestly could not remember.

"It's because all the meat is packed in barrels of salt," he informed her, not noticing her distracted mood. "There's two kinds, salted pork and salted beef, all in barrels. Oliver showed me."

"Oh, he did, did he?"

"Yes," he replied, oblivious to her sarcasm. "When he carried me to the galley he showed me." Then he frowned. "I wish I had a pair of shoes. The men all stared at my foot." He began to wriggle both his feet back and forth beneath the bed cover.

"If anyone of them says anything unpleasant to you, Aubrey, you just tell me. I'll take care of them."

"It's all right, Eliza. Oliver looked after me. He made the others show me *their* scars. Did you know that Oliver has two scars on his belly, right next to each other? He got them in two different fights." He jabbed at the air as if he held a dagger in his hand, then grunted twice in feigned agony. "Oliver is first-rate, don't you think?"

Eliza grimaced in distaste. "First-rate? Well, I suppose so. A first-rate thief. A first-rate liar." Then when she spied his crestfallen expression she relented with a sigh. "Don't mind me, Aubrey. I'm just tired, that's all. And more than a little frustrated by our predicament."

He resumed the rhythmic fluttering back and forth of his feet. A week ago he'd not had nearly that much flexibility in his injured foot, she realized. "So tell me," she said. "Why do you think Oliver is first-rate?"

"Well, first off, he knows everything about ships and sailing. Did you know that each sail and each rope on the entire ship has its own name? And he can run right up the riggings as quick as the monkeys I saw at the bazaar at Charing Cross," he exclaimed.

The glow in his eyes was more than excitement, she glumly realized. It was hero worship. Master Aubrey Haberton, heir to a wealthy Baron, had as his idol a flippant sailor—very likely a pirate, she feared. Considering the future Cyprian Dare forecast for the child, however, perhaps Oliver *was* a good role model, the ironic thought occurred to her.

"Right up the riggings," she echoed. "I hope you don't get any foolish ideas, Aubrey."

He grinned, an excited expression that she hadn't seen on his face since . . . since before his accident during the summer. Eliza straightened a little from her perch on the side of his bed and peered suspiciously at him. "Aubrey." She stretched out his name in a warning tone. "What is going on in that devious ten-year-old mind of yours?"

His face immediately turned innocent—except for the dancing light in his merry eyes. "I was just thinking that my foot is getting stronger, that's all. Climbing the riggings is mostly a matter of strong arms, anyway. If I cannot walk so well, nor ride, at least I could learn to climb riggings."

"Don't you dare!" she exclaimed in horror. "Why, you could fall and hurt yourself even further. Or worse, you could drown. You could tumble into the sea and drown!"

"Oh, ballocks," he scoffed. Then he clapped his hands over his mouth as if he'd said something he shouldn't.

Ballocks? she wondered.

"Now you listen to me, Aubrey Haberton. Oliver Spencer is a charming rogue, but a rogue nonetheless. If I should discover him tempting you to dangerous adventures—"

"He fancies you, you know."

"What?" Eliza drew up in surprise. Then she rolled her eyes. "Oliver fancies every woman alive, or so I've been informed."

"Well, that may be. But he likes you far better than all the rest. Truly."

"He said that?"

"Well, no," Aubrey admitted. "But he asks all these questions about you, all the time. Things I don't even know the answer to." He eyed her speculatively. "What *is* your favorite flower anyway?"

Cyprian stood on the quarterdeck just above the pair of rooms occupied by his two captives. He took a long pull on his cheroot, then tossed the remaining fragment into the crisp wind. It was getting cooler. In a matter of days they would put in at Alderney. Then what would he do with the troublesome Miss Eliza Thoroughgood?

A murmur and a faint giggle drifted up from their rooms. Clearly neither she nor the boy suffered so greatly that they could not wring some pleasantness from their situation. The irony, he thought sourly, was that he should be celebrating triumphantly but could not.

He'd been so eager to take the boy, so sure of the satisfaction it would bring to capture Haberton's heir. But the boy's cousin—the prim and luscious little guardian—had thrown him completely off-kilter. He ought to be feeling victorious. Elated. But all he felt was frustrated and restless. Why had he allowed her to stay? And what was he to do with her, anyway?

He grimaced at that. He knew what he wanted to do with her. But then what? Put her ashore in Devon with sufficient funds to hire a coach home?

He ran his fingers through his dark hair. You'd think he was no more than a randy youth, the way she roused him. No better than Oliver. "Bloody hell," he muttered. "Bloody, bloody hell."

Xavier glanced up from his perch on a coil of rope. But he didn't say a word. He knew better.

Oliver, however, was not so wise. One side of his mouth curved up in a smirk. "Somebody's feelin' a trifle horny, I'm thinking."

Cyprian glared at him from beneath lowered brows. But the fierce expression that would have silenced the young man a week ago did not work so well this evening. For Oliver met his captain's lethal stare with a belligerence Cyprian had never seen on his former cabin boy's easy-going countenance.

"Is there something you wanted to discuss, Oliver?"

The younger man poked his tongue into his cheek,

clearly considering his words. Then he cleared his throat
and spit over the rail.

"The thing is, Miss Eliza's a lady, not some doxy to
play fast and loose with."

Cyprian held himself very still. "I hadn't known you
recognized the difference."

Oliver jerked to his feet. "I bloody well know the difference. Better than you, it seems. And I won't let you
hurt her," he finished, his hands clenched into fists.

"Jesus, God," Cyprian swore under his breath. What
had ever possessed him to keep the bloody wench on
board? Not only was she interfering with his plans and
wreaking havoc on his famous self-control, now she was
creating dissension in his crew.

"I have no intention of hurting her. So you can shed
the white knight image you've been cultivating of late."

"But you *do* intend to seduce her," Oliver main-
tained, his outrage not in the least abated.

"And your intentions are more noble? What are you
planning, to marry the troublesome wench?"

As soon as he said the words, Cyprian regretted them.
If Oliver hadn't considered that possibility before, it was
patently clear he did so now. The boy's belligerence fled
as the idea took hold in his head, and Cyprian groaned
out loud.

Hearing his captain's reaction, Oliver frowned.
"Eliza's not the sort you fool around with; she's the sort
you marry. Xavier married Ana, so why can't I marry
Eliza?"

"First tell me, why would *she* ever agree to marry
you?"

"Well, love, of course. People who love each other get
married. Look at Xavier and Ana," he pointed out once
more.

Cyprian's initial anger at Oliver faded beneath the
young man's simple explanation. For all his rough upbringing, he was, at least on this matter, a complete

innocent. Oliver's famous accomplishments with ladies in ports up and down the Atlantic coast had been matters of uncomplicated lust. This girl, however, seemed to touch some deeper chord in the lad.

Cyprian sighed and began to pace, and his voice lost its sarcastic bite. "She's a lady, Oliver. Her father's titled and she's wealthy beyond anything you can even imagine. She lives in a grand house—several grand houses. Her father has probably turned down dozens of men he deems too inferior for her. What do you think he'd say to the likes of you?"

"That doesn't matter. Not out here," Oliver reasoned.

Cyprian shook his head. "I'll admit that's true. But tell me, do you think *she* would consider an offer of marriage from a poor sailor? Besides, she already has a fiancé."

But Oliver refused to concede the point. "If I had the chance to court her properly, I could convince her. If you would leave her alone," he added, as belligerent as before.

Cyprian gritted his teeth in irritation. What in hell was wrong with the fool? The fact that an irritating voice in his head said that Oliver was right about Eliza —that she was the type to marry and raise a nursery full of rosy-cheeked children with—only increased his anger.

He glanced at Xavier, but the big African offered no help. In fact, he had an odd grin on his face as if he enjoyed watching his friends spar over the same slight woman.

"Just stay away from her," Cyprian finally growled at Oliver.

"And watch you ruin her?" Oliver advanced toward Cyprian, his body stiff as if he meant to challenge him right there. Only then did Xavier intercede. He blocked

Oliver's progress with one unyielding hand on the young man's arm.

"I shall ensure Miss Eliza's security as long as she's aboard the *Chameleon.*" His steady gaze went from Cyprian to Oliver and back to Cyprian. "I vowed as much to her, and I make the same vow now to the both of you. Think of me as her father, if you will," he added with a returning grin.

Cyprian wanted to curse the two of them as they stared at him. What was it about this one little slip of a woman that she could set his two most reliable men at odds with him?

"See to the watch," he finally muttered. But even as he departed the deck, Cyprian vowed to himself that before this voyage was done he would have the high and mighty Eliza Thoroughgood in his bed. Lady she might be, but he was no less deserving of her favors than her precious Michael was. Had his father but claimed him, he would be considered more than fitting as a suitor for her hand.

The fact that his father hadn't claimed him only goaded him more sharply to take what she had to offer. She could be made willing. He knew that already.

As for Xavier and Oliver, if either of them interfered too much he would put them ashore in La Coeuna and continue on to Alderney without them. Just him and Eliza Thoroughgood and a crew that knew when to shut up and look the other way.

Eliza had her nightgown on. She'd washed it earlier and it had dried quickly in the brisk southwesterly winds that drove the ship forward. Before her clothes had always smelled of the lemons she used to scent them. Now the soft cotton smelled of fresh sea air, salty and quite different from home.

Aubrey had fallen asleep swiftly, and now slept the sound slumber of a healthy child who has put in a long and satisfying day outdoors. She too was exhausted, but it was less from physical activity than from emotional turmoil.

Cyprian Dare was positively the most maddening man in the entire world. At one moment he was calm and controlled—almost eerily so. Then at the next he was tossing her down upon his bed and ravishing her. Or at least starting to ravish her. Once again he had stopped, and though she was relieved at the abrupt salvation, she could not help but recall him stopping once before in just such an unexpected fashion.

Was it something about her? Something ultimately unappealing to a man? Since she did not believe it could be anything approaching a conscience on his part, it must be something about her as a woman that in the end turned him away.

But as quickly as that foolish consideration came, so did she dismiss it. The sea air must be affecting her brain, she decided as she climbed into her bed. First of all, she did not care *why* he stopped, only that he *did*. Secondly, there was nothing wrong with her. He was immoral, unprincipled, and wicked. If he found her lacking, it was probably because she was still innocent of men.

But she was fast learning all sorts of things from him. She pulled the covers up to her neck and stared at the solitary lamp still burning and swaying from the hook in the low plank ceiling. He was teaching her things she did not want to know. Physical things about her own body. And if she hadn't thrown Michael in his face, who knew how far things might have progressed?

Michael. Of course. That was why Cyprian had halted.

But that made no real sense either. An unprincipled sea captain bent on the ravishment of a woman would not stop on account of a woman having a fiancé. Oh, but it made no sense and she turned her thoughts away from Cyprian and toward Michael instead.

How was Michael going to react to this . . . this adventure of hers? No one in society would blame him a bit if he cried off now. Whether or not anything actually occurred—physically, that is—she would certainly be ruined anyway, at least in everyone's eyes. Perhaps her parents could keep the whole disaster quiet. That was assuming she and Aubrey could be rescued in the first place, since it was clear Cyprian had no intentions of ransoming them. Or perhaps they could escape.

A sudden knock at the door—three sharp raps—drove all thoughts of escape right out of her head.

"Who is it?"

"Cyprian. May I come in?"

"No!" Her voice came out as a squeak.

"Eliza, we both know I don't *have* to ask. But I am. May I please come in?"

Eliza's heart pounded so hard she thought her chest inadequate to contain it. She clutched the light coverlet to her chin as her thoughts raced. He was right, of course. He didn't have to ask because the lock on the door was on the outside, not the inside. It was meant to keep her in, not him out.

"I . . . I'm not dressed properly."

"That's all right."

"I'm already in bed."

Was that a chuckle she heard? "That's all right too. This won't take long. Besides, your lantern is still on."

"Oh, ballocks," she muttered, unconsciously adopting Aubrey's words. If Cyprian really wanted to come in, he could. Perhaps it was better to agree to his request while he was still in a good mood. "If you'll just wait a moment."

She climbed out of bed, angry and frightened, all at the same time. With a yank she pulled the top cover from her bed and wrapped it around herself like an oversized shawl. Then, determined to hold her ground, she braced one hand on a built-in dresser and bade him enter.

It was hard to read Cyprian's expression when he finally stood inside her small cabin. Though he smiled and outwardly appeared almost courtly—if such could ever be said about a man intruding upon a lady's bedchamber—she could sense a fine tension in him. He stood with his legs spaced apart, a posture so absurdly masculine that it sent a funny shiver up her spine. And all the while he studied her with eyes that seemed to see far too much.

She pulled her makeshift shawl tighter around her throat and shoulders. "Well? What did you want?"

"I came to bring you these." He extended a small bundle to her. "More things for you to wear. You and the boy," he added.

It was not what she'd expected. But then Eliza could not rightly say *what* she'd expected. When he extended the bundle to her again, she stepped forward and took it, for that seemed the only course open to her. "Thank you," she murmured, completely confused by his generosity.

He shrugged. "Perhaps I've been a little harder on you than I should have been."

At that rather understated admission, a surge of righteous anger replaced her initial fear. "Yes, perhaps you have. Is this your way of apologizing?"

He took a step nearer. Somehow he managed to fill the cabin with just the force of his presence. He bowed his head slightly, and she was unaccountably reminded of some great sovereign making concession to a minor personage under his rule. She peered at him suspiciously.

"And does this mean I no longer have to worry that you . . . that you . . . " She couldn't quite put her meaning into words, but the hot color that stained her cheeks must have conveyed it to him.

"That I will try to kiss you again?" he prompted. He smiled then, a sincere expression meant, no doubt, to banish all her fears about him. And it very nearly did, for her stomach suddenly went all fluttery.

"I should not have done that, Eliza. However, in my own defense, you did look incredibly fetching in that blouse. If I was too forward, well, I must plead a momentary madness."

Eliza tried very hard to ignore the sudden flare of awareness that ran up her backbone, due simply to the rumbling quality of his flattering words. He was a practiced rogue and she'd best remember that. Oliver had very likely learned all his tricks at Cyprian's sleeve.

"Momentary madness," she repeated, struggling to concentrate on their conversation. She needed to change the subject, she realized. And fast. "I'd thought that kiss was just your peculiar way of punishing me since my uncle was not handy at the time."

That gave him pause, but he didn't rise to her deliberate baiting. Instead he smiled and took another step toward her. "I have no intentions of punishing you for his actions."

Eliza swallowed hard and backed up, but the built-in bed caught the back of her thighs. "Well." She fumbled for words, her eyes darting about for a way to escape.

But Cyprian raised his hands in a calming gesture. "I do not intend to kiss you now, Eliza. You have nothing to fear. I only wanted to give you those items for you and the boy."

She was not disappointed to hear that. No, indeed not, she told herself. That was relief she felt deflating her chest, not disappointment. She cleared her throat. "Well, that's . . . that's good. As for Aubrey, there's still the matter of you kidnapping him, isn't there?"

Cyprian considered his response, all the while staring

at her. So far, so good, he thought. She had opened her
cabin to him and accepted what he considered his peace
offerings. For his part, despite her appealingly disheveled appearance, he was restraining himself most admi-
rably from sweeping her into his arms and seducing her
right on the spot. It wasn't easy, though. He consoled
himself with the reminder that when it finally happened
he wanted *her* to come to *him*.

He wanted Eliza to want him despite his lack of title
and standing in her world. To have Haberton's niece
succumb to him would only sweeten his triumph over
that bastard and the society he stood for. So he'd considered in advance the best way to deal with Eliza, and
he'd decided that Aubrey was the key. As long as she
believed she might sway him in his dealings with the
boy, she would pursue him.

"I have given some thought to what you said—about
him being innocent of my argument with his father." He
paused and watched for her reaction. When her expressive eyes filled with hopefulness, he knew he'd struck
upon the best way to draw her out.

"Have you decided to release us, then?"

Careful now. "I haven't decided anything. Not yet.
Your uncle cannot be excused for what he's done," he
added, a trace of anger rising in his voice despite his
best efforts to restrain it.

"But what precisely has he done?" Eliza asked. She
set the clothes upon the bed and moved closer to him.
Her face turned up so prettily to his, her eyes shone
with such an earnest need to understand, that he was
torn between triumph at how easy this was, and chagrin
at his duplicity. But drowning out those emotions were
the twin desires: revenge against his father, and lust for
the woman before him.

"What lies between him and me is none of your concern," he growled, willing her to back away from him.

She considered his words, studying him with serious

eyes, eyes that were a deep gray color, he saw. The gray of storm clouds upon the sea, yet streaked with the silvery white that so often backlit those same clouds. Between them tension crackled as sharp and dangerous as the mightiest streak of storm-borne lightning.

"All right, then," she agreed. "It is a matter between you and him—neither my concern *nor* Aubrey's," she added with emphasis.

Their gazes still held as she waited for his reaction, and Cyprian felt the thud of his heart against his ribs. She could be made willing. No matter Oliver's interest or Xavier's interference, he could make her willing. And he would.

"So we shall call a truce between us?" he murmured, unwilling to break the thread of tension building between them.

Eliza blinked and licked her lips. Just that innocent little gesture and he could feel himself growing hard.

"I'm not certain I can trust you," she said, her voice a breathless, husky caress between them. If she were any other woman that simple phrase would have been the teasing harbinger of the exact sort of witty byplay he enjoyed. The advance and retreat of a lusty, experienced woman who knew what she wanted but meant for the man to earn his way between her legs.

But with Eliza . . . she had no idea how powerful a weapon she wielded. She had but to lick her lips like that. Or lick his.

With an inner groan he marshalled his thoughts. "What can I do to convince you?"

"Well." He watched as she considered, shifting her weight from one bare foot to the other. Her toes were small and pink—just like her tongue. Just like other delectable parts would be.

By Jonas, but he'd better stop thinking like that!

"Would you have breakfast with Aubrey tomorrow? Aubrey and me?" she added.

"Certainly," he agreed without hesitation. Anything to soften her opposition to him. To draw her nearer— eventually into his bed.

A small smile curved her lips at his quick agreement, small and reserved, but a smile nonetheless. It was a start.

After he left, Cyprian went on deck, to the place along the rail that was directly above Eliza's bed. The smooth top of the glass prism that brought sunlight through the deck and into her cabin during the day glowed now beneath his feet from her still burning lamp. Though he could not see through the six-inch-thick prism, his fertile imagination could imagine what she was doing.

She would lay the blanket she'd clutched about her shoulders aside. Her sweetly shaped breasts would lift the soft cotton of her prim nightgown with every breath she took, just as they had during their first interview.

Then the yellow glow blinked out and his imagination leaped to more lurid images. She was climbing into the high bed, her firm little derriere outlined by the clinging fabric. Now she was sliding beneath the linen sheets, her legs parted negligently, her gown hiked high to reveal slender ankles, shapely calves, and soft, smooth thighs.

How warm and sweet she would be as she slept, sprawled in the innocent repose of sleep. Only a true profligate would be aroused to think of her that way.

But chastising himself had no effect whatever on Cyprian's lusty thoughts. He hadn't been with a woman in weeks, he told himself. That was why he wanted her so badly that it hurt. Besides that, the women of his acquaintance had always been of an entirely different sort from Eliza Thoroughgood. Experienced women all, they enjoyed the sharp intensity of a toss in bed, then got up and went on with the rest of their lives. What they lacked in manners and refinement, they more than made up for in enthusiasm. With them sex was a delicious meal he consumed greedily, then forgot about until the hunger struck again.

But Eliza whet his appetite in an entirely different way. Partly it was her innocence; partly her delicate beauty. But mostly, he told himself, it was her standing in society. Her good breeding was obvious, even when she stood frightened and barefoot before him in her bedraggled gown. She was a novelty, something he'd never dealt with before. And she was Haberton's niece. That was why he burned to possess her.

It was the only explanation that made any sense, for innocent virgins were not normally to his taste.

But Eliza Thoroughgood certainly was.

Whatever it took, he meant to have her. But though she might hope eventually to win the boy's freedom, Cyprian knew that was one promise he could never give her. He would do or say anything else in order to gain access to the passionate depths of her, but he would not give up Haberton's son.

He forced himself to take stock of the slant of the wind and the position of the moon. He meant to seduce Eliza no matter what it took, for in the end he knew it would be worth it. The waiting would only heighten the pleasure. Both his and hers.

He consoled himself with the thought that if he pleased her as thoroughly as he intended to, she would probably forgive him. Even if she didn't, he would simply put her ashore. Once he'd had his fill of her he would set her free. She was, after all, only a diversion, nothing more.

For a moment a twinge of conscience prodded him. His mother had been just that for Lloyd Haberton, a diversion swiftly abandoned and completely forgotten. What he intended now for Eliza Thoroughgood was no better, and that made him just as heartless as his bastard father.

But Cyprian buried that unpleasant thought beneath

the vow that he would at least acknowledge a child, should there be one. He would claim it as his and, indeed, be the sort of father he'd never had.

He frowned at the thought of becoming a father and began to pace. It wasn't what he wanted, but if it came to that he wouldn't shirk his responsibilities. He never had, not to his friends, his crew, or his mother. Especially not to his mother.

And this plan he'd set into motion—this revenge against Lloyd Haberton—was just a part of that responsibility. He paused and stared down at the deck, at the thin layer of wooden planks that separated him from the young woman who so consumed his thoughts. Eliza Thoroughgood was part of Lloyd Haberton's world. She should thank her lucky stars that he didn't intend to wreak punishment against her as well. Instead he meant to introduce her to a different world, a world of pleasure such as she'd never imagined could exist. He had no reason to feel guilty about Miss Eliza Thoroughgood, he told himself as he turned his face into the cold wind. No reason at all.

Chapter Ten

"*W*hy do I have to have breakfast with *him?*"
Eliza parted Aubrey's hair and tried to smooth down the unruly curls with the comb Xavier had brought her. "I should think you'd want to meet the captain of the *Chameleon.*"

"Well, I don't." His brow creased and he began rotating his ankles in tandem, first one way and then the other.

Eliza studied his bowed head, his sturdy arms and shoulders covered by his plain nightshirt, and his thin legs in their cuffed and belted breeches, several sizes too large for him. Who would ever guess this urchin were the son of Sir Lloyd Haberton? How little separated the privileged upper classes from their more common neighbors. The quality of their garments. The phrasing of their words. Money and education could make of any child an Aubrey Haberton. Or an Eliza Thoroughgood. And the lack of it could make of them an Oliver—or a Cyprian Dare.

"And why don't you?" she pressed Aubrey, not wanting to wonder why Cyprian Dare had become the man he now was.

The boy turned a worried face up to her. "He's the one who had Oliver and Xavier kidnap us. He's the one that stole into my cabin that other time, isn't he?" He didn't wait for her answer. "Oliver and Xavier—and all the rest of the crew—they just do his bidding. But he . . . he's the one who hates me."

"Oh, no, Aubrey. He doesn't hate you. He—" She broke off, not sure how wise it was to tell him. But the doubt and confusion on his young face convinced her. "He . . . he's had a dispute with your father, it seems. It has nothing to do with you, though. With you or me."

Aubrey's face screwed up in a frown. "With my father? He knows my father?"

Eliza sighed and sat down on his bed beside him. "Yes, though I don't know how. But whatever the reason that he holds a grudge against your father, I'm afraid you have now become like a bone between two dogs, Aubrey. Two large, jealous, and angry dogs," she added glumly.

"In a fight between them, I'm afraid my father cannot hope to win. Though they're much the same height, the captain is younger, and no doubt stronger."

"I don't think it shall come to a physical fight," Eliza hastened to say. In truth, however, she was not at all so certain. She held out no hope at all that her father and Uncle Lloyd could find them on their own. The sea was simply too vast. Though she hadn't any idea what Cyprian's final goal was, logic nevertheless deemed that a ransom must eventually be demanded. If Sir Lloyd supplied the necessary funds, surely Cyprian would release Aubrey. And her.

Still, logic had not aided her yet in her dealings with the enigmatic Cyprian Dare. Who knew what his demands might be?

"I want you to be pleasant and friendly at breakfast," she told Aubrey, trying to shake off her worries. "Be on your very best manners, all right? Though he can appear very fierce, he is not always as menacing as he appears."

"Like Xavier?"

Eliza smiled and stroked Aubrey's recently tanned cheek. "Yes, like Xavier." How healthy her cousin appeared lately, she thought, studying him closely. How robust. In spite of their trials, he grew stronger everyday. When they finally returned home to England, his parents would be amazed at his progress.

A smart rap on the door drew her attention before she could succumb to homesickness. "All right. We're coming."

As if that were an invitation to enter, Oliver came right in. "Ahoy, mate. Ah, and a bonny good morning to the bonniest lass alive," he added, bowing like some court dandy might.

Eliza dismissed him with a roll of her eyes. "Your attempts at gallantry are noble, Oliver. But they're quite wasted upon me."

She expected some flippant rejoinder, or at the least, a bold wink and wicked grin. To her surprise, however, the young man stared at her in the most serious fashion. "I suppose you are accustomed to blokes far more gallant than I know how to be."

Eliza paused, scrutinizing him. Oh dear, was there something more to his flirtations than she'd thought? Could it be that he did "fancy" her as Aubrey had said? In confusion she turned toward her cousin. "Could you carry Aubrey, please? We're to take breakfast with the captain," she explained, steering the conversation in a more neutral direction.

But Aubrey had other plans. When Oliver approached him he grinned at his friend. "Eliza's used to being around all sorts of highfalutin blokes. All the honorables and milords. She's supposed to marry one of them," he continued. "But she doesn't really like him. Or any of them. Even at her own birthday party she didn't want to be around them—"

"Aubrey!"

"—and that's why she came up with the idea for us to

go to Madeira. To escape. That's very likely why she kept on pretending she was ill, even though she's never acted ill around me."

"Aubrey Haberton, just you mind your tongue. You don't know what you're talking about. And anyway, Oliver doesn't want to hear any of this."

"Oh, but I do, Eliza." Oliver left Aubrey where he sat upon the bed and snatched up both of Eliza's hands. "I want to know all about you. I . . . I think you're quite the loveliest woman I've ever known. And the purest." He stared imploringly at her and his brown eyes were more earnest than she would have credited. "You're far too good for the likes of me," he added.

A footstep in the hall put an end to Oliver's sincere avowal, much to Eliza's relief. But when Cyprian appeared, then stared pointedly at their joined hands, her relief immediately turned to chagrin.

"Yes, she's quite too good for the likes of you, Oliver," Cyprian agreed, his voice like ice.

Eliza yanked free of Oliver's warm hold at once, but she feared the damage was done, for animosity fairly bristled between the two men. They were jealous of each other and all on account of her!

Given her reputation as the shy and retiring sort, and the fact that they were pirates—or at least smugglers—the situation was so farfetched as to be ludicrous.

Ludicrous or not, however, she still could not allow it to continue.

"I am quite able to make my own decision as to who is 'good enough' for me, without any assistance or advice from either of you. That is why I plan to marry Lord Michael Johnstone. He is as fine and good a gentleman as can be found anywhere in the empire," she stated with as much hauteur as she could muster. "Now, if we are finished discussing my tastes in men, I, for one, would like to have my breakfast."

She wasn't certain she had pulled it off. Oliver still

glared at his captain, while Cyprian regarded the younger man with an expression that somehow managed to convey both a cold anger and a dismissive nonchalance, as if the boy's interest in Eliza was more an amusement than anything else. The very arrogance of it angered Eliza as nothing else could. Where did he come by that superior attitude of his? That insufferable self-assurance?

Oliver turned stiffly to Eliza. "Shall I carry Aubrey to—"

"I'll do it," Cyprian cut him off.

"No!" Eliza practically shouted. "No," she repeated in a calmer voice, though her heart raced. *Please don't let them come to blows.* "Oliver can help Aubrey." She hooked her arm in Cyprian's, tugging him toward the door almost desperately. "Come along. I'm starving."

When Cyprian pivoted on his heel she could have cried with relief. Though the arm beneath her hand was rigid with tension, he was doing as she bade. They made the short sojourn down the narrow companionway side by side, bumping shoulders and hips in a manner altogether too familiar. But it was small enough concession in order to avoid a full-fledged battle between the two men.

That they should get their hackles up over her was hard to fathom. Eliza Thoroughgood was not the sort men fought over. Her fortune, yes. But for herself? Hardly. Yet here she was, barely keeping peace between them. Truly she did not understand the male of the species at all.

"Put him down here," she murmured when Oliver followed them into Cyprian's cabin. His lair, she'd privately begun to label the chamber. She gave Cyprian a little shove in order to get her arm free of his possessive hold, then turned to Oliver. "Thank you, Oliver. That will be all for now," she added, pleading with her eyes for him to just go quietly.

He didn't smile, but he did as she asked. "Call for me if you need anything," he said. Then without even glancing at Cyprian, he turned and left.

Thank a merciful God for that, Eliza thought. Then bracing herself to deal with Cyprian's formidable temper, she faced him. "Was that entirely necessary?"

His jaw flexed once while his eyes appraised her with cool detachment. "I'm captain here. If the boy cannot remember that, he can seek a position on another ship."

"He's not a boy," she countered. "And he is as entitled to his feelings as you or I."

"No, he's not a boy," Cyprian replied slowly, still standing on the other side of the table from her. "That's why I told you to avoid him. But instead it seems you have been encouraging him."

"Encouraging him! I am not encouraging him. Or you either—" She came to an abrupt halt when she realized that from his seat on a chair between them, Aubrey was following their conversation much as he might follow a tennis match, his head swinging back and forth between the two adversaries.

She took a slow steadying breath, though in truth, it did no good. "Let's just dine, shall we?"

It was one of the most unpleasant meals she could recall having. Even the night before, after he'd terrified her with his passions, then demanded that she serve the meal as if nothing whatsoever had happened, she'd not been this completely uncomfortable. Then they'd conversed awkwardly, about subjects she'd hardly recalled. The *Chameleon*'s tonnage. Her speed under full sail. Her draft. But at least it passed for conversation. But at this meal—this horrible breakfast—there was no conversation at all. The metal utensils clinked against the pewter plates. From outside the occasional voices of the crew wafted to them. The steady rushing sound of the wind, and the water breaking against the bow were a constant background. But inside there was a cold and difficult silence.

She felt a nudge against her ankle. "May I have another biscuit?" Aubrey whispered.

She smiled at him in what she hoped was a reassuring manner and patted his hand. There was no need to whisper. Yet considering the tension seething in the small room, she certainly understood why he did. "Of course you may." Then she turned a much cooler expression on Cyprian. "Would you please pass the biscuits to Aubrey?"

He did, and for a moment his eyes swept over the boy. But they swiftly turned away and returned to her. He was still angry, she realized. And all because of Oliver's misplaced affections. Well, if he was already angry, what harm in antagonizing him further?

"You know, Captain Dare, I thought you might relate to Aubrey those same fascinating facts you entertained me with yesterday evening. He is very taken with sailing, in case you hadn't noticed. What was it you told me about the *Chameleon*'s draft?"

"She has a draft of twelve feet," he replied after a pause that nearly unnerved her. But aside from the briefest of glances at Aubrey, he kept his attention on her.

"Ah, yes. Twelve feet," she repeated, growing angrier with him by the second. Why wouldn't he speak directly to Aubrey? He hadn't even looked at the boy, not really, only those sidelong peeks, as if he didn't want to look at him at all, but couldn't help himself. Was Aubrey some oddity to him, then? If he thought to keep his distance from his captive, why had he agreed to share a meal with him?

She stared down at her half-eaten meal. He'd probably agreed only as a way to get into her good graces. He'd brought her the clothes last night and he'd been quite disarming in his manner, even raising her hopes that she might be able to convince him to abandon this cruel plot of his. Could this silly argument with Oliver have affected his humor so adversely? She decided to try a new tack.

"I was wondering. I would like to continue giving Aubrey his lessons, and since we're . . . we're confined here," she said, trying hard to keep any hint of accusation out of her voice, "I thought we'd work on world geography. Have you any maps or charts we could borrow?" It was her turn to nudge Aubrey with her foot, though she smiled directly at Cyprian.

"Um, yes," Aubrey mumbled. "I . . . I should very much like to learn about charts and navigation. Sir," he added, though he sounded less enthusiastic than Eliza would have liked.

Once again Cyprian's gaze flickered briefly to Aubrey, then returned to Eliza. He acted as if the boy weren't there. Or as if he wished he weren't. Was it because he wished for the two of them to be alone, without the watching eyes of her youthful chaperone, Eliza speculated? A wave of heat rose in her cheeks at the very thought. Yet there was something more restraining Cyprian. She was sure of it.

"Just tell Xavier what you need. He'll provide it."

"I thought they'd be in here," Eliza persisted. "Can't you show them to us?"

Cyprian's jaw flexed. Twice. So, she *was* irritating him, she realized. Good. But she wasn't sure *why* he was irritated. Again his eyes glanced briefly at Aubrey before returning to her, and in that almost furtive movement, Eliza suddenly found her answer. Cyprian ignored Aubrey; he practically pretended the child was nonexistent, and she realized why. Because he didn't want to know the boy. He didn't want to know him or like him—or feel guilty for what he was doing to an innocent child.

At last. A weapon she could use against him!

Eliza smiled, a full-blown, warm and friendly smile.

"Please, Cyprian," she said, using his given name as he'd requested she do. "Unless you're truly too busy, Aubrey and I would much rather you explained the charts to us. Please say you'll do it. Please?"

Aubrey watched the odd byplay between the two adults with a skeptical eye. He'd much rather have had breakfast with Oliver and Xavier than with their unsmiling captain. And now Eliza was acting daffy in the extreme, even using the man's given name. He stared at her in disgust. Not that he was an expert or anything, but he could swear she was flirting with the stern-faced Captain Dare. He'd seen his older sisters lead enough suitors around by the nose to know that when a woman leaned forward that way, her eyes sparkling and her mouth opened in an encouraging smile, that she was doing some serious flirting—or wheedling, if the target was a father or brother. He, of course, was never in the least affected by their ploys. His father, however, could be had. Aubrey had witnessed that often enough.

But whether Eliza could pull it off with a man who was neither her father or brother, or her suitor either—

He stopped short on a loathsome thought. Could she possibly view Captain Dare as a potential suitor? But what about Oliver?

Aubrey turned a suspicious gaze on the captain, a gaze that swiftly escalated to a glare. The man was staring straight at Eliza, as if he might have her for breakfast or something, the bloody blighter!

A sudden twitch of Aubrey's arm was all it took to send his tumbler of apple cider over, spewing the amber colored liquid across the small table.

"Oh, Aubrey."

"Son-of-a-bitch—" Cyprian muttered.

Eliza quickly dabbed at the spreading pool with her napkin, then grabbed Aubrey's as well. "It's just an accident. You needn't curse," she rebuked him as she sopped up the mess. Aubrey repressed a grin when the captain muffled another curse. But Aubrey's smugness faded when the captain answered her.

"I'm sorry. I'm not accustomed to having a lady onboard. Or a child," he added as an obvious afterthought. Then he smiled at Eliza, and Aubrey's expression changed to a glower. His spur-of-the-moment plan, meant to put an end to Eliza's moon-eyed absorption with the captain had failed. If anything, the man's obviously insincere apology had wooed her more effectively than ever.

"Can we go now?" he complained, tugging at her sleeve.

"But we haven't finished eating yet," Eliza answered.

"I'm not hungry."

She let out an exasperated sound. "But what about the charts? The geography lesson?" She glanced at the captain. "You never said whether you would show them to us."

The man looked ready to devour her right then and there, and it was beyond Aubrey's capacity to remain calm any longer. He wanted Eliza to marry Oliver, he decided on the spot. And to bring Ollie home with her to England. Wouldn't that throw the whole family into a snit!

"If you really want to see them," the man said, smiling into Eliza's shining eyes.

"Well, I don't want to see them!" Aubrey burst out.

When they both turned to face him he shoved his plate away and crossed his arms on his chest. "I'm sick to death of lessons. And I hate this meat. It's too salty."

"Perhaps you would prefer the gruel we feed to the rest of our prisoners," the captain growled, his voice low and menacing.

Frightened now, as well as angry, Aubrey grabbed his cousin's hand. "I want to go home, Eliza. I want to go home right now. Make him take us home!" he wailed.

In a moment she was kneeling beside him, her arms

thrown around him for comfort. "It's all right, Aubrey. Everything is going to be all right."

"But I want to go home. I hate him! I hate him and his smelly old ship and nasty old food and . . . and everything! I want to go home."

"We will, sweetheart. We will. I promise you."

With his face buried in Eliza's shoulder, Aubrey didn't see Cyprian's furious expression. Or Eliza's imploring one. But he heard the man's chair scrape back and the sharp progress of his boot heels across the floor.

"The charts are in that trunk in the corner." Then the door closed with a solid thud.

For Eliza it was a dark, defeated sound. But Aubrey heard the clear ring of victory. At least for now.

Chapter Eleven

"*I* hate him."

Eliza scowled at the chart spread before her. That heavy line to the right must be the westernmost coast of the African continent. That would make the group of islands to the far left the Madeiran group. Yes, there was the bay where the town of Funchal lay, and the smaller island called Porto Santo.

"I said I hate him."

Forcing herself to a calm she hardly felt, Eliza lifted her face to meet her petulant cousin's frown. "Yes, well, I'm not pleased with him either, but behaving like a spoiled infant is not likely to soften his feelings toward us, is it?"

"I don't care," the boy persisted.

"Well, you had better care, Aubrey Haberton. In case you've forgotten, we are his prisoners. You may be having a grand adventure with Oliver, but we are nevertheless here by force. I am trying—with no help from you, I might add—to find a way to change Captain Dare's mind. To convince him to release us. Don't you see?" Her voice softened. "If he likes us it will be harder for him to follow up with whatever unpleasant plans he may have for us."

Aubrey looked down at his hands knotted in his lap,

and she recognized indecision in his crestfallen features. "But he's so mean," the boy muttered.

"He was starting to be nicer today."

"He threatened me! He said I'd have to eat gruel."

"But only after you complained about the meat."

Aubrey began to waggle his feet back and forth at the ankles. He was getting very good at it, she realized. The movement in his injured ankle was nearly as strong as the other's, though still not so wide ranging.

"Aubrey," she began. "Tell me about your foot. Have you tried standing on it yet?"

The feet moved faster. "Yes."

"And?" She leaned forward hopefully.

"And it hurt like the devil."

"But were you able to stand up?"

He reached down to rub his injured ankle. "A little." Then he shot her a lopsided smile. "Actually, Oliver and I were going to surprise you."

"Surprise me?" Excitement colored her face and lent a sparkle to her eyes as she grasped his arm. "You've already surprised me, you little imp! But tell me, were you at all able to walk?"

Aubrey grinned, his good humor restored. "Just a few steps, and it hurt powerfully bad. But Oliver said I should just buck up and take it like a man. Did he ever show you those two scars I told you about, from his knife fights?"

Eliza rolled her eyes. In his own peculiar way Oliver Spencer had done wonders with Aubrey, but at the same time, he'd shown the boy another side of life, a rough-and-tumble world made up of a far less privileged people than Aubrey had ever known existed. When they finally were returned home, Aubrey would no doubt shock his family with more than just a renewed ability to walk.

"No, he has not shown me his scars. Nor do I ever wish to see them."

Aubrey frowned and squinted at her. "Why don't you like Oliver? He is quite the finest chap I've ever known, but you act as if he is less than nothing at all."

"I *do* like Oliver," Eliza protested.

"But you like that grouchy old captain better—even though you *say* that you don't."

Eliza sat back in her chair. Did it show that clearly? She wanted to groan. How was she to get out of this? "Well, I suppose I like them both—even though I don't approve of what they're doing. But the captain is just—"

"He kidnapped us, don't forget."

"And don't *you* forget that Oliver played a considerable role in the whole escapade."

"But he was just following his captain's orders."

"He lied to us. He duped us—pretending to be a servant. What if I hadn't been awakened and come along with him and Xavier?"

"He wanted you to come along, you know."

"Who, Captain Dare?"

It was Aubrey's turn to roll his eyes. "Not him. Oliver. He wanted you to come along because he fancies you." He paused, giving her a thorough and rather adult examination with his dark eyes. "You know, Eliza, you're different now from how you used to be at home." Then he grinned. "I think Oliver would like to marry you."

Marry her! Eliza gaped at the boy but managed somehow to refrain from laughing. "I'm marrying Michael. You know that. So does Oliver, for that matter."

Aubrey pursed his lips. "Does *Cyprian* know it too?" He dragged out the name in a derogatory manner.

She straightened the chart with her fingers, aligning it with the edges of the desk. "Of course he knows. But my marriage plans have nothing to do with anything."

"I think Captain Dare fancies you too. I think that's why Ollie was so out of sorts earlier. You'd better be careful though, Eliza. Jessica likes to play one fellow against the other and look where it got her. That's why she didn't marry that baron's son. He got mad at her and tossed her over for somebody else."

"I am nothing whatsoever like your sister," Eliza declared. Jessica Haberton was widely renowned as a heartless flirt, while Eliza Thoroughgood had always been rather a wallflower.

But Aubrey obviously disagreed. "If you continue to encourage your darling Cyprian, then you're just like her."

Eliza slapped her hands down on the desk and jerked to a stand. "He is not my darling! And if I appear to be encouraging him, it's only for *your* benefit. You are the one, after all, who was kidnapped. I'm your guardian, at least on this trip, and it's my responsibility to do whatever I must to ensure your safety. Instead of criticizing me, I should think you'd be thanking me. And cooperating with me."

She rolled up Cyprian's chart with hands that shook with anger—or was it guilt? She really didn't want to know. "I believe I'll take a stroll above decks. Since you're doing so well with your exercises, I'm sure you can get back to your own cabin under your own power."

Oh, but she was too cruel, Eliza thought not one minute later. She'd fled Aubrey and his far too astute remarks. But once on deck, with a good dozen sailors eyeing her every move—some discreetly and others not even remotely so—she wanted nothing but to return to the boy. He might be in pain. He could fall. He might be reduced to crawling, dragging himself in a humiliating fashion down the narrow companionway on his hands and knees.

She pushed away from the starboard rail, determined to go to him, only to confront Oliver. More trouble.

"Miss Eliza?" He yanked a red and white striped knitted cap from his head then tried in vain to control his wind-whipped hair with his other hand. "Is everything all right?"

Eliza steeled herself. She'd never been in the position of having to let a suitor down easy, and she had no idea at all how to begin. "Everything would be all right if Aubrey and I could be set free. All I want is to go home, marry Michael, and never again set foot on a ship, so long as I live."

He blanched. Even under his nut-brown tan, she saw him pale, and his Adam's apple moved reflexively.

"What if—I'm sorry to bring this up, Miss. But what if, you know, this Michael bloke, he cries off? Because of the kidnapping and all."

"And all. You mean, of course, because my reputation will be in shreds and any decent man might consider me ruined?" She pinned him with her eyes, refusing to give in to the urge to let him off easy.

After a long, uncomfortable pause he nodded.

She was conscious of Xavier heading in their direction, so she hurried on. "Michael and I are—how shall I say this without sounding vain? We are quite madly in love. As for my reputation in the rest of society, my father is quite wealthy enough to squelch any unpleasant rumors which might surface. Or to buy them off," she added. If she were going to lie, best do it up right.

"Oliver. See to the crow's nest," Xavier ordered, before even saying a word of greeting.

Oliver did as the first mate told him, much relieved, Eliza was certain, by Xavier's rather curt interruption. When Eliza turned to the huge man, however, she was taken aback by the clear disapproval that showed in his frowning face.

"Truly I am angering everyone today," she began, not curbing her tart tone. "Cyprian. Aubrey. Oliver, and now you. Pray tell, what have I done now?"

His sketchy black brows raised in surprise. "How have you angered Oliver?"

"Oh, so you care more that I anger Oliver than that I continue to irritate your esteemed captain."

"Come now, Miss Eliza. Let's not argue, we two. Just tell me why Oliver should be angry with you."

In the face of his calm manner, Eliza's aggravation quickly faded to frustration. Her shoulders slumped and she sat down petulantly on a heavy coil of ropes. "I made it clear that I could hardly wait to be reunited with my fiancé."

"And he took it badly. But that is really for the best. You know it is."

She sighed and looked up at him. "I know. But I don't enjoy hurting people that way."

Xavier levered himself down beside her and leaned back against the rail as the ship rocked an endlessly gentle rhythm. "Shall you now dismiss Cyprian in the same manner?"

Eliza shot him a narrow-eyed glare. "Would it do any good if I did? The man pays absolutely no attention to anything I say."

He chuckled and shook his head. "Ah, my innocent little girl. Cyprian Dare pays attention to everything you do or say. Everything."

His words should not have affected her so profoundly as they did, but there was no pretending otherwise, at least not to herself. But to Xavier she only said, "If he pays attention to me, 'tis only so that he can determine how best to unnerve me. He blows hot and cold, menacing one minute and then all smiles the next. He terrorizes me, then turns on the charm until I don't know—"

She broke off, aware she'd said too much already. But Xavier just reached for her hand and gave it a reassuring squeeze. "Tell me about this man you plan to marry."

"Why?" she asked suspiciously. She pulled her hand free from his and from the lulling sense of security he always managed to surround her with. "So you can then relate it all to Cyprian?"

His soft rumbling laughter made her feel the ungrateful wretch. "Eliza, as first mate it is my duty to see to everyone's well-being. Yours and Cyprian's also."

"Well, the two have nothing whatsoever to do with one another. And anyway, it's Aubrey's well-being which is of paramount importance."

"That's true enough," he conceded, gazing upward, following Oliver's monkeylike climb up the swaying rigging to the tiny crow's nest perched high on the main mast. "But it seems the three are intertwined. Your welfare; Cyprian's. Aubrey's."

Another truth. But she did not know precisely why it was true. "Maybe . . . maybe if I knew why Cyprian hates Aubrey's father so. . . . "

The first mate's gaze jerked back down to hers. "No, no, no, Miss. You will be better served turning that pleading look upon Cyprian, not me. 'Tis his feud, not mine. 'Tis for him to explain it to you, not I."

"But he won't."

"Then you must try harder."

"Try harder?" Eliza frowned at him. Even in her sheltered position the wind buffeted her, but not nearly so much as her careening emotions did. "You are throwing us at one another, aren't you?" she accused. "You are like some . . . some overgrown cherub bent on matchmaking." It was so ludicrous she could scarcely believe it and she began to laugh. "Oh, Xavier, I believe your captain and I are far, far too unsuited."

"Perhaps. Perhaps not."

Her joviality faded in the face of his enigmatic halfsmile. She'd tried to ignore Cyprian's change of attitude toward her, but Xavier made it even harder. Between Cyprian's late night visit—ostensibly to bring her the clothing he'd found—and his half-hearted attempt to be a good host at breakfast, he'd hardly behaved like the wicked captor with his hapless victims. It didn't help that somewhere, buried deep inside her, she felt the most inappropriate stirrings whenever he was around. Whenever she even thought of him, if the truth be told.

But Xavier couldn't know that. Could he?

"I think I'd better see to Aubrey," she said, unwilling to continue any farther with this conversation.

"That shall not be necessary," Xavier replied, looking past her. "It appears that he has come to you."

Eliza turned, curious, then scrambled to her feet, unable to believe the sight that met her eyes. Aubrey stood in the opening that led below. His face was flushed from exertion and his two arms braced against the wooden frame. But he was standing and he was grinning, and the sight brought tears to her eyes.

"Oh, Aubrey! Dear, dear Aubrey!" she cried as she dashed up to him.

"Be careful, Eliza. If you even touch me, I'll fall. Five steps may not mean much to you," he panted good-naturedly. "But they felt like a mountain to me."

Had it not been for the shining light of triumph in his bright blue eyes, his nonchalant attitude might have rung true. But Eliza knew he was even more elated than she.

"Never fear, I shall be careful not to topple you over. But you must be exhausted. Do you want to sit down? Xavier can help you up—"

"No. I can do it myself." So saying he pursed his lips in concentration, then lifted his crippled foot over the threshold. His fingers tightened on the door frame; his knuckles whitened from his efforts. Then he heaved upward with a grunt, and in less than a heartbeat, he stood on the deck. And all by his own effort.

Eliza couldn't help herself. This time she did throw her arms around him, though she was careful not to unbalance him.

"Well done, my boy," Xavier said, grinning.

From up above there wafted, "Ahoy, mate! Good job!" Oliver waved down and Aubrey, squinting up into the brilliant autumn sky, waved an enthusiastic response with one hand while leaning on Eliza with the other.

Just beyond them on the poop deck Cyprian stood looking down at them. Had he seen how hard Aubrey had worked to get up those steps? Eliza wondered. She hoped so. When his eyes met hers, however, she deliberately turned back to Aubrey.

"My goodness," she exclaimed. "Where would you like to go now that you're topside?"

With a grin Aubrey glanced hopefully up at Oliver's distant figure, so high above them, swaying crazily in the tiny crow's nest.

Eliza gasped in dismay. "Don't even toy with such an idea, Aubrey Haberton."

"If I were you, I'd turn a deaf ear to her warnings," Cyprian said, drawing her attention again, and everyone else's too. As they watched, he descended the short run of steps, looking far too . . . too elemental, Eliza decided on a flight of fancy. He was every inch the daring sea captain. Call him a smuggler or even a pirate. Whatever, he was the most purely masculine creature Eliza had ever laid eyes upon. And he scared her to death.

She felt Aubrey stiffen and she automatically edged nearer him. Oh, please, not another conflict between the two of them. But to her surprise, Aubrey's expression was more cautious than antagonistic. And curious.

"So you mean you think I *should* climb up there?" the boy addressed Cyprian directly. Belligerently, even.

"I don't see why not, once you're strong enough. Besides, all sailors have to know how to climb the riggings."

Eliza wanted to tell Aubrey no, but the slow smile that spread across his childish face was too excited, too wondrous. She couldn't dash his hopes just yet. Not now when he'd just begun to walk again.

Besides, she realized, it was not likely her word would carry any weight with Aubrey, not if both Oliver and

Cyprian were urging him to more and more reckless feats. As she stared at Cyprian, puzzled and yet pleased by this first glimmer of interest he'd shown in Aubrey's improving health, Cyprian turned his enigmatic gaze on her. "It appears that life at sea suits your cousin far better than either of you could have guessed."

The relative harmony between Aubrey and Cyprian put Eliza in much too good a humor for her to argue that Aubrey's improving health did not exonerate Cyprian for his crimes. "The change of scenery has been very good for him," she conceded. "And so has Oliver. Oliver has worked with him quite faithfully of late and deserves much of the credit."

"So he does," Cyprian responded, though noncommittally.

"Perhaps Aubrey would benefit from pulling up along the riggings," Xavier put in. "What do you say, lad? Shall we give it a go?"

Aubrey's face was an almost comical reflection of his disparate feelings. How he wished to go along with Xavier, Eliza realized. To test his growing strength against a new adversary. But his suspicion of Cyprian and the man's intentions toward Eliza held him back.

Still, Cyprian's encouragement had clearly made inroads against the boy's defenses. After a long moment of indecision, when Aubrey's eyes flitted from Cyprian to Eliza, and back to Cyprian again, he turned finally to Xavier, a grin on his eager face. "How high might I climb today?"

"Not high at all!" Eliza exclaimed.

But Cyprian interrupted. "Xavier is the best one to judge the boy's strength. He's trained many a fine sailor. Including Oliver. Oliver started as a cabin boy too," he added.

A hopeful expression crept onto Aubrey's young face. "Am I to be a cabin boy as well?"

Eliza felt a pang of worry. Please don't let Cyprian

rebuff the boy now, she prayed. But she had no need to worry, for Cyprian had clearly rethought his animosity towards his young captive. "Everyone on a ship must work. Since we've had no cabin boy since Oliver outgrew the job, you appear the likeliest choice for it."

How cagey he was, Eliza realized as Xavier and Aubrey made halting progress across the deck. Cyprian had but to hold Oliver as an example before Aubrey and the boy was hooked, as surely as her brothers hooked pike in the Colne River at home. She bit her lip in worry as she watched the incongruous pair that the African giant and limping child made. Aubrey *was* getting stronger. . . .

"Come stroll with me, Eliza?"

Just that brief request from Cyprian and Eliza's heart began a painful thudding. She met his polite, almost bland expression with one she feared was far less composed, then decided to be forthright. "Why are you suddenly being nice to Aubrey?"

Their gazes met and held, but they did not clash for a change. He even grinned, though faintly. "Shall I give you the complete truth, I wonder? Or just a portion of it?"

"The complete truth," she answered at once, though a part of her knew that his reply would somehow unnerve her. She swallowed convulsively and repeated, "The complete truth."

This time his grin was not nearly so hidden. With just that tilt of his lips, that slight show of white even teeth and the relaxation of his stern expression, he became more approachable. Almost boyish, she imagined, though nothing would ever be able to quell that tautly masculine aura that surrounded him. Boyish smile notwithstanding, he was the most intensely male being she'd ever encountered.

"All right. The truth." He took her elbow and subtly steered her toward the starboard rail. "The truth is, I handled that scene at breakfast with, shall we say, an unaccustomed lack of diplomacy."

"I would not have supposed you were used to being diplomatic," she replied, not bothering to be diplomatic herself.

He chuckled. She could feel the faint vibration of it even in his light touch on her arm. It made her tremble. "Your barbs are showing, Eliza. But nevertheless, it may be only that I have of late become accustomed to having everyone jump at my command. Besides, despite my comments to the contrary, I would not see the boy become a crippled beggar on the streets."

That gave her considerable relief. "The boy has a name, you know," she suggested in a softer tone.

They stopped and he turned to face her. But he kept his hand on her arm and took her other arm in his hold as well. "So he does. Aubrey Haberton. But I would rather speak of his cousin, Miss Eliza Thoroughgood."

Had she thought her heart pounding before? This time it fairly beat its way right out of her chest.

"But . . . you . . . that is—" She took a sharp breath. "You haven't answered my question yet."

"What was the question again?" he replied, drawing her closer. Or did she lean into him of her own accord?

Indeed. What *was* the question?

"Why . . . why are you being nice to him now? The truth," she added breathlessly.

"The truth." His eyes held hers as if with a force not defined by earthly means. "I want you to like me, Eliza. If I must improve my behavior, polish my manners, then so be it. I have not treated the boy very well, but I mean to do better."

His admission was enough to make her heart cease altogether. He wanted her to like him! Could Xavier be more right than she'd imagined?

Only belatedly did she remember her duties as Aubrey's guardian. "And . . . and shall you set Aubrey free, then?"

His gaze shifted away then, and for a long moment he stared at the horizon. "In time I will set him free."

His tone was so even, so devoid of any emotional inflection that Eliza would have pressed him further. But then he turned back to face her and his eyes dropped to her lips. Eliza was certain her knees began to shake.

But I will not free you, his possessive gaze seemed to say. *You I shall keep.* And in that moment Eliza had no desire to be set free.

"He . . . he is getting better. Perhaps his father will be . . . grateful," she stammered, unable to think straight for the sensual aura he created around them.

"And you?"

"I . . . I am getting better too," she whispered.

He pulled her closer. "No, Eliza. I meant, will you be grateful too?"

"Oh." She nodded, fearful of what her admission might reveal, but unable to disguise it.

"How grateful?"

Where were her defenses? Where had her sense of self-preservation fled to? But her heart beat at such a dizzying pace Eliza was quite unable to think straight. Even when she put her hands up to hold him off, her two palms pressed against the solid wall of his stomach, and all she was aware of was the firm, warm flesh beneath that thin layer of linen. It made her fingertips burn and the most disconcerting sensations curl up in her stomach.

The ship pitched in its endless rolling rhythm, but Cyprian's strong hands held her steady before him. Then his head descended, slowly, giving her more than sufficient time to protest. But the words she could have said—wait; no; don't you dare—died unsaid against his lips.

The man was hard in every way. His body. His heart too, she feared. But his lips . . . His lips were firm and yet incredibly soft as well. Molding to hers. Enticing hers.

The wind gusted, lifting her hair in waves around both their faces, hiding the rest of the world from view. Somehow her hands slid up the warm expanse of ridged stomach muscles and contoured chest. Somehow she was pressed fully to him so that her thighs brushed his and her head tilted back as he kissed her insensate.

But none of it was forced. Indeed, there was a sort of restraint and caution in his manner which quite perversely provoked the most unseemly response from her. For it was she who parted her lips so their kiss could deepen. It was she who, tentatively at first, then more urgently, wound her arms around his neck. It was she who would willingly have kissed him forever had he not drawn slightly away.

But though their lips no longer clung, their gazes now did, and in his heavy-lidded study of her, Eliza experienced even more intimacy than in their kiss. Confused by her own perversity, she averted her eyes, bowing her head in an effort to avoid his now painful scrutiny. When his lips moved against the crown of her head, however, kissing the part in her heavy hair, she only grew more confused.

"That grateful?" He murmured the words against her tangled hair. "If I'm not careful, Eliza, I shall find myself performing all sorts of gallantries, just so you will show me more of this sweet gratitude of yours." Then cupping the side of her face with one hand, he tilted her head back up, planted a kiss on her trembling lips, and pushed her away.

For one dazed moment Eliza just stood there, staring at him. Then Aubrey's jubilant cry pierced the edges of her consciousness—as well as the other sounds of a ship under full sail—and reality struck her with all its humiliating truth. She had stood here, practically in full view of the entire crew, and kissed him.

And wanted not to stop either.

She turned sharply and clutched the thick rail in complete dismay.

"Look, Eliza! Look at me!"

She stared toward the voice, seeing Aubrey waving at her from two knots up on the rigging, but with Xavier safely at his side. Raising her arm she waved back, but she was more conscious of Cyprian's presence, still so near her, than anyone else's.

"It appears he shall heal well aboard the *Chameleon,*" Cyprian said, so noncommittal that it served to increase her discomfort even more.

She swallowed hard, for her mouth had gone as dry as cotton. Still it was better to speak of Aubrey than of her conflicting feelings about what was happening between her and this totally inappropriate man. She closed her eyes, trying to picture Michael, and though she was not entirely successful, she managed at least to recall how and why she'd ended up on a smuggler's ship. And who was ultimately responsible.

"It seems odd that a man who would steal another's child should then help heal that child," she said, pursing her lips and staring straight out to sea.

He moved right up beside her again. She saw his strong brown hands on the rail just inches from hers and it took all her aplomb not to jerk her own hands away in fear. If he touched her again she could never maintain her distance from him.

"One of life's little ironies, I suppose. But then, the boy—Aubrey, that is—came to Madeira to heal, did he not? And you as well, I take it." He turned and leaned his hips against the rail so that he faced her, his legs casually crossed at the ankle, his arms braced behind him. But still Eliza stared at the endless gray-blue swells that rolled on until forever.

"Tell me, Eliza. What illness do you heal from? For I confess, you do look every inch the picture of good health. From the roses in your cheeks, to the lovely sheen of your glorious hair, to the sweet vibrancy of your body against mine, you appear filled to overbrimming with vigorous good health."

With every word he uttered, every compliment that played up the intimate way he'd come to notice those aspects of her appearance, Eliza's cheeks burned hotter. She wanted to deny everything he said, yet his flattery was something she hungered for. She, the meek and bookish Eliza Thoroughgood, the sickly young woman who shrank from social interaction, gloried in the attentions of a rakish sea captain. It was madness to believe him and yet . . . and yet he made her believe his every word.

In truth she'd never in her life felt better or stronger than since they'd left England. Perhaps she was well now.

"Eliza?" Cyprian prompted. She took a shaky breath.

"I . . . I have suffered all my life with a malady of the lungs called asthma. Sometimes when I'm nervous or alarmed—or for no reason whatsoever—I have these attacks. I can't breathe at all then. But I've been better in recent years. Much better," she added, as breathless as if she were right now in the midst of one of those attacks. But it was not illness that caused it now. No, not illness but something far worse. Lust for Cyprian Dare caused her to feel this way. Though she should be ashamed, the plain truth was, she wanted more of these breathtaking feelings. Much more.

A wry smile curved his lips. "It would seem that you've had several opportunities to feel alarmed since you've come on board the *Chameleon,* yet you've not had one of those attacks. Perhaps being on my ship has been as good for you as it has been for Aubrey." He paused and she watched in fascination as one of his hands moved to cover hers. "You've shown me your gratitude for Aubrey's improving condition. Will you give me as much credit—and gratitude—for your own blossoming good health? Say, at dinner tonight?"

Then he raised her trembling palm to his mouth and kissed it.

Eliza had read on many topics, including scientific articles about human physiology. So far as she knew, there was no direct connection between a person's hand and the secret depths of her nether regions. There was no scientific explanation at all for why his lips pressed so warmly to her tender palm should feel so intimate or arouse her to such wicked, heated feelings.

But it did arouse those feelings down low in her belly until she felt hot and melted inside. Then Cyprian released her hand and gave her a devastating smile.

"Till tonight, Eliza. Till tonight."

Chapter Twelve

*E*liza peered out the small round window, the only one in her cabin. The sun would soon touch the horizon. Already long irregular fingers of salmon and gold glinted off the restless swells of endless ocean.

It was cooler. But then it was late November and they were heading north. Where would Cyprian finally put ashore, she wondered.

Of more immediate concern, however, was what were his intentions tonight?

Eliza took a finely knitted shawl, one of the garments Cyprian had given her, and wrapped it around her shoulders and arms. Though it warmed her, however, she suspected it would prove a less than adequate barrier to any seductive attempts Cyprian might make. Like her flimsy willpower, the shawl would fall away at his least provocation. The very thought of how easily he could draw her in sent both alarm and an unforgivable spark of anticipation skittering down her spine.

Nervously she smoothed a crease in her skirt and checked for loose tendrils in the single plait she'd worked her hair into. She had to be prepared for anything tonight, and she had to have her own plan to counteract whatever he might try.

First of all, she'd already decided to decline anything

more than one glass of wine. Then, if he should touch her in too familiar a fashion, she would bring up the subject of her betrothal and her fiancé. And if he tried to kiss her, she would mention her uncle's name. That always irritated him.

But what if he did none of those things? What if he was simply polite and charming, smiling at her with his lips curved so enticingly and his dark eyes so . . . so seductive?

Eliza swallowed hard and drew her shawl tight around herself. More than anything else she must fear his good humor. When he behaved like a gentleman, with the full force of his attention focused solely on her, that was when she must most beware succumbing. Like today on deck.

"Oh, dear," she murmured out loud. It occurred to her that she was in a far greater dilemma than she'd been in before. The angry and threatening Cyprian was of far less danger to her than the handsome and beguiling one. What was to be her defense against that sort of seduction?

She paced the short length of her cabin. Maybe if she demanded an accounting of his plans for Aubrey, the ensuing discussion could take up a goodly amount of the mealtime. But even as Eliza forced herself to march to the narrow doorway, open it, and step into the hall, she was not as confident as she would have liked. All she could do was try to take the initiative tonight and never let Cyprian Dare get her at a disadvantage. And she would begin by not waiting for him to summon her.

Her knock at his door was forceful enough to be painful to her knuckles. When Cyprian called entrance, however, a sharp wave of panic nearly sent her fleeing back down the hall. Only the thought that he would then come for her prevented her flight. With her hand trembling, but her chin held high, she gripped the brass door handle, gave it a twist, and entered the lion's den.

Cyprian had expected one of his crew. When he spied
Eliza standing in the entrance to his cabin he whipped
the piece of toweling from his shoulder, wiped the last
vestiges of soap from his jaw, and thrust both the towel
and the razor onto the built-in chest behind him.

"You're early."

"I'm sorry," she murmured, starting to back away.

"No, no. It doesn't matter." He stuffed the tail of his
shirt into his breeches with one hand while he gestured
for her to come in. "I've been looking forward to your
company all afternoon, Eliza. I'm not about to send you
away now that you're here."

When she bit her lower lip but did not move, he knew
he was pushing too hard. Too fast. But for the life of
him, Cyprian didn't know how else to act. Flatter her.
Smile at her. Try his damnedest not to sweep her into
his arms—and into his bed—when that was what he ultimately wanted. When had he grown so impatient? But
she looked so skittish standing there with the darkness
of the companionway framing her fragile beauty. She
looked like a wild young fawn, prepared to leap away in
panic, yet curious too. He just had to play to that curiosity. To draw her in and put her at her ease.

"Is Aubrey still on his feet?" he asked, knowing that
discussion of the child was his best chance of settling her
down. He walked slowly toward her, keeping his expression carefully pleasant. Not too eager. Not too possessive.

But she would be his, he swore. She might not recognize that fact yet, but he damned well did.

There was no logic in it, he knew. By rights she was
not his sort of woman at all. Yet from the very first
touch he'd been drawn to her. Though he'd tried to pass
it off to pure lust, he was no longer so sure. She was shy
and yet she could be brave. She was prim, yet fire flowed
in her veins as well. She was the sort of woman who,
once committed, would never veer in her affections.

And though she was a lady, right now she looked more a gypsy dancer. Ah, but she was one of a kind and he would make her his, come hell or high water.

When she still did not answer him, he gave her a wry look. "Come in, Eliza. I'm not going to bite you." *At least not yet.*

He felt it a victory of sorts when she finally stepped in and pulled the door closed behind her.

"Sit down. Here." He pulled out a chair. "Please. Can I offer you a drink?"

She sat, her spine straight and her posture prim, with her ankles neatly crossed. His mother had sat like that. Even when everything else in her life had been horrible, she'd retained the good manners she'd been brought up with. But Cyprian threw off thoughts of his mother. The last thing he wanted to think about at this moment was how easily a man could destroy a woman's reputation, and thereby her entire life.

"I'll have a glass of wine, but not until the meal is served," Eliza responded.

He smiled. He couldn't help it. "Are you worried I'll get you too drunk to remember to say no, when what you really want to do is say yes?"

"No!" She gripped the arms of her chair in hot denial, but her cheeks flooded with appealing color. "I did not come here to discuss . . . to discuss things we should not discuss at all. If that is your intention, then I'm afraid I must leave—"

"Wait, Eliza. Don't leave. I was only teasing. Tell me, are you also going to hold it against me if I tell you how lovely you look? Even the most proper gentleman is allowed to compliment his dinner companion, isn't he?" he asked as he picked up his best frock coat from the back of his chair and slipped it on. He kept his eyes on her when he spoke and when her gaze slipped momentarily to his chest, then lingered to watch him slide each arm in, he felt a surge of pure lust for her. She was curious all right, and she was ready.

And she would soon be his.

But with her very first words she brought his soaring hopes back to earth. "Since you've already brought him up, I'd like to discuss Aubrey with you. Specifically, where this ship is going and when you intend to return him to his family."

Cyprian hid his frown by turning away to pour himself a glass of wine. A full glass. When he sat across from her, his expression was carefully blank, and carefully pleasant.

"I intend to take very good care of the boy. Of Aubrey," he amended. *Of my half brother.* "By the time he is reunited with his family he'll be walking on his own, healed and whole again." *And a man fully grown.*

At his confident statement about Aubrey's good health her suspicious expression softened and she shifted in her chair. "Did you ever send word to my uncle that you had Aubrey?"

He nodded once. "I did."

A faint frown creased her brow. "He must be so worried. Aunt Judith too, and Aubrey's sisters. But you know, Cyprian, when he finds Aubrey walking again, Uncle Lloyd might be grateful enough to drop any charges against you and to convince the authorities to do so as well."

As if he gave a damn about the authorities. But Cyprian smiled at her, determined that nothing should ruin this evening. "In the end, Eliza, I'm sure everything shall turn out for the best."

She nodded, quite earnest. "I hope that's so. But really, Cyprian, you'll have to let him go soon. Once we land somewhere, perhaps you can send word to Uncle Lloyd that you intend to return his son." She leaned forward, resting her laced hands on the table between them. "Where shall we put into port first?"

He leaned forward too. "We sail for the Channel Island, Alderney."

"But we'll head on to London after that, won't we?"

"Yes." *But not for a long time. Quite a long time.*

When she smiled, a sweet happy expression that lit her serious gray eyes with sparkling light and seemed to energize her entire body, Cyprian felt the first twinge of conscience. He'd not lied to her. Not a word, he rationalized. If she read more into what he said than she should, well, that was her misfortune.

But he could not entirely shake off the guilt feelings that had crept up on him. He lifted his glass and drank deeply. Then taking a chance, he covered her hands with his.

"You speak of Aubrey and of seeing him returned to his family. But what of you, Eliza? Are you anxious to return to your family—and to this Michael of yours?"

At the mention of her fiancé's name she tried to pull her hands from his. But he tightened his grip and held onto her. "Why did you flee from him all the way to Madeira, anyway?"

He knew he'd hit upon the truth when her hands went absolutely still. "Tell me the truth, sweetheart," he urged, separating her hands so that he could twine his fingers with hers. "Are you really so eager to return to England and everything you ran away from?"

"Yes," she answered, on a shaky breath. But everything else about her—her eyes, her tense posture—said no.

Cyprian drew her hands to his lips and kissed the knuckles of first one and then the other. "I'm willing to give up the boy. But you . . . "

It was a calculated seduction. An experienced man sweeping an innocent young woman into a world of sensuous delight. Cyprian was aware of everything he was doing and how it affected her, for her eyes were wide and dark, and color stained her cheeks to rosy heat.

Even her breathing, shallow and ragged, revealed her state of mind to him.

But he had not expected to be so aroused himself. Nor so close to losing control. By the blood of Jonas!

"I . . . I don't think you should say such . . . such things to me," she finished in a whisper.

"Are you so afraid of the truth?"

"Not the truth, no. But—"

"But what?" He kissed the backs of her hands again.

"Don't! Don't do that, Cyprian."

He smiled but he did not release her hands. "I love to hear you say my name. Say it again for me."

"No." She shook her head and tugged her hands free of his. "This is all wrong. It's . . . it's not at all proper."

"Then how can we make it proper?"

"We can't. I mean, I don't know you—or your family."

"I have no family left."

"Oh. Well . . . "

He watched as she thought, her brow puckered as she cast about for more reasons why his courtship of her was unacceptable. But he had no intentions of giving her time to argue.

"I'm all alone in the world, Eliza. Perhaps that's why I'm so drawn to you."

"Oh." She swallowed again and her mouth formed a little O which he dearly wanted to kiss into submission. He reached over and touched her lower lip with the tip of his finger and rubbed it lightly.

"I . . . you . . . " She sat back in her chair abruptly. "Maybe . . . at least you could *tell* me about your family."

Ah, yes. He was getting closer.

"What do you wish to know?"

"Well." She traced the edge of the table with the tip of her forefinger. Without asking this time, he poured her a goblet of wine and slid it toward her. She took it as if she needed something to hold onto. But she didn't drink right away. "Tell me about your parents."

Cyprian flexed his jaw as he calculated just how much of the truth to reveal. "My mother, God rest her, died when I was a boy. She was a remarkable woman who lived a hard life, yet she managed to do the best she could. Despite her complete devotion to him, my father left her early on," he added, wanting to forestall any questions about him. "He was a successful man of business who nevertheless did not value her love. He was unwilling to accept his responsibilities toward her. And me."

"He abandoned you and your mother?" Eliza's face reflected her shock. How protected a life she'd lived. "Were there other children too?"

"No. Just me. You know, I think you would have liked my mother, Eliza." He leaned forward, surprised at the sincerity of his own words. "You would have liked her and she would have liked you. You both have the same refined manner, the same serene carriage. And yet, like her, you also possess an irrepressible spirit."

"Irrepressible spirit?" She laughed at that. "At home no one would ever say that of me. I've always been the quiet, retiring one."

"Then your stay on the *Chameleon* has been just as good for you as it has been for Aubrey. Tell me." Once more he covered her free hand with his. "Will your family be as grateful for the changes in you as Aubrey's will be?"

She cleared her throat nervously, but she didn't try to remove her hand. "It's hardly the same sort of thing."

"Maybe. Maybe not. Are *you* grateful?"

"I . . . I don't know. Cyprian, please," she added. "I think we'd be better off sticking to the subject at hand."

"And what is the subject?"

"Aubrey. Aubrey is the subject."

"No, it's you and why you fled England."

"I didn't flee."

"No? Tell me then, when is this wedding set to occur?"

She pulled her hand away and gripped the stem of her goblet again. It was clear the subject of her forthcoming marriage unsettled her. "Well, Eliza? When are you to marry this fine fellow your parents have selected for you? They are the ones who selected him, aren't they?"

"Well, yes, they are. But I'm quite content with their choice," she retorted. "We are to wed next summer."

"So why didn't you stay in London to plan the blessed event and be with this fellow your parents picked out for you?"

Eliza didn't answer until she'd drunk deeply of her wine. She licked a drop of the red liquid from her bottom lip in such an innocently provocative manner that Cyprian wanted to curse out loud. She was driving him to distraction, without any understanding of what she was doing!

"I chose to accompany Aubrey because I thought I could help him."

"Anyone could have come with him. His own mother seems an obvious choice. So why you?"

He stared straight at her, not wanting to give her an easy out. She looked so distressed he thought she might even cry, though it had never been his intent to hurt her that way. But she took a fortifying breath and her sweetly rounded chin lifted to an almost belligerent angle.

"If you must know, I wasn't completely pleased to be marrying Michael Johnstone. Not at first, that is. But now I believe we will do well together."

"Do well together?" Cyprian chuckled and stretched back in his chair. "But what of passion, Eliza? Don't make the mistake of leaving passion out of your life."

"Who are you to advise me?" she snapped right back

at him. "Judging from your behavior up to now it seems you would choose passion over commitment. Passion over trust. Passion over genuine caring between two well-suited individuals."

He smiled at her vehemence. "If you would taste of passion but once, my dear, you would know better than to compare that most violent and supreme of emotions to the blander ones you seek to sanctify."

At that her gray eyes glittered with righteous anger. "You of all people should know better than that, Cyprian Dare, for it sounds as if your mother was undone by that very sort of passion. She married a man who obviously was not committed to her, nor worthy of her trust. Why do you suppose that was? Could it be that she confused her passion for him with all the finer emotions, the ones that make for a good and solid marriage? You were raised without a father and your mother lived a hard life, as you put it, and all because passion probably ruled her choice of a man when a more rational approach might have served all of you far better. Michael may not make my heart race, but we shall do well together. And at least he'll not abandon me!"

That quickly did she cast ice water over the rising flames of his own passion for her. In a fury of frustration with her and anger at the wreck his father had made of their lives, Cyprian spoke without weighing his words.

"Did I say she married him? Forgive me for conveying the wrong impression, Eliza. My father did not go as far as to wed my mother. I fear you see before you a bastard, to put it plainly."

His words were calm but they were glacial, and she was as silenced as if he had shouted. She swallowed and fiddled with her goblet, before licking her lips nervously. "I'm . . . I'm sorry. I . . . I didn't know."

Cyprian pushed up from the table. Son-of-a-bitch, but he was making a fine mess of things. He hadn't meant to tell her that. He hadn't meant to tell her anything except what might draw her closer to him. He'd intended to stay in control, seducing her with words and just the force of his will until she was finally his. Instead she was controlling him, until he'd become a victim of his own emotions. She had but to taste a drop of wine from her lower lip and he was as horny as a goat. She used his mother's wretched life as an argument for avoiding the dangers of passion and he turned furious. Then her tongue darted out to moisten her lip and he was once more gripped by desires so strong that he felt about to burst with them.

He ran a distracted hand through his hair. If he didn't do something soon he was going to explode.

He took a harsh breath and sat down. Without saying a word he refilled both their glasses. It had been his experience from very early in life that backing down from a challenge was always a mistake. Whether that challenge came from some youthful bully, a more powerful adversary, or just a lovely young woman who had his emotions inexplicably tied in knots, going on the offensive was inevitably the best tack.

Of course, determining your adversary's most assailable vulnerability was essential to success. With a street bully, a knee to the groin always worked. Lloyd Haberton's weakness was his only son. But for Eliza Thoroughgood . . .

Cyprian raised his glass as if in toast. He studied her apprehensive expression, then smiled. "It appears we have reached an impasse on this matter, Eliza, so I have a proposal for you."

Chapter Thirteen

"A proposal?" Something in Cyprian's smile caused Eliza's heart to sink. And yet that same contrary portion of her anatomy seemed intent also on beating its way right out of her chest. She clutched her wine glass tighter. "What sort of proposal?"

He shrugged as if it were of no great moment. "Your criticism of my mother and the choices she made in her life showed a profound lack of knowledge and understanding on your part."

"I only meant—"

"No, hear me out. You speak of passion as if it is something to be avoided, a lure that can ruin your life. While it is true that my mother's life could have been easier, she never once gave me the impression that, given the chance, she would have acted any differently. She actually loved the man," he added, though a bitter edge had crept into his voice. "Her one regret was that she had not been able to keep him with her."

Eliza bit her lower lip. "Perhaps . . . perhaps if she'd not succumbed to his . . . his—you know. Maybe then he would have married her and stayed with her."

"And maybe he would have simply gone on his merry way until he'd found a more willing woman. Then where would *I* be? Never born at all. But that's not the point.

At least my mother had a taste of passion, brief as it was. I would hate to see you settle for a dull fellow like your fiancé without ever knowing what other possibilities life holds."

"Michael is not dull," she objected. *What he is, is too perfect to believe.*

"But he does not fire your passions."

"Not yet! But in time I'm certain, well, that . . . that he will," she finished weakly.

"But I already have."

Eliza's breath caught in her throat and her eyes widened with both embarrassment and shock. "You . . . you do not," she protested, though she knew it for a monstrous lie.

"Oh, yes. I do," he countered, his smile and his posture so confident that she wanted to cry. "I can tell by the way your eyes grow so dark, so sparkling." He leaned over the table. "I can tell by how you breathe: fast and shallow, sometimes not at all. I can tell, Eliza, by the way you kiss me. All that passion wrapped up in such sweetness. I think it's past time for you to loose that passion from its strict bounds. And I'm willing to show you how. I'm willing to teach you all of the pleasures—and passions—that a man and woman might share."

No, I can't allow you to teach me any such thing. But the words she meant to say aloud did not come. Instead she just stared at him, terrified. Fascinated. She should be repulsed. She tried to think of his mother and the ruined life she'd led. But all she could think of was how Cyprian's kisses had roused such strange and fiery emotions inside her. Michael and his gentle kisses had hinted at such feelings. But Cyprian's . . .

"Does this silence of yours indicate that you are giving my proposal consideration?"

"No." Her reply was little more than a mouthing of the word. Then she gave herself a strong mental shake and took a sharp breath. "No, I cannot consider your proposal—whatever it actually is." She took a long drink of her wine, though even as she did so, she knew it provided only a false sort of courage. Too much to drink, and she quickly would lose all her perspective. She pushed the glass away and clasped her hands together instead.

But that proved not so wise a move, for Cyprian once again covered both her hands with his. As she stared at him, unnerved by just that warm touch, he smiled deeply into her eyes.

"Come now, Eliza. You know you like me. We both know it. And I like you." He paused as his gaze roamed her face. "I like you far more than I ever would have thought possible."

"I will not . . . will not listen to this," she stammered even as she drank in his every word. He liked her? He really liked her?

As if he saw the doubt inside her, his thumbs began to make small circles against her wrists. Small provocative circles. "You're the most fascinating woman I've ever known, Eliza. Shy and yet bold. Prim and yet passionate. There is no limit to the pleasure we can find if we search for it together."

The beguiling rasp of his voice set Eliza's heart to hammering so hard her chest hurt. "You . . . you speak of passion. And of pleasure. But . . . but there is no future in that. None."

His eyes were so dark, so deep and compelling as he stared at her that she felt as if he were pulling her into himself. Her will. Her heart. Certainly her traitorous body.

"Tell me, Eliza. Does your Michael profess to love you? The truth now."

The truth? No. Nor did she pretend she loved him either. But to admit as much to Cyprian Dare was tantamount to yielding to his preposterous proposal—which

she wasn't entirely sure she completely understood anyway.

But he clearly took her silence for the admission she
sought to avoid. "So he does not. Do you love him?"

"I . . . I have not had sufficient time to fall in love
with him. Yet," she added, hoping desperately to salvage
something from this disastrous conversation. "But I'm
sure I shall."

One corner of his mouth quirked up and it gave her a
hint of what he might have looked like as a boy. But that
only increased her fear that she was sinking into a warm
web of his creating.

"Can you fall in love with a man upon command,
then? Could you decide just as easily to fall in love with
me?" he asked in a huskier tone.

This time she had no voice to answer. Everything was
spiraling out of control. Though her mind might tell her
to say no—to jerk her hands from his, to run out of his
cabin just as fast as her shaking legs could carry her—
every other portion of her anatomy conspired to oppose
such rational action. She could only sit there, mesmer-
ized by his eyes, and overwhelmed by the urgent feelings
inside of her, all clamoring for release.

Somehow he came around the small table. Somehow
she was standing before him, her hands still in his. Then
he bent down to touch his mouth to hers.

It was not a violent sort of kiss, like before. Their
bodies did not touch. She did not strain up to him, nor
did he seek to deepen the kiss. But by its very restraint,
that kiss was her undoing. He exhaled and she drew the
same air into herself. Her shawl slipped away and the
two of them swayed in tandem to the ship's movement.
Then she exhaled against his mouth and she knew the
intimacy had been exchanged. He'd touched her as no
man ever had—both her body and something much
deeper than merely her skin.

"Let me show you how good it can be," he whispered the words against her mouth.

"Shh," she replied, kissing him harder. She didn't want him to speak because then she must reply, and if she replied she'd have to think and be rational—and responsible for her actions. But if they didn't speak, this could be almost a dream. . . .

Her arms crept up around his neck as his slid around her waist. They embraced fully, legs entangled, loins pressed close. Her breasts flattened softly against the hard wall of his chest. And the kiss deepened.

It *was* a dream that she could feel such soaring, unlikely feelings, caused solely by his touch. Like a fever overtaking her entire body, he infected her with the passion of which he'd spoken so freely. It took over everything, her skin, her heart, her fingers, and her lips. Her mind. Her emotions.

Oh, but it was her emotions that suffered worst, for locked in his arms, submissive to his strengthening kiss and emboldened by the fire roaring in her veins, she could almost believe herself in love with this wicked and dangerous man, that all of these insane feelings *were* love. As she opened her mouth fully to the onslaught of his tongue, to the rhythmic stroking of it, she could imagine him professing a returning love, and vowing to cherish her and amend his ways. . . .

"You see?" he whispered between hot, sweet kisses along her jaw and neck and ear. "But this is just the beginnings of passion. The tip of a vast and depthless ocean of pleasure for us, Eliza."

She shook her head faintly, not wanting to hear any of this. But what *did* she want?

Cyprian seemed to know.

"I'll give you a taste, sweetheart. And yet let you preserve your purity to give as a gift another day." He circled her sensitive ear with the tip of his tongue until she squirmed in unconscious joy. "And maybe you shall give it to *me.*"

He didn't allow her a chance to respond. Instead he lifted her to sit on the trunk where he kept his charts. He continued to kiss her, more forcefully than before, until her back was against the wall and she clung to his neck with tightly clasped hands. Meanwhile, he used his legs to part her knees.

She should stop him, she thought, even as she met the bold encroachment of his tongue in her mouth. She was too vulnerable like this. Too exposed.

Yet that managed perversely to increase her excitement, so that when one of his hands slid up her leg, past her knee and under her skirt, she thought she might faint from the intensity of it. His touch was as smooth as velvet, as hot as molten lava, and as unerring in its goal as a homing pigeon.

When his thumb neared the apex of her opened legs, she stiffened. When she felt him brush the cover of curls down there, she twisted away from his demanding kiss. "No—stop—"

"Don't be afraid, Eliza." His words came low and urgent. With his other hand he caught the back of her head, forcing her to face him. Then he pressed that thumb of his deeper, past the protection of her curls, into a place even she hardly touched.

"Don't—" she protested again, swallowing hard as her sense of propriety did fierce battle with the violent emotions careening around inside her. "Wait—"

But Eliza's protest died when his thumb slid lower, then came back and began the oddest motion. Something—she could not say what—was happening to her. Her legs began to tremble. The air seemed to abandon her body, as did all her strength. She clung to him, her head back, her eyes wide with disbelief. And as she stared almost panic-stricken at him, he kept up that small rhythmic motion.

"Do you like what I'm doing, sweetheart?" he whispered.

She nodded, unable to do anything else. His eyes were so dark, so glowing, with an inner fire of their own. Was she supposed to do something like this to him, too?

She slid one hand down his chest to his flat stomach and lower. To do what, she did not know. She was operating on pure instinct now, for nothing she'd ever heard or read had hinted at what was happening between them.

But Cyprian caught her hand before she could do anything with it. "We'll save that for another time, my fiery little girl. For now—" He kissed her hard, thrusting his tongue in and out of her mouth with such an urgency she thought she would explode. At the same time he slid his thumb somewhere . . . somewhere that felt like it was right up inside her!

"Just concentrate on how your body feels when I do this," he murmured against her ear.

Once more he began that rhythmic motion, that thrumming sensation, as if he were playing some musical chord—some magical musical chord—that drowned out the entire world until only he and she were left to hear. Her entire body was filled with the song he played upon her. Oh, God, but she was filled to bursting with it. To bursting . . .

Then with a final surge of heat, the fire erupted. *She* erupted.

Like a puppet, Eliza jerked against Cyprian's hand, again and again and again. As if he'd pulled all her strings and controlled all her limbs, she raised off the trunk, her legs clasping tight around his hips.

At once Cyprian pulled her against him so that the incredible center of all the fierce conflagration pressed hard against him. He held her with his hands beneath her buttocks, rocking her almost desperately against the hard bulge in his breeches.

"Oh, God," she cried, as the agonizing fury at last began to subside. "Oh, dear God in heaven." Her head fell limply against his shoulder as she clung weakly to him.

He groaned too and thrust against her. In the dimmest recesses of her mind Eliza knew that the momentous event that had just occurred had forever changed her. But she also realized that the same sort of stupendous reaction had not happened to him. At least not yet. She lifted her head and met his eyes and recognized that besides the fierce triumph she saw, hungry desire still burned there. And frustration. At once she understood the rigid arousal kept separate from her only by his tautly stretched breeches for what it was. A man's need, rampantly displayed, still unsatisfied.

What could still be left between them? And yet somehow she knew. She'd seen the hunting hounds. And the sheep. Even the stallions. . . .

Her eyes must have grown huge, for Cyprian laughed, though his voice held a strained and almost painful note. "I think we shall save that for another time, my beautiful little innocent."

Tears unaccountably sprang to her eyes. She, who never cried, felt the unlikely burn of tears. "I . . . I'm not so innocent—"

Cyprian's grasp on her changed, growing gentler. One of his hands still circled her waist while the other stroked then cupped the side of her face.

"You are still quite the innocent, Eliza. Beautiful and innocent," he murmured, smiling directly into her eyes. "Your maidenhead has not yet been breeched—unless you and your Michael . . . "

"No!" she exclaimed, trying to back away from him, though the wall rather effectively prevented her from succeeding. "He has never—no one has ever—"

His smile grew warmer. Then he kissed her gently and yet with a hunger she could not mistake. "Good. I'm glad to be the first. I plan to teach you everything there is of passion and desire. Every erotic secret a man and woman can share—"

"No. No, this is not right." Yet even as Eliza made her feeble protest she knew how pitiful it sounded. Here she sat, her legs bared and wrapped around the lean hips and strong thighs of a man who'd just made her body feel the most incredible things. A man who held her captive on his ship—and captive with the unimaginable sensations he roused in her. Her whole world had come undone and she was unable to put things right. Once more tears threatened, but she fought them back.

"I . . . I think I would like to return to my cabin," she whispered, pulling her arms from around his neck. She didn't know what to do with her hands, so she buried them in her skirt—the skirt which was pushed high on her thighs and caught between their two pairs of legs.

She kept her eyes downcast and tried to control her ragged breaths. "Please, I . . . I need to be alone."

Cyprian inhaled deeply, then slowly let it out. He didn't want to let her leave, that was plain to her. But he did. He pushed back from her and turned away while she clamped her knees together and shoved her skirt down over her exposed limbs.

When she stood up, however, her legs were so shaky she was afraid to move toward the door. How could she ever escape him if she couldn't even walk the width of his cabin? She stared fearfully at him, at his broad back and stiffly held posture. His head was bowed and he too seemed to struggle with his breathing.

"I . . . I have to go," she muttered, mortified by the incredible intimacies she'd just shared with this man.

Cyprian nodded, then finally turned to face her. "What about dinner?"

She shook her head. "I don't think I could possibly eat right now."

At that, one of his brows arched and he gave her a

wry grin. "I suspect that within the hour, Eliza, you will find yourself more ravenous than you've ever thought possible."

"No. No, I don't think so."

"We'll see," he replied with a knowing look. "Meanwhile, I'll save a plate of food for you, just in case. The door will be unlocked," he added.

Eliza sidled along the wall. She knew very well what he meant, but despite the amazing things he'd done to her, she was fully determined not to come knocking at that door of his. Not for food, nor for anything else, either.

"Thank you for a most . . . most illuminating—" Most illuminating what? Lesson in the facts of life?

"No, Eliza. Thank *you*. You were exquisite," he continued, all trace of humor gone as he stared intently at her. "Passionate beyond my wildest hopes."

It was just too much. With a small cry of utter despair, Eliza fled him and the sensual aura that surrounded him and affected her so powerfully.

Passionate beyond his wildest hopes? She slammed the door to her cabin, climbed into her bed, and pulled the coverlet high, right over her head. Somehow she didn't think she was supposed to be passionate at all, let alone with such a man as Cyprian Dare.

Chapter Fourteen

*I*n the ensuing days Eliza lost weight. She simply could
not eat. They held a northern course for six more
days before making the turn to the east and into the
English Channel. Six more days where she could not
avoid Cyprian for more than a few hours at a time. He
seemed always to be on deck when she went up for a
breath of air. He met her coming and going in the companionway, or when she tended his cabin as was one of
her duties. And even when she stayed in her cabin, sewing small repairs for the crew—deliberately avoiding
Cyprian—she recognized the sound of his step and
caught the timbre of his voice in the chill breeze.

To make things worse, he'd taken to leaving small
tokens for her in her cabin, gifts with no notes, but she
knew they were from him. A length of Spanish lace. A
silver buckle. Though she knew she should return them,
she did not. She hid them beneath her pillow, more
confused and miserable than ever.

Yet still she clung to her plan to keep her distance
from temptation, for that's what Cyprian Dare was,
she'd come to understand. She'd suffered no temptation
in the past. Despite her ill health, she'd lived a life of
ease, with everything she could ever want provided to
her. But this trip, conceived as it was in her unfair

avoidance of dear Michael, was the Lord's way of setting her straight. She must rise to the challenge Cyprian
Dare presented her, and thereby prove herself worthy of
the good man who awaited her in England.

But why did she dread her union with Michael as
much as ever? More even?

Cyprian's laugh drifted down from the poop deck and
Eliza swallowed a lump of confusing emotions. Every
portion of her body seemed to respond to him, no matter how minimal the provocation. He laughed and she
shivered. His eyes locked with hers—though she was as
careful as possible to avoid that happenstance—and she
trembled. Thank God he'd not had occasion to touch
her again, for there was no predicting how she'd react.
Ever since that disastrous dinner—a dinner that was no
dinner at all, but a seduction—she'd stayed strictly out
of his reach. Not that he couldn't grab her if he was of a
mind to do so. But he hadn't, and that, perversely
enough, only added more to her confusion.

What *did* he want of her?

Or perhaps, she thought in uncomfortable honesty,
she should question what it was she wanted of him. But
she didn't know.

"Eliza! You're not paying attention," Aubrey complained.

"You should never interrupt a person's daydreams,"
Xavier admonished the boy while giving Eliza a scrutinizing look.

"But I want to show her how far I can twist my foot
around. And all because of Oliver," he added in an ex-
aggerated tone.

Eliza forced down thoughts of Cyprian and let her
sewing fall to her lap as she focused on her young
cousin. In the past week Aubrey had labored at any
number of tasks: swabbing decks, reweaving frayed
lines. He'd washed pots and fetched for the cook and
for anyone else who needed him, and in the process

he'd grown stronger and stronger. He could walk quite unaided now, though he displayed a pronounced limp. Still, he was mobile again and with his regained mobility had come the return of his ebullient nature. He'd become a complete monkey on the lower riggings, and quite a favorite of the entire crew. Even Cyprian.

She grimaced at that. Maybe Aubrey had forgotten that they were prisoners, but she had not. Only she was captured as much now by her distressing emotions as by the fact of their physical confinement. There were her physical reactions to him, too—

She abruptly veered away from that subject and peered at Aubrey with sincere interest. "I'm sorry if I was distracted just now. Go ahead, Aubrey. I'm watching."

He began his demonstration, flexing his foot in all directions, pedaling his legs in the air, and generally kicking and flailing about like a windmill caught in a whirlwind.

"That's wonderful," she exclaimed, overjoyed at his amazing progress.

"And I don't get so tired anymore either. I hardly rested at all today."

"And wore me out in the process," Xavier chuckled.

"Well, if Oliver weren't always confined to the crow's nest or down in the hold or given some other boring task, you wouldn't have to oversee what I'm doing. And anyway, aren't I doing a good job?"

"A very good job," Xavier conceded. "But as the first mate aboard the *Chameleon*, it's my duty to make sure everyone does his job well."

"Yes," Aubrey persisted. "But if you're the first mate, why not let Oliver on deck with me? Then you could watch everyone else while he watches over me."

Xavier's glance fell upon Eliza. "This is a working ship, Aubrey. We're not on some holiday sail. Besides, the order to keep Oliver busy comes down from our captain."

"But why?" Aubrey pushed to his feet and stomped around the deck in an angry and slightly erratic circle.

"Because Cyprian is captivated by your lovely cousin," Xavier replied, ignoring completely the embarrassed rush of color his words brought to Eliza's face. "He fears she might fall prey to Oliver's, shall we say, blandishments?"

"Xavier!" Eliza exclaimed.

"Is that true?" Aubrey asked, frowning as he stared at her. "Could you fall prey to Oliver's . . . his—"

"No!" Eliza cut him off. Then she glared at Xavier, who was grinning at her discomfiture. "Why are you putting such ideas in his head? I have absolutely no interest in Oliver Spencer. You know that. He's just a friend who has been most helpful to my cousin."

"'Tis not *I* who put ideas in anyone's head. Cyprian is to blame for that. He is the one so taken with you that he cannot bear any man's attention toward you but his own."

"He doesn't mind *you,*" she countered, trying to ignore the funny feelings beginning to knot in her stomach.

"Ah, but he knows my affections are already engaged by my lovely Ana—whom you shall both meet shortly."

"Does that mean we shall put into port soon?" Eliza asked, wanting to steer the conversation in another direction. But Aubrey was not so easily distracted.

"If he is so taken with you, why doesn't he spend more time with you? No one is stopping him."

Eliza fiddled with the embroidered edge of her sleeve. How was she to explain? And why must she, anyway? "I suppose *I* am stopping him."

"Oh." Aubrey's brows furrowed in thought. "So you want him only as a friend, too. Like Oliver. Is it because of Michael?"

"Yes, Eliza. Is it because of this Michael?" Xavier echoed Aubrey's query.

Eliza compressed her lips and stared past the deck rail and out to sea. How was she to answer that?

But Aubrey spoke again before she could. "Michael is probably too boring for Eliza, at least now that she's been to sea. I mean, what does he do but go to fancy receptions and balls and things like that?" He stared at her seriously, his expression far too wise for his tender years. "I know I shall find England quite a bore when we return. I'd much rather be a sailor."

"Well, I wouldn't," she vowed with much heat. "And anyway, Michael is hardly boring."

"You do seem a little indecisive about him," Xavier said. "In all honesty, I think you should give serious consideration to Cyprian's suit. You'll not find a better, truer man anywhere."

"His suit!" Her eyes widened with incredulity, then rolled in disbelief. "I'd hardly describe his attentions as—"

She broke off when she realized Aubrey was taking in every single word. "His . . . his attentions are not . . . serious," she finished lamely.

"I think you're mistaken on that score," Xavier replied, as calmly as if they were discussing the weather or what to have for dinner.

"Stay out of this, Xavier," she snapped, unable to hide her agitation.

"But Eliza," Aubrey demanded when Xavier only raised his brows in mild surprise. "Why should you marry someone as boring as Michael when you could marry a dashing sea captain—"

"He's a pirate," she retorted. "Or at the very least a smuggler."

"He's brave and daring. Like his name. And he has his own ship."

"Your father owns ships too, Aubrey Haberton."

"Yes, but he never sails anywhere on them."

"Well, maybe he hates them. I know I do. I hate ships and I hate the sea!"

Aubrey shook his head and addressed Xavier. "My sisters act this way too, whenever they've had a tiff with their latest beau. I think she likes the captain."

"So do I," Xavier replied, grinning. "And I know he likes her."

If Eliza had been vitally aware of Cyprian's whereabouts on the ship before her conversation with Aubrey and Xavier, afterwards she was excrutiatingly so. The day was cold and the wind blew in strong erratic gusts out of the north. But she wrapped up in the heavy knitted pullover Xavier had provided for her and stayed doggedly at her perch on deck. She had to understand what was going on between her and Cyprian, but given the fact that her own emotions were so wretchedly confused, how was she to make any sense of *his?*

But Cyprian must have sensed her new level of turmoil, for while Aubrey worked with one of the crewmen, learning how to tie several of the myriad knots used aboard a sailing vessel, Cyprian unexpectedly sought her company.

"We'll make land soon," he began, standing beside her on the protected starboard side of the charthouse.

Eliza chanced a quick glance at him. But though she swiftly averted her eyes, studying her slightly ragged nails, she'd seen enough to set all her senses off-kilter. He wore dark breeches, fitted well to his long lean thighs. His short leather jacket with the white shirt showing at his wrists and neck served somehow to emphasize the width of his chest and shoulders. He was completely covered by his clothing, and despite the handsome figure he cut, by rights he should not have aroused her in the least. But there was the expression on his tanned face to consider. And the glint in his dark eyes.

Eliza swallowed her nervousness as best she could. "And where shall we make land?" she asked in what she hoped passed for a calm and unaffected tone.

"Alderney. I have a house there."

That brought her gaze back up to his. "A house? You're taking us to your house?" Panic joined the myriad emotions that already held her in their grip.

"Did you think I spent all my time on my ship?"

Eliza frowned. "I hadn't thought about it."

"Actually, I think you'll find it an extremely comfortable abode. Somewhat like that villa you rented in Madeira."

Like their villa in Madeira? Her brow furrowed. "When did you ever see our villa in Madeira?"

He turned so he faced her, leaning his hips against the wide wooden railing while his legs splayed apart for balance. "I made it my business to know every aspect of your life before taking you aboard."

"Don't you mean Aubrey's life?" she asked, rather tartly.

He cocked his head in mild agreement. "That too. It appears now, however, that I am more interested in you."

It was a miracle that the entire ship did not go up in flames right on the spot, she thought with the one rational bit of her brain that still functioned. With his blunt words and positively scorching gaze, a sizzling heat welled up from somewhere deep inside her. From the same place where he'd touched her that time, the place from where all those agonizingly erotic sensations had burst forth—and which festered anew with a fire even hotter.

She tore her eyes away from his and stared out at nothing. Though only sea and sky rose before her eyes, her mind perversely painted Cyprian's image before her. "I don't understand you," she confessed softly, for she knew nothing else to say.

Beside her she was vitally aware of his presence. "There is little enough to understand, save that I have missed you this past week."

Eliza's heart roared like thunder in her ears. "I . . . I have been here the whole time," she whispered.

He squatted down before her and took her hands in his. Their eyes met and held—and passed a hundred messages between them. "There's no reason for us to stay apart any longer, not when we both want to be together."

How could Eliza deny that? Yet still she cast about for a reason. "What of Aubrey—and your revenge on his father? My uncle," she added.

"That's unimportant."

She shook her head, trying to clear her thoughts. But that was impossible when he held her hands so warmly, and her gaze so forcefully. "But it *is* important."

"All right, it's important. But it has nothing to do with how we feel about one another."

"What . . . what do you feel?" she whispered, afraid of his answer, yet needing desperately to know.

Cyprian paused only a moment before answering. The past week had been so long, so impossible to bear with her always nearby and yet beyond his grasp. He'd tried to court her the way she deserved, with little gifts and courtesies. He'd wanted to give her time, to make her want him more, to be ready to meet him fully and become the woman he knew she could be. But now he could see that it was he who'd been the more tortured of them both. Just holding her hands and staring into her expressive gray eyes was enough to send him right over the edge.

"I'm desperate for you, Eliza. Desperate to keep you. Desperate to make love to you."

He heard the breath catch in her throat, and her eyes grew dark. "I . . . " She took another breath. "I don't know," she answered. He could see the indecision on her face, and the yearning as well. She wanted him, all right. But she was afraid.

"Come on," He pulled her to her feet, then with one hand at the curve of her back, steered her toward the hatch that led toward his cabin. But though she tensed, she did not really resist him.

The wind blew harder than ever out of the north, bringing winter's icy blast fully on them. Clouds hid the sun and the world was a dull gray-blue of sea and sky. But inside Cyprian the sun burned with unbearable heat. This proper young lady, this well-to-do daughter of one of the best families in England wanted him, Cyprian Dare. Ne'er-do-well bastard. She was going to gift him with her virginity. And he was going to make sure she was not sorry.

That last time had only been a hint of what could pass between them. But as he'd hoped, it had been enough to whet her appetite for more.

Before they even reached his cabin, when they had barely descended the short flight of steps from the deck, he couldn't help himself. He turned her roughly and pressed her back against the plank wall.

"I burn for you," he murmured, seeking her lips with an urgency that would not be denied. "Damn, but I burn—"

And if the way Eliza responded to him was any indication, she burned too. For after only a moment of frozen shock, she responded with all the innocent passion she felt. Her lips opened to his, allowing his tongue to take ravening possession of her mouth. Her sweet young body pressed up, eager and trembling, so that her breasts flattened against his chest. It was enough to drive him mad.

"I'll have you now, my Eliza. Here and now, for I cannot wait—"

So saying, he pressed her fully against the wall and insinuating his knee between her legs, he thrust his demanding arousal against the yielding softness of her belly. She gasped and he swiftly deepened their kiss, slanting his head, fitting them closer and closer together. He wanted to devour her, to suck her right into himself, to possess her in every way it was possible for a man to possess a woman.

It passed briefly through his mind that perhaps a man should marry a woman he felt that intensely toward, if only to make sure she could never slip away from him. Was that what he wanted of her, to make her his wife? He raised his head as a spray of icy water gusted in through the open hatch. "Eliza—"

But she raised up on her toes and pulled him down for another kiss. Rain and the salt spray of a temperamental sea misted them again, but it did nothing to douse the inferno building in that dark and narrow passageway. The turbulent ocean was nothing compared to the tempestuous emotions buffeting Cyprian. The storm building outside seemed only a meek version of the violent passion gripping him.

She would be his. This very night and every night thereafter.

More water doused them, a minor deluge. But it had no effect on his burning desire for her, or on her sweetly eager response—until Xavier's booming voice intruded. "We've sighted land, Captain. But this gale—"

"Deal with it," Cyprian growled, using his body to shelter Eliza from his first mate's view, though he knew it illogical to do so. Who else would he be embracing?

But Xavier stood firm, his face wet with rain but revealing nothing of his thoughts. "The boy is coming below. Now," he added with emphasis.

"Son-of-a-bitch!" Cyprian had been angry at other times in his life. He'd been frustrated and he'd been horny, and he'd been in brutal fights as he'd struggled to survive. But never had he felt the intensity of emotions he felt at this moment. So when Eliza let out a strangled cry of alarm, then pushed frantically at his chest, he knew a disappointment and a rage so pure he thought he'd explode from it.

"Cyprian, please. We can't—"

"We can," he cut her off emphatically.

"But Captain," Xavier protested. "The boy—"

"See to him. We'll be occupied elsewhere," he retorted as he steered Eliza toward his cabin. The increased pitching of the ship would have tossed her from side to side except that he held her steady. But at his door she balked.

"No." She stopped short, bracing both of her hands on the door frame. "I must be with Aubrey. You don't understand. He'll be afraid because of the storm and—"

"He'll survive, Eliza. But I won't," he added in a hoarse voice. His hands slipped around her waist and he pulled her against his erection. "You're killing me, woman. I need you."

She wavered. He could tell by the soft way she curved into his embrace. But she turned away from his seeking lips.

"This is wrong."

"It's right. Nothing I've ever done has been as right as this."

"But Aubrey, and the storm—"

"Xavier will see to things."

"No, Cyprian."

"Yes." He caught her damp hair in his hand and forced her face up to his. "Yes, Eliza."

"Eliza! Oh . . . " Aubrey's surprised voice stole her back just as Cyprian was certain she was giving in. The dark passion in her eyes cleared to a dismayed recognition of reality.

"Aubrey!" she squeaked, pushing Cyprian away once more. Barely suppressing a vicious oath, Cyprian reluctantly complied.

"Are . . . are you all right, Aubrey?" she stammered. "Are you . . . are you very wet?"

"A little," the boy responded, approaching them with his uneven gait and a speculative look in his eyes. "What are you doing down here?"

Eliza broke away from Cyprian completely at that, slipping from between him and the door to his cabin, and leaving him to lean heavily on his hands and fight down the painful pressure in his loins. So close. He'd been so close. If ever he'd wanted to drown a body he wanted to drown Aubrey. And Xavier, he added, glaring at his first mate and the barely repressed grin that lurked on the man's dark face.

Cyprian didn't hear Eliza's fumbling retort to her young cousin. He didn't watch as the two of them made their way to their own cabins. He only concentrated on his breathing, counting slowly and evenly as he fought down both passion and rage.

They'd sighted land. If he could not have Eliza tonight, then he'd have her tomorrow night—and every night thereafter. He'd ban the rest of them from his villa, if necessary, even the boy. And he'd have Eliza in his house and in his bed—and all to himself at last.

Chapter Fifteen

"Someone's kidnapped Eliza?"

Michael Geoffrey Johnstone stared disbelievingly at the man who was to be his father-in-law. But Gerald Thoroughgood's haggard features confirmed the unimaginable truth.

"What the bastard's done is kidnap my son. My Aubrey!" Lloyd Haberton swore, his face almost purple with his fury.

"But he's taken my daughter as well," Gerald said. "The devil take him, he's stolen my Eliza—and done God knows what to her," he trailed off, going even greyer, if that were possible.

His eyes met Michael's and the two of them shared the same sickening stab of fear. *God* knew what the depraved beast would do to her—and they feared *they* knew too.

Michael reached for a decanter and poured a full glass of something—anything. His hand shook as he lifted the glass and tossed the contents back in one burning gulp. It shook as it tightened on the tumbler in a painful grip, and it shook as he threw the vessel blindly and the glass shattered on the marble hearth.

"Eliza!" he cried in a misery of desperation. He should never have let her go. He should have tried harder to put her at her ease. But she'd been so remote around him, like some porcelain doll, meant only to be admired from afar, never to be touched or played with. Only as she was departing had he sensed her beginning to warm ever so slightly toward him.

Though he'd wanted her to stay, he'd let her go, hoping that time and separation would bring her around even more. Twice a week he'd written her since she'd left, though he'd known she'd probably receive the letters in batches. But now it seemed she'd never receive any of them at all. Oh God!

"Is there a note?" he demanded of Sir Lloyd. "How did you learn of this? How can you be sure it's even true?"

Lloyd passed him two sheets of parchment, creased and folded in the manner of messages come a long way. "They came together. One from my cousin, Agnes, with a short note attached from the ranking English citizen in Funchal. But this one." He threw a third page on the tabletop as if it were contaminated. "This one is from the bastard who did this foul deed—" He broke off with a sob and turned away, one hand covering his eyes.

While Lloyd Haberton composed himself, Michael scanned the sheets. Cousin Agnes had cried over her note, a rambling, incoherent message that revealed only that some young man named Oliver Spencer was involved. The letter from a Lord Roland Bennington told little more, save that the island was being searched high and low for the villains—and their victims.

But it was the other note that revealed much more. It was addressed to Lloyd Haberton, no title, no formal address. "We have unfinished business, you and I, and through your son I will finally see it done."

It was signed, Cyprian Dare, and by its very brevity the seriousness of the situation was magnified. No threat. No ransom demand. What was the man's purpose, then?

Michael looked over at Lloyd Haberton. "Who is this Cyprian Dare? Why does he take this sort of revenge against you?"

"I don't know. I don't know!" Haberton ran his hands through his wild gray hair. "I don't know," he muttered brokenly.

"But think," Gerald Thoroughgood insisted. "You *must* know him. No one plans such a hideous deed for no reason."

"It must be for money. What else could there be? He's taking his time about a ransom note in order to increase my desperation. So I'll pay more for my son's return."

"But why would he take Eliza?" Michael demanded angrily. He threw the note down. "Why in the name of blazes would he take *her?*"

But they all knew why, or they feared they did. She was young; she was pretty. She was a fresh and innocent flower ripe for the plucking. And some unholy wretch had undoubtedly already done just that.

Michael thrust his fingers through his hair and tightened his hands into fists as he paced the length of Thoroughgood's well-appointed study. This could not be happening, not to his fiancée. It was simply inconceivable.

"We've got to find them." He glared at the other two men. "We've got to get them back!"

Gerald Thoroughgood's red-rimmed gaze held with Michael's for a long moment. "You'll help us then."

"Of course I will. Every contact and resource at my disposal is yours," he vowed in answer.

"But . . . but what about afterwards?" Eliza's father pressed. "Once she's back, what then?"

The older men both stared at him. There was no need to elaborate further; Michael heard the unspoken question. No doubt she'd been raped by now. All of society would consider her ruined. But Michael was too frightened for her safety to worry about that right now. "I will do everything in my power to see her returned to us. I have no intentions of reneging on my vow," he added earnestly.

Gerald nodded and gratitude shone through the grief on his face. "We cannot wait on further correspondence from this madman. We intend to pursue him and we welcome your participation."

"But where will we begin? Have you contacted the authorities?"

"We can't involve the authorities," Sir Lloyd said. He cleared his throat. "Not if we've any hope of preserving Eliza's reputation. I've hired private investigators. We already know the man is a ship's captain."

The men pulled chairs up to a table. All of them felt much better pursuing a course of action than just raging at the injustice of it all.

"What ship?" Michael asked. "Flying what nation's flag?"

"An English brig. The rogue ship, *Chameleon.*"

The *Chameleon* rode out the storm on the lee side of the Isle of Alderney, well away from her dangerous rocky shore. Though the sails were taken in and the hatches all closed down against the violent weather so that the sleek vessel had but to bob on the ocean's heaving surface like a well-stopped bottle, the crew nevertheless remained on full alert. They were too near the French coast and the irregular Channel Islands for complete comfort.

Aubrey slept through most of it. Xavier had advised Eliza to give the boy a mild dose of the same sleeping potion that had worked so well before. But though Eliza was relieved that Aubrey would neither succumb to sea sickness nor be frightened by the storm, sitting alone in the close confines of the dark cabin with the entire world pitching and churning around her was awful. She was terrified that they would sink, bruised by the rough and relentless heaving of the ship back and forth, and beset by shame in enormous proportions.

This storm was God's way of punishing her for what she'd been about to do. Where had her good sense fled? And her pride? What on earth had she been thinking?

And then what about Michael? What about his pride and his honor? He did not deserve this from her.

She clung to the edge of her sturdy canvas hammock as it listed and her cabin careened wildly around her. She'd learned to keep her eyes fixed upon the rope tie at the foot of the hammock. To close her eyes brought on waves of nausea, and looking about was almost as bad. Only by fixing on a solitary, rather stationary point was she able to keep the queasy feelings at bay.

So she stared at the double half hitch of straw-colored rope and wondered if Cyprian's hands had tied the knot. They certainly had tied enough knots in her heart, she thought with aching honesty.

Beyond the ship's sturdy wooden walls, the wind moaned and tore. The ship rose up on the storm-driven waves, then fell away into yawning voids, creaking as if it would split apart at any moment. Every now and again a shouted order could be heard. Cyprian's voice?

Hours passed. Perhaps she slept. She wasn't sure at all, but whatever the time, Eliza realized with a start that the worst of the storm must be over. Rain still fell. But the waves were more regular now—deep, slow swells. With care she extricated herself from the hammock, bracing herself on the low ceilings and built-in furnishings as she made her way to the tiny porthole window.

She could see no land, only the vast stretch of a turbulent sky and sea, both gray and purple. But the clouds were high now and the deep lavender came as much from the approaching night as from the aftereffects of the storm. Had the storm buffeted them a full night and day?

When the door opened without benefit of a knock, she knew at once that it was Cyprian. The remains of their own private storm still lingered, she thought, without turning around. But now it must be dealt with.

"How have you fared, Eliza?"

She sighed and squinted at a sea bird of some sort in the distance. Where did the birds go when neither sea nor sky offered them refuge? "I'm fine."

She heard him move nearer. She felt it too, like some homing instinct that always knew where he was in relationship to herself—at least physically. Why couldn't her emotional landscape be as easy to chart?

"The night will be easier. We'll wait to dock in the morning."

She nodded and pressed her lips together.

"Eliza." She heard his weary sigh when she did not respond. "Eliza, turn around. Look at me."

If she did that, everything would start again. She knew it. But still she could not help herself. Slowly she turned, though she leaned back against the wall as if to find some sort of support there.

The boat heaved—the whole world was tilting around her, she thought as she finally looked up at him. Though she struggled to hold onto her old life and the old secure values that gave it structure, every time she looked at Cyprian—or touched him, or kissed him—his hold on her grew stronger until she feared she would abandon all propriety, just to get closer and closer to him. She knew it was wrong, yet she simply did not have the will to fight it.

"I'm fine," she stated, for wont of anything else to say. Then her brow creased as she stared harder at him. He looked weary beyond words. "Cyprian?" She pushed away from the wall and approached him. "Dear God, but you look terrible."

That drew a small smile to his lips. "Why thank you, my dear."

"No, seriously. You're soaked. And when did you last sleep?"

He shook his head as if he wasn't sure, but the smile stayed in place. The ship rocked a little deeper and he reacted unconsciously by grasping one of the ceiling beams for balance. Despite the fact that his sea legs functioned automatically, he nonetheless looked ready to drop.

Eliza reacted without hesitation. "Here. Sit down," she ordered, drawing his oilcloth slicker from his shoulders as she pushed him toward the cabin's only chair. "Have you eaten anything?"

He shook his head. "Not yet. I thought you might join me." He took her hands into his, untangling her fingers from the nervous knot she'd made of them.

But other knots tightened in their stead—in her stomach and somewhere else, down lower. Warmer too. "Listen, Cyprian. I—"

"I love the way you say my name." His eyes swept over her face. "Say it again."

"I don't think—"

"Please, Eliza."

Her heart hurt, it beat so violently. "Cyprian," she finally whispered.

He let out a long sigh and his thumbs caressed the back of her hands. At the same time, her eyes caressed his features. His ebony hair was wet and plastered to his head. Beneath the slicker his shirt and vest were damp and clung to his wide shoulders. His face bore the marks of a long night and day spent battling the sea for possession of his ship. But he'd won and now, though weary, he nonetheless appeared triumphant.

Unaware of it, her pull against his grip lessened and when he drew her nearer, she came.

"You need to sleep," she protested in little more than

a murmur. But sleep made her think of beds, and beds
made her think of something else entirely. She swallowed hard and self-conscious heat stained her cheeks.

He seemed to read her mind. "I need a bed," he
conceded with a lopsided grin. Then he tugged at her
wrists just as the ship lurched, and Eliza landed sitting
down in his lap. His arms swiftly came around her waist,
and before she knew it, he had her fast in a wet, yet
undeniably comfortable embrace. The side of his face
rested against her hair and he inhaled deeply, as if the
very scent of her calmed him.

That simple sound eased her need to protest their
intimate position like nothing else could have.

"You need to sleep," she repeated, overcome with the
most inappropriate compulsion to care for him.

"I need to sit here just a few more minutes, Eliza.
Just a few more." He shifted her to a more comfortable
position, sitting sideways across his lap. His breath came
slow and steady, a hot shivery sensation against her
neck. Yet for all the violent emotion that shredded her
nerves and reduced her body to quivering jelly, Eliza
found the oddest sense of peace in the shadowed cabin.
Even when one of his hands settled on her hip and the
other drew small, irregular circles on her folded hands,
she felt an undeniable rightness.

She'd never before been so at peace in a man's presence. Though everything that was rational warned her
away from him and the seductive web he always created
around them both, just by his honest weariness—the
salty smell of his long day's labor and the warm strength
in his work-hardened body—he deafened her to a lifetime of warnings about unsuitable men. Men like him.

He needed her right now in a way that no one had
ever needed her before. How rare a thing that was, she
realized in dawning amazement. All her life she'd been
the needy one and her family had always been there, to
nurture her when she was ill as well as all the rest of the

time. She'd never nurtured anyone in return though, except perhaps for Aubrey these past weeks.

In contrast, Cyprian had probably never had anyone to nurture him, at least not since his mother had died. He always appeared so strong and capable, so utterly self-contained. But he needed her right now, that was plain. He needed her comfort and her understanding, and her touch to put him at ease. It was far too powerful a lure for her to resist.

Eliza relaxed against Cyprian's arm that circled her back, and slipped one of her arms around his neck, albeit shyly. But when he looked up, putting their faces but inches apart, she did not glance away. His eyes looked black in the fading light, but they nonetheless appeared lit with a glow from deep within. His gaze dropped momentarily to her lips then raised back to her face. The light in his eyes, however, had grown decidedly hotter and she was conscious at once of everywhere their bodies touched.

His hand slid up her left arm. "What is it about you, Eliza?"

She shook her head slightly, confused by feelings that she could not explain. The true question was, what was it about him? Why was she drawn to him when there were so many reasons for her to fear and even despise him? Yet even cataloguing his faults—he'd kidnapped Aubrey, after all—she could nullify them too. He'd made Aubrey work and in the process the coddled little boy had grown strong again. He was a hard man, but he could be incredibly tender.

His hand moved again on her arm. "You know where this is headed, don't you?"

Her eyes widened but she did not answer. How could she?

"You know that I intend to make love to you, despite the fact that you're a noblewoman and I'm just a sea captain; despite the fact that you're young and innocent

and I've been hardened by the world. That you're promised to another. You know that, don't you, Eliza?"

Eliza closed her eyes against the fire building in his
eyes. Why was he saying this? Was he trying to scare her
off?

But though he did scare her, she was unable to run
from him. She opened her eyes. "I know it's all wrong,"
she whispered.

But he shook his head. "No, it's not wrong. It couldn't
be more right." Then his mouth caught hers in a hungry
kiss. It was salty and it was possessive and it dissolved
what little doubt remained in Eliza's mind. Her free
hand came around his neck and she arched into his
body as fear and the most intense feelings of desire sent
erotic shivers through her.

Just like that other time, she thought, as every part of
her body remembered what he'd roused her to before.
She'd tried not to remember, or at least not to dwell on
what she'd allowed him to do to her in his cabin. But
here it was, happening again, and the wanton feelings
that gripped her increased tenfold.

Cyprian seemed to shed his weariness as he deepened
their kiss, as if he took strength by their very contact.
His mouth took complete possession of hers; his tongue
delved deep, exploring every crevice with an amazing
sort of passionate energy. Nor were his hands idle. One
slid low on her hip, curving beneath her derriere and
wreaking havoc with her heart's pace. The other cupped
her face with excruciating tenderness, stroking her neck
and circling the soft hollows of her throat with a touch
that felt like fire.

Just that quickly were all her brave resolutions abandoned. The hours since their lovemaking in the companionway had been interrupted by the storm
disappeared as well, so that all Eliza had left was her
need to be close to Cyprian, her need which grew with
every caress, every kiss, and every incoherent murmur.

"Cyprian—"

"Touch me," he whispered against her lips as he guided one of her hands down his side and toward his waist.

Eliza was consumed enough by passion to do anything he said. But when his hand then cupped her breast and his thumb brushed over her sensitive nipple once, then again, she was unable to follow through on her intentions. She went completely still—at least outwardly—unable to protest or twist away, or even lean into the warm pressure of his palm. Inside, however, every part of her leaped and twisted and clamored for more. More of these extravagantly forbidden feelings.

"Do you like that?" he whispered, breaking away from her lips to brand hot kisses along her cheek and neck and ear. "Do you like it?" he repeated, grazing his thumb back and forth across the now rigid nub.

"Yes," she breathed, hardly aware she'd answered.

Somehow her sweater and blouse were pulled up; she couldn't say how it came about. But all at once his work-roughened hands were no longer separated from her skin by the cotton and wool garments. He cast the pair aside and feasted both eyes and hands upon her naked breasts.

"By damn, woman. No mermaid conjured in the most desperate sailor's dreams could be as beautiful as you," he murmured as he filled his hands with her breasts, this time teasing both nipples to unimaginable pleasure.

It was not the sort of compliment a proper young English woman should expect to hear, but it did things to Eliza—both to her heart and to her body—that she could not begin to understand. Whatever his reasons for wanting her, Cyprian never let her doubt that it was strictly for herself.

She pressed fully into him, and kissed him with complete abandon. This time she did the exploring, slipping her tongue between his teeth, experimenting with that exquisite thrusting motion he'd used on her.

At once he pressed upward, pushing his now rigid loins against her bottom. Then before she knew what was happening, he lifted her into his arms and with a quick movement, stood up and crossed to her bed. While the ship heaved back and forth in the rhythm she'd become so used to, he laid her in the bed and deftly untied her skirt. As quickly as he flung it away, so did he shrug out of his damp vest and shirt.

Then he pulled her hands to rest against his stomach —his hard, warm stomach, with its narrow streak of hair leading from chest to groin—and rubbed her palms just above the waistband of his breeches.

"Touch me," he ordered once again, though the raspy demand was closer to a plea.

Eliza's first reaction was to cover herself, to shelter her nude breasts and the bared place between her legs from his view. But he wouldn't allow it.

"Don't hide from me, Eliza. I want to see you. Every bit of you. I'm going to touch every bit of you too. And taste you." Again he rubbed her hands against the line where his muscular stomach met the coarse wool of his breeches. "I want you to do the same to me."

Eliza swallowed hard, suddenly afraid of all these overwhelming feelings. "I don't know—"

"But you will," he broke in. His eyes, dark with passion, compelled her. "Touch me, Eliza."

She was unable to refuse. Slowly her hands moved down the rough wool. He released them and stood over her, one foot on the floor and his other knee on the bed, tense and trembling ever so slightly. Then her fingers encountered the thickened evidence of his desire and he went utterly still. She felt the buttons of his trousers, all five of them, as she slid her hands lower. But her eyes remained locked on his face, for there did the strength of his feelings show even more clearly. His eyes closed and his strong throat flexed convulsively. The planes of his handsome face were taut with tension, and she could see his pulse, hard and fast, throbbing in a vein along his neck.

She felt it too beneath the wool and the buttons, in the raging arousal that strained for release. Then he grabbed her hands away and held them down on the mattress alongside her head.

"Eliza—" He broke off and kissed her instead, hard and almost punishing, it felt. Perhaps she shouldn't have done that, she wondered as desire made her dizzy. But she had no time to worry about that, for with an inarticulate groan, Cyprian tore off his boots and stripped his breeches down. In an instant he lay over her, all hot, hard muscle from his clenched jaw and solid chest, down to his iron-hewn thighs. But it was the jutting muscle between those thighs that drew her attention. For it lay burning and heavy between them, and she knew what must come next.

He broke their kiss and pulled a few inches away. "Eliza," he began again. But like before he did not continue with whatever he'd meant to say. Instead he used one of his knees to spread her thighs and began an altogether different sort of conversation.

The engorged length of his manhood slid between her widespread legs, but Cyprian did not press her too quickly. Instead he rubbed one of his fingers along her lips and then slipped the fingertip into her mouth.

"Suck it," he whispered, all the while using his tongue in the most erotic fashion on her ear.

Eliza squirmed against him, wanting to get away and get closer, all at the same time. But she pulled his finger into her mouth just the same.

When his finger was wet he pulled it free, then snaked it down between their bodies. Just one touch with that slippery finger directed unerringly to the place he'd found that other time, and Eliza nearly came off the bed.

"Ah, you like that, don't you, my sweet Eliza?" he murmured in hot breaths. "You're all wet and ready for me."

She felt as if she'd been ready for him all her life. Her hands ran up and down the rangy muscles in his arms and shoulders and along his straining back. She feared she was ready enough to explode.

But he seemed to know, for he guided himself toward the source of all her need and all at once her eyes came wide open. He was inside her.

But not all the way, she quickly realized. Slowly, in rhythmic little thrusts he slid deeper and deeper, filling her with an odd sort of pressure. It was like the ship being tossed helplessly upon a mighty, surging sea. She feared she would splinter apart, and panic welled up. But again he seemed to sense her fear, for he slowed the pushing and caught her face in his hands. "Just relax, sweetheart. Just relax and you'll see, it'll be easier."

"I . . . I can't," she answered, ashamed of her fear and the tears pooling in her eyes.

Cyprian only smiled, though she sensed a strain behind the smile. "It may hurt a little, Eliza. I'll be as gentle as I can. After that, though . . . " He moved a little deeper and she gasped. It was uncomfortable, but she didn't want him to stop either.

"After a little while it'll feel much better than anything you've ever felt before."

"Better than . . . better than what you did that day?"

His grin widened and he kissed her, hard and triumphantly. "Better even than that."

"But . . . " Eliza swallowed, lured by the promise of something even better than those incredible feelings. Was it possible? "But what about you?"

"Don't worry about me," he said, his smile fading. He

pulled out a little, then thrust back in, eliciting a gasp from Eliza, and causing sweat to bead up on his brow. "Don't worry about me at all." Once more he pulled out, then thrust his hips forward. But this time he drove all the way in, past her meager virgin's barrier. She gasped at the sharp tearing pain. But it was quickly over and with a growing sense of wonder she realized that he now rested fully inside her.

But he didn't rest long. Before Eliza could catch her breath and adjust to the completeness of their joining, he began to slide out again.

"No, wait—"

She stopped abruptly when he slid all the way back in. "Oh." Her eyes widened as he repeated the movement, and another surprised sigh escaped her. "Oooh . . . "

"Damn," he muttered. As if he couldn't prevent himself, he began to move faster.

Eliza's eyes fell closed and without realizing what she did, she wrapped both arms and legs around him. "Cyprian," she whispered, pressing kisses to the hot, salty skin of his neck and jaw. His unshaven skin prickled her lips but that only added to the exquisite myriad of sensations gripping her. His whole body was hot and straining and damp with sweat. Precisely how she felt on the inside.

"Cyprian," she whimpered as he moved faster and faster. In and out again. Filling her and withdrawing. Stroking and building with every stroke an inferno she could not control. Hotter and higher. And then the explosion.

Eliza arched and cried out as her body seemed to shatter apart. All the light and heat and sound in the entire world centered right there between them, and in the following seconds, Cyprian was consumed by it too. He cried out, words she couldn't understand, as he drove into her like a man possessed.

It happened so fast and furiously, so violently, that in

the aftermath Eliza could have believed herself dead and gone to heaven, though a heaven quite unlike anything her religion lessons had ever prepared her for. Cyprian rested on her, spent and gasping, his body collapsed. But she was collapsed too. And as the roaring in her ears subsided to only the creaking of the ship and their own mingled breathing, she knew that nothing could ever be the same again. Not her. Not them.

Nothing.

Chapter Sixteen

*T*hey anchored in a quiet bay early in the afternoon. They would row to shore, Aubrey had told Eliza when he'd come to awaken her. And where had she been at breakfast, he'd inquired, for it had been nearing the noon hour by the time she'd arisen.

It was a question Eliza had not been ready to answer. Even now as she pulled on the men's wool hose she'd been given, and slipped the heavy fisherman's sweater over her blouse and skirt, she could hardly believe where she had been—or rather, with whom she'd been, and doing what.

While Aubrey had eaten breakfast with Xavier and Oliver, she'd been sprawled in a sated stupor, wondering at Cyprian's insatiable appetite for her. She'd been the main course of his breakfast. And he'd been hers, she thought now, with hot color staining her cheeks. He'd touched and tasted and even nibbled on every portion of her anatomy during the long night and the morning that had followed, and she'd learned how to do as much to him. Giving him pleasure had been every bit as exciting as when he did it to her.

Later in the morning, after he left, she'd bathed herself with a sponge and bucket, and she'd witnessed the evidence of their near violent joining with her own eyes.

The reddened skin of her breasts where his stubbled jaw had scraped. And the inner skin of her thighs too. A small bruise on the side of her throat no doubt had occurred that second time they'd made love, when he'd gone slower and longer and yet had driven her to writhing ecstasy. He'd held her down with the weight of his body, and kissed and sucked every part of her body in the process.

And then there were her nipples. They were pink and swollen and bigger than she'd ever remembered them being. Just to think of what he'd done to them with his lips and fingers and tongue caused them to stiffen again in lingering passion. Something deep inside her tightened too, and she knew that were Cyprian to walk through her door, she'd want to do all those things again, right this very minute.

She closed her eyes with a groan and sat back on the bed—the scene of her fall from grace.

Dear God, was she truly the same Eliza Thoroughgood who'd set out on this journey because she feared her coming marriage to Michael? If someone had just told her what pleasure she might find in the marriage bed, she would never have wanted to delay her wedding.

Yet Eliza knew, somewhere in her woman's soul, that what she felt with Cyprian, she could never feel for Michael. To even think of herself lying with Michael that way—

She shook her head and frowned. Their marriage would have been a huge mistake. Or at the very least, rather passionless. Yet knowing that, she nevertheless felt an awful stab of guilt. She could never marry Michael now. Not that she wanted to. Cyprian was the only man she could ever conceive of marrying.

But he hadn't spoken a word of marriage—or of love.

Eliza gnawed her lower lip, but with her new heightened sensitivity, that sent a tremor of remembered passion burning its way through her. Was what she felt for him love? Or was it passion—the same sort of passion that had brought his mother to ruin?

Now she was ruined too, she realized as desolation washed over her. He'd seduced her and she'd not put up much of a fight. He had no reasons to make promises to her, did he?

But even if his intentions towards her were not the most honorable, at least his intentions toward Aubrey were changing, she consoled herself. He'd contacted Uncle Lloyd, and they were heading for London soon. She may have sacrificed her good name and reputation to him, but he'd said that Aubrey would soon go home.

As Aubrey's guardian she should rejoice in that one victory. Shouldn't she?

Cyprian watched the dinghy all the way to shore. He'd waited until just before the turning of the tide to send them, when the sea was calm and there was little risk of the boat being swamped.

Cyprian had wanted to take Eliza ashore himself, but after the night they'd just spent, he feared he'd never be able to concentrate on the boat. Just the two minutes he'd spent on deck with her this afternoon had proven that.

He groaned aloud to even think of it. Her face had been pale, then had turned the loveliest shade of rosy pink when she'd spied him. Her eyes had been huge, and their serious gray had changed in a matter of moments to a darker, more passionate color. She'd been both embarrassed and aroused at the sight of him, and it had been all he could do to get out an intelligent greeting.

What had he said anyway? Something about fair skies and a fortunate wind; about going ashore soon, and had she slept well.

"Bloody hell," he muttered now, realizing why she'd

looked down and refused to meet his gaze again after that. Had she slept well! When had he become so completely muddle-headed over a woman?

The answer was obvious. Since the unlikely Miss Eliza Thoroughgood had found her way onto his ship and under his skin. For that's what he concluded it must be. He was obsessed with her and the incredible night he'd spent with her had only magnified it. He'd had her all night long, and yet he wanted her now all the more. Just the thought of covering her lovely body with his made him hard all over again.

Scowling into his spyglass, he willed his arousal away. When he saw Oliver lift Eliza out of the boat and wade ashore with her in his arms, however, Cyprian's frustration turned to unreasoning fury. If he could have reached out and grabbed Oliver, he would have strangled the young sailor for taking advantage of her that way!

But once on the beach the boy put her down and after a few bobs of their heads, Oliver turned back for Aubrey who was splashing ashore under his own power. But Cyprian's attention remained on Eliza. He could not get enough of her, not even from this distance. He'd only let Oliver go ashore with her because he was the strongest swimmer on board. If the boat had tipped over, Cyprian wanted Oliver there to save her. He'd sent Xavier to keep Oliver in check. But Cyprian had to admit—though reluctantly—that lately Oliver's behavior toward Eliza had been completely blameless. He'd taken Cyprian's threat seriously, it seemed. And Eliza had never encouraged him.

By damn, but she was a rare one, his Eliza.

His Eliza.

Cyprian removed the glass from his eye and stared at the small group as they made their way across the beach toward the stone steps that led up to his fortresslike house. His Eliza. Was that what he wanted, for her to be his?

As he prepared to leave the *Chameleon,* assigning a skeleton watch and making one last check of the ship, Cyprian firmly suppressed any thoughts of what he wanted from Eliza, beyond the obvious. He'd told Xavier to put her in his bedroom. For now that was enough.

The bedchamber was huge. It boasted not only a gigantic bed dressed with the finest bed linens of Indian cotton, a Turkish carpet big enough for three normal-sized rooms, and a view of the bay and the *Chameleon* at anchor, it also had a sumptuous bathing chamber attached to it. And the generously sized roll-edged tub that stood in the middle of it was already filled with gently steaming water.

"When I saw the boats coming ashore, I began heating the water," the housekeeper said. She'd introduced herself as Ana, but Eliza had already guessed that. For when the woman had come racing down the narrow steps and thrown herself into Xavier's widespread arms, there had been no doubt that she was his wife. Their complete absorption with one another had been a beautiful thing to see—and painful too. Eliza realized that was how she wanted Cyprian to feel about her.

"After weeks at sea," the almond-eyed Ana was saying, "the first thing I always want is a long luxurious soak. I'll leave you now, unless you want something else?"

"Oh, no, this is wonderful. Just wonderful," Eliza replied, smiling. Then she hesitated. "Oh, but I don't have any clean clothes."

"Do not concern yourself with that, miss. You bathe and I'll lay out fresh garments for you on the bed." She left with an encouraging smile and a ripple of her straight, hip-length hair. Eliza could only speculate about Ana's heritage. Indian, perhaps. Or Oriental. No matter the woman's home country, however, Eliza was certain that if Ana and Xavier should ever have children, they would turn out exquisitely beautiful.

Eliza wasted no time in shedding her clothes and climbing into the big bathing tub. Rose petals floated on the surface, and once she'd submersed herself, she surfaced just enough that her nose protruded above the water. Her hair spread around her like a silky blanket, undulating in dark waves.

How utterly divine it felt to bathe again, though in truth she was not bathing. Not yet. She was soaking. Floating in a fragrant sea. She'd applied neither soap nor wash cloth to her skin, though myriad choices were laid out on a hammered copper tray beside the tub. Judging from the luxuries Cyprian surrounded himself with, he was a man of some wealth. Though not excessively showy, his home was extremely comfortable and reflected excellent taste, though the decor was completely masculine. It suited him very well, she decided.

The question was, did *she* suit him, for she already knew he suited her.

Eliza sat up in the water and smoothed her heavy hair back from her face. For a moment she just stared blankly past the rolled rim of the tub.

On the surface they were so totally mismatched. He was a sea captain, a man who worked long and hard for his living. Hardly the sort her father would invite to dine with his family, let alone marry his only daughter. Cyprian had been raised without a father, by a woman ostracized from polite society. It was a far cry from her sheltered family upbringing.

But then, maybe their differences were the reason for the strong attraction between them. Maybe what he needed was a family, a warm, loving family circle to fill in the empty holes in his life. And perhaps what she needed was simply to be needed, and to be the genesis of a family for him.

Eliza swallowed hard and pulled her knees up close to her chest. When he arrived from the ship, maybe she'd be able to judge, for they'd had little enough time to speak today. But how was she to broach such matters in conversation? And then, what if she were misinterpreting everything? What if all he really wanted was to bed her with no future beyond those intense moments of passion?

But Eliza didn't want to think about that possibility. Once more she sank beneath the water, shaking her head so that her hair moved around her like a living thing. All over her body her skin tingled with delicious heat. When she finally surfaced, she let out a sigh of pure satisfaction. But a distinctly male chuckle jerked her out of her pleasant lethargy and she sat upright with a splash.

"Cyprian!" Eliza pulled her knees up to her chest then circled them with her arms. "You . . . you didn't knock," she stammered, hoping the water adequately concealed her state of complete nudity.

"You were underwater. How could you have heard?" He straightened from where he leaned against the door frame and moved in slow steps right up to the edge of the tub. Leaning down he tested the water, then ignoring her shocked expression, he stroked the side of her cheek. "May I join you, my lovely mermaid?"

"J—join me!" Eliza choked out.

"Yes, join you," he repeated, shrugging out of his vest and shirt, all in one motion.

Eliza averted her eyes the moment his bare chest came into view. A part of her knew she was overreacting. Considering what had passed between them last night, a shared bath should not shock her in the least. Nevertheless it did. For one thing, it was still daylight. No shadows hid her from his view nor him from hers.

Unable to stop herself, she glanced sidelong at him. He'd already removed one salt-encrusted boot and was drawing off the second. Then he stood, meeting her tentative gaze with a wink, and she felt as if the bath water increased in temperature from pleasantly hot to positively steaming. His body could only be described as beautiful, she decided even as she tried to drag her eyes away. Big and muscular, with hard planes and intriguing ripples. He was as purely a male creature as she could imagine had ever existed.

And he was unfastening his breeches even as she watched.

This time she did look away, turning her head with a jerk and searching wildly about for a towel or a robe. Anything to cover herself with and make her escape.

But there was nothing, and anyway, it was too late. For with his own sigh of pleasure, Cyprian stepped into the tub and sat down opposite her.

Eliza stared at him in dismay. "You can't do that."

He sighed again and stretched his legs out so that his feet rested on either side of her hips. Then he leaned back against the tub and rested his arms along the sides. "I've already done it, Eliza. Besides, I would love nothing better than to have you scrub my back." Then he grinned again. "Well, maybe *one* thing better."

Eliza couldn't help it. She blushed scarlet, from her chest, up her neck and across her face. Her arms tightened around her legs and she tried to make herself as small as she could. Yet even as she cringed from the overt intimacy of their shared bath, an unmistakable frisson of fiery passion began to curl and grow in her nether regions. The heated water was nothing compared to the wonderful burn of desire that sped through her veins with frightening speed. Her breath grew short, her nipples pebbled and her toes curled in unconscious longing. Every caress they'd shared last night came back to her. As the bath water moved languidly against her skin, it might have been Cyprian's palm or fingertip, or his lips and tongue, so excruciatingly vivid was her memory.

She stared at his handsome, weary face, and her lips parted in unconscious longing. At once Cyprian reached for her hands.

"Come closer, mermaid." He drew her arms apart and tugged just enough for her bottom to slide forward on the slippery tub floor.

Eliza glanced frantically toward the tall window and the streaks of afternoon sun that poured their winter warmth into the room. This could not be proper. Not by anyone's standards!

But Cyprian laughed as if he sensed her very thoughts. "It feels even better in the afternoon," he murmured.

Better than last night? Her eyes widened and despite herself she wondered if that was even possible. But as Cyprian unfolded her bent legs so that they rested across his own legs, then pulled her right up to him, her protests died. This was what she wanted; why pretend otherwise?

Still, as Cyprian began to work his magic, she resolved to draw him out afterwards, to talk to him and begin to understand him—and understand what they might come to mean to one another. More than anything she wanted to make him happy—to make him happy with her.

Chapter Seventeen

Not an hour later Eliza clasped the length of a fluffy white towel around herself, clutching the ends to her chest. "No, Cyprian. Absolutely not. We cannot possibly share the same bedchamber."

"We can and we will," he stated. He stood with his arms crossed and his legs splayed. And not one stitch of clothing to cover him.

Eliza glared at him with what she meant to be an inflexible fury, but which she feared came across as helpless pleading. Considering that he'd just proven to her that it *could* be better in the afternoon, she was hard-pressed to be stern with him. "It's . . . it's just not right," she argued rather lamely.

"I say it's right, and anyway, it's my house. What I say goes."

"Just like on the *Chameleon?* Oh, Cyprian. You revel in breaking all the rules. But I—" She broke off and looked away, suddenly miserable. She'd always done what she was supposed to do, until now. She'd always been a proper young lady and an obedient daughter.

Unaccountably she thought of Cyprian's mother. She'd been a proper young lady once, and probably an obedient daughter too. But that hadn't prevented her from bearing a child out of wedlock. Was that to become her own fate, too? Eliza lifted her chin and stared back at him, fearful now. "What would happen if I were to become . . . you know, to become with child?"

His face closed in a frown, chasing away the smug confidence that had been there before. "That's not going to happen. There are ways to prevent it. Ana will help you—"

"But what if it *does* happen?" she insisted. "After all, it happened to your mother."

She knew at once that she'd angered him with her words, for he yanked a clean pair of breeches from a tall wardrobe and pulled them on with jerky movements. "I won't abandon you, if that's what you're worried about. How can you even think that of me?"

Though Eliza took some solace in his response, it did not really solve anything. "You would let a child of yours be raised a bastard?" she asked very softly.

"No!" He advanced on her as if he meant to shake some sense into her, but he stopped just short of touching her. "No," he repeated, clearly struggling to regain his calm. "No child of mine will be raised a bastard."

"I see," Eliza sighed, fearing she truly did see. He'd marry her, but only if she should accidentally become pregnant. Was she now to wish for or dread just such an occurrence?

"So it's agreed. You'll share my room." His expression gentled and he reached up to smooth a long wet curl from her bare shoulder.

But Eliza shook her head and stepped back. How could she make him understand? He would dismiss her concerns about what the others might think. Even Aubrey. But she couldn't dismiss them, so she said the one thing she hoped would sway him.

"I never once, in all my life, imagined that I would become a fallen woman."

He let out an exasperated sound. "You're hardly a fallen woman, Eliza. That's just a lot of religious crap."

"All right, then, perhaps 'kept woman' is a more appropriate term."

His brows lowered in returning anger and he grabbed her by both shoulders. "You worry too much about what others think. You and I are the only ones whose opinions matter here."

"That's easy for you to say," she retorted as she tried fruitlessly to pull free of his iron-hard grasp. "You have no family to worry about you—to be ashamed for you. But I do. I do," she repeated in a lower tone when he straightened up and slowly released her arms.

She backed away, then holding tight to the damp towel around her, she turned and moved to the window. Outside afternoon had given way to the early dusk of winter. But even in December the expansive grounds that surrounded the stone-walled estate were green and verdant. Late-blooming flowers still showed here and there, pink moss roses and nodding cream-colored chrysanthemums. It was very like the magical island in the story Aubrey loved so, where boys needed never to grow up. Aubrey imagined he could become one of those boys. But Eliza feared that Cyprian already had. He denied she could become pregnant, and refused to understand that her concerns for propriety were valid. It seemed a natural part of his personality to thumb his nose at society any way he possibly could.

She heard his footfall as he approached and she shivered in undeniable yearning when his palms slid slowly up and down her arms. "Don't fight me on this, sweetheart." He kissed the top of her damp hair and pulled her so that her back rested against his chest. "We don't have to answer to anyone here, just each other. I please you. You please me. Together we're good, Eliza, better than I could ever have believed possible. Don't ruin it now when it's only just begun."

Eliza closed her eyes and struggled to remember why

she was fighting him. "It's just begun, but where shall it end?"

"Why should it ever end?" he answered, turning her in his arms. He tilted her chin up and kissed her with unbearable tenderness. But though Eliza rose into his kiss and reveled in the thrilling quiver that began again, a part of her knew, nevertheless, that he was wrong.

It had to end and eventually it would. But for her to think it could end in marriage—with their children tumbling happily about this lovely house, and she and Cyprian growing old together—was foolish beyond words. Her father would never allow it for one thing, and anyway, Cyprian did not really want to marry her.

She pulled out of his embrace and once more turned away from him.

"This has to end eventually. We cannot go on in this suspended state. You and I . . . " She shook her head in frustration. "And there's Aubrey. He must be returned to his father. You know that."

He didn't reply for a long moment, and she was too afraid to turn around and face him. Finally she heard him sigh.

"None of these decisions needs to be made right now, Eliza. We're both tired. You're upset. We'll talk about this later—tomorrow—after we've both had a good night's sleep."

He came up behind her and planted a light kiss on the side of her neck. "I've a few things to see to now. If you need anything just ask Ana. She'll take care of everything."

Eliza nodded and slowly he stepped away. She heard the sounds of him dressing but she continued to gaze blankly out the window, for she feared the powerful hold he had on her. Just a touch, a kiss, a smile, and all her arguments died.

He left the room with only a brief goodbye, but Eliza felt his departure as keenly as if her heart had been torn from her chest and departed with him. She knew, however, that she must hold onto her own will, for her future and Aubrey's depended on it.

They were on British soil now, and their real lives awaited them. If only she could convince Cyprian of that. He had to release Aubrey, and he had to accept the reality of the relationship he was forging with her. Until then the least she could do—if she retained any shred of self-preservation—was to maintain the semblance of propriety. They might make love in his huge tub in the afternoon, but she must have her own bedchamber, whether he liked it or not.

Still, that would not solve the greater problem that faced her: she was becoming emotionally entangled with Cyprian. It wasn't just physical anymore. And while physical entanglement was already foolish in the extreme—after all, she could become pregnant—an emotional entanglement was an invitation to utter disaster. He was not a man who desired marriage. That was far too conventional for him, especially marriage to a woman like her. The fact was, her social standing might very well be the larger part of his attraction to her. Through her he could mock her uncle and all he stood for. By ruining her he once more thumbed his nose at them all.

It was an enormously depressing thought and she had to quell an unexpected sob. She was a fool to stay here any longer. Though something in her dreaded that truth, it was no longer avoidable. The time had come for her to return to her old life. Despite her foolish reluctance, it was the only choice left to her.

Aubrey stared down at his feet and the plain work brogans Oliver had brought for him. "It feels strange, after going without shoes these past two weeks." He grinned up at Oliver as he tried them out. "Look, my limp doesn't show nearly so much."

"I expect in time you'll have no limp at all," the young sailor answered from his sprawling position in a cane-backed planter's chair.

"And I expect my father will be so pleased that I shall have anything I want. And the first thing I shall ask for is a sailing vessel all my own."

Oliver raised his brows. "Is he so rich as all that?"

Aubrey shrugged. "He's got lots of ships that trade all over the world. I know. I know! You can be captain of one of them and teach me everything about sailing. I can be the first mate." He jumped up and down, grinning at the sharp sound of new leather striking the wood floor of the bedroom he'd been given. "Where's Eliza? I want to tell her all about my new plan."

A narrow crease appeared on Oliver's forehead. "She's with Cyprian."

That slowed Aubrey's madcap dance around the room. "Is she going to marry up with him?"

Oliver shifted in the chair. "I couldn't begin to guess at that."

But Aubrey only stared harder at him. "If he were to ask her, I'm thinking she would say yes."

"Say yes to what?" Xavier asked, entering the room through the open door.

"To marrying Cyprian," Aubrey replied. "I think Eliza would, if he asked her."

"So do I," Xavier agreed. Then he too turned his scrutiny on Oliver. "Don't you have an opinion on that?"

Oliver shot him a dirty look. "He's not likely to ask her, so there's no point to your question."

Aubrey moved to stand before the sullen Oliver. "You could marry one of my sisters, you know. Jessica is in desperate need of a husband, at least that's what I've heard my father say. And all the young lords think she's quite beautiful."

Oliver rumpled the boy's hair affectionately. "And do

you think your father is desperate enough to choose a penniless sailor like me for a son-in-law?"

"But you'll be a captain, remember? You'll be captain of my ship, just like Cyprian is captain of his ship." He nodded earnestly. "I think it's a very good idea, Oliver. Don't you, Xavier?"

"I've known of more unlikely pairings than that. Pairings that have brought immense happiness to both halves of the mismatched couple." He clapped one huge hand on Oliver's shoulder. "Can't you be happy for Cyprian and Eliza, Oliver?"

Oliver stared up at his longtime friend. "If Eliza is happy with Cyprian, then yes, I can be happy for them. I know that she doesn't care for me in that way," he admitted. "But I will not see him hurt her," he added more forcefully. "And I think that's just what he'll do."

"I will not let him hurt her either," Xavier promised. "But unlike you, I have hope for them. It may take time for our captain to recognize how valuable she is to him, but it will do neither of them any good if we interfere too swiftly. Let us just enjoy our homecoming, shall we? And see where circumstances may lead us."

Cyprian decided to leave Eliza to her own devices for a while. Though she hadn't argued further with him, he knew she was not yet resigned to her position in his household. Perhaps a little time to herself would help. And it would allow him the chance to pursue some important private business.

Though it was the dinner hour, Cyprian's man-of-business answered his summons at once. They sat in Cyprian's teak panelled study, with two squat tumblers and a finely cut crystal decanter of Barbados rum between them, the doors closed against interruption.

"They received word even faster than we expected. A special messenger was dispatched on horseback, straight from the harbor at Portsmouth. He arrived in London four days past and Haberton has since learned that you are captain of the *Chameleon*. He and Miss Thoroughgood's father and fiancé have wasted no time in beginning their pursuit of you."

Cyprian's hand curved around his glass of rum, but he did not lift it to his mouth. Her fiancé was searching for her. Did the man not realize that her reputation must be destroyed by now? Or did it not matter to him?

His fingers tightened on the cool glass. Could the man want her as badly as he himself did, to the point that he'd have her back no matter what might have happened to her?

"What do you wish to do?"

"Send him to the bottom of the sea," Cyprian muttered, gulping the rum angrily.

"You said you'd not hurt the boy!" The solicitor jumped to his feet. "You promised—"

"I'm not going to hurt the boy!" Cyprian snapped.

"But you just said—"

"I was speaking of someone else. Not the boy!" Cyprian struggled to repress his irritation and control his tone. "I was thinking of someone else. I have no intentions at all of harming young Aubrey."

The man sat down, mollified but not entirely reassured. "What do you intend to do about the boy, then?"

Cyprian sighed. Time to put his plan into motion. "I'll write another letter to Haberton. Something about his son working as a cabin boy—perhaps on a slave ship. Or I could say he's been sold to a press gang."

"But I heard he is crippled. Would his father believe you?"

"He's no longer crippled—only a little lame. Anyway, it hardly matters. His father will run in circles searching for him, and that's all that counts."

"What of the girl?"

Cyprian never did answer that. He wrote a note which the man assured him would be delivered within two days time to Lloyd Haberton's primary residence in London. Then the man left and Cyprian was alone with his grim thoughts.

The game was on. But his joy in it was not nearly so satisfying as he'd expected. Yes, he had Lloyd Haberton where he wanted him, frantic and mad with worry. But Cyprian couldn't savor his triumph, for his thoughts centered more around Eliza than they did his bastard father.

He'd not been able to gauge her mood today. While they'd been making love in the steaming tub he'd had no such problems, for when she gave herself to him physically, she held nothing back at all. The prim English miss disappeared and an exquisitely passionate wanton took her place. But afterwards . . . afterwards her resistance had been frustrating.

She still had expectations of returning to her family—and to her fiancé. Christ, but he'd gladly kill the bastard! Anything to drive him out of her thoughts. But that would only alienate her further.

Short of doing that, his only other option seemed to be to get her with child. Though he'd rather have her all to himself for a while, he feared that pregnancy was the only sure route to possessing her fully. Her family would abandon her if she were pregnant and she'd have only him to turn to. She'd have to marry him if she were pregnant though she'd made it clear today she feared the very idea of pregnancy.

He stared down into his empty glass. He was hardly the sort of man she'd ever envisioned marrying, but though that rankled, he was certain he could change her mind. She didn't want to become pregnant. She didn't want to share his room. She hadn't wanted him to join her in the tub either. But he had, and in the end, once she'd relented, her innately passionate nature had taken over from that cautious side of her. Once she was aroused by his lovemaking, she threw all that caution to the winds.

He poured himself another glass of rum as he sat alone in his office. It would be his self-imposed task to keep the difficult Miss Thoroughgood thoroughly aroused and thoroughly sated. He would make love to her morning, noon, and night, no matter her feebly worded objections. He would get her with child and then he would get her before the nearest priest or vicar or even a shaman if she so chose.

Her objections to him would disappear in the face of the impending birth of their child, for she would not be able to envision marriage to her fiancé then, and her family would have turned away from her in shame. He was sure that Eliza would do the proper thing and marry him, if only for the sake of their child.

Their child.

For the first time since he'd left her alone in his room, Cyprian felt an easing of the tension inside him. Their child. The very thought of them creating a child together brought an unexpectedly satisfying feeling to his chest. Their child.

Cyprian smiled and placed the stopper on the decanter. Whether it was a son or daughter, he had no doubt at all that Eliza would make a wonderful mother. And he vowed to be the sort of father he had always wished for. Unlike Lloyd Haberton, he would be there whenever his child needed him. He would take the child everywhere and answer all his questions—or hers. He and Eliza together would create the perfect home for their child. For their *children*, he amended, unaware that he'd begun to smile.

With that thought buoying him up, he went in search of Eliza.

Chapter Eighteen

The room she found was not nearly as large as Cyprian's chamber. But it was spotlessly clean and the bed was soft. And it had a lock on the inside of the door.

Eliza lay on the bed and stared at the door through the nighttime gloom. Would he come looking for her? But she knew the answer to that. He would, and with a vengeance. It was for that reason, hoping to protect Aubrey from the unpleasant scene which surely must result, that she'd decided not to retreat to Aubrey's room. She'd thought of asking Ana and Xavier for help, but she'd ruled that out as well. It wasn't fair of her to pit them against their employer. Besides, they had their own reunion to celebrate. As for Oliver . . .

She rolled onto her side and determinedly closed her eyes. Cyprian was suspicious enough of Oliver. No need to fan that particular fire any hotter. So she'd found this empty room in a back corner of the house all on her own. She fully intended to make it hers so long as she remained in Cyprian's house, but at the same time, she also knew she must find a way to leave. The very thought filled her with intense sorrow, but she knew that's how it had to be.

A clock somewhere in the house chimed the hour.

Then, before the final tone could sound, she heard him. As if mimicking the rhythmic tolls of the tall clock, doors slammed, one by one, as he made his way down the hall.

"Eliza!" Slam.

"Damnit, woman!" Another slam.

Eliza jerked upright and folded her legs beneath her as she backed up against the high headboard of the bed. He was coming and her heart raced in fear—or was it more accurately termed anticipation?

"No," she muttered. He would have to understand that what he expected of her was impossible. She simply could not flaunt this intimate relationship before everyone's eyes. He'd made it clear enough that he would only marry her if she should accidentally become pregnant—

Another slam, and she winced. Her father would never allow her to break her betrothal anyway, especially not to marry someone so patently unsuitable as Cyprian Dare would appear to be. But would her father feel differently if she *did* become pregnant? Would he demand that she accept Cyprian's unenthusiastic offer of marriage?

Somehow marrying Cyprian under such circumstances seemed even worse than marrying Michael. Those were not the conditions under which she wished to keep Cyprian in her life.

Suddenly the door shook and Eliza gasped. But the sturdy lock held against Cyprian's fury.

"Unlock this door, Eliza. Now."

She swallowed hard and swiftly weighed her options. She couldn't avoid him forever. But then she wasn't trying to. She was just trying to avoid him for the night.

The door rattled again. "Eliza." When she didn't respond right away he hit the stout oak panel and she jumped. "Damnit! I know you're in there!"

"Go away," she demanded, though her voice was quite without the force it should have had.

"Unlock this door, Eliza. Unlock it now."

"I want to be alone."

There was a pause. "Just for tonight?"

She clutched a pillow to her chest as she considered her reply. "I won't share a bedchamber with you, Cyprian. It's not right and I won't do it."

In the silence that followed that statement, she thought she might have heard him sigh.

"Eliza. I don't want to have this conversation through the door. Let me in. Please," he added in a more conciliatory tone.

All things considered, Eliza deemed it best to comply. He would not relent. She was certain of that. And if she angered him too much, he might go so far as to break the door down. Then there would be no reasoning with him at all.

"Eliza!"

"All right! All right, Cyprian. I'll open it," she declared. She hesitated before the door. "But only to talk."

Her hand trembled as she slid the iron bolt back. Her heart pounded like angry waves against a rocky shore, but she didn't want to examine just why. They would discuss this matter sensibly and somehow she would make him understand how untenable a position he was trying to force on her. He would listen to her this time and he would have to admit that she was right.

No sooner was the bolt free than the door slammed open with a jerk. It crashed against the plaster wall, almost hitting her in the process. But the door was no real threat. Cyprian, however, was another matter altogether. If the terrible expression on his face was any indication, he was livid with anger, and Eliza stumbled back when he barged into the room.

"Don't you ever bar a door to me again," he warned

in a voice that was made all the more terrifying by its unearthly calm.

"And don't you threaten me," she snapped in frightened reply. Then her backward motion was halted by the edge of the bed and she unceremoniously sat down.

In an instant he stood over her, tall and furious. Before she could utter a word of protest, he pushed her prone upon the bed and braced himself over her.

"This is my house. My word is law here." He caught her hand when she tried to strike him, then pressed his weight fully on her to still her struggles. "I'll never hurt you—I swear it—so you have nothing to fear."

Eliza stared up at him, dismayed by her body's betrayal. And her heart's. "You're hurting me now," she whispered, conscious of the heat and power in his hard masculine form.

At once his grip loosened and he raised up a little on his elbows. That brought a bitter smile to her lips. "I don't mean physically."

He frowned. "Don't try to convince me—or yourself—that what we've shared is repugnant to you—"

"Oh, you're just too thickheaded to ever understand!" Once more she tried to escape his disturbing nearness, but that only lodged him more intimately against her. "Get off me!" she cried in complete frustration.

"If you wouldn't fight me—"

"If *you* would stop ordering me around—ordering *everyone* around!"

He cut her off with a kiss that came just short of being brutal. As a means of silencing her, it was most effective. But it did far more than that, for as his lips fitted to hers and his tongue sought entrance to her mouth, he began to silence all the warning bells going off in her mind too. This was not the way to convince him she would not be his mistress, by giving up her position at his very first caress. He would never take her seriously if she parted her lips so easily and curled her arms around his neck, as if she were eager for him.

But she was eager. His body weighed down on hers and she reveled in the intimate contact. Something hot and seething inside her cried out that quickly for relief, and she had learned by now that only Cyprian could provide it.

Yet still, in another more sane part of her being, she clung to the conviction that this was not right, feeble though that conviction was becoming.

"No, Cyprian—" She tore her mouth from his, then shoved at his shoulders. "Get off me."

"No."

She turned her head away from his seeking lips, but he caught her hair roughly in his fingers and held her steady. "Don't fight me, sweetheart. You can't win."

Eliza stared up at him through the darkness of the room, past the darkness of spirit that quickly descended to shroud her soul. "This should not be a contest between us, nor a fight," she whispered as he lowered his head, presumably to plunder her mouth once more. She wasn't sure she could fend off the carnal pleasure of it if he did, so she was relieved when he paused.

"I don't *want* to fight you, Eliza. I just don't see why *you're* fighting *me.*"

"Because you think you can take whatever you want," she cried, putting voice to her frustrations. "Me. Aubrey. You're the captain of your ship and your word is law there. You own this house, and you think your word must be law here too. But what about us? What about what *we* might want?"

She felt him stiffen. "You want this, Eliza. Don't try to deny it."

"No." She shook her head and searched for words that might make him understand. "No, I don't want it. Not in my heart or my head. But you . . . you know how to make me willing. How to make my body want your body. It's not the same thing," she finished in a small voice.

Silence reigned for a long uncomfortable moment. But he didn't move from his dominant position over her. "You wanted it before. On the ship last night. In the tub this afternoon."

Eliza closed her eyes. "Maybe . . . maybe I did—on the ship. You . . . you were so tired—"

"Not *that* tired."

"And you needed me," she finished, ignoring his interruption.

"I need you now just as much as I did then."

"No." She shook her head again. "It's not the same."

"It is for me," he retorted, impatience clear in his low voice.

"Well, it's not for me," she countered. "Not anymore."

He let out a low, exceedingly foul curse. Then, to her utter surprise, he rolled off her and stood up. Eliza lay still a few seconds. She was relieved; how could she not be? Yet the absence of his weight somehow left her with the most forlorn ache inside.

She pushed upright, then watched as he lifted the glass from a bedside lamp and used a phosphorous match to light the candle within. As the pale flickering light cast its golden hue over them both, she crawled over the bed to stand on the floor, then backed as far away from him as she could get, clutching the thin silk wrapper around her. As if that could protect her from him.

He turned to face her, his legs spread wide and his arms crossed over his chest. "I think it's time for you to tell me just what in hell this is really all about."

In the meager light he looked even more forbidding than in the dark. He'd removed his jacket before coming to search for her, and now his shirt was open at the neck and partially pulled free of his janus cord trousers. He looked big and angry and extremely dangerous.

"I . . . I've already explained. Although you have a way of . . . of making me willing, I don't really want . . . this."

His eyes narrowed. "Why not?"

Because that's all you want of me: my body willing and ready for yours. Because you'll only marry me if I accidentally should become with child. But Eliza couldn't bring herself to say that to him. "I already explained. It's wrong."

"That's a bunch of crap and you know it." He advanced on her. "What we have—you and I—is rare. It's like nothing I've known with any woman before. And it's sure as hell you'll never know it with that dandy you're engaged to."

"You don't know that. Besides, Michael has nothing to do with this. You're just trying to cloud the issue."

"Oh?" He stopped just inches from her. "Then what the hell is the issue—besides the fact that we're both horny and we'd both feel a damn sight better if we worked all this energy out in bed."

"Is that all you think about?" she cried. "What goes on in bed?" She tried to step to the side and put some distance between them, but he trapped her with one brawny arm on either side of her. Breathing hard from frustration, she tilted her head back against the smoothly plastered wall and met his hot, hungry gaze. "When are you going to let Aubrey and me go?"

His jaw tensed, once and then again. "Soon. But you'd do better asking me that when I'm in a good mood, Eliza. I thought that was something women knew instinctively. You ask a man for favors *after* you make love to him."

"How could I possibly know that?" she replied though her heart was breaking. "I've no experience with whoring. Until now."

Quick anger brought a scowl to his face. "This does not make you a whore!"

She laughed, a harsh, brittle sound, devoid of any mirth. "I'm consorting with the enemy, aren't I? Trying to buy my young cousin's freedom with my body."

She could tell by the glitter in his eyes that her words had struck their mark, and hurt. He grabbed her chin in his hand. "If that's what you're doing, then I suggest you get on with it."

"Oh!" She swung at him and although the sound of her palm cracking against his face held a certain satisfaction, it obviously destroyed the last of his self-control. With a cry of pure rage he swept her up in his arms and in three quick steps crossed to the bed. Before Eliza could utter a word of protest or scramble away from him, he had her flat on her back, with both gown and wrapper yanked up to her waist.

"I wouldn't want you to feel like a whore, Eliza, so fight me." He pushed her legs apart and thrust up against her. "Fight me," he ordered, biting her neck, when she twisted her face away from him. He caught her hair and pulled her head cruelly around so that his face hovered inches above hers. "Fight me if you're so repulsed by what I'm doing."

She tried. Truly she did. She tried to free her hands from the viselike grip he had on them, but to no avail. She tried to kick him, to buck him off—to clamp her legs back together. But she failed. As if her struggles were of no real consequence, he kept her hands trapped above her head and her legs widespread.

Then he began to touch her. The side of her leg, from her knee, up her thigh to her hip. Further, up her waist and alongside her heaving ribcage. Eliza kept her eyes clenched shut and her face tilted hard to the side as she twisted and turned. She knew her struggles were futile, but she simply could not acquiesce. When he pushed himself a little higher on his elbow, however, and slipped his warm palm up to cup her breasts, she went absolutely still.

"Cyprian—" The words she meant to say died in her throat when she met his burning gaze. His hand moved in a slow, sultry circle, and Eliza fancied that she felt every one of his work-hardened calluses stroke across her puckered nipple.

She gasped, a small, sharp intake of breath, as the most sizzling wash of lethargy stole through her. Lethargy that put to rest all her protests while another feeling that was hot and alive and, oh, so wonderful took over her entire being.

He made that circle again, molding her breast to the curve of his hand, and this time he moved his fingers across the straining tip. One, two, three, four—all his fingers flicked over it, each more arousing than the last. Then his thumb moved back and forth, and she turned her face away once more.

He was doing it. He was making her willing and God help her, she couldn't ignore it. His thumb worked back and forth slowly, teasing the tight peak to new levels of excitement. But he moved it too slow. Too slow.

"Cyprian . . . " She murmured his name again. Was it a curse or a plea? She could not say. But she knew she wanted to cry. From frustration. From a yearning so intense it must surely kill her. From a heart that was breaking.

"Eliza," he whispered against her ear. "Do you like that, sweetheart?" His thumb moved a little faster and to her chagrin, a tiny whimper escaped her lips. She liked it far too much.

He nuzzled past her hair and began to kiss her ear, to nibble on it and run the tip of his tongue along it and even inside it.

Another whimper broke free. She could hear the rush of blood in her veins and her own labored breathing. Then his hand abandoned her breasts and moved down

between their two bodies. He fumbled for a moment—
to open the front of his breeches, she realized when the
heated length of his manhood pressed against her thigh.

She tossed her head restlessly, but he caught her
mouth in a hard kiss that demanded every bit of her
attention. His lips parted hers; his tongue pushed fully
into her mouth, starting a rhythm she recognized at
once.

It was going to happen and she . . . she was glad.
No, more than glad. She felt as if the world would come
to a complete standstill if they could not finish this act
that he'd initiated.

Though he yet restrained her hands, Eliza arched up
into the kiss. She was succumbing to him; he was making her willing, just as he'd threatened from the very
first. But from some wellspring of feminine knowledge
—something come from her very bones, or maybe from
her soul—Eliza knew that even in surrender she could
find her own manner of triumph.

So she kissed him back, mimicking the possessive way
he thrust and withdrew. She met his tongue and they
dueled and danced—and she felt his arousal grow even
harder. Her hands twisted in his relentless grasp until
she could stroke her fingertips across his knuckles.

He was not idle either. His free hand slipped between
their bodies, and after sliding his palm up and down
between her legs, parting the soft curls with his fingers,
he deepened the caress.

The whole world came to an abrupt halt—or else
tilted off its axis. He slipped one finger deep with her,
then out and up, drawing her own moist heat to slide
across the inflamed nub hidden there.

Which was worse—or better—she wondered as sensations too powerful to endure rippled through her body.
When he slid right up inside her, she felt as if she were
melting. When he touched that small spot, she seemed

to erupt. Both sensations were too wonderful, too exquisite . . .

His grip slackened and one of her hands turned so that she clasped it to his. Palm to palm, with fingers entwined, she held onto him. He raised his head, breaking the kiss, and for one long moment of perfect union, their eyes met and clung.

"Eliza—" He broke off as if he did not know what to say. Then he shifted, just a little, and she felt the hot, probing tip of his manhood against her. In the golden candlelight they poised that way, their bodies ready to join, their eyes already having done so. But he did not move; he just devoured her with his hot blue gaze.

Not until she arched, drawing him closer, did he finally begin the excruciating pattern he'd taught her before. Thrust and withdraw. Enter and retreat. It was as if he'd been waiting for her permission—or more likely the final sign of her capitulation, she thought, as the remnant threads of their battle lingered.

But the rising passion between them pushed the last of their earlier struggle into the background. They fought a new battle now. Together. On the same side. Their bodies strained together, a harmonious rhythm, hot and damp and ever faster. Their hands held tight, both of his clutching hers now, palm to palm. Soul to soul, she preferred to believe.

And for that moment she did believe it. As the apex neared, as they rushed faster and higher, until she had no choice but to leap out into the unearthly void with him, she knew their souls had connected in a way that could never happen with anyone but him. Love, desire, happiness, and the search for forever all came together in that blinding burst of passion. He thrust over and over and over, filling her with the finest gift a woman could ever hope to have from the man she loved.

The man she loved.

In that instant Eliza knew she loved him, and that she

wanted a child from him—no matter the cost to her life in the years to come. And there would be a cost, she knew. She would have to trade her old life away for one that was scary and unpredictable.

Finally Eliza understood Cyprian's mother and why she'd had no regrets. When you loved a man there could never be regrets.

Chapter Nineteen

*H*e stayed with her all night. And in between brief, entangled naps, he made love to her again and again. It was as if he were proving his rights to her, his possession of her. But Eliza did not mind. Every time he touched her, every time his lips or fingers or tongue explored some new and highly sensitive portion of her body, she felt as if she too were possessing him. For his violent anger of before had dissipated into an exquisite tenderness. She'd done that. She comprehended little enough else about him, but she knew that everything between them had changed the moment she'd begun to stroke his hand.

She sighed now and rolled over, fitting her back against Cyprian's strong, warm body, but keeping her eyes closed against the early morning light. With an echoing sigh he turned too and pulled her close so that her derriere nestled against his groin. When he flexed the hot length of his manhood ever so slightly, she let out a sleepy chuckle.

"Are you laughing at me?" he growled, a husky morning caress against the back of her neck.

In lieu of an answer she wiggled her backside against him, and when he responded with an involuntary thrust against her, she giggled again.

Before she knew what he was up to, he'd rolled her onto her back and lay over her, propped up on his elbows. It was a position she'd learned to love.

Smiling, she slowly opened her eyes and met his devouring gaze. "Don't you ever get tired?" She ran her hands along his side and then around to the lean muscles that rippled down his back.

"You're killing me," he admitted with a wonderfully wicked grin. "But I can't do anything about it. My life is in your hands." Then the banked fire in his vivid blue eyes leaped to flame. "What would you do with me if I put myself entirely in your hands? And what would you have me do to you, Eliza?"

At once the most erotic visions crept into her mind. Them together upon the fore deck of the *Chameleon*, near the figurehead of the woman and the serpent. Them naked and lying upon a nest of fallen sails and riggings. The two of them tangled in the ropes. Him tangled; her tangled.

Embarrassed color stained her throat and cheeks, and she averted her eyes. How could she even imagine such a thing? She could not meet the intensity of his eyes. Then, as she stared elsewhere—anywhere—it gradually dawned on her that they were in his grand bedchamber. In *his* huge bed.

As if a chill wind had suddenly blown over her, a shiver ran up her back.

"Well?" he persisted. He smoothed an errant curl back from her cheek, then wound it around his finger and gently tugged. "What would you ask of me, my sweet mermaid?"

She turned her head, but there was no teasing in her tone now, and the color had drained from her face. "How did we get here in your bedchamber?"

His expression stayed determinedly pleasant. "I brought you."

"When?"

His knuckles slid up and down along her jawline. "I think it was after you made love to me that last time." He smiled down at her. "Does it really matter when?" His head lowered, as if he meant to kiss her, but she turned her face away.

"It matters to me." She pushed at him, then scrambled out of the bed when he let out an exasperated breath and obligingly rolled away. When she realized she was naked, however, and that none of her clothes were in the room, she began to panic. She grabbed at the first thing she saw—his jacket—and though she would have preferred anything else, she donned it as fast as she could. Then, wrapping the loose lapels across her chest, she faced him.

He lay on his back, propped up on the pillows. But he wasn't looking at her. Instead, he faced the ceiling with one arm flung across his eyes. Was he so disinterested in her feelings as all that? Eliza's fury magnified with this new hurt.

"You knew how I felt about this."

"But there's no need—"

"I didn't want Aubrey to see us—" She broke off, angry and humiliated.

"For Christ's sake, Eliza. The boy's going to see a whole lot worse than the two of us before he grows up."

But that callous remark only raised her ire to a new pitch. His words might be true in the larger sense, but Aubrey was still a child and he was her responsibility.

"No matter my reasons, you knew I didn't want to share this room with you," she accused him once more.

He let out a sigh. "I thought last night might have changed your mind."

"Oh really? Now who's behaving like a . . . like a . . . a whore?" she sputtered. When he moved his arm and glared at her she glared right back. "Isn't that what whores do, use their bodies to get for themselves what they can't get any other way?"

"Damnit, this is hardly the same thing, and you know it!" He flung the sheet back and stood up, as naked as a man could be—and more beautiful than he should be, she noticed, though unwillingly. "You're too damned obsessed with whores. First you're one, then I am. Son of a bitch, why can't you just see things the way they really are? We both wanted what happened last night. And we'll both want it again tonight!"

She stared at him a long, awful moment. There was a certain truth to what he said, but that was not the point. She steeled herself. "I wonder if your father used that same argument with your mother."

She knew at once that she'd struck a nerve, for his face darkened in fury. "Leave them the hell out of this." He bit the words out.

"But it's true, isn't it?"

He let out a vile oath, but Eliza could not rejoice in her little victory. A wave of utter sorrow struck her then, and she felt suddenly exhausted. This was all so hopeless.

She lifted a hand toward him, then let it fall to her side. "I won't share this chamber with you, Cyprian. I won't. And nothing you do or say is going to change that—"

"Do you want me to marry you?" he snapped. "Is that it?"

When she only stared at him, struck speechless by his unexpected words, he went on. "If I marry you, will you share this bedroom with me then? Because I warn you, woman, I don't hold with the custom of separate suites for a husband and wife."

If she were married to him she'd never want to sleep anywhere but in his arms. But . . . but what about love? What about all the other emotions that a marrying couple should share? She'd had a half-hearted betrothal once before. Though Cyprian's reasons for making this frustrated offer of marriage were nothing like Michael's, they were just as disappointing. Even more so. She loved Cyprian, she admitted with a sinking heart. But he only desired her.

"I . . . I'm not sure that marriage is a very good idea," she muttered, tightening her arms across her chest. Then she turned and fled toward the door. Her heart was shattering and she needed desperately to be alone.

But Cyprian was too fast. He caught her and wheeled her around to face him. "You don't think it's a good idea?" he repeated. "Why?"

Eliza lifted her chin and pressed her lips together, trying hard to stop their trembling. Why couldn't he ask her to marry him as if he really wanted her to? Outside a bird called in high-pitched tones. But in the stone-walled house all was silence.

"My . . . my father would never allow it."

"To hell with your father. This is between you and me."

Because you don't love me! she wanted to cry. But instead she said the only thing she could think of. "We have nothing in common."

His dark brows arched. "We have sex," he drawled out sarcastically. His hand jerked his jacket down on one side, baring her shoulder and the upper swell of one breast to his eyes. "We have hot, steamy sex."

"That's not enough!" she cried.

"Hell's bells!" He shoved her away from him. "I must have been crazy to think a spoiled little girl like you—" He broke off and turned, then snatched up his breeches and pulled them on, one angry jerk at a time. When they were on he fixed her with a piercing glare. "You'll make the perfect wife for this fiancé of yours. You'll wear the right clothes, know the right people, give the right sort of parties. And in between times, while he makes his long-winded speeches in the House of Lords, you and your latest lover can fuck each other's brains out."

She winced, not at the profanity, but at the gruesome picture he painted of society life. "No, I would never—"

"Oh, yes, you will. The first time you catch your esteemed Michael with his pants down in one of your friend's beds, you'll do it, all right."

"Not everyone is like that!" she cried. "Just because your father—"

"My father." He let out a chilling laugh and shook his head. "My father is the perfect example. He's living proof that everything I've said is true. Even you can't deny that."

"He's just one man."

"One man who happens to be your uncle."

"My uncle—" Eliza stared at Cyprian as she struggled to comprehend what he implied. *My uncle?*

Slowly she became aware that her heart was pounding faster than it should. Her mouth had gone dry and she licked her lips to moisten them. Cyprian turned away and reached for his shirt, as if he wished all at once that he hadn't revealed that. But he had, and now, as Eliza watched him gather up his boots, she felt a growing horror. Cyprian was Uncle Lloyd's son? But if that were true, then that made Aubrey his . . . his half brother!

"But, I don't understand. You've . . . you've stolen your own brother?"

He raised his head and stared at her with a face wiped clean of any emotion. Neither anger, nor pain, nor even lust showed in his night-blue eyes and carefully controlled features. "My half brother. I suppose that makes us cousins."

"Only by marriage," she answered automatically. "But Aubrey—"

"He's my half brother and I'll do a damned sight better job raising him than Haberton ever will."

"But he's a Haberton too. And so are you," she added, still stunned by his news.

His eyes narrowed. "I'll never be a Haberton," he swore.

"But you *are.*" She moved toward him as it all began to make sense. But he stopped her with his next words.

"Would that make me acceptable in your eyes, Eliza? If I carried the Haberton name and held the same place in your precious society that Aubrey is supposed to inherit, you'd jump at the chance to marry me, wouldn't you?"

"That has nothing to do with anything," she began, but he cut her off with a cynical snort.

"Doesn't it?" His eyes raked her with insulting thoroughness, making her uncomfortably aware of her near naked state. She clutched his coat all the tighter about her and tried to gather her scattered wits.

"Cyprian, you have to let Aubrey go," she said, trying to refocus on the main issue again.

"No."

"But what's the point of this now?"

"The point, my dear Eliza, has not changed in the least. Your uncle—my bastard father—has lost his most prized possession. His one male heir."

Eliza didn't quite believe that, however. She pinned him with her eyes. "But things have changed, haven't they? You never expected to like Aubrey, did you? You told me once that you would make Aubrey into the same sort of monster that Haberton made of you. But you can't do that anymore, can you? You can't torture your half brother." She gave him a bitter smile. "You're not quite the monster you make yourself out to be, Cyprian Dare."

She saw the hesitation in his dark eyes—or she thought she did. He bent down to put on his boots before she could be sure. When he straightened again, however, he was the commanding captain of the rogue ship, *Chameleon,* self-assured and devoid of any emotion save for vengeance.

"Would you like me to prove to you again what I'm really like, Eliza? Would you like me to throw you down on that bed, and take you against your will?"

She swallowed hard. "It . . . it was never against my will," she whispered, praying she could break his icy control with that soul-baring admission.

But he only gave her a cold smile, edged with bitter triumph. "I told you from the beginning that I like my women willing. If they're not willing, then I make them willing."

His words were like an arrow to her heart. Was that what he'd done with her? Was that all it was? Eliza was too confused to be sure. He'd asked her to marry him—but maybe that was only to put an end to her objections about sharing his bedchamber.

Terrified by how he might answer, she nonetheless had to ask. "What . . . what were your true intentions toward me?"

There was a long awful silence, and she thought he did not mean to answer. She shivered as gooseflesh prickled her arms and her exposed legs. Gone was the warm, exciting lover of the night just past. In his stead towered the man who'd stolen her and Aubrey from their beds. Vengeful. Frightening. Yet still, she knew she loved him.

Finally he spoke, no hint of emotion in his voice. "At first I thought you were a nuisance. Then I decided you'd be a useful messenger." His eyes moved over her but in a cool sort of appraisal that seemed to measure her value as some commodity. She shivered again. "In the end I decided you'd make an entertaining diversion. Life at sea tends to get boring," he added as a final thrust to her heart.

Eliza's sob caught in her throat. She wouldn't let him

hear it. She couldn't! But it burned so cruelly for release that she feared she'd suffocate.

A diversion. That's what she'd been to him. A diversion.

Trying her best to control her trembling, she lifted her chin and gave him her coldest, most seething glare. "Well, then, I suppose that's just as well, for that's exactly what I considered you." Then her voice broke and she was unable to maintain that facade any longer. With an anguished cry she turned and fled.

She shouldn't cry over him, not such a despicable, heartless unfeeling wretch as Cyprian Dare. But Eliza did cry. She couldn't seem to stop. Every hurt—every hope dashed, every tender look and fiery caress—came back to her as a new and painful betrayal until she was overwhelmed with such a crushing sorrow that she could do nothing but cry.

She fled down the hall, then blindly descended a narrow stairway, not able to stay even one of her tears. At the base of the stairs she shoved at a door, then finding herself outside, ran down a pebbled path. She was in a garden still abloom, though winter was supposed to be upon them. But this was the Isle of Alderney and none of the rules of real life applied here, she realized when she slowed her headlong pace. She sank to her knees in a bed of lacy ferns and covered her wet face with her hands. Her whole body shook with the force of her sobs. Here it was still springtime. Here proper young women forgot a lifetime of propriety and turned into wantons. Here men proposed marriage in one breath, then broke hearts in the next.

In her misery she huddled in a ball, crying as she'd never cried in her entire life. But then, what had she ever had to cry for? Her life had been so lovely, so pleasant and easy. Now . . . now she hurt so badly she thought she might die from the pain.

Her hair clung in snarls to her wet cheeks. It tangled about her face and arms and caught in the buttons of Cyprian's coat. At once a new wave of misery engulfed her. She still wore his coat—and nothing else. His scent clung to it. Spicy. Salty. She fancied that the heat of his body still permeated the fine merino fabric.

She raised her head and ruthlessly scrubbed the tears from her eyes. She sat in a bed of yarrow, she realized. In the kitchen garden. The house was behind her, and beyond a low stone wall, a hill lifted, spotted with jagged gray boulders and still green heather.

Where was she to go? she fretted as she pulled her knees beneath herself and shakily pushed to a stand. She could not go back there. Not to his home. Not after what had passed between them. But she could go no-where else either, not with only his coat to cover her nakedness.

It was Ana who came to Eliza's rescue. As if she'd been watching for Eliza, Ana appeared at the garden gate, and upon spying her, hurried to her side.

"I . . . I've quite ruined the . . . the yarrow," Eliza choked out, wiping once more at her tear-stained face.

"It will recover," Ana replied, her olive-skinned face serene and understanding. "You will recover as well," she added. She moved a wet strand of hair back from Eliza's cheek, then smiled reassuringly. "Come, I will take you to my home and we will talk there."

"But I—my clothes—"

"I will tend to that," she said, turning Eliza and steer-ing her toward the garden gate. "I'll tend to everything."

How Eliza clung to Ana's words. She'd been so confi-dent, so cocky, when she'd suggested this journey to Madeira. And look what it had come to. She was ruined —her reputation destroyed and her heart shattered. And Aubrey—kidnapped by a man who claimed to be his half brother.

She followed Ana woodenly, holding Cyprian's coat

tight around herself, and excruciatingly aware of her bare legs. But as her feet hurried along the narrow stone walk to Ana's home, her mind turned around and around that one shocking fact. Cyprian was Uncle Lloyd's natural son. Though never acknowledged— though he'd been utterly abandoned, it seemed—he was Sir Lloyd Haberton's firstborn son.

No wonder he hated Aubrey and everyone else who'd lived the privileged life he'd been denied. No wonder he'd used her so shamelessly.

Yet he had offered marriage, albeit not in a very loverlike fashion. Then again, maybe he hadn't meant it. Maybe he'd thought only to put an end to her objections with that wretched proposal of his. Oh, but she could make no sense of any of it at all.

"Come in and sit down," Ana ordered when they reached a charming little cottage. Red roses clambered up a trellis arching over the front door. Inside the wood plank floor gleamed and the scent of lemon oil and fresh bread pervaded.

Like a wooden puppet, Eliza followed each of Ana's commands. When the exotic woman pushed her into a chair, she sat. When Ana tucked a woven blanket around her legs, Eliza shifted as necessary. When she pressed a hot cup of tea into Eliza's hands, she drank, though without any real enthusiasm. Only when Ana began to question her did she balk.

"I can't talk about it. Please, don't make me," she implored.

But for all Ana's tender ministrations, in this the woman refused to be gentle. "If you cannot tell *me* your troubles, Eliza, who can you tell? I am your ally, the only woman in this domain of hardheaded men. If we are to prevail, we must help one another."

"What do you mean, prevail?" Eliza asked, as confused by Ana's attitude as by everything else.

"Prevail? I mean, get our way. What *we* want." She

shrugged and smiled. "We must teach these men that what we want will make them far happier than what they think *they* want."

Eliza shook her head. "I don't think you understand about Cyprian."

"Oh, but I do."

"No, it's too complicated—and too hopeless. You see, Aubrey . . . Aubrey is his brother," she revealed, still finding it hard to believe.

"His half brother," Ana corrected her. "Xavier told me." She stared at Eliza with her dark, almond-shaped eyes. "Does it bother you that Cyprian is a bastard?"

Eliza lowered her cup. "No. No," she repeated.

"Well then, does it bother you that he has no title, that he earns his way in this world through his own hard work and ingenuity?"

"No, of course not," Eliza snapped. "That has nothing to do with anything." She sat the cup on a side table and stood up. "You just don't understand!"

"Are you in love with him?"

Eliza's chin began to quiver and she had to clench her teeth to make it stop. "That has nothing to do with anything either. He doesn't love me and he never will. Oh, but I must get away from this place." Then to her enormous chagrin, she began to cry once more.

Ana pressed Eliza back into the chair. But her expression was not in the least perturbed. In fact, she was smiling. "Well, that is good to know, though I expected as much. Now you just drink your tea. I'll get clothes for you so you can dress and comb your hair. Xavier will be back soon to eat. If you truly want to leave this place, he'll find you passage home. And if you truly love Cyprian," she paused and her smile broadened ever so slightly. "Well, if you truly love Cyprian, maybe Xavier will send you home anyway."

Eliza shook her head. "But I don't understand—"

Ana tilted her head and gave Eliza a wise look.

"Sometimes love needs a little help. That's what friends are there for—to help."

"You can't help with this," Eliza replied morosely.

But the woman only smiled. "We shall see. We shall soon see."

Chapter Twenty

*W*ith Ana pushing, things happened so fast that Eliza's head seemed to spin. She donned a simple gown of gray and white striped linen and at Ana's command used a brush and comb to work out the tangles in her hair. Meanwhile Ana continued her work as if nothing at all out of the ordinary was happening. She added onions and peppers to a pot of veal stew simmering on the hearth. By the time Eliza was reasonably presentable, the stew smelled delicious, the kitchen table was set for five, and bread, butter, ale, and fresh milk were set out as part of the meal.

Ana gave her a critical glance. "Wash your face." Then she smiled. "Things will work out, Eliza. I feel it here." She touched her chest with one hand.

Eliza forced a smile for Ana's sake, but she could not share her confidence. When a footstep sounded on the walk, she stiffened. But when Xavier entered, she wasn't sure whether relief or disappointment was the stronger of her emotions.

"Eliza. I hadn't thought to find you here—" He broke off and peered at her more closely. Then he glanced questioningly at Ana.

"A lovers' quarrel," she answered his unspoken words.

"That's not true," Eliza countered. "We're not—that is—this . . . this is not just a quarrel," she finished lamely.

Xavier raised his ebony brows and looked from Ana to Eliza and back to his wife.

"Cyprian told her about his relationship with Aubrey, and now she means to leave Alderney," Ana explained. "Can you arrange for her to leave?"

"Ah." Xavier nodded in understanding, but then he frowned and moved to stand directly before Eliza. "Still, you cannot leave, Eliza. Cyprian would be very angry—"

"I hate him," she swore, and at the moment she almost did. Almost. But she ignored that fact. "I cannot stay here a minute longer. I will not!"

"I think Oliver should take her back to London," Ana remarked.

"Oliver? Oliver!" Xavier sputtered. "Cyprian would kill the boy if he were to take—" He broke off and he and his wife shared a long look. Then he smiled. "Oliver," he repeated in a most considering tone. "She *would* be safe in his care."

"I thought so."

"I don't want to get Oliver in trouble with Cyprian," Eliza said.

Xavier shrugged and moved to the table. "Ollie's always in trouble with Cyprian. But he always forgives him."

"Do you really think he'll help me?"

"He and Aubrey are coming in now," Ana said. "You can ask him yourself."

When Oliver and Aubrey came in, all smiles and towering good humor, Eliza couldn't help staring at her young cousin. The similarities between him and Cyprian were there, she realized. The same black curling hair, and they both had blue eyes, though Cyprian's were darker. And Cyprian was tall like her Uncle Lloyd, just as Aubrey probably would be.

But she wasn't going to tell Aubrey, she decided on the instant. That news must come from either Cyprian or Uncle Lloyd. It was not her place to reveal such awkward news to the boy. She turned instead to the subject of her departure.

To her surprise, however, Oliver was not nearly so eager to help her as she would have thought.

"I don't think you should flee Cyprian on account of one disagreement," he advised her as they all sat down to eat. "If Ana had done that to Xavier, where would they be right now?"

Xavier nodded and Ana smiled her serene smile, but that only made Eliza more adamant. "This is not the same thing. I . . . I have a fiancé waiting for me," she explained after searching her mind for some pressing excuse for leaving. Not that there weren't any number of good reasons. Her parents. Her brothers. In truth, Michael had nothing at all to do with her need to flee. Especially now. There was also Aubrey's family to consider. She leaned forward with an earnest expression on her face.

"Aubrey and I must escape, Oliver. We cannot stay—"

"You said nothing about Aubrey," Xavier interrupted.

"Well, I just assumed—"

"I'll help *you* leave, but Aubrey must stay," Oliver stated. Xavier and Ana both nodded their agreement.

"It's all right, Eliza. I'll be fine," Aubrey piped up. "I like it here. Only I hope Oliver won't be gone too very long."

"But Aubrey *must* come," Eliza cried. "You must," she repeated to him as she took his two arms in her hands and bent down to stare into his young face. "You're the one who was kidnapped. You're the one who must escape."

But neither Oliver or Xavier, nor even Ana would

agree to helping Aubrey flee. In the end she had no choice but to accept their terms, though she was infuriated by their obstinance. Weather permitting, they would set sail in Xavier's single-masted sailboat at the turn of the tide, the men decided. Oliver could easily manage the sturdy vessel alone, and within a day and a half they should make land at Portsmouth. While Ana assembled food and clothes and other gear, Xavier and Oliver plotted their course. Eliza was so stunned by the swift progression of events that she could only sit silently amid the hubbub around her.

When Aubrey approached her, limping only a very little, she took both his hands in hers. "Aubrey, I can't bear to leave you here. There must be a way to smuggle you onto Xavier's boat."

But the ten-year-old only shook his head and shrugged. "You needn't worry, Eliza, for I'll be just fine. Truly. Only you must send Oliver directly back, all right?"

"Once I am returned to London I'll tell them all where you are," she said. "Your father will come for you right away. I know he will."

"Well, don't tell him or mother that I can walk now. I want to surprise them." He gave her an impish grin.

"But they will want to know how you are faring."

"Just tell them that I'm having a jolly good time. You see," he added matter of factly, "if I walk up to them on my own, I'm thinking that my father will be so surprised and pleased that he'll forget all about being angry at Cyprian."

At the mention of Cyprian's name, Eliza blinked and looked away. "Yes, well, perhaps that's a good idea," she murmured. But though Uncle Lloyd might eventually forgive Cyprian Dare, she didn't think she'd ever be able to.

To cover the sudden rush of embarrassing tears, she drew Aubrey into her arms and gave him a tight hug.

"Everything will turn out all right in the end," she whispered. At least for him, she silently added.

"Not so tight," he complained, but good-naturedly. "Oh, and Eliza, be sure to tell Father to give Oliver a big reward, all right? A very big reward."

Cyprian watched them cast off from a hill above the house. He could make out the several figures on the shore, especially the two that boarded Xavier's sailboat. Oliver was taking her back—and he was letting it happen.

He shrugged and turned away from the distant scene, but despite his every attempt to feel indifferent to what was happening, he could not. With a sudden curse he spun on his heel, snatched up a jagged bit of rock, and flung it with all his strength at them. At Eliza.

She could have stayed. They could have sorted things out. But she was fleeing from him the very first chance she had.

Well, damn her to hell. Damn her and his father and all of them.

Damn them all to bloody hell.

They set sail in the late afternoon. Xavier, Ana, and Aubrey saw them off, but there was no sign of Cyprian. That was good, though. Truly, it was. For even if he did not order her to stay, he would most certainly take odds with one of his men taking her back to London.

Even knowing that, however, Eliza could hardly bear the knowledge that she would never see him again. She sat in the cockpit of the little sailboat, gripping the rail with both hands and staring back at Alderney's rocky shore as it slowly receded into the sea.

In the long hours on the vessel Oliver taught her how to sail, though little enough of it sank in. She was too mired in her bleak thoughts. He explained about the wind and tacking, about the sails and the rudder. But

not once did they speak about what it was that had sent
her fleeing. Nor did Oliver flirt with her in other than
the most mild of fashions, the way he did with Ana, she
realized. Somewhere along the way he'd acceded to
Cyprian's claim on her. Had she not been relieved that
she didn't have to fend him off, she would have been
even more depressed. Xavier, Ana, and now Oliver.
They all paired her with Cyprian, even though they
should know better than anyone why it was an impossible match.

And it was impossible, she told herself. Even if he'd
been the least bit honest in his feelings toward her—
even if he'd gone so far as to fall in love with her—it
would never have worked. They were too different, too
vastly different. She'd tried to convince herself that was
an advantage, but she knew now it was not. How many
fellows had her parents dismissed as potential suitors
for her who were far more suitable for her than Cyprian
could ever hope to be?

Then there was the cold hard fact that Cyprian did
not love her. That he'd only enjoyed her company for a
few hours. That he'd used her.

As the dark sea swelled up beneath the little boat and
the wind pushed them ever nearer her home, she rued
the day she'd ever set off for Madeira. She should have
been content with the future planned for her. Now . . .
now who knew what her future held?

They sailed through the night, all the next day under
a dreary gray sky, and into the next night. Dawn was
approaching when the lights of a small town guided
them toward shore. Though Eliza was alarmed at the
idea of docking while it was still dark, Oliver was obviously well-acquainted with this particular harbor. When
he handed her ashore, she swayed a little, disoriented
and exhausted.

"There's a posting house up the hill. We can take a
room and then catch a coach to London as soon as we

can," Oliver said, hoisting their meager bags in one hand and supporting her elbow with the other. "Can you make it?"

She could and she did, but barely. She fell asleep half-clothed in the room he eventually guided her to, and when his knock sounded later in the day, it was all she could do to rouse herself from the stupor of sleep.

The remainder of the day passed in the same sort of thickness. Eliza did as Oliver told her, including boarding a coach, but she felt as if she were sleepwalking. The next day was better. Perhaps it was the bitter cold that wiped away the cobwebs from her mind. Whatever, by the time the laboring team of horses made their way into London, she was alert, albeit tired and sore from the long ride.

Diamond Hall was lit as if for a ball and a manservant stood sentinel on the front steps, lantern in hand. He was waiting for her, Eliza realized, for Oliver had sent word ahead that they were coming. Before the coach ceased its swaying, her entire family tumbled forth through the pair of mahogany and brass front doors.

Had she ever been so happy to see them? Eliza did not think so. Despite the pervasive weariness that had gripped her the past three days, she fell into the bosom of her family, laughing, weeping, and holding each of them as if she would never let them go.

"Oh, my darling," her mother cried against her neck. "Oh, my dearest little girl."

"We've been waiting forever!"

"What an adventure you've had!" Perry exclaimed. "You must tell us every little detail."

Then her father swept her into his arms. "Eliza," he whispered, squeezing her so tight she feared her ribs might crack. "Eliza."

When she finally surfaced, the Thoroughgood brood was herded by the beaming butler, Tonkins, into the foyer. It was then that she spied Aubrey's parents.

Aunt Judith was as pale as death. Her eyes were huge and she'd lost enough weight that her dress hung loose on her. Uncle Lloyd too was thinner and somehow shrunken. In his blue eyes there showed a fear that she'd never seen before. A fear for his absent child. At once she broke away from her parents' embrace and made her way to her grieving aunt and uncle.

"He is fine," she said in the quick hush that fell. "Truly he is. Healthy, happy—"

"Happy? How can he be happy—" Lloyd Haberton broke off when his wife turned weeping into his arms. Eliza berated herself for her poor choice of words. As she cast about for a better explanation, she caught Oliver's eye. He'd sidled into the house with the rest of the crush, but up to now he'd been ignored. Now, seeing the desperation in Eliza's eyes, he came to her rescue.

"Aubrey's quite well," he announced above Aunt Judith's muffled weeping. All eyes turned at once to him.

"This is Oliver Spencer," Eliza explained. "He's the one who delivered me from . . . " She trailed off, uncertain how to term Cyprian. Her captor. Her lover.

"From that Cyprian Dare," Uncle Lloyd supplied the name in a stinging, contemptuous tone.

Eliza nodded but her uncle was staring at Oliver. "Why couldn't you have delivered Aubrey as well?"

Oliver raised his brows and Eliza feared for a moment that he would make some flippant reply, or else reveal something he shouldn't. Such as the fact that Aubrey could walk now, and that he was having a glorious adventure.

But Oliver must have recognized the caution in her eyes, for he cleared his throat and addressed the older man respectfully. "It was impossible, sir. We had to sail the channel in a tiny boat. And I thought we would capsize a dozen times," he added.

"Oliver is a most talented sailor," Eliza put in before the young man could elaborate any further.

"You're sure Aubrey is not being mistreated?" Aunt Judith asked. The misery and hopefulness on her face made Eliza's heart ache. How happy she would be to hear Aubrey was walking again. But the boy had exacted a solemn vow from her to allow him that privilege. And besides, it might aid Cyprian's situation with his father when Aubrey was finally returned home.

"Your son is tan and fit, and he exercises his foot daily," Oliver said, smiling reassuringly at Aubrey's mother.

"Does he get enough to eat?"

"All he needs. He's not mistreated at all," he repeated. "In fact he's quite a pet with the entire crew."

"Then why—" She broke off again, stifling her sobs with a crumpled lace handkerchief.

"Yes, why?" Lloyd demanded, his anger at Cyprian focused on Oliver instead. "Why in the name of God would anyone use a child—a *crippled* child—to hurt someone who doesn't even know him?"

"I can explain that. But first," Eliza said, "I would like to sit down. And could we have tea, Mother?"

By the time they settled in the front parlor, their numbers were thinned to her parents, her aunt and uncle, LeClere, Perry, Oliver, and herself. But even that made for too many, she realized. "I need to speak to Uncle Lloyd. Alone," she added, staring only at him.

"But why?" He glanced at his ashen-faced wife, then closed his mouth on the rest of his words. "May we use your study, Gerald?"

Once alone in her father's study with her uncle—Cyprian's negligent father—Eliza had an attack of the jitters. She didn't know quite how to begin.

"Has he . . . has he done something hideous to my boy?" the man asked in a voice that unaccountably trembled.

Eliza frowned. "Something hideous? No. No, I told you, Aubrey is unharmed."

"Then what?" he exploded, pacing back and forth and tugging at the thick facial hair that ran along his jawline. "What is it you cannot say in front of the rest of them? In front of his mother?"

"He's your son!" Eliza shouted back at him. She was no longer sorry for her uncle but instead furious. It was clear he loved Aubrey, but what about his firstborn son? What about Cyprian?

"Of course he's my son! He's my son and crippled or not, I'll kill to have him back. I'll kill that bastard who took him!"

Eliza shook her head. "No, Uncle Lloyd. You don't understand. I didn't mean Aubrey. I mean Cyprian. Cyprian Dare is your son. And as you so eloquently put it," she added, a sarcastic edge in her voice, "he may indeed be a bastard. But he's *your* bastard."

"What? What do you mean?" he sputtered. Then his eyes grew large and his face drained of all color. "What . . . what exactly do you mean?" he finished in a whisper.

"I mean that he is your son, your firstborn son," she revealed, filled unaccountably with righteous fervor for Cyprian's situation.

He sat down on the oxblood leather settee and stared disbelievingly at her. "But . . . but how could that be? Who—no." He stood up scowling. "No. No, I don't believe it."

"Well, I do," she said, angry that he could deny it. "He looks like you. And Aubrey looks like him," she added for good measure.

"But how could that be?" he repeated, still fighting the truth.

"It probably occurred in the usual fashion that bastard children are made."

At her tart reply, he focused back on her. "You

should not speak of such things. It's unseemly." When she only glared at him, he hesitated. "Well, it is," he finished weakly.

"I don't think you have the right to criticize anything about my behavior, Uncle Lloyd."

He ran a hand through his wiry gray hair and stared distractedly about. She'd stunned him, it was plain, and Eliza felt the first meager glimmer of sympathy for him. "Didn't you know you had another son?"

"No. No, of course not. Another son? But with whom?"

Her sympathy fled. "With whom? Was she so forgettable, then? Or were there so many women that you cannot recall them all?" She began to pace, anything to vent the quick anger—and quick fear—that welled up inside of her. Years from now would she be only some forgotten woman in Cyprian's past? She didn't want to believe it, but faced with her uncle's attitude, it was impossible to ignore. She wrapped her arms around her waist and focused all her fury and terror on her uncle. "Is it possible there could be even more Haberton bastards out there?"

He seemed to shrink even more, for his head sunk low between his shoulders and he clasped his hands between his knees. "No one has ever told me that I . . . that she . . . " He looked up at her, the perfect picture of misery, and she was reminded of Aubrey before he'd relearned to walk, when he was unhappy and frustrated and knew he'd behaved shamefully. Sighing, she crossed the room and knelt before him on the plush carpeting.

"Cyprian is angry with you. He feels . . . he feels that you abandoned him and his mother."

"No." He shook his head. "No, I did not. I would not . . . "

"Do you know who his mother was?"

He did. She could see it in his eyes. But he didn't want to admit it could be true. "This man, he could be lying. Does he have any proof? Did you speak to his mother?"

"She's dead."

"What? Cybil is dead?"

Cybil. Somehow having a name made the woman even more real to Eliza. "He said she was a vicar's daughter. Oh, Uncle Lloyd. How could you have ruined a vicar's daughter?"

"I didn't know! I was . . . I was young—not even twenty yet—and very stupid. I . . . I was on holiday and . . . and I fancied myself in love with her."

How Eliza's heart ached to hear his painful confession. Cybil, Cyprian, and now her uncle Lloyd, all of them tortured and ruined by passions run amuck. And she was in no better straits. She might already bear Cyprian's child. Would her family abandon her if she did? Would Cyprian never try to learn the truth? Would her child grow up to despise his own father?

Oh, God, but she could not bear for history to repeat itself so horribly.

"I didn't know she bore the child," her uncle said, gripping her shoulders. "She said she knew a woman in a nearby village who . . . who helped girls in trouble. I gave her the money. . . . " He trailed off at her confused expression. "Oh, it doesn't matter. Not now. But tell me, Eliza." His hands tightened painfully. "Will he —this man, my . . . my bastard—will he hurt Aubrey? Will he return my son unharmed to me?"

Eliza shook off her uncle's hold and rose to her feet. To hear her uncle refer to Cyprian as his bastard in the same breath that he called Aubrey his son struck her as somehow distasteful. "They are both your sons. Cyprian should not be blamed for the circumstances of his birth. That is clearly *your* fault. And as for what he plans for Aubrey . . . " She paused and sighed. "I only know that he will not hurt him."

"But I want him back!"

Eliza glared at him, and in that moment she was almost glad that Aubrey was with Cyprian. Lloyd Haberton did not deserve his son—he didn't deserve *either* of them.

"Cyprian plans to raise Aubrey as he was raised, to be a survivor amid adverse conditions. To be strong. To be a fighter."

"But he has no right! And anyway, Aubrey is crippled now."

"You forget that they are brothers," she pointed out, forcing herself not to reveal Aubrey's recovery.

"Does he want a ransom? Is that it?"

"No." She sighed again, suddenly overcome with weariness. She turned for the door, but he caught her before she could leave.

"There must be some way for me to get him back. He must want something, Eliza. Didn't he say anything?"

Eliza shook her head, sad for him now instead of angry. "I'm sorry, Uncle Lloyd, but he didn't say anything about a ransom or any other compensation. I don't know what Cyprian Dare wants. I never have."

Chapter Twenty-One

*E*liza stepped from her bath wrapped in a thick towel, and padded on bare feet through the door to her bedchamber. Her mother stood before the window, staring out at a moonless winter sky. It was cold out there, Eliza knew. But it was warm in her room. And it was no doubt warm on Alderney.

She shook off that thought and forced a small smile when her mother turned.

"Oh, Eliza." Constance Thoroughgood smiled as she'd been smiling all evening, a trembling smile of pure happiness, misted over with just a hint of tears. "You cannot know, my darling, how we have worried."

"Mama." Eliza enfolded her mother in a hug that tightened as her own feelings of love strengthened. How blessed she'd been. She had her parents; she had Perry and LeClere, and all her aunts and uncles. And this home. The list was endless.

But Cyprian—and too many others like him—had not been nearly so blessed. "I love you, Mama," she whispered. "I love you and Papa. More than you can ever know."

Against her cheek she felt her mother's damp smile. "I know, my darling. But you are only at the beginning of your life. You've so much yet to learn about love—

about how strong it can be. For a man. For your child."
She pulled away and stared into Eliza's eyes. "I love you
beyond all understanding. And . . . and I can see that
you've changed," she added in a more hesitant tone.
"Do you wish to talk about it at all?"

Eliza knew at once what she meant. Could it possibly
be that obvious? Still, she pretended not to understand.
She pulled out of her mother's embrace.

"Changed? Well, I suppose that I am," she said, con-
centrating on drying her arms and legs. She donned a
warm, flannel wrapper and slid her feet into a pair of
matching mauve bedroom slippers, then found her
comb. "I'm much healthier now. Did you know I didn't
have any attacks, even though it was all most stressful,
and I was outside most of the time. Dr. Smalley is
bound to be impressed."

"You're thinner."

Eliza glanced over at her mother. "I'm stronger too.
There's no longer a need to keep this chamber for me
on the main floor. Being outdoors so much and on a
sailing vessel—"

"Eliza, you must tell me," her mother broke in with
unaccustomed force. "I am your mother, after all, and
no matter how—no matter how you may have suffered
at this man's hands, we will weather the storm together."

Eliza couldn't help it. At her mother's vow of such
unswerving loyalty and support, she burst into tears.
Why couldn't poor Cybil's mother have been as wonderful as her own? If Cybil's parents had loved their daughter better, so much unhappiness could have been
avoided. If she'd just held her daughter the way Constance Thoroughgood was holding *her* daughter right
now.

"Hush. Oh, hush, my darling. My baby. It will be all
right. You'll see. It will," Constance crooned to the sobbing Eliza. "I'll make everything all right."

Slowly Eliza's sobs eased. Eventually she told her mother everything. About how she'd insisted on accompanying Aubrey when he was kidnapped, and about how she'd fallen in love with Cyprian.

"That's not love," her mother angrily countered. "You're not in love with him. No one falls in love with a man who . . . who rapes her," she choked out.

"No, it wasn't like that." Eliza grasped her mother's hands urgently as they sat side by side on her settee. "It wasn't like that at all. He didn't force me. I wanted—"

"No, daughter. You're wrong. He's older than you and vastly more experienced. He knew precisely what he was doing and he took total advantage of your innocence. He seduced you and though to you it may seem entirely different than rape, it isn't. Not really. If anything it's even worse," she stated, beginning once more to tear up.

"Mama, no. You don't understand."

But Constance was not to be convinced. In the end she smoothed her daughter's tangled hair and managed a weak smile. "Well, I suppose it doesn't really matter how it occurred now, does it? The outcome is still the same." She sighed as if the weight of the world rested on her narrow shoulders. "Your father will have to speak to Michael."

Eliza bowed her head. It was one thing to defend Cyprian to her mother. Michael was a different situation altogether. "I'm glad he wasn't here tonight," she whispered.

"He wanted to be, but your father decided it would be best for me to speak with you first."

"I . . . I suppose you'll go tell Father now."

"You're his daughter; it's his right to know, for he'll have to determine what we're to do now." Constance stroked Eliza's hand, then took it in her grasp and twined their fingers together. "You must tell me, darling. Is there . . . is there any chance that you could be

. . . with child?" She finished the last in a pained whisper.

Eliza shuddered, partly from fear and partly from a longing she could not explain, either to herself or to her mother. "I don't know," she confessed in a mumble.

Constance compressed her lips as if to prevent them from trembling. Then she burst out. "Oh, I hate that man. I hate him!"

"Please, Mother. No. How can I make you understand?" Then she had a ludicrous thought. "You realize, of course, that he's family, don't you? He's my cousin by marriage. And your nephew."

Constance drew back as if struck. "He is nothing to us—"

"No, Mama. Don't say that," Eliza interrupted with much heat in her voice. She lurched up from the settee and pulled her wrapper tighter against a sudden chill. Then she faced her mother. "You may hate him, if you must. But never say he is nothing. Not to me."

Her mother stared at her in shock. "But Eliza—"

"No, just heed my words. For better or worse, I am not the same girl who left here. In the marriage mart I suppose it's for the worse. But in other ways I am changed for the better. So . . . " She swallowed hard. "So tell Father to summon Michael. But also tell him that I will speak to Michael myself. This is, after all, a matter between him and me. No one else."

Constance stood and did as her daughter ordered. She crossed the room and backed out the door. But the entire time she kept her surprised stare focused on her daughter, her strong, tanned daughter, who stood so straight and firm. Eliza had changed, she realized, from a girl into a woman. Her father might not like it, but perhaps, with the grace of God, Michael Johnstone would.

* * *

Gerald Thoroughgood looked nervous. But then, Michael was nervous too. Eliza was back and he'd tossed and turned the whole night, worried about what they'd done to her. Delicate creature that she was, there was no telling how she would be affected. That was, no doubt, why her father had made him stay away yesterday. But they'd sent word late last night for him to call in the morning. Come dawn he'd scarcely been able to wait. But although it was still early now, Gerald was awaiting him in the marbled foyer when the butler showed him in.

"Michael. So good of you to come." Gerald shook his hand then cleared his throat. "Eliza is—"

"Is she all right?" he demanded, searching the older man's face for some sign. Had she been ruined by them? Had she?

"She is . . . ah, well. But she wishes to speak to you herself. So . . . so I'll just show you into the conservatory."

Michael didn't wait for Gerald Thoroughgood to show him the way. He knew well enough where the conservatory was and he hurried there without another word. The mahogany door stood open, but he closed it fully after he entered. At the click of the heavy brass latch, Eliza spun around.

For a moment he hardly recognized her. It was the sun behind her, he rationalized, for it backlit her, outlining her slender figure and leaving her face partially in shadow. But there was something more, he realized. Something he couldn't name. He felt a slow sinking in the vicinity of his chest.

"Michael. Thank you for coming," she said in a voice that she probably meant to sound calm, but which nevertheless revealed a trace of nerves.

"I would have been here last night, but your parents suggested that I wait." *What did those bastards do to you?*

"Yes. Well." She moved away from the tall windows, and meandered restlessly past a tall potted palm. Michael's eyes narrowed. There *was* something different about her; something in her carriage, in the tilt of her head.

"Are you all right?"

She looked up at him with a pained smile. "I am . . . well," she finished after a brief hesitation. "However I thought it only right to offer you the . . . the opportunity to withdraw your offer of marriage to me."

He crossed to stand before her, but at the startled look on her face, he refrained from actually touching her. "Why should I wish to do that?"

But he knew why, and the hot color that flooded her face confirmed it.

He'd kill the man, Michael swore as uncontrollable anger swept over him. He'd kill this Cyprian Dare for what he'd done to her!

But right now he had to deal with Eliza herself. Before she could turn away, he grabbed both of her hands. "I know you must have suffered terribly at the hands of your captors, Eliza, but that means nothing to me. I will stand by my offer of marriage as staunchly now as ever."

She blinked and for a long moment she simply stared at him, clearly stunned. No doubt she'd expected him to acquiesce at once, relieved to be let off the hook. But if he did that now, what would happen to her? His defection was sure to confirm what everyone would already suspect.

"Eliza, none of this matters to me," he repeated. "You've come back safely, just I've prayed you would. There's no reason for wedding plans to be altered."

"But . . . but you don't understand," she whispered. She looked away as her cheeks turned an even more violent hue.

"I do understand," he said as gently as he could. "You

needn't ever speak of it. Whatever happened—whatever that bastard—"

"Don't call him that!" She jerked her hands free of his and spun away from him.

In the sudden silence Michael stared at her, at the long tumble of her dark hair and the yellow ribbon that held those luxurious waves in place. She *had* changed. She was no longer the beautiful but shy girl he'd thought so well suited to him. She was stronger now, with a will of her own. And it sounded as if she were defending the monster who'd ruined her! How could she?

"What do you mean?" When she only stiffened he turned her forcibly to face him. "Why do you care what I call him, Eliza?"

She met his gaze reluctantly, yet even in that he could see the changes in her. It was not shame that shone in her lovely gray eyes, but defensiveness. "Cyprian Dare may be my uncle's bastard son, but I will not have him reviled for it in my presence."

"What? Your uncle's bastard?"

She squared her shoulders. "He is, though my uncle probably would prefer that such knowledge be kept private."

Michael frowned, taken aback by this newest and most shocking disclosure. Young Aubrey Haberton had been kidnapped by his father's bastard son, Aubrey's own half brother. Then he had a thought. "That makes this man your cousin—at least by marriage. Does your uncle plan to acknowledge him? Because if he does, that would save your reputation. Our wedding can occur as planned."

She didn't refute his words, but he could read opposition in her expression and stiff posture. She didn't want to marry him. But why?

"Must I be blunt?" she finally asked, lifting her chin to a pugnacious angle.

"Perhaps you should," he replied, calling her bluff. And it was a bluff, he knew when her eyes darted away from his. She'd expected him to play the gentleman and let her off easily without a full explanation. But he had no intention of doing so. He'd admired her before, for her quiet beauty and unassuming manner. They were a perfect match in temperament, social standing, and fortune. But now he felt a stirring he'd not felt before. Was it simply jealousy, or perhaps disbelief that she could actually turn him down? He didn't care. She had agreed once before to marry him and he would not release her now without a fight.

"Well, Eliza? I'm waiting for some explanation."

With a muffled cry of frustration, Eliza shook her head at Michael. Why was he being so obtuse? Did he want to hear all the details in excruciating description?

"I just . . . can't. That's all."

"Did he rape you?"

Eliza cringed to hear him word it that way, but she also felt guilty for the righteous anger that filled him on her behalf. "No," she mumbled. She turned away and began stripping the foliage from a fern, one narrow leaflet at a time.

"No?" She heard the enormous relief in his voice, and also the confusion. "No? Then . . . then what?"

She didn't want to tell him, and yet it suddenly seemed unfair not to. Summoning her courage, Eliza turned to face him. He was handsome. He was kind. She should be grateful to still have the opportunity to become his wife. But she simply could not do it.

"He . . . he did not rape me. But all the same, I am . . . no longer a virgin."

For one long second he did not comprehend. Then he drew back and his face lost color, and she knew he understood. They stood that way, staring at one another with the weak light of the winter morning slanting through the glass doors, until finally Eliza had to look away. He knew her for what she was now.

Yet with his next words he proved her mistaken. "He seduced you."

"He cannot bear all the blame."

"Oh, but he can. And he will, for I shall kill the bastard!"

Eliza flinched. "I told you not to call him that."

"Why?" he demanded to know. "Why should you care what I call him? It's what he is, after all. A bastard intent on ruining his own family."

"That's unfair!" she shouted, desperate to defend Cyprian against Michael's accusations. "Who's to say how you or I would behave under the same circumstances?"

"I would never kidnap my own brother, nor rape my own cousin!"

"It wasn't rape!" she cried, as tears of frustration stung her eyes. "It wasn't! I wanted it. I wanted *him.*"

At Michael's crushed look, she bowed her head. "God help me, but I love him."

Cyprian Dare supervised the reprovisioning of the *Chameleon* with practiced ease. Water kegs. Salted meats. Wine and rum in kegs. They were traveling light with the hold filled primarily with ballast, for he expected to bring a full load of smuggled goods aboard near Royan, France, for delivery to one of his contacts in Littlehampton. But his main reason for departing his Alderney stronghold was because he could think of nothing else to do.

Haberton would be fast upon him, no doubt. Between Oliver and Eliza, Haberton would soon know precisely where his son was, and Cyprian had no intentions of letting the man off the hook so easily. Yet his cat and mouse game with his bastard father brought him no satisfaction any longer. Aubrey was enjoying himself too much. And Eliza was gone.

He paused in the middle of checking the eyepiece of his sextant and stared vacantly into space. She must be back in the bosom of his family by now. And rejoined with her fiancé. How had he taken this whole situation? Was this Michael of hers a pompous ass? Had he rejected her or had he welcomed her back with open arms?

Cyprian's fingers tightened on the brass navigational instrument. Neither scenario pleased him and if he weren't so furious with himself he would have laughed at his own perversity. She'd fled from him at the first opportunity, yet his anger at her and everyone who'd helped her hadn't lasted even a day. He'd known she was leaving; he'd driven her away.

Yet the thought of her wed to this Michael Johnstone was enough to drive Cyprian mad. He wanted her back, even though he knew it was impossible.

"When do we sail, Captain?"

Cyprian looked up at Aubrey's bright call. The boy wore torn breeches and an overlarge cable knit sweater. Plain stockings covered his skinny legs and a pair of brogans protected his feet. He needed a haircut, but then who was to say how a sailor must wear his hair?

"We go on the next tide."

"Will you leave word for Oliver, so he knows where we are?"

Cyprian gave the boy a wry look. "Don't worry. He'll be told."

Aubrey eyed him keenly. "You're not still angry with him, are you? We're all to blame, you know. Me and Xavier and Ana too."

"I know who's to blame," Cyprian answered, his smile fading.

"If Eliza hadn't—"

"I don't want to talk about your cousin," Cyprian cut him off.

Aubrey drew back a little at his sharp tone, but the boy's gaze remained fixed on Cyprian. "Well, she could have married you instead of Michael." When Cyprian didn't respond he went on. "You asked her, didn't you?"

"Mind your own business. If you haven't enough to do, I can find some additional tasks for you."

Under threat of extra chores Aubrey left. But his question lingered after him, accusing Cyprian with its complexity.

Yes, he'd asked her. But he knew it had been in the most insulting way he could term it. What had he been thinking? Why had he felt the need to hurt her that way?

But then, why had he done any of the things he'd done to Eliza?

He didn't want to examine his motives. He didn't want to think about her at all. Yet he seemed perversely unable to do anything but. She consumed his thoughts, waking and sleeping. He could not enter his own bedchamber without imagining her in his bed. He could not bear the sight of his big bathtub, or the door to her tiny cabin on the *Chameleon*, so near to his own. Worst of all was to see Xavier and Ana together, for their happiness in one another managed to magnify the emptiness he now felt.

"Son of a bitch." He set the sextant down and ran his hands through his hair. He'd driven Eliza away when the last thing in the world he'd wanted was to lose her. If he'd only known how desolate he would feel. How bleak.

But how could he have known she would get under his skin that way? And why? Why had such an unlikely woman so thoroughly beguiled him? If he could just answer that question, maybe he could shake off this lachrymose mood that hung over him.

He picked up the sextant again and stared at it, remembering. She'd thrown it at him once. She'd been terrified of him, but not enough to bury her absolute fury.

What a brave little fool she'd been. But he'd been impressed by that bravery, just as he'd been impressed by her tenacity and her sweetness—and the passion she hid beneath that demure exterior of hers.

He'd not expected those qualities from a woman like her, wealthy, well-educated, and sheltered from the harsher side of life. Maybe that was why he wanted her so. He was no one of consequence, a bastard who'd clawed his way from puny cabin boy to powerful captain. He owned three ships and a sprawling and comfortable estate. Not a paltry accomplishment, all things considered. But for a man like him to possess a woman like Eliza . . .

To possess her would make everything else worthwhile. To possess her would be to prove his worth to the entire world—his father included.

Then Cyprian scoffed at his own perversity. He didn't need to prove his worth to Lloyd Haberton. He had the man's heir in his control; that was all that mattered. As for Eliza . . .

As for Eliza, it did no good to dwell on why he felt such an overwhelming need to have her back in his life. She was gone and she would not be back. He'd broken her heart with his cruelty. It was too late for regrets.

Chapter Twenty-Two

*E*liza paced the library, fingering an occasional tome, but not really interested in books. Perry sat at the huge library table, books and papers and inkwell spread out as he concentrated on the lastest assignment his tutor had given him. But every few minutes he glanced up, studying his sister far more intently than he had been his books.

"You never used to pace," he pointed out.

Eliza stopped, then sat down on a wine-colored leather reading chair, making a careful show of arranging her skirts. It was true, of course. She never used to pace. She used to be happy to sit quietly, to read or do needlework, or play board games with one of her brothers.

But no more. She'd changed. Her body had somehow healed—or perhaps she'd been better all along and just not realized it. It was her heart that was afflicted now. Rent in half. Shattered.

As quickly as she'd sat down, she stood up again. "If I'm distracting you, perhaps I should leave."

"No. No, don't leave. I'm bored with Plato." Perry pushed away from the table and crossed to her. "I'd much rather have a nice talk with you."

Eliza frowned. "I'm not feeling particularly nice today."

"You *have* changed, haven't you."

"I've broken off with Michael."

Perry just shrugged. "Mary Lena Blevins has been chasing him as if he were a fox and she a first-class hound ever since you left. She'll help his broken heart heal."

"Mary Lena? Oh, she's not his sort at all," Eliza said dismissively.

"She's any fellow's sort, Eliza." He gave her a leering grin so reminiscent of Oliver that she should have laughed. But nothing could make her laugh today.

"Where's Oliver?"

Perry chuckled. "Cornered in father's office. Uncle Lloyd is browbeating him for not bringing Aubrey out with him, while Father is trying to determine where this Cyprian Dare fellow might be off to next."

"I told them both not to blame Oliver for any of this."

"Well, he was the one who revealed how he tricked you into hiring him to protect Aubrey," Perry pointed out.

"He was just following orders."

"Cyprian Dare's orders," Perry said, giving her a rather odd look.

"Yes, Cyprian Dare," she replied, warning him with her eyes not to pursue that subject any further.

But Perry was clearly oblivious to it all, or else deliberately baiting her. "So, where do *you* think he's off to? They don't expect him to sit around Alderney and wait for them."

Thoroughly annoyed with him, as well as every other male of her acquaintance, Eliza let out an inelegant snort and stalked the length of the room. "They're wasting their time trying to track him down. Anyway, that's just what he wants, for Uncle Lloyd to follow him, to exhaust himself trying to regain Aubrey."

"You have to admit, Eliza, that it's awfully good revenge, given the crime Dare holds our uncle to."

Eliza gave him a sharp look. "How did you learn about that? It's supposed to be confidential."

His face pinkened. "I . . . um . . . I overheard someone speaking about it."

"Perry, I cannot believe you are still listening at keyholes. I thought you would have outgrown such childish pranks by now. And who was incautious enough to be speaking of it where they might be overheard?"

"Why, you," he retorted with a smug grin.

"Me? But the only one I told was—" She broke off as the realization struck her. "You overheard my conversation with Michael." Her hand went to her throat in dismay. "How . . . how much did you overhear?"

Perry was a terrible liar. His blushes and his inability to stifle them were a family joke, and he'd long ago learned it was better to just admit to the truth. Now he gave her a sheepish look. "Well, I s'pose I heard pretty much all of it."

"All of it?" She swallowed a lump of despair.

He nodded. "All of it."

"So . . . so you know why . . . that is, why I . . . " She couldn't continue. She was too mortified.

"I know you love the chap," he said, generously avoiding what else he knew of her dealings with Cyprian. "How does Aubrey get on with him?"

"Aubrey?" Eliza laughed, a little hysterically, she realized. "They get along very well. He's made Aubrey his cabin boy."

"His cabin boy? But how does Aubrey manage? That chair of his must be awfully difficult to manipulate on a ship."

"He doesn't need the chair," she said, still disconcerted by how much her younger brother knew of her personal relationship with Cyprian.

"Can he walk then? Was he cured in Madeira as you'd hoped?"

"Not exactly," she demurred, realizing she'd let Aubrey's secret slip.

"Does he use crutches now?"

Eliza threw her hands up in the air. "You are the most troublesome brother a girl ever had!"

But Perry only laughed and ruffled the top of her head. "You know you missed me," he teased as she swatted his hand away. Despite herself, Eliza laughed too.

"Oh, yes, I dearly missed having you mess up my hair and listen in on my private conversations."

"How am I to know what's going on in this family otherwise? Everyone treats me as if I'm still a child. But I'm sixteen now. Sixteen and a half."

Eliza looked at Perry, really looked at her baby brother who was almost a head taller than she now. He was practically a man, she realized with a start. Old enough to be interested in girls—women, she amended. For all she knew, he might already have had an alliance with one of the maids or some other creature of loose morals— She broke off at the unpleasant thought that she had no right to judge others. *She* was a creature of loose morals herself, now.

"Yes," she managed to say. "Yes, I can see that you're no longer a child."

"I wish you'd tell mother and father as much."

Eliza nodded. "I will."

"You will?" His thick eyebrows raised hopefully. "If you'll do that, Eliza—convince them to treat me as the man I now am—why, I'll . . . I'll do something equally generous for you. I'll find something."

"Yes, well . . . " Eliza resumed her pacing. How she wished he could do the one thing she truly wanted, make Cyprian come for her. Make him come to London, return Aubrey to his family, and take her back to

Alderney with him. She'd go anywhere he wanted, live anyplace he liked, even aboard the *Chameleon* if he would only say that he loved her and ask her to marry him as if he really meant it.

Come live with me and be my love. The line from the poem came to her and she focused on the shelf of books beside her. She had nothing else to do today. Perhaps she'd just read poetry and become more maudlin than ever. But that was stupid, she decided. She squared her shoulders and looked at Perry.

"Let's go and rescue Oliver from our father and Uncle Lloyd. I think you'll like him once you get to know him."

Within the hour she knew that had been an understatement. If Perry had emulated Michael before, to watch him now with Oliver Spencer was to actually witness a slow transformation. By the time the three of them had toured the stables, taught Oliver how to play lawn tennis and collected fishing gear and trekked down to the river, Perry's speech was peppered with "mates" and his walk had taken on a definite swagger.

Their parents would be appalled, but Eliza was perversely comforted. Perry was no snob, and neither was she—despite Cyprian's accusations to the contrary. Not that it mattered, of course. Not anymore.

From her perch on a bench, she gazed at the two young men fishing in the icy river as if they were old friends. Perry had taught Oliver how to cast; Oliver let Perry use his lethal-looking knife to gut the three fish they'd caught between them. It was like a replay of Aubrey and Oliver. Maybe the idyllic life of England's landed gentry was too serene for young men. Maybe a little excitement was good for the soul. And the body, she added, thinking of her own returned strength and Aubrey's. She should thank Cyprian for having snatched her and Aubrey away from their boring lives, for they'd benefitted in so many ways.

She'd never be able to thank him for letting her go, however. She'd never be able to thank him, or forgive him.

Dinner would have been a somber affair except that Perry kept pestering Oliver with questions about life at sea. LeClere too, after an initial reserve, warmed to Oliver. To his credit, Oliver swiftly adopted the manners appropriate to a formal dinner in a house like Diamond Hall. Between Perry and LeClere he was suitably dressed in a dark gray suit and a pale blue figured waistcoat and snowy linen shirt. His hair was washed and combed, and to anyone who'd not seen him in his sailor's garb, he was every inch the gentleman. She saw his quick gaze as he watched to see where to place his napkin and which utensil to use. He held his crystal wine glass lightly and drank sparingly. Except for the one surreptitious wink he gave her, he was almost as proper as Michael Johnstone himself.

"Where are you from, Mr. Spencer?" Eliza's mother asked. Despite her initial reserve toward him, she'd begun to thaw and that was all the opportunity Oliver needed. Now Eliza's mother was quite charmed by him.

"I was born and raised my first few years in Lynton. That's in north Devon along the Bristol Channel. My father was a cooper and my mother did laundry," he added, not in the least concerned that such an upbringing should brand him unworthy of the likes of the Thoroughgood family. But he didn't care and neither, it seemed, did anyone else. He was, after all, the one who'd saved Eliza. It warmed a small part of Eliza's frozen heart to know her family could be so generous.

"Oliver said he went to sea when he was eleven," Perry threw in.

"Eleven?" Constance Thoroughgood frowned. "That's awfully young."

"My parents died suddenly," Oliver explained. He

glanced at Eliza. "Cyprian knew my father and he took me in. Made me his cabin boy."

Like he'd done with Aubrey.

The unsaid words hung in the air a long, awkward moment. Everyone's eyes flitted toward Eliza, then away, as if they expected her to swoon at the mention of Cyprian's name—or else to dissolve into tears. She looked at her mother and caught the sorrowful expression on her face, then looked at the other end of the table toward her father whose lips had thinned in anger.

"If Aubrey fares even half so well as Oliver, then he shall do very well," she stated as matter-of-factly as she could manage.

"But this man Dare was a friend of Mr. Spencer's father," Gerald Thoroughgood grimly replied. "He's not so kindly disposed towards our family."

He meant his brother-in-law, Lloyd Haberton, of course. But Eliza feared he meant her too, and it roused her ire.

"Cyprian will not hurt Aubrey. In fact, he's already helped him enormously."

"Helped him?" Her father set his glass down with a thunk and wine sloshed over the lip. "How can you say such a thing—"

"Gerald!"

He broke off at his wife's sharp tone.

"This is unsuitable dinner conversation," she rebuked him.

"But she's not behaving at all like she used to," Gerald complained to his wife. "Ever since—" He stopped of his own accord this time, but Eliza knew what he implied. So, she feared, did everyone else, and her face grew warm with embarrassment.

To her surprise Oliver cleared his throat. "Cyprian's led a hard life, but he doesn't take advantage of helpless people."

Gerald stood up, quivering with anger. "He took ad-

vantage of Eliza. No matter what she may say, he took
advantage of her!"

"That's not true."

Every eye turned her way. Her mother knew the
truth, as did Oliver and her eavesdropping little brother.
Though her father didn't want to believe it, she must
convince him. She couldn't bear for him to judge Cyprian so wrongly.

"Cyprian did not take advantage of me," she stated
slowly and succinctly.

"You don't know what you're talking about," her father sputtered. "You're just an innocent child who—"

"I'm a woman, Father. Just as Perry is no longer a
school boy but a man, I am no longer a girl. I'm a
strong, healthy woman and Cyprian Dare must receive
a large part of the credit."

"Credit! Why, when we catch him I'll have him drawn
and quartered!" He threw his napkin down on the table
as if it were a glove and the linen-covered table was
Cyprian's face. "The man should be shot for what he's
done to you and Aubrey."

"Beggin' your pardon, sir," Oliver put in mildly. "But
I think you ought to know that Eliza's in love with Cyprian." He ignored Constance's gasp and Eliza's groan of
dismay. "And he's in love with her," he added, shooting
Eliza a lopsided grin.

It was positively the last straw. With a cry that was
half frustration and half despair, Eliza pushed away
from the table. "How can you say such a lie, Oliver
Spencer? If I thought it was true—"

She couldn't finish. Instead she wheeled around and
ran from the room, embarrassed, ashamed, and so consumed with sorrow for herself that she thought she must
expire from it. If only Oliver's words were true. If only
they were.

But as she hurried down the hall, clutching her shawl

around her shoulders, then jerked open the front door and dashed down the steps, she knew that Oliver was wrong.

She flew headlong around the house and hurtled down a garden path until her side ached and her breath frosted the cold night air. She collapsed onto a wooden garden bench and pressed her hand to her side. No one had followed her. She was all alone and free to contemplate her awful manners and otherwise reprehensible behavior.

Whatever she'd been before her ill-fated departure for Madeira, she was no longer the same girl. She'd fallen from grace—and fallen in love with a rogue. But he didn't love her, no matter what Oliver said.

And yet . . . and yet even if she never loved again, and no one ever loved her, the fact remained that she might very well already bear a child of Cyprian's. She moved her hand down to her stomach and held it there. Her reputation was already ruined, so would it really matter if she did, she wondered. She could always move to her dower house in Surrey and live a quiet life there with her child.

But everyone would know her child as a bastard, she reluctantly admitted. Though she felt she could bear being ostracized by society, the thought of an innocent child being treated so was too awful to contemplate. And anyway, why was she even thinking such thoughts? Why was some stupid, emotional part of her actually wishing she could bear Cyprian a child?

It was that which finally brought tears stinging to her eyes. Cyprian didn't love her. He never had. And any baby of theirs would always be called a bastard.

She cried hard, hurtful tears in the cold loneliness of the brown, winter garden, her misery wrapped around her like an icy blanket. She didn't see her mother silhouetted in a second story window watching over her.

Nor was she aware that Perry stood guard as well, hunched over in the shadows of a bare-limbed beech tree. She only knew that everything had gone wrong and it seemed it could never be put back to rights.

Chapter Twenty-Three

Morning started as miserably as the previous day had ended. Eliza's monthly courses began.

Constance was understandably ecstatic. Eliza, however, sank into depression. She lay abed all day, trying to blot out the sounds of life beyond her room, muted through they were. Clothilde brought breakfast. Lunch, too. But Eliza waved her away. Her stomach cramped and hurt, but the pain seemed somehow cathartic. She wanted it to hurt, for the physical pain was at least real. She could press her two hands over her lower stomach and know exactly where the pain was. Her other wounds were not like that. The rest of her ached in less tangible ways, yearning for things she could not have. There was no comfort to be found for such deep, pervasive pain.

So she lay in bed most of the day, pretending to be asleep whenever anyone peeked past the door. Not until her mother shook her shoulder sometime in the early afternoon did she relent and open her eyes.

"I don't wish to get up," she muttered, pulling the coverlet over her shoulder and rolling to face the wall.

"There is a messenger here, Eliza, and he won't give his message to anyone but you. Get up," Constance demanded, tugging the warm coverlet back. Then her lips thinned and her nostrils flared. "He says he's from that man."

That man. The only person her mother referred to in such a distasteful manner was Cyprian Dare.

Eliza sat bolt upright and kicked free of the heavy bed linens. A message for her from Cyprian?

"Your father has threatened to throttle the hapless fellow, but he nevertheless refuses to give the message to Gerald. We've sent word for Lloyd and Judith to come round, in case there's word about Aubrey."

Constance grabbed for the wrapper Eliza meant to don. "You cannot see him in that!"

Eliza glared at her mother, then thrust her unraveling braid behind her shoulder. "I doubt he cares what I wear."

Constance let out an uncharacteristic snort of disbelief. "Dear God, but that man has truly addled your senses. Put on a dress, Eliza. Here." She threw the first frock she could lay her hands on at her daughter. "And you'll *have* to comb your hair."

Eliza did as her mother asked, shedding her nightgown without the least thought for her more normal modesty, then pulling on her discarded chemise from yesterday. She gave her mother a warning glare when she stepped into the skirt, foregoing any petticoats or slips. She tied the tabs then thrust her arms into the simple wool bodice and turned so her mother could do up the buttons on the back.

"Hurry," she muttered, tapping her foot in a jittery motion. "Hurry."

"No. You slow down, Eliza. Just look at you," Constance accused, once she finished the buttons and began to release the rest of the braid. "You mope around as if you're dying, then that man sends word and you're suddenly bursting with energy." She picked up a hairbrush and began to brush Eliza's hair in long determined strokes. "Besides, this will give your aunt and uncle time to arrive."

Eliza suffered her mother's ministrations in silence while her anxiety increased. Her mother was right, of course, and she was a fool to react so at the first mention of Cyprian's name. But she couldn't help it. Besides, she was as concerned about Aubrey as anyone, she rationalized.

"Sit down and I'll dress your hair."

"Oh, that's completely unnecessary," Eliza cried, coming to the end of her patience. With deft fingers she caught her hair in one hand and tied it back with the first bit of ribbon she spied.

"A green ribbon with a blue dress?" Constance complained. But Eliza ignored her. Without waiting for her mother, she hurried from the room, oblivious to her appearance, her cramps, or anything else. Cyprian had sent a message to her. To *her*. That was all that mattered.

She found her father, both her brothers, and a man she didn't recognize standing in her father's office. He looked more a solicitor than a messenger boy, and she frowned in confusion.

"Miss Eliza Thoroughgood?" he asked, clearly relieved to see her, for the atmosphere in the office was decidedly frosty.

"Yes. Give me the message. Please," she added as an afterthought.

He cleared his throat. "Could we speak in private?"

"No!" Gerald burst out. "I will hear every word that man sends to my daughter."

"But Father—"

At that precise moment voices in the hall heralded the arrival of the Habertons with several of their daughters in tow as well. For a moment pandemonium reigned. Her uncle Lloyd was shouting. Her aunt appeared ready to dissolve into tears. Jessica and Augusta Haberton corralled LeClere and Perry, both urging their cousins to fill them in on the details. Then Oliver strolled in and while attention diverted momentarily to him, Eliza grabbed the messenger's arm.

"Tell me," she hissed. When the man's eyes darted about, she squeezed his arm all the tighter. "Tell me now!"

"He demands a ransom for the boy. Fifteen thousand pounds."

"That's all?"

He looked at her as if she might be a little mad. "That's a rather goodly sum, miss. He wants it delivered to the Bear and Claw Inn in Lyme Regis on Wednesday coming. Someone will lead the bearer to a meeting place where the boy will be released." He sighed, as if glad to be done with his job, but Eliza could not believe that was all he'd been charged with saying to her.

"That's all?" she repeated. "He . . . he said nothing else?"

She caught a glimpse of comprehension in the man's face, and a trace of sympathy as well, but he still shook his head. "No, miss. Nothing else."

Lloyd Haberton stepped up at that moment and pulled the man away from Eliza. "Tell me!" he demanded. "Tell me what he said. What does he want? Is my boy all right?"

Sorrow should have been Eliza's consuming emotion at that moment. Sorrow or anguish or some equally devastating sentiment that Cyprian hadn't cared enough to send word to her. At the very least she should have felt relief, that Aubrey would be freed on Wednesday to return home. But in that instant what she felt most was anger. How dare he? How dare he make her love him, then ignore her! How dare he send a message to her with no personal word whatsoever!

Her hands closed into fists. If Cyprian had been there instead of his emissary, she would have slapped him hard enough to make his head spin.

"Tell me what he said!" her uncle demanded in a threatening tone that drew her attention. And just that fast did she decide what to do.

"Quit berating the man," she ordered her uncle, stepping between him and the shorter messenger. "Captain Dare has sent word to me that he wants fifteen thousand pounds for the return of Aubrey."

"Thank God," Aunt Judith cried.

"Fifteen thousand pounds!" Uncle Lloyd bellowed.

"Yes, but I'm to deliver it myself. It's the only way he'll do it," she added, unobtrusively pinching the messenger's arm.

To his credit, the man didn't make a move to contradict her. As the crowd in the office all began to talk and question and offer their disparate opinions, Eliza was more conscious of the messenger's silence than anything else. If he'd objected to her impulsive lie, she didn't know what she would have done. But he didn't say a thing.

As for the rest of them, it didn't matter what they said. Aunt Judith would force Uncle Lloyd to pay the heavy price; Uncle Lloyd would convince his sister-in-law to let Eliza go; and Constance Thoroughgood would prevail upon her husband's concern for young Aubrey to make him agree. But even if they all said no and Eliza had to go to the Bear and Claw Inn all alone and without a penny of the ransom money, she meant to be there come Wednesday. Nothing in the wide world could prevent her from being there.

" 'Tis a good thing we're not trying to go unnoticed," Oliver smirked as he and Eliza exited the first of the two coaches that had carried their party from London to the small port town of Lyme Regis. Eliza was truly thankful for Oliver's presence, for he was the only one besides herself who was not out for Cyprian's blood. Well, Perry wasn't either, but he didn't count. Still, Oliver had insisted on coming as had both her parents, her aunt and uncle, and her two brothers.

Fortunately, the two older couples had traveled in one coach and the younger foursome in another. Eliza was not certain she could have borne being confined with her Uncle Lloyd for the duration of their lengthy trip.

As she stepped down from the coach, she pulled her hood up against the frigid mist that hung over the town. Despite the foul weather, however, there were signs of activity. In their carriage Oliver had told her, Perry, and LeClere that Lyme Regis was a small but busy resort town on Lyme Bay, once a favorite haunt of smugglers. Perry had pumped him for information about the lucrative smuggling industry and as Oliver had warmed to the task, spinning out his tales of dangerous chases and narrow escapes, even LeClere had become spellbound. But all Eliza could think was that somewhere in this very ordinary place, Cyprian was waiting with her cousin—at least she hoped he was here. He could have sent Xavier with Aubrey, or anyone else, for that matter.

But somehow she knew he wouldn't do that. She'd had an awful lot of time during the last two days to ponder this strange turn of events. Cyprian had not kidnapped Aubrey for monetary reasons. It had never been Lloyd Haberton's money he'd wanted. What he'd wanted had been his own unique sort of revenge. The fact that he was demanding a ransom now struck her as a rather large compromise on his part. Obviously he'd come to the conclusion that Aubrey must be returned to his family, but his need for revenge was not entirely gone. That must be why he was demanding such an ungodly amount of money from his father. In Cyprian's eyes, Lloyd Haberton had to pay in some painful way.

The fact that he'd sent the demand through her, however, was harder for Eliza to understand. That he wanted her to know what he was doing was obvious. But why? So that she might see him in a more favorable light? So that she would come herself? But if that was so, why hadn't he sent her a message of some sort?

Eliza paused at the entrance to Darnell's Posting House, while her father herded everyone else inside. He meant to take rooms for them for the night, and they all prayed that Aubrey would join them soon. Eliza prayed also that Cyprian would want to see her. But even if he didn't, she was here. Beyond that she had no further plan. She could only go on to the Bear and Claw and wait.

She didn't have to wait for long.

Oliver had delivered her to the Bear and Claw and sat downstairs in the public room while she waited alone in a private dining room. A serving girl brought her hot tea and stoked the fire. Now as Eliza shed her heavy cloak, the girl gave her a frankly curious look.

"No, no. Don't take off your cloak yet, ma'am."

Eliza stared at her. "Are we going someplace else?"

"Yes, ma'am," the girl replied. "I've been given instructions. If you'll just follow me, I'll show you to the backstairs."

The backstairs? At once Eliza understood. Cyprian was just making sure no one followed her. She nodded and did as the girl instructed. But her heart began to race in nervous anticipation.

"Don't forget your satchel," the maid reminded her when Eliza would have left her uncle's ransom money sitting on the floor beside the hearth. Then with money in hand and her hood pulled up about her face, she hurried down a narrow servants' stairwell behind the maid, through a series of storage rooms, and out into a small rear courtyard.

The door shut behind her with a dull thud, and for a moment Eliza was alone, unsure where to go. Then a sharp whistle sounded and a wiry old man in the stable doorway gestured her toward him.

He didn't speak but only pointed at a rough cart with a canvas cover when she drew near. Eliza climbed inside without voicing the myriad questions that clamored inside her. Where were they going? How was Aubrey?

When would she see Cyprian?

The man closed the flap so that she could not be seen from the outside, nor see out either. Then the wagon creaked and shifted as he climbed on board, and with another short whistle, the team of draft horses started forward. Eliza braced herself with a hand on each side of the narrow cart, but after a short jouncing ride along the cobbled stone streets, the ride turned easier. By the time the cart rocked to a halt, however, grim clouds hung low, darkening the entire world, and when Eliza crawled out of the vehicle, she had no idea whatsoever where she was. But surely Cyprian must be near.

When she spied a coach waiting with another driver in place, however, and her taciturn driver ordered to get in it, she objected. "Where is he going to take me? And where is Cyprian?"

"I don't know nothin' 'bout nothin'" the man grunted. "Get in."

When Eliza finally complied, it was with the greatest of misgivings. She was getting scared. To make it worse, the carriage was pitch black inside, and before she could even get settled, it took off with a lurch, unbalancing her completely. She lost hold of the satchel when she tried to right herself. But she was unable to prevent herself from toppling over anyway.

When she fell, however, it was not onto the hard edge of one of the seats, but against the solid form of a man sitting on that seat.

Cyprian!

Chapter Twenty-Four

"*C*yprian."

Eliza was hardly aware she'd uttered a word. All she knew was that it was him. No doubt clouded her mind at all. The hand on her waist was his. The impossibly hard thigh beneath her hand as she tried to push upright was his. The warmth that threatened to envelop her was his. Oh, but it was most assuredly Cyprian Dare.

Once she was on her feet, however, he shoved her unceremoniously into the seat behind her. Then he barked out a sharp command.

"Drive!"

The carriage jerked forward again and Eliza nearly slid off the leather bench seat. Between peering avidly at Cyprian's shadowed form and trying to keep her seat, she was completely discombobulated. But when it seemed he did not intend to speak again, a feeling of dread crept up her spine in cold, little shivers.

"Where . . . where is Aubrey?"

"The last time I saw him he was on board my ship."

He sounded furious. But why? Because she was the one who'd come? Could that be it?

"And where is the *Chameleon?*" she persisted, for it was far easier to discuss Aubrey than their own peculiar circumstances.

"Somewhere at sea, I'd guess."

"At sea? But you were to bring him here in exchange for the ransom. Here!" She shoved the heavy satchel at him. "Here's your money. Now give me my cousin!"

She heard him shift in his seat, and stow the heavy satchel to the side. He drew back one of the window shades and in the meager light it afforded, she saw the glint of his eyes and the flash of his teeth. Then she felt the undeniable touch of his gaze upon her.

"Aubrey is nearby, Eliza. We came on another of my ships—lest your uncle have the authorities detain the *Chameleon*. You and Oliver have no doubt given him all the information he needs to find both my home and my ship."

Guilt stung her, for there was a certain truth to his words. Still, if he hadn't kidnapped Aubrey, no one would be searching for him or his ship.

"My uncle has not involved the authorities. But he has sent men of his own."

"No authorities?" She heard the amusement in his voice. "Was that your father's idea, perhaps? To protect you from the scandal that would surely ensue should it become public knowledge that you'd been several weeks in the company of a band of sailors—and unchaparoned at that?"

"I don't know," Eliza muttered, though she suspected as much. "They have not involved me in their planning."

"Really. Then how is it that *you* carry the ransom money, and not one of the men of the family?"

How, indeed. What had she foolishly thought to accomplish by such a bold act? Faced now with his cold questioning, it seemed she'd invented a depth of feeling between them that was entirely one-sided.

Eliza clutched the door post when they hit a nasty rut. "Why did you send your ransom message to me instead of to my uncle?" she countered.

"I didn't—" He broke off, but Eliza was not left in

confusion for long. "Xavier." He laughed, a hollow, mirthless sound that killed what little was left of her hope.

Xavier with his infernal matchmaking had been the one to send the messenger to her. Not Cyprian. How foolish of her to misread the situation. But then Xavier had also misjudged his man, for Cyprian was obviously not interested in her anymore.

"So, did he also change the content of the message to say *you* must deliver the money?"

Eliza wanted to lie. She wanted to say that she'd only come because she'd thought she had to in order to secure Aubrey's freedom. But she couldn't, and as the silence stretched out, revealing the shameful truth, she heard Cyprian sigh.

"How did you convince them to let you do it?"

Eliza swallowed hard and stared down at her hands. "I . . . I told them you demanded it. That it was the only way you'd agree. . . . "

He digested that for a moment. "What about the messenger?"

"He . . . um . . . he had whispered the message to me and I . . . well, I just changed it that little bit. He was kind enough not to make a liar of me."

"I see."

No doubt he did, Eliza thought miseraoly. He saw a foolish young woman flinging herself at him—and he was not in the least interested. At least not any longer. He'd had what he wanted of her—but he was hardly willing to give her what *she* wanted of *him*.

A sob rose in her throat but she ruthlessly forced it down. No tears for him—especially not in front of him.

His fingers drummed a tuneless rhythm on the door post. "So, how has your fiancé taken all this? Or has your father been able to keep your . . . adventure a secret from him also?"

His cavalier words propelled her from sorrow to utter

fury. "Michael has been an integral part of the search for Aubrey and me. From the very beginning—"

"So he still intends to marry you," he broke in. "I must say, he rises in my estimation, Eliza."

"Rises in *your* estimation? Don't you dare patronize him or me, Cyprian Dare. Michael Johnstone is ten times the man you are! At least he offered to marry me, whereas you—"

"He offered. Didn't you accept?"

Eliza snapped her mouth closed. She didn't want to tell him anything else. But he moved across the small space to sit beside her, then caught her chin in his hand.

"Tell me, Eliza, has a date been set? Have you agreed to marry him, or not?"

She tried to turn away from his piercing eyes. Truly she did. But he was too strong to fight off, and anyway, his gaze had captured hers and would not release it.

"You turned him down," he whispered, surprise evident in his tone. "You turned him down, didn't you?"

"Yes," she admitted in a small voice.

"But why?" Then his grip on her chin tightened. "Are you with child?"

"No!" This time she broke his mesmerizing hold on her. And yet in the carriage there was no place to flee. Though it was a foolish gesture, she scooted across to the facing seat and shrank back into the corner farthest from Cyprian.

To her relief he remained where he was, though his watchful gaze was nearly as unnerving as his touch. "You're not with child," he mused. "So why did you come when there was no need? Why did you lie to your father and uncle?"

Eliza tried to control her runaway emotions. How was she to answer that? Certainly not with the truth.

"I . . . I wanted to see Aubrey. To make sure you didn't renege on your deal," she added more belligerently.

"I see. And what if that was my plan all along, to take Haberton's money and keep his son just the same? What could you possibly do to prevent it?"

"I don't suppose appealing to your honorable side would do, would it? For clearly you possess none," she spat.

He laughed then, a full, hearty laugh that was more welcome to her ears than manna to a starving man. It warmed a cold, shrivelled part of her heart even as it drove a dagger through it, for he was laughing at her, not with her. The two were a world apart.

"I suppose, Eliza, that to a protected English miss like yourself, I could not possibly possess a shred of honor. But in the society I inhabit, honor is a double-edged sword. There is honor to be had in noble gestures, very like your Michael's offer to marry you despite the ruin I brought up on you. But there is also honor in vengeance, in righting a wrong left too long untended. I see my revenge against your uncle as honorable though I doubt you could ever understand that." A change in the coach's motion stopped him. "Ah, we have arrived."

The carriage had slowed, then turned. The muffled thud of the horses' hooves turned to a clatter on the paved surface of a small courtyard. Eliza had no time to argue with Cyprian, to convince him that she did understand about him and his father. The metal-rimmed carriage wheels added their noise to the arrival, and in a moment the side door was opened, the step had been lowered, and Cyprian alighted.

He did not help her down, but left that task to a beaming Xavier. But Xavier's welcome face fell into a confused frown when Cyprian strode away and Eliza remained silent in the depths of the carriage.

"Come. Come, Eliza." He reached a hand to her, urging her out. Once removed from the carriage, Eliza struggled for composure. "The . . . the coins—they're inside," she whispered, watching Cyprian disappear into a neat two-storied stone house.

Xavier hefted the bulky satchel then took her arm and steered her after Cyprian. "He doesn't care about the money. He cares about you. I'm so glad to see that you came."

"No, Xavier, this has got to end. He doesn't care about me, no matter how much you or I want him to. He doesn't care."

"So you *do* want him to care."

Eliza threw her hands up and let out a muffled cry of despair. "So what if I do!"

"Then tell him," the huge African said. He smiled at her so sweetly that Eliza could not doubt he believed that such a simple declaration by her would solve everything. He loved his Ana so much that he believed his own domestic tranquility could be achieved by others just as easily. If only it could be so.

"What have you to lose?" he continued, as if he knew all the doubts that plagued her mind.

"My pride. My self-esteem," Eliza answered morosely. Then her tone turned bitter. "No, I've already lost those just by coming here. I give you credit, Xavier. You certainly predicted my reaction, didn't you? Too bad you couldn't have foreseen his more accurately."

"Ah, Eliza," Xavier chided her. "You fought more strenuously for Aubrey than you are now fighting for yourself—for yourself and for Cyprian."

Eliza stared resentfully at him. Was that true? She didn't want to know. "Where is Aubrey, anyway?"

After a long steady look that made her glance uncomfortably away, he shook his head, then gestured toward the house.

Aubrey's laughter led her to him. He and Ana were playing a board game before a merry blaze in a cozy parlor. At the rush of cold air they both looked up, then with a glad cry the boy leaped up and flew to her.

"Eliza!" He flung his arms around her. "Eliza! You didn't tell me she was coming," he accused, craning his neck to look at someone behind her.

"I didn't know she was." Cyprian's voice so nearby sent Eliza spinning around, flustered anew.

"Come, Ana," Xavier interjected. "I'll help you in the kitchen." Without giving Eliza time to protest, the pair disappeared, leaving Eliza staring at Cyprian, with her happy cousin the only buffer between them.

"Why didn't you send word you were coming?" Aubrey turned his question upon her.

"I didn't know where you were." She combed her fingers through his shaggy curls and tried to ignore Cyprian's unnerving presence. "You look very well."

"Oh, I am." He disentangled himself from her embrace. "My limp's improving. Slowly," he admitted. "But I can tell."

She watched him show off the growing strength of his injured leg. His parents had missed him so much. But having him return to them so much better might make everything they'd suffered seem worthwhile, in the long run.

"I've come to take you home," she blurted out.

Aubrey stopped his antics and his face grew serious. "I thought that was probably the case." He glanced at Cyprian. "Did Father send a ransom, then?"

Cyprian nodded and stepped nearer to Eliza. "May I take your cloak?"

She backed up, hugging the heavy garment to her as though it afforded some sort of defense against him. "There's no reason for us to linger. We can return to Lyme Regis in the carriage now."

He took a step closer. She stepped back. "It's a long, cold ride. Surely you'll want a bowl of Ana's vegetable soup and freshly baked bread first."

Eliza shook her head. "No, I wouldn't."

"Well, Aubrey would. Right, Aubrey?"

"Well . . . " The boy hesitated, switching his curious gaze back and forth between the two adults. "Actually, I am hungry—"

"Don't try to force Aubrey into the middle of this," Eliza demanded.

"He's already in the middle," he replied so calmly she wanted to scream.

"Only because you're so consumed with revenge," she accused. All her heartache—all her fear and doubt and yearning—knotted inside her, knotted and seethed, then bubbled uncontrollably to the surface. "Only because you think to hurt your father through Aubrey! But Uncle Lloyd never knew about you. He never knew she bore him a son—"

"Is that supposed to exonerate him, that he gave her the money to be rid of me?"

Before she could respond she felt a tug on her arm. "I . . . I don't understand," Aubrey whispered. At once Eliza realized what they'd revealed. She stared at him, wide-eyed and sorry for her hasty words. But she knew from the boy's expression that it was too late. They'd said too much.

"You said hurt *your* father, but . . . " The child looked from Cyprian to Eliza, then back to Cyprian. "Does that mean . . . is my father also . . . also *your* father?"

Cyprian took hold of Aubrey's shoulders then squatted down before him. "We are half brothers, Aubrey. I didn't want to tell you because I didn't know how you would feel about it."

"But . . . but I don't understand."

"It happened long ago, before your mother married your father."

Aubrey frowned for a moment, then his eyes widened in sudden comprehension. "Oh. But then, who is your mother?"

Cyprian's hands moved up and down Aubrey's thin

arms and he released a slow, drawn out sigh. "Her name was Cybil and although she was a lovely woman, she was not the sort of woman your father had planned to marry." He paused and Eliza saw a muscle flex in his jaw. To state the situation so mildly to Aubrey clearly took a huge effort. "But she took good care of me," he added.

"That's why you stole me, isn't it? Because my father didn't marry your mother. He married mine."

Aubrey backed away, his young face a mask of confused emotion. "That's why you hate me."

"I don't hate you—"

"But you did. You did at first."

"I tried to hate you," Cyprian admitted. "But you made such a good cabin boy." He grinned at the child and received a small answering grin in return. "You worked hard. You made yourself get better. And besides—" Again he paused and Eliza caught her breath. "And besides, you're my brother."

"Your half brother," Aubrey corrected, his face still vulnerable.

"My *only* brother," Cyprian stated.

For a long stretched-out moment the boy and man stared at one another. They were so alike, Eliza thought as love for both of them swelled in her heart. Dark hair, blue eyes. Both determined—hardheaded, really.

Then Cyprian opened his arms and Aubrey charged into his older brother's embrace.

"I always wanted a brother," Aubrey whispered in a voice that trembled with emotion.

"Me, too," Cyprian replied hoarsely, holding Aubrey tight.

Tears rose in Eliza's eyes at the sight of the two. Who could ever have predicted such an emotional scene between captive and captor? But then, she should have guessed, for hadn't she been as much Cyprian's captive as Aubrey? And hadn't she become as inexorably in-

volved with him? Unlike Aubrey, however, she did not
have any ties to Cyprian. He was not her brother. He
was not even her cousin, at least not by blood. He was
just the man who'd taken her virginity—and her heart as
well. But that didn't mean as much to him as it did to
her, she reminded herself.

She hugged her arms around herself, when what she
really wanted to do was throw her arms around Cyprian
and Aubrey. As if he sensed her emotional state, Aubrey pulled a little back from Cyprian and looked over
at her. Chagrin and joy and a tiny bit of accusation
showed in his little boy's face.

"Why didn't you tell me before, Eliza? Why did you
keep it a secret?"

Eliza glanced from her young cousin to Cyprian,
searching for an answer that made sense. For now that
the truth was out, it seemed foolish to ever have hidden
it from Aubrey. It was Cyprian who answered the child's
question, though his fathomless eyes remained locked
with hers.

"Eliza thought she was protecting you, and I . . . I
had a hard time accepting the fact that I was using my
own brother to get even with my father."

Eliza's heart began to pound in her chest, to race with
painful speed. Was he trying to say that he was sorry,
that he'd been wrong to seek this sort of revenge against
his father?

"But . . . but why do you want to get even with my
father?" Aubrey asked, drawing Cyprian's attention
back to him. "He's your father too."

Cyprian released Aubrey and stood up, and before
her eyes Eliza watched him transform back from caring
brother to vengeful son. From apologetic captor to pi-
ratical sea captain.

"He's never been a father to me," he said stiffly. He
glanced at Eliza. "Whether he knew about my existence
or not doesn't matter. He ruined my mother's life.

Though I was unwise to involve you in my revenge, nothing has changed."

"But you don't have to take his money," Aubrey argued. "One day it will be yours anyway. You're the oldest son."

"I'm his bastard, Aubrey. Not his legal heir. And anyway, I don't want or need his money."

"Then why did you demand a ransom—"

"Because it pains him to give it to me!"

He snatched up the heavy satchel Xavier had left beside the door and flung it violently across the room. It struck near the hearth and burst open, spilling a clattering, glittering array of coins and jewels out onto the planked wood floor. Truly it appeared a pirate's booty.

In the awful silence that followed his outburst, Eliza and Aubrey stared dumbfounded at Cyprian. He was, Eliza thought, more furious in that moment than she'd ever seen him, for he actually shook with the force of his rage.

Then, as if he could not stand there one more moment without exploding, he jerked around, yanked open the door, and quit the house. The fact that he left the door standing open seemed somehow more depressing than if he'd slammed it right off its iron hinges.

Chapter Twenty-Five

"**C**ome along, Aubrey. I'll find the driver and tell him to take us back to Lyme Regis directly. Go find your coat now, and let's get on our way."

"But what about supper? Ana made supper. And what about Xavier?"

"We'll tell them goodbye. I'm sure Ana will give us something to take with us to eat in the carriage." She took his elbow and urged him toward the door that Xavier and Ana had left from. "Hurry, Aubrey. We have to hurry."

"But why?" He dug in his heels and twisted out of her grasp. "Why do we have to hurry? Didn't you hear him? He's my brother." His small face crumpled suddenly into tears. "He's my brother and if we leave now, I know I'll never see him again."

The onset of Aubrey's tears, when he was struggling so hard to restrain them, brought fresh tears to Eliza's eyes as well. Damn Cyprian Dare for finding a new way to hurt Aubrey! And damn him for managing to bring her to tears more times in the past weeks than she'd done in her entire life!

She gathered the weeping child in her arms, then sat down on a rush-bottomed settee, holding him still. "Please don't cry, Aubrey. It's all for the best, anyway.

You'll see. Think about your mother and father and how happy they'll be to see you again. Your sisters too." She finger-combed his dark unruly hair. "And Oliver came with me. He's waiting at the Bear and Claw right now."

"Oliver?" Aubrey raised his head and wiped his eyes with the back of his sleeve. "Yes, I would like to see Oliver." Then he met her concerned gaze with his damp blue stare. "You know, if Oliver found out he were Cyprian's brother, I bet he wouldn't let Cyprian go off forever. He'd find a way to stop him." His chin jutted out stubbornly and for a fraction of a moment he was the very image of Cyprian at his most frustrating. It brought a grudging smile to Eliza's lips.

"You see?" he continued. "Even you must admit he would. Ollie's like that. And so am I," he decided.

He stood up and crossed to the forgotten spread of riches on the floor, then knelt and began to gather everything back into the much abused satchel. "If I take the ransom with me, Cyprian will have to follow us, won't he? Then perhaps I can convince him and Father to be friends."

Eliza shook her head in dismay. "I don't think that will work, Aubrey. Besides, perhaps Cyprian is entitled to some of your father's wealth."

Aubrey glanced up at her though he didn't pause in his self-appointed task. "If you were to marry him, that would probably help to smooth things out even more."

"Marry him?" Eliza pushed out of the settee and began to pace. "Marry him! Aubrey, the fact is, Cyprian does not wish to marry anyone. Least of all me," she added in a smaller voice.

"Xavier says he does."

"Xavier is a complete and foolish romantic."

"Ana says so too."

"That figures," Eliza muttered, pacing the length of the cozy parlor. "Hurry up, Aubrey. It's past time we left this place."

"You'd marry him if he agreed, wouldn't you?" Aubrey persisted, ignoring her last words. "You keep saying *he* won't, but you never once said *you* wouldn't marry him. You want to, don't you? You do!"

"So what if I do!" she exclaimed. "It takes a bride *and* a groom, in case you aren't familiar with the process!"

He scowled at her sharp tone and for a moment he looked like the petulant little boy who'd flung his drawing of the white cliffs over the railing of the *Lady Haberton.* But then his face cleared and he became the bright, mischievous boy he used to be—and had become once more. "I'm not ready to go," he stated. "First I'm going to put this satchel in the carriage. Then I'm going to have my supper. Then I'll bid everyone a proper goodbye. It's only polite, Eliza. You know I'm right."

They ate in the kitchen at a massive oak table that had, no doubt, seen a century of meals served on its scarred surface. Eliza was too jumpy to eat. Or so she thought. But the warm cheer of the old-fashioned kitchen, the fragrance of soup and bread, and the golden glow and soft popping of the generous blaze in the huge fireplace did much to soothe her shattered nerves. Added to that, Xavier's hearty good humor and Ana's ever-present serenity were like a balm to all Eliza's wounds. How she wished she could settle into this delightful cocoon of love and security they managed to create, no matter what the circumstances.

As Cyprian's friends they understood the perverse workings of her heart—why she was so drawn to the vengeful sea captain. But they foolishly attributed more caring on Cyprian's part than actually existed. They refused to understand that she had to leave. Of course, once home, she would then become the recipient of her mother's doleful stares and her father's regretful ones. Everyone would treat her as if she were some fragile doll, just as they'd always done, though this time it would be for entirely different reasons. Her body was strong now. It was her heart that suffered.

The thought of the dull and depressing existence awaiting her in London was too horrible for Eliza to contemplate, and she set her spoon down in her half-empty bowl of soup.

"Have you had enough?" Ana asked, studying Eliza with almond eyes that always seemed to see too much.

Eliza swallowed and nodded her head.

"I suppose you want to leave now," Aubrey said. "Well, I want to write down my address first. So Cyprian can find me. *And* the ransom," he added belligerently.

"That's a very good idea," Xavier said solemnly. "Write down Eliza's address too."

"Oh, stop it!" Eliza cried. She pushed away from the table then stood up and leaned forward, bracing herself on her hands and glaring at them all. "He knows your address, Aubrey. He knows everything there is to know about you and about your father. If he truly wanted to be a brother to you, nothing would stop him. But he doesn't. All he wants is to hurt your father—*his* father. And he doesn't care who else he hurts in the process!"

She took an angry breath. Then as abruptly as it had come, her anger gave way to crushing despair. "Come along, Aubrey," she finished in a somber tone. "It's time to leave."

It was a dismal company that trekked out to the carriage. A dreary mist hung in the air, not quite rain, nor could it properly be called a fog. It fit Eliza's mood perfectly.

Aubrey had insisted on carrying the heavy satchel, though its broken hinge made it awkward. Xavier helped him, a faint frown shadowing his dark face. But once they reached the carriage which stood beneath a shed and devoid of any horses, he grinned. "I'll have to find the stableman. It may take awhile. And it's getting late, almost dusk. You shouldn't be setting out so late—"

"If you can't find the stableman you'll have to harness the team yourself," Eliza ordered in her most haughty tone. She was sick to death of dealing with Xavier's ceaseless matchmaking. Didn't he realize it was not going to work?

"I'm a sailor," he said, drawing himself up regally. Then he winked at Ana. "I don't know a thing about harnessing a team of horses."

"Well, Aubrey does," Eliza retorted.

"My foot hurts," the boy responded, sitting on the folded down carriage step. He began earnestly to rub his ankle above the worn cuff of his brogans. "It hurts in the worst way."

"Oh, botheration!" Eliza glared at the two of them, then turned to Ana in final appeal.

But that one only raised her brows in mild response. "Cyprian knows how to harness a team of four. He worked as a stable boy once. Perhaps he'll help you."

"Perhaps he would, if he were here," Eliza snapped back. "But he's gone—"

"I think *fled* is a better word. He has fled your presence, just as you are fleeing his."

Eliza opened her mouth to retort, then shut it. She wanted to deny that she was fleeing, but they'd all know it for a lie. She *was* fleeing Cyprian. But he could hardly be said to be fleeing her. Could he?

She stared at Ana as quick doubt assailed her. What was it that Xavier had once said of Cyprian? That he had much pain in his heart.

Xavier tossed the heavy satchel into the carriage and at the solid thud of weighted leather against wooden floorboards, Eliza turned to stare at it. Cyprian did not want the huge amount of riches contained within that broken satchel. Not really. He wanted revenge—or at least he thought he did. But look how quickly he'd warmed to Aubrey. They were brothers though Cyprian had fought the idea at first. Maybe it was as she'd once speculated: what Cyprian Dare really needed was to belong to a family.

Maybe if she tried just one more time. . . .

"Where did he go?" She turned back to face Ana and Xavier. "Where did he flee to, as you call it?"

Xavier shrugged and worry showed on his downcast features. "That I do not know. The horse he hired is gone from its stall. But I'm certain he'll be back if you will just wait awhile."

"Yes," Ana put it. "You wait for him here, Eliza, while we deliver Aubrey to the Bear and Claw."

"I want to wait, too—"

"We *will* be waiting," Ana cut Aubrey off. "But we'll wait with Oliver at the Bear and Claw. I'm sure Eliza can bring Cyprian around if she has a little time alone with him. Besides, your parents must be desperate to see you by now." She rumpled the boy's hair fondly. "Think how surprised they're going to be when you walk up to them."

Aubrey grinned at that. "They will be, won't they? All right, then, let's be off. But what about the ransom money?" he added.

"Better leave that with me," Eliza answered. "Your father owes Cyprian that much at least."

"I don't think he'll want it," Xavier said. He smiled at her, the gentle smile that was so at odds with his otherwise fierce appearance. "He's been seeking treasure all his life, but I don't think it's the kind of treasure you can carry in a satchel."

Color crept into Eliza's cheeks despite the bitter cold of the gray December afternoon. Xavier meant her, of course. But though she wished fervently that he was right, she just was not sure. There was so much against it—primary among them Cyprian's hatred of his father.

Only it wasn't really hatred, she realized. It was all that pain in his heart. Maybe Xavier had been right all along.

But as Xavier finally searched out the stableman and Aubrey roused the driver, Eliza nevertheless was paralyzed by fear. Cyprian might be hurt by his father's neglect, but that didn't mean she was the one he could find comfort with. She and Ana hauled the ransom back into the house while the horses were put into their traces. Then the driver boarded and it was time for them to leave her all alone to wait.

"You need not fear Cyprian," Xavier whispered as he enfolded her in a smothering hug. "He will come around."

"That's right," Ana added, planting a farewell kiss on Eliza's cheek. "After all, Xavier came around, didn't he?"

Eliza met Ana's knowing gaze. "If I thought Cyprian could care for me even half so much as Xavier obviously cares for you—"

She couldn't finish. But then she didn't need to, for Ana knew. "He will," she whispered. "He will."

Eliza's last hug was for Aubrey. "I'm glad you're finally going home. Your parents will be overjoyed." She fingered his dark curls fondly. "I only wish I could be there to see their reactions when you walk up to them unaided."

"I intend to run—or perhaps skip," he said, his blue eyes dancing. "While you are working on Cyprian, Eliza, I shall work on Father. And I shall look forward to the day when they are reconciled with one another."

If that day ever comes, Eliza thought as she waved them off. If that day ever comes.

Chapter Twenty-Six

Cyprian sat the rawboned saddle horse under a dreary sky, in the meager shelter of a yew tree. Most of the countryside was barren, the stripped skeletons of trees and the brown remains of heather and nettle stalks, all shivering in the bitter blasts of the north wind. A solitary bird—a raven, it appeared—fought the wind, but otherwise, he and his horse were alone. The restless animal stamped a fore foot and blew a plume of frosty breath into the frigid air, but Cyprian ignored the horse's impatient desire to return to its warm stall. The carriage had turned out from the gate. Eliza and Aubrey were leaving.

The window curtains were closed, all but one, and Cyprian caught a glimpse of Aubrey's face, pale against the dark carriage. Then the curtain fell, and in a minute the vehicle was gone, round a bend of century old hedgerows.

It was for the best, Cyprian decided as he shifted in the saddle and tried to work the stiffness out of his back. Maybe now he could get on with his life. Maybe now he could get a decent night's sleep again. Once he got the hell out of England, things would be better and he would forget about his half brother—and about his cousin-by-marriage.

But Cyprian knew that would never happen. He would never forget. Not entirely.

With a violent curse he turned the eager horse and urged it into a reckless gallop. Across the field gone brown and dry, even in the hanging mist, he pushed the rangy animal until they seemed to fly as one across the frozen earth. It was almost like sailing, he thought as the icy wind tore at him and stung his eyes until they teared up. He could use the power of this horse like he used his ship, to swoop down on the unsuspecting and to escape his pursuers.

But there was no one to swoop down upon today, nor anyone to escape either. With another curse Cyprian slowed the plunging animal, then gradually brought him around, and urged him back toward the cottage. Time to return to his ship. Though it was late, he could not stay here tonight. He'd let Xavier know he was going. Then he'd be off no matter the dark, the weather, or anything else. He'd get out of England and as far away from his father and brother—and Eliza—as he possibly could get.

A light burned in the kitchen when he rode up. Or perhaps it was just the fire in the hearth. Cyprian shivered. He was wet and cold. Maybe Ana would heat him a stein of mulled wine before he left. A big one, enough to warm his body and dull his mind.

"Rub him down well," he told the stableman. "And give him an extra portion of mash. We'll be off again soon."

"Aye, Sir. I'll see to his needs. Reckon the missus inside will see to yours," he added with a wheezing chuckle.

"Yes," Cyprian agreed absently. Ana would see he was well fed, but she'd probably give him her own version of a tongue lashing about letting Eliza leave. Though she seldom said much, when she fixed her dark slanting eyes on a person, there was no doubt whether it was approval or disapproval she felt.

But he had no intentions of enduring her black stares this evening. He'd eat, then he'd leave. And if Ana and Xavier didn't like it, the hell with them.

The kitchen was empty, but the smells of dinner lingered and Cyprian's stomach growled as he latched the door behind him. He was grateful for the solitude and surprised also to see that Ana had bothered to leave a setting for him at the big table. But even as he approached the pot of soup and lifted the lid to sniff, his stomach rebelled. He was hungry but he couldn't eat.

With a sigh that was more a groan he put the lid back and turned to look for something to drink instead. Warm, cold, he didn't care. He just wanted something strong, something that would deaden his mind and kill the emotions that tore at his insides. But as he started to remove his gloves, a sound drew his attention and he turned around.

"Ana, where are you hiding the—"

The fact that Cyprian stopped in midsentence could be interpreted one of two ways, Eliza grimly thought. Her fingers tightened together in a knot that she pressed harder against her stomach. He was shocked and pleased, or else shocked and extremely annoyed to find her still there.

"Eliza."

"Hello, Cyprian."

A long, awkward silence ensued and Eliza cast about desperately for something to say. "Let me help you with your coat." But when she stepped forward, he did not make a move to cooperate.

"You're still here," he muttered, more to himself than to her, it seemed.

"Yes. Xavier and Ana took Aubrey to his parents. I stayed," she added quite unnecessarily. Cyprian's face was still; his expression was unreadable and his eyes—

his beautiful dark blue eyes—were shuttered so that she
could not read any facet of what he was feeling.

"Why are you—" He cleared his throat and began
again. "Why have you stayed?"

Eliza turned away. She was suddenly unable to bear
the intensity of his stare. Why had she stayed? If she
answered honestly she would bare her very soul to him,
bare it and leave herself completely vulnerable. But
then, she'd known it would come to this when she'd
decided to stay.

"The thing is . . . " She paused and took a shaky
breath. Then she turned and faced him. "The thing is,
Cyprian, I . . . I love you. There's no use pretending I
don't."

He stiffened, just a little, but she saw and it was like a
cruel slap across her face. He clasped his hands behind
his back and rocked back slightly on his heels. "I think
you're attracted to me, Eliza. But that's just physical. It's
not love."

"Yes, it is!" she burst out. "It *is* love. The only reason
you deny it is that you have no idea of what love is.
You've hated for so long that you can't understand love.
But I understand it, so don't you *dare* tell me that what I
feel for you is only lust!"

In the aftermath of her outburst he only stared at her
with a confused expression on his face, as if he could not
understand or else did not want to. More than anything
Eliza wanted to flee that look, to flee the fact that he
was not responding the way she wanted him to. He
hadn't said he loved her. But she was done with fleeing,
she reminded herself. She'd started this confrontation;
she might as well finish it.

With a courage borne of desperation—and the most
intense longing she'd ever known—Eliza loosened her
tightly clenched hands, took a slow, steadying breath
and forced herself to walk right up to him. Then she

reached for his left arm and drew it from behind his back.

Without saying a word she began to remove his leather glove, tugging at each of the fingers in turn until she could slide the entire glove off. She held the leather garment in both hands for a moment, aware of his warmth lingering there. Then she placed the glove on a nearby chair and raised her gaze up to meet his.

She removed his other glove the very same way, but their gazes remained locked this time. And with every tug, every slide of his fingers from the fine leather, Eliza felt some small barrier between them slip away. For him it might simply be lust, but for her it was love. No other word came close to explaining this all-consuming emotion, this mingling of desire and adoration and an insane need to soothe all his hurts, past, present, and to come. She wanted to make him happy, for perversely enough it seemed the only possible way for her ever to be happy. It was mixed up and impossible to explain, but Eliza knew it was true.

The second glove came off and she set it aside. Then with fingers that shook, she reached for the buttons of his overcoat.

"Eliza." His hand came up to circle her wrist and stay her movement. But she continued at her task even within the warm hold of his hand.

One button; a second. A third. And all the while his eyes grew darker until they seemed to suck her in. It was a dangerous thing to seduce a man, the one sober part of her mind recognized. Dangerous when so much more than merely your body was involved. Then she parted the front of his damp cheviot coat and slid both her hands against his waistcoat, palms pressed to the warmth and hardness that lay just below the pekin and the fine wool challis of his shirt.

He muttered low, an epithet muffled by a groan that seemed wrenched from the deepest part of him. One of his hands lifted to her hair. He stroked it once, then again before he frowned and began to pull the pins free. He removed her snood and watched almost distractedly as the thick twist of her hair spilled free down her back. Once more he stroked her hair with the gentlest of touches, all the way down to her waist, and all the while Eliza stared up at him, her breath caught somewhere in her midsection, her eyes held by the tortured look on his face. He was the same fierce man who'd terrified her less than a month before. But now he was the one who looked terrified. No, not terrified. Torn. He was drawn to her; that was plain. But he was torn by the vast differences between them. If only she could make him forget all the ways they were different and dwell instead on all the ways they were alike. All the ways they were so well suited.

"I love you, Cyprian," she whispered again as with renewed effort she worked the buttons of his waistcoat free and slid her hands beneath it to circle his waist. "Even though you don't want me to, I can't help it."

Without warning his arms came around her, crushing her to him as if he meant to draw her right inside himself. As if he meant to hold onto her forever.

"I want you to," he muttered against her hair. His lips moved, kissing her brow, her eyes, then finding her mouth.

Eliza wanted to dissolve into that kiss, to wallow in it, to drown in it and never come up for air again. But even as his hold on her tightened, Cyprian drew back just enough to stare deeply into her eyes. "Ah, damn, Eliza. You're so innocent. This will never work."

"You want me to love you," Eliza countered, smiling up at him. Her heart swelled almost to bursting with joy at the implication of his reluctant words. He wanted her to love him! "You want me to love you, Cyprian, and I do."

"I wanted you to, yes. But how much chance does a

sheltered woman like you have against a man who deliberately sets out to seduce her?"

"How long are you going to continue to confuse lust and love?" she demanded, not in the least deterred by his continuing resistance. She could taste love on his kisses and it was the thrilling taste of the sweetest sort of triumph.

She gripped the loose edges of his waistcoat and tugged until he bent down to her and their faces were but inches apart. "You could never make me fall in love with you. You made me willing in other ways," she admitted. "But loving you . . . " She paused as her emotions rose to form a lump in her throat. "Loving you was my own idea. You didn't make me love you, Cyprian . . . and you can't make me stop."

Their gazes held for one long torturous moment. If only he would believe her.

If only he felt the same.

Then with a groan of capitulation his mouth came down on hers. Eliza's eyes closed, but she did not need to see to know, nor even to hear the words he murmured in incoherent snatches between kisses. He cared about her. Whether he called it love or not no longer mattered to her. He cared, perhaps as much as she did.

He swept her up in his arms, all the while devouring her with kisses. Her lips parted and he fit his mouth ever closer, sliding his tongue inside, drawing hers back into his mouth. He tasted and searched and delved deep, rousing her to fiery passion in a matter of seconds. All her fears that he'd reject her, that he'd turn her overture down, dissolved now into a soaring, sizzling triumph.

Then he sat down on a bed—when had they gone up the stairs and found the bedchamber where she'd laid a fire, fearing to anticipate success, but needing to? He nestled her on his lap and circled her with his arms. "I'm sorry, Eliza, for everything I said before."

"It doesn't matter. I love you."

"I shouldn't have walked out—"

"You came back. I love you."

"No, *you* stayed. There's a big difference."

"I love you. I love you, Cyprian Dare. I just couldn't run away from that fact any longer."

He looked down at her. The room was dim with only a faint light coming in through the open door. But Eliza could see everything she needed to see. Cyprian's face had never been so earnest; his eyes had never been filled with such a clear emotion. She could feel the intensity of it in his touch even. He fairly thrummed with it, and she thrummed with an answering intensity. She circled his neck with her arms, seeking to pull him down to her. But he resisted and his eyes searched her face as if he might discover something new there. He smoothed a stray curl back from her cheek, then caught the tendril in his hand and rubbed it back and forth between his thumb and forefinger.

"I never expected . . . this," he murmured. "I never expected you."

Eliza nuzzled her cheek against his hand. "I never expected to love someone like you," she answered honestly. "Nor did I ever expect that love could be so . . . so completely overwhelming."

"Yes." He stared down at her and their eyes connected. Their souls connected. "So completely overwhelming."

Then he kissed her, a simple press of his lips to hers, of flesh to flesh, as millions of couples must have done over the course of a million years. But it was so much more than that. For Cyprian gave her his heart in that kiss; he gave his heart into her keeping. But just as importantly to Eliza, he took her heart most tenderly into his own care. She felt it in the sweet, almost chaste way his lips moved upon hers. She heard it in the steady thud of his heart beneath her fingers, and felt it in every portion of her body. I love you, Eliza, she heard. Only you. Always you.

Had he spoken the words or was it just the communion of of their souls? Eliza opened her eyes when Cyprian rolled her back onto the bed and half covered her with his body. "I hope you never regret the choice you've made, Eliza." Then before she could assure him she would not, or question him about what she thought he'd said before, his mouth came down on hers with a ferocity she knew well, and loved.

This was her man. Hers. And she would never let him go or give him up.

She opened to his plundering assault on all her senses, for only in such acquiescence would she find that soaring oneness with him. She opened her mouth to the heady invasion of his tongue, and her arms to the power of his embrace. And when he pressed hard and urgent against her belly, spreading her legs with his knees and demanding every right a man can demand from a woman, she arched up against him, demanding in her own feminine way that he take that which she offered.

He moved against her, thrusting the thick proof of his desire against her yielding softness, but his trousers and her bunched up skirts were in the way. "If we were in Madeira, we wouldn't have so many clothes on," she whispered between breathless kisses.

"I'll take you to Madeira, or Bermuda, or even the West Indies, where we can go around naked in the jungle if we want to. And I'll make love to you in the shade of a palm tree, or on a wide open beach. . . . "

Eliza let out a little cry of pleasure when his hand slid up her thigh, pushing her skirts aside until he found the damp center of her.

"I'll make love to you in the sea itself." His thumb brushed past the curls to find the tender nub, the incredibly sensitive place she'd never known she possessed. Until Cyprian.

"I'll make love to you everyday until I die, Eliza. Until I die from loving you."

There it was again. He *had* said it. Eliza stared up at him, into the face she loved so well. His thumb had found a rhythm that was raising her so high, so fast that she could feel her body begin to spin out of control. But not so much that she couldn't demand a final admission from him.

"You love me . . . don't you? Don't you, Cyprian . . . like I—oh . . . like I love you. . . . "

It was starting. That final climb; that final leap into some indescribable place. But Eliza held on, gripping the edges of his waistcoat. She needed to hear it once more.

Then he bent his head into the curve of her neck, burying his lips somewhere near her ear. "I love you," he whispered as he fought against his own physical need, all the while still urging her to new heights. "I do love you, Eliza."

Like a tidal wave it came then. Love. Desire. An explosion of too many feelings to ever put a name to. The ultimate physical ecstasy. The ultimate emotional joy. Eliza convulsed with the incredible pleasure of it, pushing up against his hand as his words played out over and over and over in her head. *I love you. I love you.*

He loved her.

Somehow in the hazy aftermath, Cyprian must have removed her clothes. Eliza recalled being turned and rolled over by hands that were both tender and urgent. He shifted her legs and arms about, and managed to remove skirt and bodice, petticoats and chemise, boots and stockings, and everything else without quite ripping the garments apart. Or maybe he did rip them. She didn't know, nor did she care. She only knew that though the room was chilly, she was flushed with warmth. Her skin radiated a heat that welled up from inside her until she felt she would surely go up in flames.

Still caught in the sultry afterthroes of what he'd brought her too, Eliza opened her eyes and stared up from the center of the bed to where Cyprian stood over her. He had paused in the process of shrugging off his waistcoat, and his eyes slid slowly over her, from her wildly disheveled hair down past her bare breasts and naked belly, all the way to her wantonly splayed legs. He saw everything, for she wore not a stitch of clothing. Though her first thought was to cover herself, to grab a bit of sheeting—anything—and hide her nakedness, Eliza forced herself to lay there and let him see her. Her skin turned even more rosy, though with embarrassment this time, but still she lay there, gazing up at the man she loved, hoping he knew that she would never deny him anything again. Never.

She saw him swallow, a reflexive movement. Then his eyes lifted to meet hers and if she had any lingering doubt about his feelings for her, the look on his face chased them away once and forever. For everything about Cyprian—the intensity of his midnight eyes, the hungry expression on his harshly handsome face, the straining impatience of his finely honed body—all spoke of love. And all focused upon her.

"Cyprian," she whispered, wanting him next to her. Within her. "Cyprian . . . "

The waistcoat was flung aside; the shirt tugged off almost before the waistcoat hit the floor. His boots flew in different directions, and in a moment he peeled the snug-fitting breeches down from his hips and thighs.

Then he stood before her, naked and proud. But still he hesitated. Was he giving her time to visually savor him as he'd savored her? It was almost more than she could bear. Her breath came short and fast. Her heart pounded a painful rhythm, fueled of desire for this man whom she loved.

Finally she raised a hand to him, beckoning him to come to her, to relieve the pressure that knotted anew in her nether regions and radiated out to encompass every square inch of her body. She needed him now. Why was he waiting?

Cyprian took her hand, but still he held himself away from her. She could see his erection, hard and jutting. Ready. She knew he wanted her as badly as she wanted him. Then he bent his head and kissed her hand, each knuckle, each fingertip, and, turning it over, kissed also her sensitive palm.

"I'm sorry, Eliza."

"Sorry?" Her heart paused in its mad racing. "Sorry for what?"

"For everything. Everything I put you through." He paused and swallowed again. "Every cruel act and harsh word."

With a rush her heart resumed its solid, loving beat. For a moment she'd been afraid he'd changed his mind. "I don't care about any of that, Cyprian. It's all in the past. It's the future I care about." Then her eyes moved over his magnificently masculine body. "And the present," she brazenly added.

"But I put you through so much. Even today—"

"Then make it up to me now." She turned her hand in his so that their fingers twined and their palms were pressed together. "Make it up to me right now," she repeated, tugging him closer.

He came down upon her slowly. First his eyes moved over her, caressing her in a way that felt purely physical, for her nipples tightened and she squirmed beneath that dark blue touch. Then his hand followed, stroking, teasing, tracing curves and hollows, seeking out her most sensitive spots and rousing her in the most subtly erotic manner she could ever imagine.

Eliza wanted to tell him to hurry, that she was burning up inside and liable to explode beneath his slow scorching touch. But she could hardly breathe, let alone speak. When his head lowered toward her breasts, her eyes fell closed and her hands knotted in the bedclothes. It was all she could manage.

With his mouth and tongue he teased her breasts, first one and then the other. Back and forth he moved, nipping, sucking, and teasing her until she was nearly mad with longing for him.

Somehow in the midst of her restless writhing, one of her hands found his thigh. Hard, rough with hair, she nonetheless thought it the most divine bit of human flesh she'd ever touched. Her fingers slid restlessly back and forth, then further up until she felt a hard smooth heat against her knuckles.

She didn't stop to think, for she was operating purely on instinct now. And love. She took his heavy male member in her hand, circling it with her fingers and sliding a little wonderingly up and down its length. It was so hot and so silky, given the rough feel of the rest of his body.

But before she could investigate the ridged end or the softer tip, he jerked her hand away. "No, Eliza. Don't. No." He shook his head when she protested. "If you do that now—"

He broke off and caught her mouth in a kiss that told her more than words could. He was as ready to ignite as she was. His mouth forced hers open and his tongue thrust inside in a feverish rhythm that presaged their ultimate joining. Even as she submitted to the glorious domination of his lips and tongue, he parted her legs with his knees and moved over her.

Eliza felt the hot weight of his arousal against her stomach and she thrust up against it in automatic response. When he groaned against her mouth, she smiled, for this was surely a woman's greatest joy: to give herself in love to the man who loved her; to know that the simple movement of her body gave him such complete pleasure. Then he pulled a little apart from her and she felt the insistent press of him as he finally sought entrance to her woman's place.

Eliza lifted her eyelids and gazed up through the gathering darkness into his sharply etched features. As he slid inside, slowly, in short erotic thrusts, she watched the play of emotions on his face. Passion was there; restraint too. And love. Love was there in the way his eyes caressed her and in the curve of his lips as he bent low to kiss her once more. It was there in his powerful straining body, in the hard line of muscles beneath her hand as she swept it down his back.

"I love you," she murmured as his mouth moved on hers in sync with his body's rising motion. But though the words were lost in their quickening passion and gasping breaths, Eliza knew he understood. And as he began the full thrusting pace that carried them faster and higher, she knew that her ultimate joy would be to give him a child—a family full of children.

She tightened her arms around his shoulders and lifted her legs to wrap around his thrusting hips. This time was for love and family, and a future they would live happily together.

"Oh how I love you, Cyprian," she whispered as the incredible rush began.

And as he pushed her past the edge, then joined her in that mad, spiraling explosion, she heard his muffled cry. "I love you, love you . . . love you."

Chapter Twenty-Seven

*C*yprian was insatiable. But then, Eliza felt the very
same way. She could not get enough of this man. A
lifetime with him could not begin to be enough.

But they did not speak of lifetimes during the sweet,
dark hours of the night. They spoke only of the present,
using lips and tongues and fingertips, and every other
portion of their bodies to speak the language of love. It
was a conversation that was at once both eloquent and
earthy, at times a ballet, at other times very nearly a
brawl. She began to understand the nuances of his very
breathing: quick and shallow when she explored him
with her fingers; hard and gasping when the rush to
completion began.

But when she returned to her earlier curiosity about
that most overt symbol of his masculinity, his breathing
halted altogether. His entire body went absolutely still,
though she could sense the fine tension that held him in
its grip. Oh, yes, there was a heady sense of power to be
had in commanding his complete attention this way.

But Cyprian only let her go so far with such inquisi-
tive searches. Invariably his stillness would burst into
near violent emotion and no matter how she tried to
slow him down, he would be over her. In her. Making

love to her as if he'd never done it before and would never have a chance to do so again.

But Eliza knew better. This was only the beginning, and there would never be an ending to it, she promised herself now as she nestled into his arms. Morning was nigh. A new day for them to spend together. A new life for them to begin, although there were any number of obstacles in their way. But they would face those obstacles together. And they would overcome them too.

Cyprian stirred behind her, pulling her more intimately into the curve of his body. Her head rested on one of his arms, while his other arm lay warm and heavy over her hip. His hand slid down her thigh, slow and sleepy, then pulled her leg up so that she was curled in a snug ball, and he encircled her completely.

Eliza felt a contentment she'd never experienced before in her entire life, and she knew Cyprian felt it too. Perhaps this was the time for them to speak of the future, she thought, though the lovely cobwebs in her brain made coherent thought a little tricky.

"Good morning," she whispered, kissing the murmured words against his muscled forearm just beneath her cheek.

"Mmmm. . . . " He nuzzled his face into her hopelessly tangled hair, then kissed the three little bumps of bone at the back of her neck. A delicious shiver worked its way down from his lips, all along the curve of her spine. Eliza could hardly believe the desire it awakened in her. Was there no satisfying this hunger she felt for him?

Then suddenly and without warning, he pulled away. She started to roll over to face him, but he cautioned her with a touch that had turned abruptly from teasing to tense.

"Stay here."

He pushed lithely from the bed and reached for his breeches while she sat up, staring at him through the cold, early morning light in open-mouthed confusion. "What's wrong? Where are you—"

"Someone's coming."

He yanked on his boots in two quick movements, then straightened and looked at her. He was the very picture of a man at full alert, while she . . . she felt fuzzy-headed from lack of sleep. Someone was coming? But who?

"Oh, dear!" she exclaimed as it abruptly dawned on her. Her father, or perhaps even Uncle Lloyd. She wasn't sure which one would be worse. And if they were together—oh, but it didn't bear thinking on.

Yet the ringing clatter of horse hooves on the cobblestones in the courtyard could not be ignored. After a quick glance past the short heavy curtains, Cyprian grimaced and turned away.

"It looks like the whole damned lot of them. Your entire family."

Her entire family! Good Lord, but this was going to be dreadful!

While Cyprian grabbed for his shirt, she leaped from the bed, searching wildly for her chemise and dress—anything to cover her nakedness and prevent everyone from jumping to the wrong conclusion. But then, clothed or not, what other conclusion could they possibly draw?

"Oh, dear," she murmured once more as the reality of what she'd done sank in. Her father would kill Cyprian. Then she glanced at Cyprian and saw him slip a small dagger in his left boot. It was more likely, she realized, that Cyprian would kill her father, if it came down to that. Somehow she must stop the coming altercation before it could begin.

"Wait for me!" she cried when Cyprian headed for the bedroom door. He paused as she struggled with her chemise, then crossed to her and took her by the shoulders.

"If I don't go down now, they'll come up here and that would be even worse, Eliza." He gave her a quick, hard kiss then set her away from him. "Get dressed and comb your hair. I'll hold them off as long as I can."

"But Cyprian, you don't understand—"

"Oh, I understand, sweetheart," he countered. "I've despoiled you, their only daughter, and now they've got to make things right."

"But Cyprian—"

"Just hurry," he ordered. Then he was gone.

Eliza heard a violent pounding on the downstairs door. "Eliza? Eliza!" Her father's agitated cry came through the solid stone walls of the cottage. Pausing only a moment, she ran to the window, thrust the curtain aside, then lifted the latch and shoved the casement window open. The morning was bright, but frigid. Below her a half dozen faces turned up when the window swung wide.

"Eliza—"

"Are you all right?"

"Unlock the door!"

She heard the rising babble and saw the icy puffs of angry breath left hanging in the winter air. Besides her father and two brothers, Uncle Lloyd and Aubrey were also there. Xavier had come too, with Ana and Oliver beside him, though they stood back, just watching. No doubt Xavier would help Cyprian should it come to that, but that did not ease Eliza's fears very much.

Her father gaped up at her as though he could not quite comprehend this reality. He took in her sleep-tossed hair and barely clad shoulders, staring wide-eyed, as if he could not believe his eyes.

But instead of filling her with shame, his stunned expression only strengthened her need to stand beside Cyprian. He was as good a man as any of them, despite the circumstances of his birth and upbringing, and she would not let any of them say a single word to the contrary.

Without responding to any of their calls, she pulled her head inside and slammed the window closed. She pulled on her skirt, tying it haphazardly over her bare legs, then slipped on her bodice without benefit of lacing. Her short jacket would hold it in place and she slid her feet into her ankle boots without waiting to don stockings.

Her hair was hopeless, she decided. Then she heard the pounding on the door stop abruptly, and she flew out the door and down the stairs like one possessed. That she must stand with Cyprian was her one overriding thought. She must stand with him though it be against everyone else that she loved.

The sight that met her eyes would have been comical under any other circumstances. Cyprian stood in the open door, barring their entrance with his legs braced wide and his fists on his hips. Aubrey stood opposite him, a slender child seemingly in charge of all the angry men behind him. But it was not Aubrey's stature that held them back, but his unlikely smile and cheerful voice.

"Hello, brother. Did we awaken you?"

"Don't call him that!" Uncle Lloyd ordered his son. "I told you to keep him away from here," he added, turning his fury on Oliver. But that one only shrugged and ignored him. Oliver shot Eliza a saucy wink, though, and it gave her immeasurable comfort. Somehow this would work out.

But when she glanced up at Cyprian she was not so sure, for he stared at her uncle—his father—with an expression that defied description. Hatred, fury, triumph and fear seemed to compete for dominance, and she sensed the brittle tension that gripped his entire body. Without pausing to think she stepped nearer and slipped her hand through his arm.

"Eliza! Come here, daughter," her father demanded when he spied her behind Cyprian. At her father's curt command, Cyprian glanced over his shoulder. Then with the insolent sort of gesture she should have expected of him under the circumstances, he pulled her against his side with a possessive arm around her shoulder. "Do you wish to speak to these people?" he asked her, as if the angry throng outside the door was of no moment whatsoever.

She responded with an exasperated glare, then forced herself to smile at her father. "Good morning, Father. Would you . . . " She faltered in the face of her father's scandalized expression. "Would you like to come inside . . . for tea?" she finished rather lamely.

Her father's face was as pale as Uncle Lloyd's was red. "What I would like is for you to come home with me. Right this minute," he added in a voice that trembled with emotion. He stepped in front of Aubrey, and in the cold, clear dawn, he suddenly looked every one of his fifty-odd years. He looked weary and beaten, and it affected Eliza as nothing else could have.

"Papa, please. You have to understand—"

"I do understand," he broke in. Then he extended a hand to her. "Come home with me, Eliza. Captain Dare and I will speak later. But for now it would be best for you to come with me. Your mother has been beside herself. She needs to see you."

Eliza stared at his outstretched hand, then turned an uncertain countenance up to Cyprian. But though his fingers tightened almost imperceptibly on her shoulder, his face was harsh and unreadable.

"Cyprian, I . . . maybe I should go to her."

"It's time for you to choose, Eliza. You can't have them *and* me."

"Come along, Eliza," her father implored. But she continued to stare up at Cyprian.

"Why does it have to be a choice? Why can't we reconcile our differences and be one happy family—"

"That's impossible." Cyprian cut her off. He looked away from her and, following his stare, she spied her uncle—Cyprian's long absent father. He stood now with Aubrey before him and his hands rested on the boy's shoulders. They were so alike at that moment that even a blind man would name them father and son. For Cyprian, she realized, the sight must have stabbed at his heart as cruelly as a razor-pointed dagger.

With a soft oath she grabbed Cyprian's shirt front and forced his attention back to her. "I came to you, Cyprian. I forsook all my pride and came to you. Will you do no less for me?" She took a shaky breath, but she continued to hold his angry glare with her eyes. "I'm leaving with my father now, but only to go back to the posting house in Lyme Regis. I shall bathe and take a nap and reassure my mother that I am well. But I shall await your company for dinner. We shall dine together, you, me, and my parents. Do you hear me? We shall work everything out then."

For a long moment their gazes held and despite his rigid composure, she saw the emotions that burned inside him. Anger was there, for he wanted her to reject all of them right then and there, to choose him without any concessions to anyone else. Fear was there too, fear that she would choose her family instead and that he would be the rejected one. But most of all there was pain, the pain Xavier had tried to tell her about that very first day on board the *Chameleon*. His father had chosen his legitimate family over his illegitimate one. As a result Cyprian saw every choice as a total committment: one or the other, with no room for compromise.

But Eliza had enough room in her heart for all of them. She just had to convince Cyprian of that.

"I love you, Cyprian. But I love my family too. I have no intentions of giving up either of you. So don't *you*

give up on *me,* do you hear?" Then she tugged his shirt
so that he was in reach, and lifted up on her toes to give
him a quick, chaste kiss.

Someone beyond them let out a sharp oath, but she
ignored it. "Come for dinner at the posting house, Cyprian. Don't disappoint me." Then smoothing his rumpled shirt front with nervous fingers, she stepped back,
turned away, and walked toward her father's waiting
arms.

Chapter Twenty-Eight

"**Y**ou should take her home now!" Lloyd Haberton stated. "Get her away from his foul influence while you can. And pray that Johnstone will still have her."

Eliza glared daggers at her uncle. If she hadn't been so completely rattled when her father had hustled her into his carriage, she would have demanded to ride in the vehicle carrying her brothers. By the time she realized her mistake, however, they were underway. Now she had reached her limit with her uncle's overbearing ways.

"You need not speak of me as if I were not present, Uncle Lloyd. For your information, I will not return to London until I am quite ready to do so. And I am not in the least interested in *having* Michael Johnstone, as you put it, no matter *what* his opinion of me might be."

"I was not thinking of London," her uncle angrily shot back. "After this shameful episode your only chance is to retire to the country and hope some good-hearted rustic will overlook your scandalous past and offer for you!"

It was a cruel blow, and it found its mark. Eliza gasped and had to fight down a monentary panic. What if Cyprian did not come . . . Then she rallied. "Is that

what you did after *your* shameful episode? Did you retire to the country and marry some rustic?"

"Eliza!"

She turned at her father's rebuke. "You are all very
conveniently overlooking the fact that Cyprian is Uncle
Lloyd's son! Call him your bastard, if you will," she said,
glaring back at her uncle's now furious face. "But the
fact remains that you abandoned his mother and there-
fore him. Our family has been cruel enough to Cyprian;
I will not be a part of any continuing cruelty toward him.
I refuse to abandon him again."

"But I did not know she bore the child," her uncle
vowed. Then his gaze shifted uncomfortably to Aubrey,
who sat silent for once all ears and eyes as the adults
around him did verbal battle. "I don't think this subject
is approprate."

But Eliza ignored the last part of his words. "What
would you have done if you had known?" She leaned
forward in the rocking cab of the coach and pinned him
with her eyes. "How would you have dealt with Cybil
then? Would you have married her?"

"I . . . well, no . . . no, I was betrothed to Constance. I could not have broken my vow to her," he
added defensively.

"You were already betrothed? That means . . . that
means you always intended to abandon them." Eliza sat
back in the hard seat, horrified.

"Father?" Aubrey put in from his spot against the
door. "Is that true?"

Lloyd's stare switched from Eliza to Aubrey. "No, no,
son. I . . . I would have provided for them. Bought
them a cottage. Seen to his schooling."

"Perhaps you should tell him that," Eliza suggested.

"That won't make any difference!" Lloyd swore. "It's
too late. It became too late the minute he stole Aubrey.
Even though my son is returned to me, he still has my
money." Then he gasped. "My money!" At once he

pounded on the roof of the carriage. "Driver! Stop! Turn around. We need to go back for my money!"

"Cyprian is your son, too!" Eliza shouted furiously. "But you value your money more than the son you sired. I'm surprised you agreed to put up a ransom for Aubrey, all things considered. And you didn't once admit that without Cyprian's involvement Aubrey might still be crippled," she reminded him in a scathing tone. Then turning to Aubrey she added, "Take note, cousin, of how much your father values his children."

"Oh, but you are wrong, Eliza," Aubrey countered most sincerely. "Father and mother were so happy to see me—and to see me walk right up to them. He cried for joy, you know. He really did."

Eliza wanted to stamp her foot in frustration. *Whose side are you on?* she fumed silently at her cousin.

But then she saw how her Uncle Lloyd stared at his son, how his eyes went to Aubrey's legs and then back to his innocent young face. How love for his child shone in his eyes despite the other emotions that contorted his features. He hesitated now in the middle of trying again to attract the driver's attention, his arm upraised and his mouth open wide, staring in sudden confusion at his young son.

Aubrey was most assuredly a master of manipulation, Eliza recognized in that portion of her mind that could still be rational and observant. The child did not say another word. He didn't need to. He just stared at his father, speaking volumes with only his guileless blue eyes.

Oh, but he was so like his older half brother. It was not just the raven-dark hair and piercing blue eyes they'd both taken from their father, but also the personality traits they so obviously shared. They were both stubborn to a fault; each had a willpower that frustrated everyone; and they both possessed an uncanny ability to manipulate the people around them. Cyprian was an expert at it and Aubrey seemed to have the same natural talent.

When her uncle fell back against the hard leather seat, Eliza turned her head toward the window. The fringe-edged shade was pulled down and laced at both corners to keep the damp December wind out. But still she stared at the shade as if through an open portal that revealed a wondrous landscape, wild and beautiful. But any scene she viewed was purely in her mind, though no less wild and beautiful. For it was Cyprian she saw in her mind's eye, and she knew there was nothing more wild and beautiful than him.

A lump rose in her throat and fear forced her eyes closed. She was cold and lonely, though in the midst of her family, and the thought that Cyprian might not come tortured her. Tears fought for release, but she willed them back. She would not cry in front of them, not even her father, for they would all know she cried for Cyprian, and that would only make things worse. They hated him; he hated them. If she were to keep *all* of them, she would need to be strong, stronger than she'd ever had to be in her short, sheltered life. But she would be, she vowed with renewed determination.

With a cleansing sigh she clutched her hands together in her lap. She meant to win in this battle of wills, though she would have to defeat her father, her uncle, and Cyprian. But she did have allies, she realized. She had Aubrey. And Oliver, Xavier, and Ana were on her side. Even Perry was leaning her way. She could only pray that together they were enough.

"Not another word." Cyprian cut Xavier off with a menacing glare. Ana, however, was not so easily cowed. She picked up a muslin apron and tied it around her waist.

"So much for men being stronger and braver than

women," she muttered, as if to herself. But she knew it carried to Cyprian.

"You don't understand any of this, Ana. So kindly mind your own business," he finished in a decidedly unkind tone.

"I happen to think Eliza is my business," she stated as she handed a bucket to Oliver. "Fetch water," she ordered. Then she began to assemble a variety of herbs and spices on the wide table. "Eliza and I have become quite close. I consider her very like a sister, and I admire her for her courage." She raised her head and fixed Cyprian with her dark mysterious gaze. "She knows her mind and is not afraid to pursue a course that will bring her happiness—even if that course is fraught with obstacles. Which is more than I can say for you," she added flatly.

Cyprian sent her a murderous look and his hands tightened into fists. "If she'd wanted to stay she could have. She *chose* to leave. I did not run her off."

"She chose to go to her mother and she invited you to dinner! That is a far different picture than the one you attempt to paint."

"Christ!" Cyprian spun on his heel and stalked to the door. "I'm leaving."

"Don't forget your money," Ana called out to him. "I know how much you value it. I only hope it brings you comfort tonight and all the long nights to come—"

The slam of the door was her only answer. Still, Ana was not perturbed, and a faint smile curved her lips.

"Was that smart?" Xavier asked, his voice worried.

But she only slanted a wider smile at him. "I think so. He is just too hurt and angry to think straight right now. But he'll come around."

Xavier grinned and walked up to her to take her in his arms. "How did you come to be so wise?"

Ana laughed. "You can ask me that after all I went through to teach you about love?" Then she glanced

over at Oliver who had watched the entire scene with
the empty bucket in hand. "Go fetch the water," she
ordered him once more. "Just because that Haberton
fellow has agreed to Aubrey's demand that you captain
a ship for him does not mean you do not have chores
around here." She smiled up at Xavier then. "Oh, and
Oliver, don't hurry back."

As he slipped out the door, Oliver heard her laugh
and the rumbling murmur of Xavier's reply. No man
was immune, he supposed as he crossed to the well.
Xavier had succumbed to love despite a mighty battle
against it. Now Cyprian was fighting it.

Whose love would *he* resist, he wondered. Then he
chuckled. Why resist? So long as she was comely, with a
fair face, long silky hair, and a ripe young body, he could
think of no reason at all to resist falling in love. Then his
brow wrinkled at the thought. He'd been a long time
without a woman. Since Xavier and Ana plainly did not
want his company, perhaps he should take a stroll and
see what the village over the hill had to offer in the way
of female companionship.

Cyprian did not ride this time. He'd worn out his val-
iant steed once already, so this time he stalked away
from the cottage on foot. He did not mark his direction;
he was too furious with Ana to care. What right had she
to interfere? If he'd wanted her advice, he would have
asked her for it.

The dry, frozen grasses crackled as he strode across a
fallow field. Beyond the barren branches of a stand of
birch, the church spire of tiny Dunlop was barely visible.
England was ugly in winter, brown and grim. Not the
sort of place he cared for, not when he could be on the
pleasant isle of Alderney or Madeira's beach of perpet-
ual June.

He slowed as he approached a roadside grotto, one of
many that dotted England's roads and highways. He

could go to Madeira, he told himself, breathing hard at his exertion. He could sail tonight if he wanted to. But what about Eliza?

Cyprian came to a halt. Maybe Ana was right. Maybe he should accept Eliza's invitation. It was plain she wanted him. Hadn't she come to him yesterday—though not without a little prompting from Xavier. Hadn't she given herself to him without hesitation, without holding back a thing? To even think of the joy he found in her embrace sent a surge of heat to his loins. Ah, Eliza.

He frowned and stared blindly about. If she did want to make a life with him . . . His thoughts were confused and his emotions a tortured maze that pitted a lifetime built upon vengeance against a future that promised a sort of happiness he'd never considered before. But Eliza came with a price. Her family was a part of her—a part she wouldn't give up, even for him.

He swore a vile oath. Why wasn't *he* enough for her? Why couldn't she forget about them—

But he understood why. It was not her way to abandon the people she loved. She hadn't abandoned Aubrey and she wouldn't abandon the rest of her family. He was the only one she had no trouble leaving behind.

Yet Cyprian knew better than that. She hadn't turned away from him. She'd extended a hand to draw him into her family.

"Ah, Christ," he muttered, raking his hands through his hair. Then a childish call and an answering bark drew his attention. When he turned, he spied a boy bent under a canvas sack of sticks that jutted out several feet on either side of him. He appeared about the same age as Aubrey, and despite his awkward load, he trotted at a goodly pace in the wake of a small, brown-and-white speckled dog.

The boy and his furry companion were oblivious to Cyprian's presence, for the little dog was busy searching either side of the path, trying to scare up a field mouse or a hare to chase, and the boy was eagerly following his pet's progress.

"Atta boy, Spot. Keep after them. Oh! There's one! Get 'im! Get 'im, fellow!"

The dog tore off after some invisible creature that scurried beneath the dead meadow grasses. The boy started to chase after them, but his wide load of kindling unbalanced, and firewood and boy both tipped over.

In a minute the dog was back with his young master, panting and licking him, while the lad heaped praise upon his pet. "Good boy. You gave him a real go there, laddie."

He was in the midst of rebalancing his load when a sharp whistle turned his head around. "I'm here, Da'."

As Cyprian stood quietly observing the scene from beside the grotto, a man pulling a small two-wheeled cart came over the hill.

"Danny, come here, lad. Up on the cart wit' you, for it's downhill from here on." The woodcutter lifted both the boy and his load up onto the already heavily laden cart. Then down the hill they began, cutting through the field on a cowpath.

The boy's laughter and the father's rumbling replies drifted up to Cyprian, as did the little dog's excited yapping. But their conversation was not what held Cyprian's attention. What drew his gaze and kept it focused upon them as they made their slow descent to the village was the warmth they exuded. Father and son.

He'd been obsessed with his own father and his hatred of the man for so many years that he'd been blind to everything else. But now he saw himself in the role of father—*really* saw himself, not just as being better at it than Lloyd Haberton, but as finding happiness in it. Enjoying fatherhood for itself, not as another sort of revenge.

He wanted to be a father, he realized, as he watched the villager and his son make their way home. He wanted to share an afternoon with his son—or daughter —then return home, cold yet cheerful, to his warm home and welcoming wife.

To Eliza.

As if an immense weight had been lifted from his shoulders, Cyprian suddenly felt buoyed up. The very thought of her bearing his children gladdened the deepest recesses of his heart. He'd never wanted that from another woman, and he never would. Eliza was everything to him, he saw with welcome clarity. She was love and home and happiness. She was his future, just waiting for him. But he had to reach out and grasp hold of that future if he truly wanted it.

The very thought of doing that, and of having to deal with his father, enraged him. But a life with Eliza . . .

He took a deep breath of the icy air and shook off his doubts. Down the hill, the woodcutter and his son were out of sight. But as Cyprian turned and started back to the cottage, the image of the pair stayed with him. By now they were home, welcomed in by a smiling woman who steered them nearer the fire and brought them bowls of hearty stew and asked them about their day. A simple enough pleasure, to dine in the presence of the ones you loved.

Suddenly Cyprian could hardly wait for the dinner hour.

Chapter Twenty-Nine

"*I* see no reason to primp for this . . . this . . . this hooligan bastard your sister's husband has turned loose on our family!"

Eliza's jaw set to hear her father's angry shouts. Her mother made some reply, but Eliza could hear little enough through the door that separated her room from her parents, only perhaps the phrase "prodigal son" and something about "to err is human."

"If that were a biblical quote instead of the simpering words of some long-dead poet, perhaps I'd take it to heart—"

The rest of his tirade ended when Eliza rapped angrily on the door. "May I enter?" she called. Then she twisted the door handle and strode in, not waiting for an answer.

Her father stood, trousers and braces on, his linen shirt fastened properly with jasper studs and his shoes already on. He was frowning as his wife helped him tie his burgundy silk neck cloth prior to him donning his striped waistcoat and black frock coat. Eliza's mother was already dressed in a gown of dove gray with crisp white cuffs and collars, and rich purple braid on the bodice. A sheer purple scarf draped her shoulders and was tied in a wide graceful bow at her chest. Though it was a far cry from the frilly sort of gowns she wore to entertain at Diamond Hall, given the circumstances, she still managed to look as lovely as ever. All in all, the pair of them were every inch the well-to-do couple. Somehow that only added to Eliza's simmering anger.

"Never call him 'bastard' again," she snapped, glaring at her father. "Not if you intend to dandle any children of mine upon your knee."

Where that threat came from she could not say, but it had the desired effect of silencing her father, though his mouth gaped open wide in shock.

"Eliza," her mother breathed in an equally shocked tone. She glanced surreptitiously at Eliza's stomach, then raised her fearful glance to her daughter's face.

"No, Mother. I do not bear a child of Cyprian's. But I intend to. I intend to fill his home and his heart with the joy of children. Your grandchildren," she added as a tide of softer emotions drowned her anger. The very thought of Cyprian cradling a child of theirs filled her with such strange and intense feelings that she felt she might dissolve with the strength of her love for him—for him and his yet-to-be-conceived children. Their children.

She sighed and sent her parents a trembling smile. "Please be nice to him, Papa."

He shut his mouth finally, then cleared his throat and turned away. This was so hard on him, she realized as he fumbled into his waistcoat and did up the buttons. After all, it was not even two months ago that he'd reluctantly seen her off, his ailing daughter, to heal on foreign shores. Now she was back, changed in ways he did not understand, stronger both physically and emotionally. She'd never shouted at him once in her entire life, nor questioned his will either, except in the matter of her betrothal to Michael. But now she fussed like a fishwife, no longer suffered any malady of the lungs, and was throwing herself at a man he considered of no consequence, less reputation, and absent of any honor whatsoever.

An inappropriate giggle bubbled up inside her. All in all, she supposed her parents were actually taking things rather well.

She stared at the two of them and suddenly saw them as they truly were: not two people intent on preventing her from finding the love and happiness she sought, but as parents who loved her in the same way she would love her own children someday, parents who wanted her secure and happy. That was all. She knew that only Cyprian could give her those things. Only with him could she find that security and happiness they wanted for her. It remained now for her to convince them of it.

A rush of love for them filled her heart and with a glad cry she flew across the room and into their startled embraces. "I love you both so much," she whispered though fierce emotion choked her. "You've been such good parents to me, though I've always been a most difficult child—"

"You were never difficult," her mother softly crooned, circling her with welcoming arms and smoothing her hair with a gentle hand.

"I was always sick."

"But you're well now," her father replied, kissing her brow and patting her shoulder with a warm but awkward hand.

Eliza gave him a damp but heartfelt smile. "Yes, I'm well now, and I'm grown up enough to know where my heart lies. Wait," she said before he could interrupt. "I know you think I'm making a terrible mistake with Cyprian. But you forget the example that you have set for me and LeClere and Perry. It's obvious to all of us—to everyone who knows you—that the two of you adore each other. It's only natural that your children want the same sort of rock solid love in their own lives. Well, that's how I feel about Cyprian."

She met her mother's wide, luminous gaze and saw in that instant that she'd won her mother over. Love was an emotion that women seemed to recognize instinctively. It was men who seemed to struggle against it, just as her father's frown showed he struggled against it now.

"You may love him. I do not doubt the sincerity of your emotions, daughter. But as for him—" He broke off and pulled away from their embrace.

But Eliza would not relent. "He loves me too, Father. The only impediment for him is my family—mainly Uncle Lloyd," she hastened to add.

"Yes, well I'm afraid your uncle Lloyd is not going to go away. He will remain your uncle and a part of this family whether this . . . this sea captain of yours likes it or not."

Eliza crossed to her father's side and took his hand in hers. "Cyprian will come around, Father. He just needs time."

"Hmph. You say that because you wish to believe it. For all you know, he may not even show up tonight."

With that one exasperated comment he struck at her deepest fear. What *if* Cyprian did not show? What if she were wrong and their love was not sufficient to counteract his lifelong hatred of his father?

Eliza could not bear the thought, so she did the only thing she could. She smothered her fears with optimism, giving her father a brave smile. "He'll be here. You'll see. Before this night is out, we will begin to mend the rifts in our family and you'll understand why I love Cyprian so much."

Her father did not respond. He only turned toward the plain oak-framed mirror that hung on the wall and began once more to fiddle with his cravat. Her mother sighed and gave Eliza a warm and hopeful smile. Then a sharp rap upon the hall door brought their heads swivelling about.

"He's here," Eliza breathed, and her heart began to pound a happy rhythm.

But the message brought by her youngest brother, Perry, was far less promising than that. "Uncle Lloyd says he accepts your invitation after all, Father. He shall dine with you tonight."

"Papa, no!" Eliza exclaimed. "If his father is there—"

"What will happen? His true nature will out? Better to know now how this man you would wed will deal with your family. *All* of your family."

"But that's not fair," Eliza protested. "Mother, please. You understand, don't you?"

"Oh, Eliza. Yes, of course I understand. But I also agree with your father. If your Cyprian loves you as dearly as you love him, he will bury his anger. His love will snuff it out and the two of you will be able to begin a life together free of any impure motives."

"But Mother . . . "

Eliza trailed off in the face of their unrelenting expressions. It was clear they had decided; it was up to Cyprian now, completely up to him. A lifetime of hatred versus the promise of a lifetime of love.

Though she tried to convince herself that love must always triumph over hate, as she followed her parents down the dimly lit hall toward the private dining room they'd reserved, Eliza was suddenly afraid. Cyprian was a man of intense emotions. He loved and hated with a fierceness that could be terrifying. Though she'd come to love that intensity, it now filled her with dread, for Cyprian was nothing if not unpredictable. Soon she would know the direction of the rest of her life. Soon she will be filled with indescribable joy, or else unutterable misery.

As she took her seat at the well-laid table, Eliza's heart beat a frightened and irregular pattern. Please come, she prayed, not to God but to Cyprian. *Please hurry to my side and please, please, tell me you'll stay forever.*

Eliza paced. Her uncle was on his third glass of wine. Her mother kept folding and refolding a square linen napkin while her father pulled out his watch for what surely must have been the hundredth time.

The door creaked and Eliza whirled. But her hopes crashed into despair when it was only Mrs. Dooley, the innkeeper's wife.

"Shall I send round the first course?"

"Yes—"

"No!" Eliza countered her uncle's word. "No. We await another guest."

"Who's not coming," Uncle Lloyd muttered.

"He is," Eliza vowed. "Go on," she ordered the puzzled woman. "And when he arrives, do not delay a moment in showing him in."

The door closed with a discreet click. Silence reigned again in the modestly furnished dining room.

It occurred absurdly to Eliza that she seemed always to spend her most nerve-wracking moments in dining rooms, and all on account of suitors. At her birthday party in the dining room at Diamond Hall, she'd been sorely upset at the thought of marrying Michael. Dear, kind Michael who deserved a far better woman than her to love him. How she hoped he discovered such a lifemate soon.

But this wait here at the plain little inn at Lyme Regis was far, far worse than the hours she'd spent dreading marriage to Michael Johnstone. It was well into the dinner hour. Cyprian should be here by now, shouldn't he? She kept her back to her parents and uncle. If only Aubrey were here, or her brothers. But they'd been given their dinner separately. It was to be only her parents, Cyprian's father, her, and Cyprian. *If* he showed up.

Another quarter hour passed, though it felt like an hour or more. Eliza stood at a curtained window, staring off into the darkness at a grove of beech trees stripped bare by the winter winds. The gray silhouetted branches reached up as if in supplication to the dark and moody sky, praying for the return of warmth and light, she imagined. Just as she prayed for the warmth and light that only Cyprian could bring to her life.

A soft rap sounded on the door and Eliza started, then as quickly, she subsided in disappointment. Cyprian's knock would never be so timid.

Sure enough, Mrs. Dooley's peculiar west country drawl intruded on the somber silence of the room.

"Beggin' yer pardons, but—"

"I'll introduce myself, thank you."

Eliza gasped and whirled. Cyprian!

He stood in the doorway, nearly brushing the door frame with the top of his head. Had any man ever looked so handsome and so virile? So dear? Eliza's eyes misted with grateful tears as she stared at him unspeaking. He'd come for her. He loved her, and oh, how completely she loved him.

Their eyes met and held, and she saw in them both love and a raw vulnerability. *I'm here for you,* his gaze seemed to say. I'm here because I love you and need you.

Then his eyes shifted to his father, and in a blink the vulnerability was replaced by a careful blankness that she knew covered a soul-deep anger. He stiffened, not stepping into the room, so she started toward him instead. But her mother caught her arm, staying her progress while her father went forward to greet Cyprian.

"Good evening, Captain Dare." He put out his hand in greeting, and although Cyprian did not at once take it, her father held it there, steady. When Cyprian finally grasped Gerald Thoroughgood's hand, Eliza could have kissed her father for the unwavering generosity of that gesture. He wanted this to work, she realized, and that meant more to her than she could ever express. He wanted Cyprian to have the opportunity to come to terms with his own father as well as hers. The opportunity to marry her. It remained only for them to mend the wounds between Cyprian and Uncle Lloyd.

She took a shaky breath, afraid to be hopeful, but unable not to be. Her mother squeezed her arm in reassurance as her father drew Cyprian into the room. The door closed. Cyprian hung his hat and his heavy top coat on a wall hook. Then he turned to face them all.

This was not easy for him, she could tell, for although he looked tall and forbidding—unapproachable, in fact —she knew him well enough now to realize that he always appeared his most intimidating when he was actually most vulnerable. Oh, how right Xavier had been when he'd advised her that Cyprian's anger hid a wounded heart. Though she'd scoffed then, now she knew it was true. But she intended to see that heart mended, and this night would see them take another step toward that healing.

"May I make the introductions, Father?" Eliza did not wait for his answer but crossed the room to stand beside Cyprian. She smiled encouragingly at him and tucked her hand in the crook of his stiffly held arm. "I would like to introduce all of you to Captain Cyprian Dare. My father, Sir Gerald Thoroughgood." She tugged him toward her mother. "My mother, Lady Constance Thoroughgood."

"Welcome, Captain Dare." Her mother extended a hand and Cyprian took it, giving her a short, courtly bow. Her mother smiled approvingly at Eliza then turned her ever gracious mien toward Cyprian. If anyone could put a person at ease, it was Constance Thoroughgood. Beneath Eliza's hand she could feel some of the tension ease from Cyprian's arm. She must remember to ask her mother just how she managed to project that lovely calm in the middle of such tense circumstances. But first they must deal with Uncle Lloyd.

Cyprian's posture once more became stiff when they turned to face his father. But when Eliza took the three steps needed to bring them before Lloyd Haberton, Cyprian stayed right beside her.

"Uncle Lloyd," she began, as she searched for the right words. "You and Cyprian met under all the worst circumstances. His opinion of you is not high," she admitted, deciding to be candid. "And I know that your feelings toward him are less than generous—"

"I do not seek his generosity," Cyprian interrupted her.

"Nor am I inclined to give it!" Uncle Lloyd snapped back at him.

"That's not what I mean!" Eliza exclaimed, forcing her way between the two of them.

"Well, if he thinks he's entitled to even a farthing's worth of my estates—"

"Your estates mean less than nothing to me," Cyprian sneered.

"Then return my ransom money!" Lloyd Haberton's face grew red with fury. "Return my ransom money to me unless you are lying!"

Eliza's eyes darted from Cyprian to Uncle Lloyd and back to Cyprian. He was enjoying this, she realized. If he could enrage his father to the point of apoplexy, he would probably consider this evening a towering success. To Eliza's absolute relief, her father interrupted the two men before a full-fledged conflict could erupt.

"I will not condone this uncivilized sort of behavior in the presence of my wife and daughter!" he thundered. Both men glared at him but at least they were silenced. "Now," he continued, yanking at the lapels of his frock coat. "It's late and I am hungry. We shall sit down and make our peace and enjoy our dinner." He turned to

Eliza's mother and extended his arm to her. "My dear, allow me to seat you."

Eliza had never been prouder of her father than she was in that moment, nor had she ever admired him more. As he seated her mother at one end of the oval table, then positioned himself opposite her at the other end, Eliza tugged discreetly on Cyprian's arm. He did not lead her to the table as she hoped, however, but instead looked down at her.

"I would like to have a word with you. Alone," he added, not bothering to lower his voice. But if his voice was unexpressive, his eyes were not.

"Cyprian," she began in an imploring whisper. Her father, however, cut her off.

"After the meal, and assuming we come to some amicable agreement, I will gladly grant you time alone with Eliza. Perhaps a hot toddy before the fire, or some other appropriate activity."

"That would be very nice," Eliza answered when Cyprian did not, praying all the while that he would go along. Then he let out a short, harsh breath and with uncharacteristic brusqueness steered her to the table.

"Here, Captain Dare, sit beside me," Constance said, smiling as she patted the chair beside hers. Her bright eyes met Eliza's, sending her hope and encouragement. "Eliza, you sit between Captain Dare and your father."

That left the place opposite them for Cyprian's father. Eliza was not certain she could endure an entire meal with them glaring at one another like furious dogs straining at their leashes.

When Lloyd took his seat, however, the situation seemed to become a little less tense. Father and son might not like it, but they were actually sitting at the same table, preparing to partake of a meal together. This was going to work, Eliza knew with a sudden surety. It might be difficult and even become ugly. But eventually it was going to work.

Mrs. Dooley appeared with a tureen of steaming chowder, platters of crusty breads, a cheese assortment, and two different wines. While she served, the conversation was limited. When the woman pulled the door closed behind her exit, however, Cyprian took charge. He addressed Eliza's father.

"Despite the awkwardness of our introduction, I am here to ask for Eliza's hand in marriage. We are well suited, despite outward appearances to the contrary. And I believe she is willing." He covered her right hand with his left one and sent her a faint smile. "I will be a good husband to her."

And I will be a good and loving wife to you, Eliza sent him the silent reply. She had anticipated arguments and stubbornness and overwrought emotions at this meal, but she'd not counted on the overwhelming feelings created in her by Cyprian's simple statement to her father. Her heart swelled with a love she never could have anticipated just a few short weeks ago.

"Well," her father responded to Cyprian, nodding his approval. "I am happy to hear that. And I am well aware that she is eager to be wed with you. But I must know more of your circumstances. Where will you live? How will you provide for her? That's why I invited your father here."

"He has nothing to do with this." Cyprian glared at his father. "I am my own man. I own three ships free and clear and I can provide well for Eliza with no assistance from him. As for where we will reside, I have a substantial residence on the Channel Islands, and should Eliza wish it, I can build her another home elsewhere."

"Well, do not expect a marriage settlement from me," Lloyd muttered, glowering at both Cyprian and his brother-in-law. "He kidnapped my son, after all, and stole my money—"

"He *is* your son!" Eliza cried, jerking upright. She

leaned over the table, shouting at him. She'd heard all
she could stand of her uncle's grousing. "When will you
accept that fact and make peace with him?"

"He doesn't want peace with me! He only wants to
humiliate me in front of my family! That's why he's marrying you, Eliza, to get at me. And you are fool enough
to—"

"Do not call her a fool." Cyprian stood up too and
Eliza feared he had finally lost the battle he fought with
his temper, for he projected an icy rage.

"No, do not call me a fool," she broke in, hoping to
head off any further escalation of their argument. "Aubrey and I are united in this matter, Uncle Lloyd. The
both of us have come to see that there is much to love
both in you and in Cyprian. He is your son, whether or
not you are willing to forgive him for kidnapping Aubrey. And he is your father," she continued, addressing
Cyprian now. "He may have abandoned your mother,
but he didn't abandon you. He didn't know she bore
him a child." She grasped Cyprian's hand in hers, twin-
ing her fingers with his. Only when he responded to her
urgent grasp with a slight squeeze did she then reach
across the table to take one of her uncle's hands.

"Enough time has been wasted. Please, let's not dwell
on the mistakes of the past. The future is all we have left
to us. I want it to be a good one." She took a fortifying
breath and prayed for the right words to break their
impasse. "You will be grandfather to our children, Uncle Lloyd. Would you throw that away?"

She could feel the resistance in her uncle's hand. Yet
as her reference to grandchildren sank in, something
changed. His frown eased a trifle and then he glanced
reluctantly at Cyprian.

"Will you let them know me as their grandsire?"

Oh, please, Eliza prayed even more fervently. Her
fingers tightened on each of their hands as she turned
her gaze on Cyprian.

He was not in a forgiving frame of mind; she could sense that. And yet as she clutched at his hand, willing herself to be the conduit between father and son, she felt the very moment when he relented.

He sighed and looked away, and she wanted to cry for joy.

"If Eliza wishes it," he stated in a stiff tone. He tilted his face down to hers. "If you truly wish it."

"I do," she breathed. "Oh, Cyprian, I do."

Her uncle cleared his throat noisily, then as if in after thought, yanked his hand free of Eliza's with an irritated frown. "Perhaps now we can get on with the meal," he muttered. "But there is still the matter of the ransom money," he added as he picked up his spoon.

"I'm sure we can make an arrangement that is satisfactory to both parties. Isn't that right?" Eliza's father asked. He stared at Cyprian until his soon-to-be son-in-law gave a grudging nod, then eyed his brother-in-law until he got the same sort of assent. Then he smiled. "Good. Now that that's settled, let us make a toast to Eliza and Cyprian."

As Eliza and Cyprian sat down, their hands still entwined, Gerald Thoroughgood stood and raised his wine glass to them. "To my only daughter, Eliza Victorine, and to her fiancé, Captain Cyprian Dare. Long life and much happiness."

"And many children," Constance added.

"Yes," Lloyd said after a moment. He lifted his glass. "Many children."

After that the meal went relatively well, although to Eliza it seemed to stretch on forever. She wanted to be alone with Cyprian even if it had to be under the most circumspect conditions. She needed to speak privately with him even if they could not touch or kiss or even embrace. There were things she was bursting to say to him, but alone.

By the time her father tried to force a dessert of

baked apples on them, she was ready to scream. But as if she read Eliza's every emotion, her mother came to the rescue. "Eliza, no doubt you and Cyprian would like to share a moment or two alone."

"Oh, yes. Thank you, Mother."

"I'll arrange for a private sitting room," her father began.

"We'd rather take a walk," Cyprian replied.

"But it's snowing."

"I love the snow," Eliza vowed. "I'll just get my cloak," she added, scooting away from the table.

"But what about your lungs? Constance," Gerald turned, appealing to his wife. "The cold is not good for her lungs—"

"I believe our Eliza is no longer the sickly girl we tend to think she is. She's a woman now, strong and healthy, dear." She smiled at her husband. "She'll be fine."

Eliza sent her mother a grateful look as she donned her cloak, pulled her hood up and searched the inside pocket for her gloves. Later she would find her mother and they would talk. Later she would try to thank her for everything she'd done to make sure things turned out so well. But now . . . now was the time for her and Cyprian.

Once quit of the inn, though, with several stern warnings from her father to stay within the forecourt and not to linger above a quarter hour, Eliza could not restrain herself.

"You came," she murmured, grasping the sleeve of Cyprian's great coat and forcing him to face her. "You came for me in spite of everything."

"He and I will never be father and son," Cyprian warned, for he knew of what she spoke. "Not in the way you would have us be." But his serious expression could not hold in the face of her loving gaze. His lips softened in the beginnings of a smile, and his midnight blue eyes

roamed her face, as if examining every angle of it, studying her, memorizing her. Claiming her as his own.

An overbrimming joy filled Eliza, a flooding warmth
that even the worst snowstorm could not chill. Were she
to will it, she was convinced she could melt the gathering snowdrifts, banish the heavy clouds, and summon
the sunshine and warmth of spring, so complete was her
happiness. It would always be springtime in her heart,
so long as Cyprian loved her. But he hadn't actually said
it to her except in the midst of passion. She wanted to
hear it now, when they were bundled in winter clothes,
and only their faces were unencumbered by multiple
layers of wool.

She stepped right up to him and laid her head against
his chest. At once his arms came around her and she
snuggled into the strength of his embrace. He held her
as if he would never let her go, and yet his hold was as
gentle and careful as if he held some delicate treasure
and feared to break it.

But she would not break. So long as he loved her, he
could never, ever hurt her.

"I love you, Cyprian." She raised her gaze to stare up
at him, up at the harshly beautiful face that was hers
now to stare at for the rest of her life. "When you came
tonight, I . . . I thought I loved you before. But now
. . . now it's even stronger." Then she laughed and buried her face against his chest, for she feared she
sounded the lovesick fool. But then, that was precisely
what she was, and what she intended always to be.

When Cyprian lifted her face with one warm finger
beneath her chin, she met his eyes shyly. What she saw
in his dark heated gaze, however, sent all thoughts of
shyness skittering away. For love shone in his eyes, clear
and unhidden, there for her to see and know and revel
in. Then he spoke the words of his heart, and the cold
and the dark and the snow really did disappear for her.

"I love you, Eliza. Against my will. Despite my every

instinct that tried to prevent it, I have lost my heart to you." His palm curved against her cheek and though he wore a faint smile, his words were serious. Almost reverent. "Since you have my heart, it remains only for you to agree to take the rest of me as well. Your parents appear to have consented, but it is your consent I need. Only yours. Say you will marry me and I will spend the rest of our lives proving my love to you."

"Cyprian." Only that one word could she utter, yet he knew it for a yes. Later she would expound on it. Later she would explain that he did not have anything to prove, that their lives together would be all the confirmation she would ever need. For now, however, she needed to touch him and be closer to him. She clutched his lapels, raising up on tiptoe to kiss him, and he bent down to meet her half way. Their lips met and clung, and parted to fit better. Closer. Deeper.

When they drew apart for breath, Cyprian caught her up in his arms, pulling her fully against him, though layers of harrington, drill, and melton separated them from the embrace they both desired.

"We must set an early date," she said, kissing his jaw, his cheek, his ear.

"Even tomorrow would be too long. Ah, my Eliza, how I have missed you."

"And I you," she answered, holding his face between her gloved hands. "Promise me we shall never be parted again."

"I promise," he vowed, taking her mouth in a devastating kiss that left her hot and breathless and more than a little disoriented. "Which room is yours?" he murmured hoarsely as he pressed kisses in her hair.

"Up above the—oh, Cyprian. You cannot mean to—"

"Oh, but I can. And I will."

He ran a hand down her back and even through her petticoats and skirts and voluminous cloak, Eliza felt the steamy rise of passion begin way down low inside her. Maybe he could, the wanton thought occurred to her.

"I'm at the corner that faces the stables. On the second floor."

A light slanted across the yard as a door opened. "Eliza? Come in now. The storm is getting worse," her father called.

The snowstorm *was* getting worse, she realized as they backed away from each other to a more circumspect distance. But the storm inside her . . . it was getting better and better. Perhaps later Cyprian would bring it to that shuddering crescendo he knew so well how to orchestrate.

"Till later," Cyprian murmured, giving her one last breath-stealing kiss.

"But not too much later," she pleaded as she tucked her hand in his arm. They ran together toward the light, toward her father who waited for her.

"Good night, Cyprian," she called as her father hustled her inside.

"Good night," he replied, watching her until she disappeared into the posting house. Then he grinned and stared up at the second floor of the solid building.

It proved to be a very good night indeed.

IF YOU ENJOYED *Heart of the Storm,* READ ON FOR AN EXCERPT OF REXANNE BECNEL'S PASSIONATE NEW ROMANCE, *A Kiss in the Storm*:

"Daphne Melerine. She's his mistress, you know," Darius Bellingham added when Adam asked who else they waited on.

Though he was careful to keep his expression bland, Adam felt an undeniable sense of anticipation. So that was her name. She'd piqued his curiosity at the cemetery, but knowing she would be joining the small group in the solicitor's office sharpened his interest even more. Daphne Melerine. An exotic name for a most exotic woman. Though he'd actually seen little of her beyond her mourning costume, all the references Hef had made to her through the years began to come back now.

An exquisite woman.

A jewel beyond value.

More loving than a wife could ever hope to be.

Hef had often stated his belief that a mistress was more attentive to her man than a wife because of the uncertainty of the mistress's position. But while that certainly made sense, Adam had never been inclined to keep a mistress of his own. He enjoyed, rather, the diversity that could be found all around him. Lusty serving wenches. Elegant widows. Other men's wives. Even an occasional night in one of the better sporting houses. He wanted no commitments beyond the hours he spent with the various women. No emotional entanglements either. And though he intended someday to marry, he suspected that no single woman could satisfy him for long.

Of course, Hef had been an older man. As the years

went by, perhaps he too would one day prefer a regular mistress to the parade of women he now enjoyed. Regardless, however, he was more than a little intrigued by the solitary mourner he'd watched at graveside.

A soft knock sounded and the door opened on silent hinges. One of the several clerks stepped back and when a woman moved forward, all the men in the office stood.

"Miss Melerine. Welcome. We've been expecting you," Bellingham said. "Please. Sit here." He indicated a dark upholstered chair adjacent to Adam's. "I believe you are already acquainted with Mrs. Hollings, Mr. Filmore's housekeeper."

Adam watched as she smiled at the older woman who was to hear the bequeathals to all the household staff.

"Perhaps you also know Mr. Carroll, Vicar at St. Luke's."

The greeting there was cooler. But then a man of the cloth could not wholly approve of a woman of Daphne Melerine's ilk, Adam thought. Further introductions were made to Hef's three men of business, all of whom were obviously known to her, and she to them. Finally Bellingham gestured to him.

"This is Mr. Adam Slater. May I present Miss Daphne Melerine."

Adam bowed and extended his hand to her, a gesture she'd plainly not anticipated. After a brief hesitation she placed her fingers in his. There was no assessing look on the pale face behind the veil, he noticed. No hint of curiosity about whether he might become a new protector for her. Considering his usual appeal to women, it caught him vaguely by surprise. Added to that, she pulled her hand away as soon as he let her.

The odd thing was, he hadn't wanted to let that hand go. Within the soft, expensive gloves, her fingers were slender and strong. And warm. The thought of her, so young and alive, lying with an aging roué like Hef struck him suddenly as repulsive.

He peered at her, trying to understand how she could have done such a thing, but after meeting his gaze for only a moment, she turned her attention toward Mr. Bellingham.

He had been dismissed, Adam realized with another, stronger sense of surprise. She showed not the least sign of interest in him. He sat down, faintly taken aback, and yet he had enough of a sense of irony to find some humor in the situation. Maybe she preferred older men. Perhaps she'd truly cared for Hef.

Or perhaps she was the sort who played hard to get— not a game he'd ever particularly enjoyed.

But it was more likely, he realized, that her interest in the contents of the will on Mr. Bellingham's desk precluded any other distractions.

He straightened his jacket and crossed one ankle over his knee. Enough of this perverse fascination with a woman whose face he'd not yet clearly seen, whose hair color was unknown to him, and whose taste in men meant nothing to him at all. He had other engagements later today. Time to learn why he'd been mentioned in Henry Filmore's will.

A Kiss in the Storm—coming from St. Martin's Paperbacks in 1996!

Award-winning author of *Creole Fires*

GYPSY LORD
He was Dominic Edgemont, Lord Nightwyck, heir to the Marquis of Gravenwold. But he was also a dark-eyed, half-gypsy bastard...
_____ 92878-5 $4.99 U.S./$5.99 Can.

SWEET VENGEANCE
Rayne Garrick had found Jocelyn Asbury among a band of cutthroats—and now he would do anything to have her...
_____ 95095-0 $4.99 U.S./$5.99 Can.

BOLD ANGEL
Saxon beauty Caryn of Ivesham was once saved by a mysterious Norman knight—but even that wouldn't make her marry him.
_____ 95303-8 $4.99 U.S./$5.99 Can.